FATE'S
INSTRUMENTS

ESSENTIAL PROSE SERIES 150

Canada Council **Conseil des Arts**
for the Arts **du Canada**

ONTARIO ARTS COUNCIL
CONSEIL DES ARTS DE L'ONTARIO

an Ontario government agency
un organisme du gouvernement de l'Ontario

Canada

Guernica Editions Inc. acknowledges the support of the Canada Council
for the Arts and the Ontario Arts Council. The Ontario Arts Council
is an agency of the Government of Ontario.

We acknowledge the financial support of the Government of Canada.

FATE'S INSTRUMENTS

❋ No Safeguards 2—Paul's Story ❋

H. Nigel Thomas

GUERNICA
EDITIONS
TORONTO • BUFFALO • LANCASTER (U.K.)
2018

Michael Mirolla, editor
David Moratto, Interior and cover design
Guernica Editions Inc.
1569 Heritage Way, Oakville, (ON), Canada L6M 2Z7
2250 Military Road, Tonawanda, N.Y. 14150-6000 U.S.A.
www.guernicaeditions.com

Distributors:
University of Toronto Press Distribution,
5201 Dufferin Street, Toronto (ON), Canada M3H 5T8
Gazelle Book Services, White Cross Mills
High Town, Lancaster LA1 4XS U.K.

First edition.
Printed in Canada.

Legal Deposit—Third Quarter
Library of Congress Catalog Card Number: 2017964541
Library and Archives Canada Cataloguing in Publication
Thomas, H. Nigel, 1947-, author
Fate's instruments : No safeguards 2, Paul's story / H. Nigel Thomas.
-- First edition.

(Essential prose series ; 150)
Issued in print and electronic formats.
ISBN 978-1-77183-260-1 (softcover).--ISBN 978-1-77183-261-8 (EPUB).
--ISBN 978-1-77183-262-5 (Kindle).

I. Title. II. Series: Essential prose series ; 150

PS8589.H4578F38 2018   C813'.54   C2018-900141-0   C2018-900142-9

For Alice Agatha Richards (Tant Alice)
whose home provided the warmth, affection
and nurture I needed at age 17

With the farming of a verse
Make a vineyard of the curse.
—W.H. AUDEN

I COME AWAKE stretched out on the couch. Realize I'd dozed off. My bladder is full to bursting. On the radio Mozart's *Requiem* is playing. I recognize it easily. It was one of Grama's favourite pieces.

First the bathroom. I smell, then see the overflowing dirty-linen hamper. I turn the fan on. I shake my head. Not today. Yesterday I said I would do the laundry today. In the mirror I stare at the bags under my eyes, the double chin. I should increase my time at the gym. Can't ignore my appearance. Not now. Certainly not now.

Next the kitchen. 15:41 the stove clock says. I've slept for more than two hours. I'm hungry. I open the fridge. It's almost empty. I pick up the milk carton and sniff it. Sour. The carcass of a barbecue chicken with pretty well all the meat gone and two dinner rolls are all that's edible in the fridge. I put the rolls in the toaster oven, grab a fork from among the dirty dishes in the sink, and rake off whatever meat I can from the carcass of the chicken.

I feel relaxed. The nap has helped. At 5:14, when I got out of bed, I thought of walking down to the gym at the Forum, but couldn't work up the energy. Today I'd intended to write, but a nightmare woke me up around 3 a.m., and left me awake and in a stupor all morning.

I'm in a prison cell in Antigua, Guatemala, in the corner where the slop pail is. Flies are landing everywhere on my body. I can't lift my hand to prevent them from alighting on my face. Juan Pablo and Lencho get up and are coming toward me. I try to scream but no sound comes.

I dream about this prison a couple times each year. Never this harrowing though. Usually it's some variant of my mother and Madam

J paying the bribe the Antigua police wanted and forcing me to say I'd give my heart to their Lord. Madam J usually has a yellow purse holding the knife she'll use to cut out my heart to give to her Lord.

The real arrest happened six years ago. I was nineteen. I excluded the prison details from the story I told Jay. He knows I got busted for buying weed and it was why I hadn't contacted him and Ma for more than a year. He suspects too that I haven't told him the full story. That boy knows me a little too well. If I'd thought about it I'd have told Bill about my prison experience. Maybe it wouldn't be haunting me still. He'd have understood and wouldn't have flapped his mouth about it. My more usual nightmare—happens once, sometimes twice, every couple of weeks—is that I have some important place to get to but can't begin the journey. Or if I begin, I get to dead ends and have to turn back until I can no longer move in any direction.

⇥ Jay hasn't called to update me on his condition. That foolish boy. I have to call Carlos and Rosa in Guatemala to find out how the funeral went.

I should write down last night's nightmare, keep track of my dreams for future reference. Maybe I should tell Jay the full story. Wonder how he'd react. Might shrug and say he doesn't see why I had to withhold it. After all I'm no novice when it comes to dealing with the police. In my teens I was taken to the Côte-des-Neiges precinct more times than I care to remember.

I get my journal from the bedroom, sit at the dining table, and record the nightmare: those nineteen hours I spent in a Guatemalan slammer, the part I hid from Jay. Trimmed it too from the confession I made to Carlos the day I found out about Ma's death and risked arrest coming home.

Wished *Lonely Planet* had info about cops posing as pushers. Not sure it would have made a difference. I'd already bought grass freely in Belize, Honduras, Costa Rica, and Nicaragua from taxi drivers or their contacts. Guess my luck had to run out at some time. At the police station the *chontes* were firm. Probably felt if they were going to be corrupt it should be worth every quetzal. Then again, the salary those guys earn—somewhere around $600 per month—and their standard of living: supporting children in private schools, stay-at-home wives, maybe a mistress or two on the side, sometimes widowed mothers, plus owning cars, they have to find—extort—extra income, and the source is obvious. *Prensa Libre* carried a long piece on it. These wanted $1,000. Not a penny less. I'd offered $500, and they suggested I could get the other $500 from my credit card. I didn't have a credit card. The older cop picked up my wallet from the counter, took out the cards, and examined them one by one, finally settling on my debit card. He held it up. "*¿Y esa?*"

I shook my head. I had just over $800 in my account and the equivalent of about $100 in quetzals in my wallet.

They knew what they were doing and were certain they'd be paid—one way or the other. I didn't know that. The older cop went on to explain that I could contact my family and get the money from them. He scribbled something onto the back of a form, pulled his cellphone from his pocket, and handed it and the paper to me. The paper had a Western Union address. The last thing I wanted was for Ma to find out that I was in police custody in Guatemala. If I could reach Jay, I would lie to him and get him to send me the money. But if I called and Ma answered I would have to hang up the phone, and the cops would have a record of the number. My hands sweaty and trembling, I deliberately dialled a wrong number. A recording said there was no service for the number I'd dialled. Their eyes were riveted on me. Even the station captain's from his desk a couple metres away.

"There's a problem: *algo técnico, pienso*," I said, trying to sound casual.

The young cop stretched his hand for the phone. He pressed redial and listened. He gave the phone to his colleague, who bared his teeth. He glanced at my handcuffs, said something that I didn't understand, and began heading toward the back. With a toss of his chin and his beckoning thumb, he signalled me to follow him. The other cop walked behind me. We exited onto a small parking lot with three police trucks. They shoved me into the passenger seat of the nearest one. The young officer took the steering wheel; the other sat on my right. They drove a short distance, to the prison I passed every day on my way to Spanish classes: a vast structure with destroyed upper floors of half-standing walls. All but the first floor was in ruins. The first time I saw it I feared for the prisoners inside should there be an earthquake. The older cop pulled me out roughly and pushed me, past the women selling snacks on the sidewalk, toward a gate of vertical steel bars. Two boyish-looking guards in grey uniforms stood with semi-automatics inside the gate. One opened it. The hinges grated. I got goose bumps and froze. The older cop pushed me forward. A large noisy fan rotated just inside the door. There was a strong urine-and-feces smell.

About two metres in from the door, a bespectacled man with a full-moon face sat hunched behind a bare desk in a steel cage. The older cop went to him and spoke. The man picked up a phone and spoke into it. The young cop remained at my side. A couple of minutes later, a burly man in a grey uniform came from the interior end of the corridor. At his right hip a bundle of keys jangled. His beady eyes peered out at me from his jowly face and stared at every part of me. Then he said, "*Venga*," beckoned with his thumb, and began walking towards the interior. With a head toss, the young cop gestured that I was to follow this man. The young cop walked behind me. The odour was now a mixture of feces, urine, and mildew, but there was some natural light at the far end of the corridor we were walking down. I heard commingled voices too. The man with the keys turned left, went a little way, and stopped in front of a door. He opened it, held it open, and motioned for the cop and me to enter. The cop unlocked the handcuffs, then left. Now the buzz of voices was more distinct. Sounds of a ball being kicked. Shouts. Prisoners playing soccer outside.

The jailer asked me if I understood Spanish. I told him a little. He ordered me to empty my pockets and put the contents onto the desk. The cops had kept my wallet. He picked up my puffer, turned it around in his hand, and frowned. He sprayed his left wrist, lifted it to his nostrils, and sniffed. I told him that it was in case I had an asthma attack — "*Es medicina para controlar mi asma.*" He put it down. Next he examined my EpiPen and shook his head. Holding it up, he stared at me, shook his head, waved a forefinger and said: "*Éste no puedes*. No can keep." What he said next, I didn't understand. He pointed to his slacks and shirt, gestured unbuttoning them and throwing them onto the floor. He unbuckled his belt, pointed to his underpants and said: "You no take off. You keep. *¿Comprendes?*" I nodded. He pulled out a bottom drawer from a narrow floor-length cupboard to the right of his desk, took a grey canvas bag from it, and with gestures told me to pick up my clothes and put them in it. When it was done, he reached for the bag and threw my EpiPen into it. From a middle drawer of his desk, he took a safety pin, a stamp and a stamp pad, and a pad of yellow post-its. He fiddled with the stamp, then stamped two pieces of paper; one piece he pinned to the canvas bag, the other he gave me with a warning. "*No lo pierdes*. Keep. No lose." On the paper was written: *Sábado 39: DT1-04*. I stuck it into the waistband of my underpants. Suddenly the noise of the prisoners outside broke into my consciousness

"*Vámonos*," the jailer said and got up. Three or so metres from his office, he stopped in front of a steel cage with bars from ceiling to floor on two sides, everything inside visible from the corridor. There was a solid wall on two sides. In the wall opposite the corridor was a space about half a metre square that opened to the outside. There were four vertical steel bars in it. The noise of the players, daylight, and a slight breeze came in through it. The jailer opened the door of the cell, motioned for me to enter, then slammed the door shut and locked it. Three men were in it: two of them, in their underwear, sat on a slab of about two-and-a-half metres: the length of the room; the third man—toothless, completely naked, emaciated, his ribs visible—sat on the floor talking to himself.

In a corner opposite the sitting men was a blue pail. The buzzing flies and the stench coming from it told me what it was. I turned to see the eyes of the two sitting men focused on me. To my right I heard the footsteps and shouts of the prisoners coming in from outside.

My mind raced. How was I going to get out of here? Now Ma's finding out about my being in police custody didn't seem to be such a big deal. I knew what went on in prisons. Back in Montreal, in high school, an ex-prisoner had lectured us about the perils of prison life.

That talk and the fear of my boss's rivals offing me had pushed me to give up drug trafficking. I didn't want to be anyone's wife. My body felt cold. My teeth chattered.

"*Venga, Chavo, Amigo, venga. Sienta vos. No es tan malo.* (Come, amigo. Sit down. It's not so bad)," one of the seated inmates said to me. He indicated the space to his left. The other shifted to the right to create more space on the slab. I took a couple of hesitant steps and stared at the speaker. He seemed in his early thirties, had a slender body, dark eyes, black hair, an oval kind-looking face, a large Adam's apple, and buck teeth. I sat as close to the edge as I could.

"*Estaba descuidado, hombre! ¿Por qué está aquí?* (You were careless, man. Why're you here?)" the fellow continued. While I tried to put an explanation together, he spoke again, this time in English. "I'm Juan Pablo."

"Paul," I said. "*Mucho gusto.*" He reached over and we bumped fists.

He looked at the other guy and said: "He's Lencho. *Es Guanaco.* Understand?"

"*Salvadoreño,*" I said.

"*Bueno!*"

Lencho slapped me on the thigh—a stinging blow—and grinned. Some of his molars were missing. He seemed to be in his forties, had very thick eyebrows that came together above his nose, heavy jowls, deltoids like cannon balls, a bulging gut, and a hairy body. His bare arm hung loosely. A tattoo of a snake on it. His head and mine reached to about the same level. Juan Pablo towered more than a full head above us.

"Lemme figure this out," Juan Pablo said. "Tell me if I'm right. They busted you for drugs, and you didn't cough up. Huh?"

I nodded.

"Where you from, *mano?*"

"Canada."

"Not sure how *chontes* deal with Canadians. If you'd o' been a *Gringo*, the American embassy would leave you swing in the wind for couple days, then come pay and carry you. Unnerstand, *mano?*"

I nodded.

"*Mano, chontes* fake the paperwork. Ain't nutten to that shit they pretend to write down. Ain't worth a rat's fart. Get my drift, *mano*? Now if you'd o' been from Europe, you wouldn' be even here. *Chontes* would o' know who to call for *plata*." He rubbed his thumb and middle finger, his eyes a lustrous black, and nodded. "And somebody'd o' come to the precinct, pay off the *lapas,* and take you away, and when you back in your country you pay 'em back. *¿Comprende?* A *mano* from *Alemania* told me so."

He said he'd lived in San Diego for five years *indocumentado*. One night the cops raided the flat he shared with a Mexican and found a gram of grass in the apartment and charged him with drug possession. The grass belonged to his roommate, who was out at the time. He spent a month in the slammer and was deported straight from prison. Today he was behind bars because he'd encroached onto someone's turf. Lencho, himself a deportee from the US, was his sidekick. (No doubt providing *la galleta*—intimidating force—that Juan Pablo lacked.) Their boss was working out their release with the *mero-mero*. He winked. They expected to be out by supper time. "Amigo, when the *chontes* bring you supper, tell them you want contact Canadian embassy. You no want stay in here. After two days they put you with others. Know what that means?" His eyebrows arched, his stare intense.

I didn't answer.

Lencho laughed.

"Man, they'll line up to fuck you. They'll turn your asshole into a *pusa*. If the guards fancy you, they'll have a go at you too. You'll be lucky if you leave here without HIV. Let your embassy get you to fuck outta here, man. In Guatemala you ain't human when you in prison. Do what you have to do to get out of here."

"*Chaquetear. Culebrear. Mamar. No importa. Lo importante es salir de aquí,*" Lencho said, speaking for the first time.

Juan Pablo translated. "Lick ass. Brown-nose. Suck off the guards ... Whatever will get you out of here without a busted arse and HIV."

My breath choked. My hand shook as I took a blast from my

puffer. Juan Pablo watched me trying to regain my breath and said that back in San Diego a prisoner that the guards hated had died because they hadn't replaced his puffer. "*Mano,* some of 'em ain't human. *Son brutos. Joden con sus madres. ¿Comprende?*" He made thrusting movements with his fist and laughed. "With their mothers, man." Then he fell silent.

The language school I was attending was closed for the weekend. In any event the contact information for it and Señora Garcia, my landlady, was in my wallet. By Monday if I didn't show up, she would contact the school, if only because the school paid her. I wondered how long I'd be here. With Lencho and Juan Pablo I felt safe, even with El Cholco, Juan Pablo's name for the man sitting on the floor.

The noise in the back was replaced by an indistinct hum of voices and the occasional shout. I suspected there were locked steel gates everywhere. If this place caught fire we'd all perish. It happened quite frequently in Latin America. Ditto if an earthquake struck.

Lencho got up and went to pee. He was even shorter than me. His back looked like a shag rug. There too his muscles bulged. He stepped over the man now lying on the floor in a foetal position. At the first frothy sound Juan Pablo held his nose and turned his head to the wall. I followed suit. The smell was intense and seemed to be coating my throat. The disturbed flies buzzed around for a while. I covered my face with my hands and wriggled to dislodge those that had landed on my back.

Lencho returned to sit on the slab. After a while Juan Pablo dozed. Lencho too, his body leaning into Juan Pablo's. Intermittent noises came from the prisoners on the right. I sat there, thinking, thinking what a fool I'd made of myself. Would I make it out of there alive, undamaged? Ma and Madam J would be so triumphant when they got the news. I envisaged Madam J, gesturing wildly, sanctimoniously saying: "Sister Anna, I did know it. Ain't I did tell you so? That bwoy heading down the path o' destruction. With bruck-neck speed." Next it would be their pastor praying before the entire congregation that Anna's boy would turn from the path of evil.

I looked at my sleeping cellmates. They seemed quite comfortable.

The cell felt colder and damper, and mosquitoes were now buzzing at my ears. Something bit me, quite likely a flea.

Suddenly the man on the floor sat up and began to scream. The two other prisoners came awake. Lencho shouted at him in a language I didn't understand and made a cutthroat sign. Juan Pablo laughed. El Cholco began to tremble and fell silent.

Now I wanted to pee. I couldn't hold it any longer. I went to the pail. The flies hit me, but the worst part was the splattering on my legs. I felt ashamed and didn't want to return to sit on the slab. I heard commotion to the right of me, the prisoners becoming louder than usual.

"*Cena*," Juan Pablo said, yawned, and stretched. He looked at Lencho, and they pounded fists.

Within seconds the turnkey came and beckoned to Juan Pablo and Lencho. They got up and followed him. At the door they turned to look at me, shook their crossed fingers, and said: "*Buena suerte, mano.*"

In my mind I rehearsed what I would say to whoever brought my supper. Now there was a veritable uproar to my right: the sound of fists pounding on tables and screams of "*¡Mierda. Es pura mierda esta comida!*"—prisoners calling the food shit. The man on the floor became alert, his head turned to the sounds coming from the right. My stomach was roiling and my saliva tasted bitter. I hadn't eaten since around 8 a.m.

A youngish, short, pot-bellied fellow, in a grey uniform brought two Styrofoam plates, each with a scoop of pureed beans and two tortillas. There was no cutlery. I told the fellow who brought the food that I wanted to contact the Canadian embassy. He said he would relay the message. When he came back to collect the plates, he said that it couldn't be done before Monday. I said that in that case I would like to contact the police officers who'd brought me here. For a while, he looked away, but said nothing.

Someone I hadn't seen before came to the cell about half an hour later. By now it was dark outside and the only light that came into the cell was from a weak bulb in the corridor. He did not beat around the bush. He said, smirking: "*Tenés que pagar. ¿Cúanto dinero tenés?Hay una factura.* (That will cost you. How much money do you have? There's a fee.)"

"None. The police kept my wallet."

He left without further comment.

What with anxiety, slapping mosquitoes, brushing off bedbugs and fleas, and itching, I didn't sleep that night. El Cholco shouted frantically in short bursts at times and at one point began pacing the cell and screaming: "*Déjeme libre, hijos de puta! Déjeme libre!* (Let me go, you sons-o-bitches!)"

"*¡Cálmate! ¡Cállate! ¡Silencio, por favor!*" prisoners from the other side shouted. But El Cholco continued until he was tired; then he lay on the floor, fell asleep, and snored like a tractor.

Sometime after dawn a guard brought more beans and tortillas and a cup of dark water that might have been coffee. He said I would be having visitors and he would come back to get me in fifteen minutes.

A turnkey, not the one from the day before, came with my clothes, and led me to a shower. It was cold water. It was early October: the rainy season. Already the morning temperatures in Antigua were between seven and ten degrees Celsius. In the bathroom light I could see the swellings all over my body where mosquitoes, fleas, and bedbugs had feasted. It was a good twenty minutes before the turnkey returned and found me shivering. He took me to the front of the building, to where the man in the cage had made the telephone call the day before. Beside the cage stood Señor Leal, the director of the language school: a willowy man, in his late sixties or early seventies, who looked at you with beady eyes and a permanent squint. A metre away was the young police officer in civilian clothes. I remembered then that a cell phone number was on the business card the school had given me.

Leal asked me how I was. I told him okay. He put his arm around me and led me a short distance away from the cage. He told me that I should find the money however I could to pay off these guys, that going to prison in Guatemala was no joke. I said that I could pay them $500 and would try to get the remaining $500 from my brother and give it to them when it came. He said to stay where I was and went to speak to the young cop. I watched them talking, Leal's gesticulation showing that he was bargaining; then he looked at me, winked, and beckoned.

Outside the prison, the cop gave me my wallet, and we walked to an ATM fronting the Eastern side of Central Park, across from where the cops had posed as pushers the day before and arrested me. He waited for me on the sidewalk. I saw that five one-hundred quetzal notes along with several smaller bills were still in my wallet. The various cards as well. I took out four of the one-hundred quetzal notes and my Medicare card and put them in my pocket. After withdrawing the money, I slipped my bank card into my pocket. Outside, the cop reached for the money and asked for my wallet as well. He took a cursory look inside, before pocketing it. He said I had to come with him to the police station. A couple metres from the station, he stopped walking and said that they knew my home address and phone number; that if I didn't honour my agreement, all calls to my number and all letters to or from me would be intercepted, and posters put out for my arrest, and if I dared to leave Guatemala I would be arrested. Grinning and slowly shaking his head, he said: "*Está atrapado, hombre. Tiene que pagar. Otra solución no hay.*"

He resumed walking and said he was taking me to Señora García to collect my passport. I told him it was in school's vault but that a photocopy of the data page was in my wallet. He stopped walking and pulled out his cellphone. His lips pursed and his eyes squinted. I held my breath until he put the phone back into his pocket. Next he pulled out my wallet, removed the data page and contemplated it. He put the page back in the wallet and shoved it into a side pocket. Warning me that they had to have the money before 5 p.m. the next day, he said I was free to go.

Suddenly, it became important again for Ma not to know about my plight, and I wasn't going to pay these cops any more money—not one dime! My passport was in my room. I left a note on my bed for *Señora García*, absconded, and remained incommunicado with everyone for thirteen months.

My impulsiveness. Wanting to win at any cost. It's how Jay sees it.

"*LA MORT DE Jack Layton* ..." I jump up from the table, pick up the remote from the floor in front of the couch, and put the TV on *News-world*. A reporter is giving a-man-on-the-street reaction to Jack's death. There's room for one more news item: the imminent fall of Gaddafi. The clip says two of Gaddafi's sons are in rebel custody. Old news. A clip I heard from VPR at 6 a.m. said Mohamed had escaped custody.

August 22, 2011. Jack Layton's dead. Jay admires him. Death. Death. Carlos and Rosa are home now. The funeral was at 10:30, 12:30 Montreal time. I have to call them. 10 p.m. should be all right. In summer Guatemalan time is two hours behind ours. Here I am still caught up in a Morales family drama. I promised to cut loose after Carlos left me. They were good to me in Guatemala. Can't deny that. Even Rosa. In spite of her bitterness and bigotry. They were my family for almost thirteen months.

Rosa had wanted to know if I was coming for the funeral, forgetting that I've been barred from re-entering Guatemala. Give her a chance tonight and she'll try to get Carlos and me back together.

≈ I need to talk to somebody. Gina is visiting her Haitian cousins in Boston. Times like these, I miss Bill. Jay, why haven't you called to let me know how you're doing? Paying me back for what I did five years ago—is that it? The fucking phone number you gave me isn't working. Whatever you do, just don't go and die in the Congo. Don't. And I have bad news for you. There's been a flood in your condo.

How could you be so fucking stupid to go and catch malaria? After the warning I gave you! Then again, you're like so damn polite. If you were here, I'd grab your collar and shake some sense into you. Why haven't you been taking your anti-malaria pills? I warned you. Told you about that bout I had in Copán Ruinas and still you ignored my warning.

I was naïve too. Thought Deet would keep the frigging mosquitoes away. Didn't want any more poisons in my body. Enough anti-asthma drugs in me, thank you.

Señor Vargas, the hotel manager—eyes like pop-out emeralds —came to see me three times during the night Saturday and Sunday and got the handyman to drive me to the doctor's office first thing Monday morning. A mere hundred metres away but I couldn't have walked it.

Vulture of a doctor stared at me shivering and sweating and envisaged gold, platinum even.

"¿Habla español?"

I shook my head. Then my Spanish was less than elementary. I'd spent three weeks studying the sounds and vocabulary from a Living Language CD.

"I no speak *mucho inglès. Es malaria. ¿Comprende?* Malaria. Pills? You no bring?"

I shook my head.

He said something to his nurse.

The office was on the second floor of a two-storey building in a block off the central square. A room no more than five square metres. The nurse's desk, about the size of a pupil's, was just inside the door. Two metres behind it was a folding screen that hid the doctor's desk. Overhead a creaking fan slowed, sped up, and sometimes paused. I don't remember seeing a window, but there had to be one: I could hear the vendors and traffic in the street below.

Dr. Francisco Aguilar. Bespectacled, round copper-coloured face, double chins, brown eyes in mounds of blubber; round-bellied, stooped shoulders, a cm or two taller than me, somewhere in his fifties; in a white unbuttoned lab coat embroidered with his name over his grey slacks, white shirt, and blue tie. He said something to his nurse: a top-heavy woman in a too-tight white uniform, skin lighter than his, bleached hair dyed blond in a single plait dangling at her back, her open mouth a sunset of gold-encased teeth. She got up from her desk, opened the door of a set of white melamine cupboards on the left beside the door, took down a mason jar of white pills, emptied two into her hands, walked to a 40-litre bottle of water on a stand in one corner, filled a paper cup, and approached me. She opened her mouth wide and pointed to it, then to my mouth. She tossed the pills into my mouth and held the paper cup to my lips while I drank.

"I give you pills *más*? *Le doy comprimas*." Aguilar pointed to the jar of pills on the nurse's desk. "*Comprende? Usted*—you—*me da dinero*." He pointed to me. "Morney." He pointed to himself. "I no give you pills. *No le doy nada*." He shook his head. "I give *papel*"—he picked up his prescription pad and pointed to it. "You go *farmacia*. You *compra*." He pointed outside. "What want?"

I must have looked puzzled. He repeated what he'd said. The nurse took over. "You go *farmacia*. You buy pills. You no go *farmacia*. *Nosotros*"—she indicated herself and Dr. Aguilar with a sweep of the hand—"sell you pills. You buy? Yes? No?"

I nodded. She went off to put the pills into an envelope.

Dr. Aguilar looked at me, belched, excused himself, then with accompanying gestures: two fingers, eating sounds, etc., said: "You eat *desayuno*. You *toma mientras*."

"Breakfast, two," the nurse said, gesturing two fingers. "*Comprende?* Two, lunch, two supper, two sleep."

"*Por siete días*," Aguilar resumed. I didn't understand what he said next. The nurse took over. This time she wrote down what I was to do. After seven days I was to take a pill every Sunday and every Wednesday for the next three months, and for now I should remain in bed for the next seven days.

"One hundred *dólares*," Aguilar said and gave me a piercing stare.

I was too weak and didn't have the language to argue with him.

I wonder if the hotel manager got a commission. It was one of those fleabag backpacking hotels: $15 per night, $23 if breakfast and supper—lots of beans, tortillas, and white bread—were included. I'd taken the second option. He'd come to look for me in my room when I didn't show up for supper. He met me shivering, returned for a thermometer, took my temperature, suggested an ice-cold tub soak along with aspirins, sent the handyman to get the ice, and got me to the doctor two days later. I'd promised to send him a thank-you note after I got back. I never did. Guess because the getting back was so complicated.

I was supposed to leave for Tegucigalpa that same morning but I stayed on for three more days. I left the hotel, my eyes still yellow, my legs wobbly, but the fever, ague, and sweating were gone.

When I got to Belize I read up on malaria on the internet and learned that some African types are already resistant to most anti-malaria drugs. Maybe that's the problem, Jay: your doctor gave you those. You're too disciplined to have forgotten what I told you. In Costa Rica, I had my blood tested in a San Jose hospital. They sent me to have my eyes checked as well, and reduced the medication to a single pill a week—all of it costing me less than US$50.

Jay, how could you let yourself catch malaria? I told you to go to a travel clinic. I'm anxious. Call me. You're probably downing all sorts of shit in Africa. Don't know how to tell people to buzz off. Feel you must please everyone. As soon as you get back here—you better not go and die—I'm marching you off to the doctor to make sure there's nothing in your gut that shouldn't be there.

I'd have gone with you until the end of August, but nowadays African governments are competing with one another to see who can impose the stiffest sentences on gays—some want to put us in concentration camps, some to kill us. Guess fucking with us is a lot easier than giving food, health care, and education to their people. I won't be travelling to any of them—that's for sure—or to any country that wants to jail or kill me because of how nature made me.

➤ I'd better take off these pyjamas and shower, rejoin civilization, and go over to the plaza to pick up some food, vegetables especially, before I come down with scurvy. Deposit the cheque I got yesterday too. The elation it brought yesterday—$250 for a short story: my first—is gone today. Professor Bram, my writing professor, would say: "Enjoy it, Joe. In this post-literate age they don't come often." He calls the males Joe and females Babs. At the beginning we frowned and cleared our throats, then grumbled about it to one another in the cafeteria, but were too afraid to tell him outright to call us by our names. I can't stand the man but Bill got me mixed up in their complicated love-hate friendship.

≥ 3

BACK HOME, I stare at the blinking light on the telephone, go to get the message, to see whether it's Jay who called while I was out. Some group begging for money for the famine in East Africa. The old messages replay and I hear one from Carlos sent three weeks ago. He began leaving them after he moved out in May. Messages in a blend of Spanish and the halting English he now insists on speaking. "*Pablo, mi buen Pablo*, I want be with you." A smacking kiss. "I sorry I leave you. I go come see you tomorrow. I love you."

You wonder what makes some people think they're smart and everyone else is stupid ... I shouldn't blame him. Think of all those Central Americans and Mexicans, including his brother-in-law, trying to get to the US and Canada. All means are valid. In his place I'd have done the same. Still it's not easy, not easy to admit that you've been duped. I still don't know what Jay thinks about him. I ask Jay, and he looks away and shrugs or repeats his mantra varying a word or two: "Paul, relationships are complex, even when they're abusive. Sometimes it's the abuse that keeps them going. Stop questioning me about Carlos. I don't know him. I'm not married to him. I rarely interact with him." Go trailing off into the fucking ether when all I want is your simple opinion, not some fucking philosophical treatise. When sorry-ass Jonathan got into trouble and came back here on sick leave, you let him stay with you.

"You care more about Jonathan than about me," I said.

"I do?"

"Yes. You're nursing him through a breakdown. What I'm asking for is a lot less: your simple opinion."

He chuckled, squinted, then gave me that smirk that used to make me want to smash his face when we were younger and still lived on Linton. "Paul, Jonathan stood by me during Ma's illness and death and while I was going crazy wondering where you were. Supporting him now is the least I can do." Instead of answering me, sends me on a fucking guilt trip. Fuck you, man. Three months later he and Jonathan spent two weeks in Guadeloupe to celebrate Jonathan's winning his case against the university. And since Jonathan got his job at UQAM last September, they've been inseparable. Says there's nothing sexual going on between them. Some Platonic friendship that, enough to make my own balls wither. Yes, he prefers Jonathan over me. He's still punishing me for the way I treated him and Ma. Just can't bring himself to say so. It's why for four days he hasn't called to say how he's doing.

↠ Carlos. What a son-of-a-bitch! When I told Bill that I was going to Mexico to marry Carlos and bring him back, he remained silent for a long time before saying he understood my need for companionship, that we all want to have someone to cuddle, that all our lives we go searching for that comforting feeling we had in the womb. "A costly search." And he related that he'd brought a Thai fellow here: Chai, and they'd "stayed together for eight turbulent years; then Chai moved out ... without warning. I came home after giving a lecture one Monday morning and met a note on the dining table. 'I took my things and left. I'm not coming back.'"

Bill stopped talking briefly and pressed his lips together. "I can't say I don't miss him. Don't know why I became so attached. Eleven years now and I still miss him. I go to the sauna every couple o' weeks and get my rocks off. It's not the same. Not the same. Definitely not the same. I feel empty afterwards, and hate myself for giving in to the urge to go. If Chai comes back today and asks me to make up, I think I'd say yes. Five-six years ago, the answer would have been no. Now, it would be a definite yes." He stopped talking and swallowed loud. We were silent for close to two minutes.

He resumed: "Sometimes, half awake, I reach over to embrace

Chai, forgetting that he's no longer in my bed. Chai. Left me for a fellow closer to his age. He was twenty-two when I brought him here. I was forty-three. This attraction for men younger than ourselves. Not sure why. Logic tells us it won't work, but who listens to logic … And we pay for our deafness. *Do we pay*! Those puppy-love songs and that asinine pop music I listened to day in day out … Thought I'd go mad. Every weekend he wanted to go dancing. When I said no, he'd say: 'You better come, or I might not come home at all.' And sometimes he didn't come home, especially in the later years. I took it all in stride or tried to. I'd be the first to tell you that sexuality shouldn't be fettered; that adults have the right to sleep with other adults—until it's your man who's sleeping with other men. And he knew how to goad me. Didn't he! When we were out, he'd look at handsome men—invariably men a lot younger than me—fantasize out loud about what it would be like to be in bed with them, and stare at me. It's a good thing he left me before the law allowing civil unions between gays was enacted. I would have done something stupid like that, to bribe him to stay with me. The trouble I've got myself into! Chai wasn't my only trial, just that I miss him most. There were three others: a Mexican, a Peruvian, and a Jamaican. I would have married them all if I could to legalize their status. In those days I would have been responsible for them for ten years."

He smiled. "The Peruvian: Enrique. Thought I was rich. Wanted an allowance of $1,000 per month. Wanted to wear designer-only clothes. Stay at home to cook and clean. But he wasn't devious. Never tried to steal anything from me. I paid a woman to marry him so he'd get permanent resident status. Left me three months later. Heard from him four years ago. He was in a hospice dying from AIDS. Paco. Mexican. Had an army of Hispanic friends. Brought them all the time—ten, twelve, fifteen—to my apartment to drink my liquor and eat my food and leave the mess for me to clean up. When I confronted him about the mess, he said I should get a housekeeper. I could afford it. Then he got hooked on cocaine and threatened me with a knife one night when he needed money for a fix. Had to call the police. He was waiting for his refugee claim to be processed. Within three days he was on a plane to Mexico. The Jamaican, Rick." He swallowed. "A body to mortgage your soul for: sleek, stream-lined, V torso, straight legs with huge thighs. The sex?" He gestured so-so. "I'd take him to the Gay Village and watch the eyes of young and old, staring, gleaming with lust. I'd smile at them and think: Eat your hearts out. Lived with me for eight months. We never had a problem until he went to the bank and tried to impersonate me. The cashier knew me. She told him she needed some more bills and went to the back and called the police." He paused and shook his head slowly. "Rick had come here on a holiday and overstayed his time by a couple of years and had decided to go back without telling me. The developing world. Poverty. Homophobia. People are desperate to escape. To better themselves and help their families. And why shouldn't they? They see how much our money buys when we visit their countries. We spend in a day what it takes them weeks to earn. They can screw us without losing sleep. We do it to them when we pay them next to nothing for the goods they sell us and the minerals we take out of their countries and leave them with nothing more than poisoned land and water."

"What happened to Rick?"

"They kept him in detention for a week before sending him back to Jamaica. I went to see him at the detention centre the day before he left. Even gave him a couple hundred dollars. Unfortunate fellow. Bright. Twenty-seven. Had already done a BA in history in Jamaica. Said he was fleeing homophobia, but was loathe to apply for refugee status. Got busted for marijuana when he was twenty. Said he was in the wrong place at the wrong time. Had a criminal record. A no-go for permanent residence here. I'd tried to get him into the MA pro-gramme at Concordia. Tuition alone was several thousand dollars."

He stared away from me, seemingly in deep thought, for almost a minute.

"Paul, I suspect that you're like me when it comes to affective dependence."

I said nothing.

"It can get you into a lot of trouble. A lot of trouble. We make fools of ourselves, because we're afraid to be without affection."

I looked at him questioningly.

"Here you are going off to marry this guy. Have you seriously considered what you're getting into?"

"What's to consider?"

"Look, I don't want to meddle in your private affairs. But when you told me you'd made up your mind to go to university and I asked you how you would support yourself, you said you'd inherited quite a bit of money from your mother and grandmother."

I nodded.

"The moment you marry what's his name—"

"Carlos."

"Half that money, half of all you own, might become his."

"Seriously?"

"Seriously."

"Even if the marriage breaks up within a year?"

"I think so."

"What should I do?"

"Good question. I don't know."

Three days later he asked me to come to his apartment. He'd spoken to a Me. Gélinas, a lawyer acquaintance who does a lot of work in the divorce area, and Gélinas had said that even though my inheritance would be protected, I should draw up a pre-nuptial contract before entering into any sort of union. Gélinas had also suggested that I bring Carlos here as a tourist and get to know him better before embarking on anything serious.

"Carlos already knows I'm coming to marry him. I can't change that."

"Well, take your chances. I would suggest as well that you let Jay help you manage your money."

"Bill, all my life, all my twenty-one years, Jay has been in charge of me. I want to break free. Jay wants his freedom too. He told me so. I want to continue living with him. He says no. I understand because I want my freedom too."

Bill smiled. "Well, if freedom's what you want, then you shouldn't be getting married."

"Come on. We're two guys. It's not as if we're going to adopt children and raise a family."

"Have you discussed that with Carlos?"

I shook my head.

"Hombre, these are things you talk about before you embark on marriage."

I said nothing.

"Want to know my honest opinion? You're not ready for any of this. Didn't Jay tell you so? Maybe Jay at your age. But you." He shook his head and twisted his lips.

Ready or not, I'm going ahead. "Listen, Bill. *On est deux mecs.* It can't be that bad. We'll keep out of each other's spaces. I'll be busy with school work. Carlos will be too. He has already applied to UQAM."

He gave me that look again, where he twists his mouth to the left. "So you want to go ahead with this?"

"Yes. I can't turn back now. A promise is a promise."

"Hombre, the only time you can't turn back is when you're falling off the cliff. You're still at the brink."

"Why're you so negative? You're always negative. You've never said one happy thing to me yet. Man, listening to you, you'd think the earth was about to crack open and swallow us up. You're sour, man. *Aigre, en hostie.* Because Chai and Rick and Enrique — all your lovers — dumped you."

His shoulders slumped and his lips compressed.

"Sorry, Bill. Sorry, man. I know you're telling me to be careful. Just that. Just that ... You know what this means to me?" I went over to the recliner where he sat, put my arms around him, and embraced him. "I got carried away. It's like you're my father and I lost my cool. Understand?" He smiled and we said nothing for a while.

"Let Jay help you manage your money."

"Tutelage! Not again. Grama thought I needed it. Maybe Ma was feeding her news about me. I don't know. Ma made her will on her deathbed. They made it quick and simple. Otherwise she too would have put me under Jay's supervision. Jay controlling my money? You've got to be kidding."

He shook his head. "That's not quite what I'm suggesting, even though I think he'd do a better job than you."

I got up to leave. At the door I changed my mind and went to sit in the couch facing him.

"Why don't you let me have a talk with Jay?"

"Okay, but that doesn't mean I'm agreeing to anything."

When I left his apartment, I was so caught up thinking about it that I went past my metro stop. Jay was sitting at the dining table when I got in. I searched his face to see if he knew what Bill and I had been discussing. But that sheepish look, a dead give-away whenever he's hiding something from me, wasn't there. I went to my room and remained anxious. Around midnight I heard him flushing the toilet and went to his room. He met me standing at the door and frowned.

"What is it, Paul? Can't it wait until tomorrow?"

I shook my head.

He snorted and motioned for me to sit down in the chair across from his bed.

I told him what Bill and I had discussed, and that I'd lost my temper.

For a while he said nothing. Then he chuckled. "You're lucky. It's like he's adopted you. I sometimes wonder how gay men without children deal with their paternal instincts." Then he exhaled loud. "Paul, I don't want to manage your money. I might steal it. I would never trust you with mine. Why should you trust me with yours?"

"You can't steal, Jay, not even from yourself."

"I'm flattered but you're foolish to think so. Grow up. I'm human. Remember, how much you loved and admired Grama? She once told Ma that she was quite prepared to horn Grandpa when he got old and couldn't perform."

"She wouldn't have. She was being flippant. After she divorced Benjamin, she remained single. Wasn't involved with anybody."

"Aunt Mercy?"

"Fanciful speculation. And even if it was so, she was faithful. I'm not here to talk about that ... I gave Bill permission to talk to you about managing my money."

"You did! Tell him there's no need to. It's hard work just getting up every morning and doing the necessary. I have enough tasks."

We said nothing for a while, but eventually he agreed to talk with Bill. I went back to my room and was able to fall asleep. In the end there was a compromise. My assets would remain in my name. I would have nothing to fear if the union between Carlos and me dissolved. Quebec law shields assets acquired before marriage as well as proceeds from those assets. It was agreed that the earnings from my investments should go into a joint chequing account with Jay. It was all worked out on June 29, 2007, three days before I boarded the plane for Mexico, where I was to meet and enter into a civil union with Carlos. Civil union rather than marriage was Gélinas' idea. Since Carlos reads and speaks French—taught it in Guatemala, I had the contract drawn up in French. He signed it without reading it.

✳ "So, you're a married man," Bill said to me over the phone two days after I came back from Mexico bringing Carlos. Four years ago, almost to the day: August 17, 2007. "Come over with Prince Charming. If he's hot and sexy, I might put my morals on hold and borrow him for a night. The honeymoon must still be on."

We'd been held up in Mexico City for six weeks while I did the paper work to obtain the civil union certificate and his temporary resident visa. Even then the signs were glaring. In restaurants he'd order the most expensive dish on the menu. There were hints too when we met in Comitán the year before. "Are we staying at the Montebello?" He frowned when I shook my head and told the cabdriver to take us to the Meson de Los Angeles—for a fifth of the price. He talked only about himself and his family and kept complaining that Comitán lacked everything: "Aren't they tired of eating tacos? Don't they have anything else on the menu?" Until I said: "But Comitán's a lot cleaner, safer, and orderly than Huehuetenango. Have you seen children shining shoes or selling trinkets in the parks and the market? No. They're in school." He'd hear me talking to Jay over the phone and wouldn't even ask how Jay was. The storm you prefer not to know about, the data you want to be wrong, that you convince yourself are wrong—long before they break into consciousness.

Three days after arriving here, we visited Bill in his apartment. I observed Bill taking his measure. We sat at his dining table and drank red wine, ate pizza, and chatted in Spanish. Carlos, fidgeting, his eyes turned away, gave mostly yes-no answers to Bill's questions. About past boyfriends, he said he'd had only one before me—eyes closed, a sure sign of lying.

"And after you've settled in, what are your plans?"

"*Quizás trabajar. Quizás estudiar.* (Work maybe. Study maybe.)" Bill pressed him for specifics.

"*Ahora, no sé,*" he said, turning away his head and rolling his eyes.

After several "*no sé,*" Bill quipped: "*Hombre,* there's a helluva lot that you don't know." Carlos's eyes narrowed and ridges formed in his lower jaw.

Bill asked me to come see him alone the next day. We went for coffee at the Tim Hortons in the Village.

Bill was silent for a long time.

"How's it going between you two?"

"Fine."

"Why's he so cagey?"

"Cagey?"

"You haven't noticed?"

"He's meeting you for the first time. Maybe he finds you intimidating."

Bill stared at the tabletop for a long while. When he looked up at me he said: "Take him to a gay bar and see how he behaves. Did you two go to any in Mexico City?"

I shook my head.

Bill swallowed. "You lived with him for almost a year in Guatemala." He glanced at me then looked away. "But that was in his mother's house." He stopped talking, frowned, and fell silent. When he resumed talking, it was about the battle by US gays for the recognition of their rights.

When I got home Carlos was on the computer emailing his friends and relatives. He broke off, and we had tamales for supper. On my way back from Bill I'd detoured to Plamondon and bought us Guatemalan food, that I felt would make his transition less difficult. Carlos ate silently. While I was washing the dishes, he said: "You were out with Bill, right?"

I turned around to look at him and nodded.

"*¿Qué piensa de mí?*"

"I don't know. He didn't say."

"*No te creo.* (I don't believe you.)"

The next evening, we visited Gina at her apartment—near the Olympic Stadium, a few blocks north of the Botanical Gardens. Her partner Emilia was away visiting her grandmother in Managua. Gúicho, from high school days, was there along with four of Gina's friends. Women I didn't know. Two couples: one Black and French-Canadian, the other South Asian and French-Canadian.

Lucky girl, that Gina. Pursuing an LLD at Université de Montréal. Paid for with oodles of bursary money. Alvin, the other genius in our high school group, was at Cambridge pursuing a PhD in physics. I burned with envy, and thought of the ass I'd made of myself in high school, while they studied and excelled.

Tortilla chips, dips, guacamole, mineral water, wine, a platter of fruit, and a chocolate cake were laid out on the kitchen counter for us to serve ourselves. We ate and talked in French, except for when Carlos and Gúicho spoke to each other. I had my first chance to observe how comfortable Carlos was with Québécois French. I was impressed. (He later told me that his French teachers at university were Christian Brothers from Quebec.) Gúicho attached himself to Carlos all evening. They exchanged telephone numbers, and I heard Gúicho saying that he lived on Lionel Groulx, down the hill from us.

"Don't believe a word of it," Gina said, trying to rile him. "Sky's his home."

Guicho bared his teeth at her, then pointed at me and asked Carlos. "Where did you meet this lesbian?"

"*La ferme, Gúicho!*" Gina said.

He touched Carlos' right breast. "You girls need a man to protect you. You look vulnerable."

"He's venting because he can't find one," Gina said.

"I'm a top," Gúicho said and smote his chest. "*Dos cientos por ciento* he-man!"

"In your dreams. A toy top."

We laughed.

"So, Meatman, where's *le mon oncle*, your brother, the vampire?" he asked, staring at me wide-eyed.

"At home. Want his number?"

"Yes, and his cock."

"Gúicho, please," Gina said. "Keep that for the sauna."

"Ok. Ok." he waved his arms dismissively. "I'll be *políticamente puritano. Cuando estoy con mojitos ...*"

Within days he and Carlos began visiting each other.

➤ Two months after arriving here, Carlos was surprised when he discovered Jay's name along with mine on a cancelled cheque. He joked about it. He remembered that I'd told him I came to Guatemala with money I'd inherited from Grama, and asked if I'd had Jay's permission for that trip: "Why Jay control your money?"

"Both Grama and Ma were worried I'd run amok. They gave Jay everything on condition that he look after me," I said joking. He said nothing, and I didn't elaborate.

Thereafter he'd jibe, in Spanish usually: "No wonder your parents put you under guardianship. You'll never grow up. You'll always be a minor. *Estarás siempre menor.*"

4

CARLOS, FIVE YEARS after our meeting. Carlos in his mother's home. In mine. Two different human beings inhabiting the same body. In Huehuetenango he'd go in search of strawberries for me. Never missed a chance to put his arms around me when no one was around. Replaced Paul with *Querido* and *mi otra costilla*. Once when his sister and her children were visiting, she asked if all gays were like us, said she was jealous, and wished her husband Federico would copy our example.

It all dried up six months after he came here. Jay had warned me that I'd see sides of him I didn't already know. Bill too. My first sense of real trouble came the day he went to register at UQAM, a mere two weeks after he'd arrived. His appointment was at 10:30, and we'd arranged to meet for lunch in Concordia's EV building around 12:30. I waited until 3 p.m. and he never showed up. The cellphone I'd got for him was off. I phoned home. He wasn't there. I became worried. Two hours later he came into the apartment smiling and asked what we were having for supper. I waited for his explanation. None came.

"Carlos, where were you?"

"*Estaba chumpipeando con Guícho en el centro.* (Been wandering around with Guícho downtown.)"

I swallowed and took a deep breath. "Weren't we supposed to meet for lunch?"

"*Sí. Pero ...*"

"And you couldn't phone?"

He shrugged and went into the bathroom to avoid answering me.

Still some things surprise you, things that stared you in the face but that you couldn't see. Things that Bill saw. Carlos never wanted to be around when Bill and I met. Said Bill pushed *su hocico* (his snout) in where it had no business and one day somebody would chop it off.

"Meaning?"

"You no understand. *Cambiamos el tema.* (Change the subject.)"

I felt he was over-possessive and jealous of my attachment to Bill. Almost never participated in the free-roving conversations Bill and I had. Bill spoke in Spanish whenever the three of us were together so Carlos wouldn't feel excluded. But Carlos would be silent or yawning or glancing at his watch, his frowning stares telling me he wanted to leave, sometimes when the conversation was most exciting. Bill and I lived a few blocks from each other—he at Chomedey and Maisonneuve, I initially at Fort and Tupper and later at Atwater and Lincoln—so I never had to worry about transportation to and from his place. At home Carlos would list Bill's grammatical errors and make fun of him, then try to replicate all the gesticulations of "Dona Sansón, *la grande folle.*" (He learned the derogatory epithets for gays very quickly, most likely from Güicho.) Next he took to calling Bill *Estrella*: the name of a rabid dog they'd had to euthanize. The first time he said it, he laughed so hard his tummy shook. At times, to rile me, he'd ask: ¿"*Tu Estrella, sin luz, sin calor, cómo está-ella?* (Your star without light, without heat, how's she?)" And chuckle.

Eventually he refused to go to Bill's place and didn't want to be present when Bill dropped by. "¿*Por qué te interesas tan a ese trapo? ¿Fuera tu primer amor? Sin duda, por dinero.*" He guffawed and his body shook.

I clenched my teeth for a few seconds. "I don't appreciate your calling Bill an old rag. And if he'd been my first boyfriend, I'd be proud of it whether or not it was for money. What do you want, Carlos? I won't end my friendship with Bill."

He grimaced, looking as if reacting to a bad smell.

On another occasion he said: "*!Qué bueno que te haya rescatado! A ti te gustan los viejos. Es evidente.*" He laughed.

"You didn't rescue me from anything. And yes, older men like Bill interest because younger men like you have nothing to say that can't be put in a tweet."

"That's what you think of me?"

I didn't answer.

"Answer me!" He was seated beside a pile of boxes in one of the two chairs of our small kitchen table in our studio apartment on Fort Street. We were getting ready to move into my present apartment, on Atwater and Lincoln. I was sitting with my back to the window overlooking Fort Street. He got up and glowered over me, all the while shaking his balled fists.

I sucked my teeth. He went into the bathroom and showered, then dressed and left without saying anything. He came back a little past eight the following morning. This was January 16, 2008, five months after he arrived here. Two hours after he came in, immigration called him to come in for his permanent resident visa. Last week when he phoned to beg me to make up with him, I re-read the entry in my journal about that day and cried.

The afternoon of January 17, when we did talk about his sleeping out, he said: "You brought me here. I live in the apartment you pay for, I eat the food you buy, but I won't let you walk all over me. "*No lo permito. Prefiero volver a mi país.*"

"Humiliate *you*! You call Bill and me names. I swallow it all. You have the nerve to accuse *me* of walking over you? By all means go back to *your country* if you want to."

I hid all this from Bill but I told Jay. Jay thought it was an overflow from the pressure Carlos was feeling from being away from his family and friends, and urged me to go easy with him.

"And his sleeping out?"

"There's probably nothing to it. An immature way of showing anger and trying to make you jealous. Maybe he wants to reach you at another level and you're not letting him. I don't know."

"And what about not wanting Bill to come to the apartment?"

"Who pays the rent, Paul?"

The next evening I invited Bill over. That night after Bill left Carlos slept on the couch. When we moved here on February 1, the room that I'd intended as an office became his bedroom, and it was the rare night that we slept in the same bed after that.

❧ I'd asked him why he spent the night of January 16, 2008 outside but never where. I wanted him to think that his behaviour didn't affect me unduly. He'd already spent a semester at UQAM, doing a major in popular culture and a minor in Spanish. He later switched to Spanish linguistics and education. I feel certain now that he'd spent that night outside to gauge how much power he had over me, to measure how emotionally dependent I was on him. He rarely slept out after that but he routinely came in at three and four in the morning. He blamed me for not wanting to go to the bars. I avoid closed crowded places because I don't know when I'll react to something I'm allergic to and begin to wheeze. On a couple of occasions at Sky, I'd had to use my puffer and so I stopped going. One time he infested me with crab lice and said I had picked it up at the gym.

❧ Four months ago, April 21, the day after he became a Canadian citizen, he told me, without ever taking his eyes off me, what happened on January 16, 2008: that Gúicho had taken him to a sauna, and they'd taken part in an orgy. "*Me gustó muchísimo.* I love it." He smacked his lips. "I went back many times, while you and Bill were having *sus aburridas discusiones.*" He gave a farting sound and a dismissive hand-wave; "Pile o' shit. *Embotados. Están embotados, tú y él. Lo digo en francés: bouchés*; y en inglés: You two corked, man, plugged." He slapped his rectum: "*Aquí,*" and grinned.

¿"*No digas nada*"?

I spread my open palms and shrugged.

"You no love me. You love Bill."

I bit my lip and pressed my hands fiercely against my thighs.

"You ice, *hielo.* You no have feelings."

That quarrel began about forty-five minutes before we had supper. He was doing the cooking: *pepián* chicken and *gallo pinto* (rice and black beans), one of three or four things he knows how to cook. I went into my bedroom and remained there for the rest of the afternoon and all that evening. When he called me for supper, I pretended to be asleep. I'd intended to proof a short story I was submitting to a journal. I didn't.

The next day I went to see Bill. He'd had to abandon teaching midway in the semester. He was waiting for some diagnostic tests his doctor had ordered and had been forewarned that the results might not be good. I began to talk about Carlos, and he said he didn't want to hear. I insisted.

"What do you want me to tell you—that Carlos has never been in love with anyone but himself? You know that already. A week after I met him I was sure this would be over in a year. I was wrong. Free food, free rent, trips in winter to Miami and New Orleans. Whoever's advising him has told him to play it safe until he gets citizenship. And his tuition fees, you pay them—"

"For the first year only. It's a loan. You know that. I followed your advice and made him sign a promissory note."

"Hold your breath." He moistened his lips. "But it has lasted almost four years, and will continue until ... until he walks out on you." He looked away. "Sorry, I don't want to hurt your feelings. I'm under a lot of pressure. Sorry."

"He got his citizenship two days ago."

Bill twisted his lips to the left, then to the right, and shook his head. "Things will get interesting now. Very interesting. The actors change, the script stays the same. Brace yourself."

"Meaning?"

"You'll soon be out of his clutches. Did I just say that?" He shook his head as if clearing it of fog. "It's all the pressure I'm under. Don't know what I'm saying. Look, I don't want to hear anything more about your problems with Carlos. I've given you all advice I can. It's for you to act on it. Maybe you can't. Can't expect people to do what they can't do." Then he fell silent.

I'd gone to his place to ask his advice regarding Carlos' confession that he frequented saunas, but in the end I never told him. I'd burdened him enough. Besides he was looking frail. He'd lost at least ten kilos in three months; his skin was folding and now had a deep creamish colour. When I began noticing it months before, I'd assumed that it was his sixty-six years catching up with him. Like most gay men, he tried to mask his age: going to the gym, dyeing his hair, which was still quite thick ... Prescient Bill.

→ Disaster has a way of coming bundled. The next day, April 23, Jay phoned around 1:15 p.m. to say that Bill wanted us to meet at his place, and whether I could come that same evening around 7 p.m. It was urgent.

Laid back in his brown leather recliner, his legs crossed, his last will and testament in his lap, he told us that he was in the terminal phase of pancreatic cancer. I began to cry. Jay moved from the couch where we were both sitting, went to stand beside the recliner, and took Bill's hands into his. News like this freezes me. I don't remember much of the conversation after that. And it was only when I expressed surprise after Jay made an offhand comment about the work involved in being Bill's liquidator that I understood that much of the conversation that night was about Bill's last wishes. I had never suspected that he didn't have friends, that he was indeed a loner, someone like Jay. I knew he and Jay had grown close. Sometimes Jay would mention that they'd gone to see a play, an exhibition at the Museum of Fine Arts, or a film, and I would feel a twinge of jealousy that I hadn't been invited. I knew it was because Carlos was in my life, and I shrugged it off with the acknowledgement that choices come with limits.

Bill died on May 31 in the ambulance taking him to hospital. From April 23 until he died, Jay slept at his house. I dropped in for an hour or two every afternoon to see if there was anything he wanted. The CLSC sent someone for a couple of hours in the morning.

Even so he followed the election campaign ongoing then and continued to express his opinions on world affairs. He looked upon the revolt in the Muslim countries with ambivalence. "More power to them if they can hold their governments accountable and keep them half-way honest. Politicians are a slimy breed. For every half decent one, there are fifty who operate like termites in the dark. Hope they

topple every last one. Governments must be accountable to their people."
He shook his head. "The challenge is to find ways to hold them accountable. Don't be fooled. Many of these clamouring for democracy today will be beheading their comrades tomorrow. My sixty-six years o' living tell me that a lot of this is about wanting to become the new hogs at the trough."

About Canadian voters he was just as scathing. "Promise them they can have everything without paying taxes and they'll vote for you. People are like bodies of water waiting for wind. One day they vote Tommy Douglas the greatest Canadian and the next they put Stephen Harper in power. Humans logical! Whom are we kidding?"

I didn't agree with his pessimism but knew I had no arguments to challenge him. We stayed silent for a long time, then he said, as if muttering to himself: "Democracy is mostly rhetoric. Reform was going to make all sorts of changes to make society more democratic if they came to power. When they smelled power they changed their tune and their name. As the opposition they championed whistleblowers. In power they muzzle them more than any other government before. They're the closest thing to a dictatorship that Canadians have ever lived under. And do Canadians mind? Not at all. If people's material needs are met, they don't care what sort of government is in power. It's one reason Hitler had so little opposition."

He asked if I'd seen *The Wind that Shakes the Barley*. I had. "Then you know what I'm talking about. Yeats got it spot on: 'Beggars change places but the lash goes on.' The only justice is that sometimes the whipping's done by those formerly whipped." In spite of his weakened condition—he wasn't able to stand in line at the polling station—he went to vote. He voted for Jack, but I doubt Bill would be one of those according him sainthood today. "The guy's a great actor," he said. "But the NDP is the clearest voice against the politics of selfishness that the Conservative Party and the capitalist media are promoting." He liked how Jack had forced Martin to put money into social housing and forced Harper's hand in the home energy refit programme. Bill even donated to the NDP, but he knew, much like he'd said when Obama was elected, that the rhetoric deployed to win power has nothing to do with exercising power. He'd voted Liberal consistently from the time of Trudeau, but stopped when Martin became finance minister. Putting the nation's finances in the hands of a capitalist, he felt, was a recipe for increased homelessness.

Jay voted Green. I'd planned to vote Liberal because of the same-sex legislation they brought in, but was one of those young people who never made it to the polls. Jay's the only one in our circle who voted. Gina turned off the television as soon as the election ads came on. She says that political platforms have been hoaxes "from as far back as when heaven was invented ... Nowadays politicians offer heaven on earth, camouflaged, but heaven just the same, and, oh boy, don't they find suckers. Even Obama does. It worked for him the last time. Can't wait to hear what he'll promise next time. Maybe he'll walk on water. Even fly. Trust me, it can be arranged, like a Batman movie. Daddy voted for Stephane Dion when he was Liberal leader, but would shake his head and say: 'What a stupid politician! If you want to get elected you don't tell people you'll raise their taxes; you tell them they won't have to pay taxes.'"

Hope I never get to be this cynical.

⤳ Bill donated his body to McGill's medical school, but he left a lot of unsettled business. He'd inherited his mother's house in Vancouver and was in the process of selling it when he fell ill. The sale was to be notarized on June 15. Jay had to fly off to Vancouver to complete the transaction. Apart from his works of art, which he gave us — six paintings and four pieces of sculpture — his possessions were to be liquidated, the money put in a trust fund, and the earnings given to The Stephen Lewis Foundation.

His illness and death threw Jay's travel plans to Africa into chaos. Jay had taken a semester of unpaid leave to travel around in Africa and was scheduled to fly out on May 24. An auctioneer liquidated the contents of the condo, and the sale of the condo was notarized mere days before Jay left for Africa on June 25. He's entrusted Gélinas, Bill's lawyer acquaintance, with setting up the trust fund.

⇥ April 29, a week after Carlos became a citizen, he asked me again why Jay was controlling my money. I told him it wasn't my money. He asked why I hadn't contested the will.

"Take my mother to court because my grandmother didn't leave me more than $6,000! Carlos, I was nineteen when my grandmother died. All the years I spent with her she treated me like a little god. And then the little god failed her. I'm even surprised she left me anything."

"You read will?"

"Yes. Together Jay, Ma, and I read my grandmother's will."

"You read your Mama will?"

"My mother's will?"

He nodded.

I clenched my teeth.

"Something about this *asunto se siente mal*. It stinks man," he said, then held his nose and shook his head.

"Change the subject."

"*¡Cambiamos el tema!* We talking our *herencia*!"

"Our!"

"*Sí.* Is my business too."

"I don't think so, Carlos." The conversation ended there that day. I was on my way to Jay's place to go over a list of agencies that could provide homecare for Bill, if it came to that. He'd fiercely rejected going into palliative care.

Three days later (the day Carlos lost his job, but I didn't know it at the time), Carlos began again. "*Tengo un conocido, un abogado, alguien que puede ayudarte.*"

"Your lawyer friend will help me with what, Carlos?"

"*¿Eres tonto?* Your *herencia*."

"I don't need your friend's help, Carlos."

¡"Caramba!" He shook his fists. Then he spoke calmly, telling me that his Salvadoran friends had introduced him to a Nicaraguan woman, Gineta; that Gineta had married a gay guy so she could get permanent residence. She and her husband never lived together, never

had sex, nothing. He'd only done her a favour. He'd been a successful businessman. Gineta had been his cleaning lady and she'd explained to him in tears that she'd lost her claim for refugee status and had been ordered to return to Nicaragua. The husband was murdered by a lover, and Gineta got his estate; she took his family to court and won. *Un amigo*—I was sure Carlos meant Gúicho—had spoken to Gineta about *my problem*, and she'd told him that the lawyer she'd hired—Alfredo Hernández—would be willing to help me.

To placate Carlos, I said I would think about it. A week later he asked me if I could come up with a thousand dollars, but wouldn't say what for. I got him to sit with me at the dining table so we could talk about it. His face half frown-half smile, the stamp of scheming, he said nothing. My mind raced. Perhaps a relative was sick: his mother, sister or one of his four nieces, and he needed the money to send to Guatemala. Eventually it was I who broke the silence.

"Carlos, what's this money for?"

His lower lip moved up a centimetre; his smile turned ironic. "I no want tell."

I pounded the table and swallowed.

"Okay. Gineta *habló*, talk with lawyer and for thousand *dólares* he go make search. I make *cita* with him: Tuesday 4 o'clock."

My chest tightened. I took a blast from my puffer. We stayed quiet while I tried to stabilize my breathing.

"There's no thousand dollars. You hear me. None! Cancel the appointment with the lawyer and stay out of Jackson family business. I don't want to hear another word about *tu herencia*. Maybe I should ask you to pay half the bills. I don't ask you for money from your student loans and bursaries or your job and you've never offered any. Whether or not Ma left me money, I too live on loans and bursaries and the allowance Ma authorized Jay to give me."

"For my mother I send all money I get. She always want car. Now she got car. I pay her car."

"Carlos, if you want to give your mother a car, that's your responsibility. I don't own a car. I don't even have a driver's licence."

He sneered.

I'd mentioned none of this to Jay. He was preoccupied with looking after Bill. Two years earlier he'd taken care of Jonathan. No wonder, he's now in hospital. Must be rundown. And nobody there to take care of *him*. Life's often like that.

But I had to talk to somebody. Next day I phoned Gina and apprised her of the situation.

"Uh huh! Meatman, this guy is hunting for money. If the lawyer smells money he'll go along even though he knows he won't win. Won't surprise me if this $1,000 isn't to con you to pay the lawyer for work on Carlos' behalf. Now that he's no longer working—"

"No longer working!"

"He didn't tell you? He's been laid off. I better keep my trap shut."

"Come on, Gina."

"I don't want to get mixed up in your affairs. I don't want anyone saying, Gina said this, Gina said that."

I walked over to Bill's place that same evening to speak with Jay. He listened and remained his sanguine self, and I had to push him to say something.

"I'm sorry Carlos turned out to be different than you thought. What do you think is happening?"

I didn't answer right away.

Bill was in his recliner, a blanket draped over him, his eyes, saffron yellow, fixed on me. "Answer your brother. Say something."

"I don't know what to say."

"Wake up, Paul," Jay said. "Carlos is getting ready to leave you and trying to find out how much he can leave with." For a while he was silent. "Quite a cleaning lady, that Gineta, and Carlos seems to be her apprentice. He has dirt to practise on."

"He won't have much to clean. After food and rent, there's almost nothing left in my—our—chequing account."

For a long time we said nothing. The conversation turned again to what Carlos might be up to. "It's possible," Bill said, "that in a probe they could find out what your assets are. Would cost a bit to do the probe though. Requires a court order, most likely."

When I got back to the apartment, Carlos was out. He still hadn't told me he'd been laid off. The message light on the telephone was blinking. I saw Gina's number. She asked me to call her when I got in, even if it was after midnight. She's a night owl. I called her right away. She said Emilia had insisted that she talk to me. "Carlos is moving out day after tomorrow. Moving in with Gúicho. By the way, two days ago, he lost his job too. I warned that boy. Goes to Sky every night. Goes to bed at four in the morning, and has to be at work some mornings at five. When his shift begins at five he never bothers to sleep. Late for work all the time. Falling asleep on the job. Dropping dishes. His boss lost his temper and told him to get out. Good thing he looks like a tub. The way he can't say no to sex, he'd be long dead ... There's more." She stopped talking.

"Gina, what are you holding back?"

She didn't answer.

"Gina?"

"I'm listening."

"You didn't ask me to call you to tell me about Gúicho's job."

"No. But I've changed my mind. You know what: you gay guys come in two groups: abusers and abused. Here's my advice: settle down and enjoy the abuse ... or do something about it, and call me afterwards."

"You're torturing me."

"Nothing you don't enjoy."

For a few seconds neither of us spoke. Then she chuckled. "Here's a joke a lesbian sister told me: When God created the first woman he gave her three boobs. She said she didn't need the third boob. So God threw it into the garbage bin but Satan retrieved it and used it to create gay men."

Ok-a-ay. There was another long pause.

"Use your brain, Meatman. Use your fucking brain. Carlos thinks you have money hidden away, and he's determined to get it. He and Gineta—you know who she is?"

"Yes, the cleaning lady."

She laughed. "Good. Well, she's advising Carlos. She brags about how *well* she did in *her* marriage. Now she's coaching Carlos to do even better in his. Meatman, if you have money left, put it far from their slimy fingers."

"I don't have money."

"What! It's all gone!" She chuckled. "The year he arrived you paid his university tuition: Thousands of dollars. Wow. Six months later you moved into a downtown two-bedroom hi-rise apartment. You pay for everything. On your spring break 2009 you took him to Miami Beach. In spring break 2010 you took him to New Orleans. You're such a fool. And all this time he was going to the sauna to pick up men. Meatman, you've been buying his affection. You guys who have issues with your bodies ... You haven't hung up! Good. You know what Gúicho says? Behind Carlos' back of course. 'Imagine, Meatman spending good money to hold on to *that*. If I'd known Meatman was a rich sugar daddy I'd o' moved in on him.'

"'Thought it was Jay you wanted,' Emilia told him.

"'The vampire. Ooh la-la! For that body. Any time. And now that I know *el pisto está en su mano*. Hmmm.'"

I was stunned.

"I have to go now," she said. "Emilia begged me to warn you. Now my conscience is clear. By the way," —she was laughing— "we know everything you two do in bed, down to the shape and size of your dick. And when Gúicho began taking Carlos to the sauna, he told us everything." She gulped. "Meatman, there are limits. There's a reason we put curtains in our windows. Did you pick up this guy in a brothel?"

I should have been prepared for this. But how? One evening coming from visiting Bill, I heard Whitney Houston's voice bellowing away in my apartment as I exited the elevator. I met Carlos and Gúicho doing dance moves to "I Want to Dance with Somebody." I lowered the volume on the stereo, and watched them for a while.

"Wanna hear my cover?" Gúicho asked, grinning.

In his version the words *dance* and *love* were replaced with *fuck*.

I left them there and went into my bedroom. Later I asked Carlos what the singing and dancing was all about, and he said Gúicho was practising to enter some sort of drama contest.

"Does he have to practise here?"

"And why not? ¿Y por qué no?"

I rolled over and went to sleep

About a month later Gina asked me what character I had in "Gúicho's masterpiece."

"In what?"

"In Guicho's skit. You mean you like don't have a role?"

"What sort of skit?"

"Thought they were practising in your living room ... Some theatre group or other is auditioning guys for a drag show extravaganza, and in a lead up to the big event they're inviting groups to come and do skits. There's prizes for the best skits. Gúicho is playing a lesbian cleaning woman who seduces her female employer. Carlos—in a blond wig, taffeta dress with lots o' sequins bought from the thrift shop, and high heels—is the female employer. You'll love it."

"Do they live happily ever after?"

"I don't know. They need a man to be the employer's husband. There's where I thought you came in. He's supposed to come and catch them in bed."

"And join in the action?"

Gina laughed. "They can't make it too over the top."

"That wouldn't be over the top; that would be the truth."

"I told Gúicho not to do that skit, to come up with something else. It reinforces the stereotype that Central Americans are cleaners."

I waited for Carlos to tell me about this. He didn't and I forgot about it until, about a month or so later, he said something about going with Gúicho to see a travesty show by The Hot Girls from Toronto. "And what about your own performance?" I asked him.

He frowned, then smiled. "How you know?"

"I have my sources."

"Gúicho was booed. *Le lanzaron objetos.* (They threw stuff at him.)"

"How come you never told me?"

"*Porque, hombre, eres estreñido;* corked man. *Deformado por el protestantismo.* You fucked up, man."

"You have the wrong Jackson."

"Jay bad. *Eres peor.*"

"Your mother should have seen *you* on stage."

He said he never made it onto the stage, that Gúicho froze on stage and forgot what he had to do. "How you know?"

"Friends told me."

"*Espiones*, you mean."

"I don't want these shenanigans taking place in here."

"Is no' my apartament too? No?"

I said nothing.

"*! Contesta-me! Caramba!*"

I didn't answer.

"*Porque pagas la renta. ¿Verdad?* You can treat me like street dog *¿Verdad?*"

"Wrong. I love peace and quiet."

"*Soy hispánico. Me gusta bailar, bromar*—happy stuff. You no like happiness, you cold, you depressed, you English, you make love like you in coma."

When he first arrived he'd scream out when we had sex, something he never did in Guatemala. I asked him to temper it. I could easily follow the conversation of the couple in the adjoining apartment. He saw nothing wrong with people hearing him. He complied while we lived on Fort but resumed when we moved to Atwater on the pretext that the new apartment was soundproof. It wasn't.

A least he knows now that not all North Americans are on a pleasure train. Guess I failed to deliver the pleasure he'd expected from *El Norte*. And he quickly fell under the influence of Gúicho, the Gúicho who says: "You guys like play gay. I'm the real McCoy. Gay in every way. Every gay man's treasure: one hundred percent pleasure" —torso slouched, arms outstretched, imitating a bird in flight. When he left high school and had to choose between going to the bars and going to college, he chose the bars. His rationale: he has to enjoy his youth, because he intends not to live a day beyond thirty-five.

"No need to worry. You won't make it to thirty. You burn your candle at both ends and in the middle too, especially in the middle,"

Gina says when he repeats his various versions of dying before thirty-five.

"Did you hear the one about ...?"

"We already heard it," Gina would say.

"The one about this bodybuilder with the perfect body who went to audition for a porno movie? Well, they loved his body; perfect in his bikini brief, yeah-yeah. They told him to take off the brief.

"'Why?' he asked.

"'They'll certainly love your body, but it's on your dick they'll get off.'

"'Then I'm keeping my brief on.'"

He stopped talking.

"That's the *joke*." Gina said. "Gúicho, I swear your jokes are flatter than your ass."

To think Carlos became the acolyte of this *chuchona*, Emilia's nickname for Gúicho behind his back. Not that saying it to his face would have mattered. Nothing could upset him.

At what point did Carlos begin to hold me in contempt? Maybe from the very beginning. The signs were always there, beginning with a day I waited for him at Concordia and he never showed up. "You no love me," he'd often say after he began staying out until three ... four in the morning. Maybe I should have had fits of anger and jealousy and beg him tearfully, on my knees, *arrodillado*, to stop making me jealous. Or go looking for his bedmates and threaten to beat them up. Like women in Latin American *telenovelas*.

⇥ After my conversation with Gina that night, I remained awake. Carlos didn't come home. There were no signs of packing. Maybe he was delaying his move. I was still lying in bed at 8:15 when the doorbell rang. The ringer identified himself as a Purolator courier. He came up and asked me to sign for a letter. On the envelope I saw the name Alfredo Hernández. The letter was a request, on behalf of his client Carlos Morales, for copies of my mother's and grandmother's wills and a true statement of the value of my assets. I phoned Jay at home. He wasn't in. I phoned his cell and got his voice mail. His students were probably writing exams. He called me just after one p.m. and came by forty-five minutes later.

We phoned Alfredo and told his secretary to tell him that our mother's and grandmother's wills were none of his business, and we would be prepared to fight his request all the way to Supreme Court.

Carlos did not come in that day or night. He showed up with four empty cartons around 9:30 on May 5, and said he'd come for his things. After packing and throwing the clothes he no longer wanted down the garbage chute, he sat down on the couch and gave me a big grin, then he began to pull at his chin. Finally he said that I had to give him a living allowance; that I'd brought him here, and even though he was leaving me, I had to continue to support him because I had been doing so all along; it was an acquired right according to Quebec law. "*Una ley de Quebec.* Lawyer tell me. I want $700 right now: *400 por la renta y 300 por la comida* (400 for rent and 300 to buy food.)"

Go fuck yourself, I felt like saying. My eyes roved slowly over his body. He'd gained about seven kilos, visible in his jowls and ballooning gut. "Alfredo will have to come in person to collect the $700, and soon after I'll begin the process to deport your ass."

"You no can. Too late. I citizen. I Canadian citizen." A triumphal grin spread across his face.

⁙ 5

HE'D JUST FINISHED his degree at UQAM and would graduate in a month. UQAM credited him a year for the work he'd done at San Carlos in Guatemala. Four months before, a blustery February day when the wind whistled around the building and a blood-chilling cold gripped the city, I didn't answer him when he mused out loud that nothing would please his mother more than to attend his graduation, that she had been disappointed that he and his sister hadn't completed university: Maria—seven years older—because she got pregnant while in first-year university and got married; he: because, in 2001, their father was branded a communist and assassinated. I knew the story, had listened to it a few times in their home in Guatemala. His father Mario, who was president of a union, and Leon, his assistant, had heard that they were on the militia's liquidation list and had arranged to go to Mexico and lie low for a while. But the assassins intercepted them half way to the Mexican border. They killed Mario and blew up the car, but they spared Leon. The company had had the nerve to send a wreath to the funeral. Rosa and Carlos disagreed over whether Leon knew that the killers were waiting for them. Everyone knew who the assassins were. One belonged to the Knights of Columbus and took communion in Rosa's church. Her *querido* Mario had been a Knight of Columbus too. But no one came forward with evidence. People remembered the 100,000 or so killed during the civil war, feared for their lives and the lives of their families and stayed mute. Carlos was in his final year at the University of San Carlos in Quetzaltenango when it happened. He gave up his studies to be with his

49

mother and went to work teaching French in a private academy to help replace the income his father had brought in.

The All Saints Day I spent with them was given over to Mario: service at church, wreaths at the cemetery, a vigil there to burn candles, and eventually eating *fiambre* at home—a day entirely devoted to *el querido* Mario. On her dressing table, beside his framed photograph, Rosa kept an 18-inch statue of the Virgin Mary. On the wall above the head of her bed were pictures of all the popes who'd come into office during her adulthood along with pictures of Carlos, Maria and Mario taking part in the Holy Week *andas*. Even so she mistrusted priests. They were on the side of the rich. I wanted to tell her that they were only carrying out the wishes of John Paul and Benedict. She went to mass regularly. The priests were corrupt but the church was holy. She reserved most of her vitriol for *los Indígenas*, because they got everything from the government while the Ladinos got nothing. She was grateful she didn't have to teach *Indígenas*, and hoped they didn't start coming to live in Hue. To me she looked Mayan: dark eyes, prominent cheekbones, dark complexion, and short stature. There were *Indígenas* in Hue all the time, especially in the stalls at the market, but they lived on the outskirts of Hue, in places like Todos Santos, and the many mountain villages between Hue and La Mesilla that produced most of the region's coffee. Her rants made me wonder how she felt about my relationship with Carlos. She never showed me any hostility. I gave them the little money I earned teaching English in her brother's language school.

Now she's back where she was ten years ago: her daughter and a granddaughter's homicides coming ten years after her husband's. Each day while I travelled in Central America I'd read the newspaper accounts of the homicides and robberies the *pandilleros* and *pandillas* committed. Meaningless statistics until I visited the thermal baths in Almolonga and heard what happened to two kids from nearby Quetzaltenango. They'd gone there to bathe, and Almolongans, evangelical Christians who bragged that they'd closed their jail and needed only a single policeman for their municipality of 12,000, doused the boys with gasoline and set them on fire because they'd stolen a radish from a plot beside the baths. No one was ever charged for the boys' murder. If the God-fearing do this, what's to be expected from criminal gangs! Their born-again Christian ex-president, E. Rios Montt, is said to have ordered the killing of close to 100,000 dissidents. He called them communists, but they were mostly the descendants of those who'd been killed or driven off their land so it could be given, sold, or leased to foreign banana and mining companies, mostly American.

After Federico left to sneak into the US, Maria began working in a Laundromat but did not earn enough to pay all her bills. Six months ago, when the second daughter got married—the first was in Guatemala City attending university, the plan was for Maria and the two remaining children—Carmen fifteen, and Karina five—to move to Hue to live with Rosa, but nothing came of it. Maybe if they had, this latest tragedy would have been averted. On two or three occasions Carlos said he planned to bring them all here as soon as he could— explaining why he's been so hungry to get his hands on my *herencia*. To this day, almost five years, since Federico left, they've had no news from him. Carlos believes it's a case of family abandonment. Federico had had to drop out of university and felt forced to marry Maria. He'd wanted her to have an abortion. Anathema in Catholic Guatemala. He'd tried to beat the last pregnancy out of her. She'd come back to Hue from Santa Elena with the three children, intending to leave him for good, but went back to him after two weeks. A week after her return, he left with his plan to sneak into the US.

Carlos thinks Federico is gay. Carlos said that, on one of Frederico and Maria's visits to them—Carlos was seventeen then, Federico had grabbed his ass and called him a cute *señorita*. Federico's closest friend from school days, Sergio, had moved to Costa Rica and returned to visit Federico two and sometimes three times each year. Whenever Sergio came to visit, Federico slept out and would come home drunk .the next day. Since Federico disappeared Sergio has been sending money to help out with the kids. Carlos is convinced that it's Federico who sends the money, that Federico is living in Costa Rica with Sergio. He'd wanted Maria to go to Costa Rica to see if her husband was there. I'm almost sure the next time Carlos hounds me for money, it will be to go to Costa Rica to find out for himself. I hope they've sent the grim news to Sergio. Or at the very least that he reads *Prensa Libre* to keep up with the news at home. Rosa told her neighbours that Federico was in Los Angeles waiting for his citizenship so he could send for his family. I wonder what they're saying now. Those who can read would have read the account of Maria and Carmen's death in *Prensa Libre*.

Ten days ago, when the deaths occurred, Gina called me at daybreak. Carlos had just phoned her to say that his sister and niece had been killed, and he'd asked her to persuade me to pay his passage back to Guatemala to be with his mother.

I did an imaginary Q&A with my grandmother. She said: Pay his passage and send some money to his mother. Kindness deserves kindness. We stand together in adversity. These conversations with my grandmother is something I keep to myself.

Two days after the murders, I read about them in full. Three months before, Carmen, sixteen, had run away from Santa Elena to Guatemala City with a boyfriend, who abandoned her once they got there. She took up with a group of *pandilleros*. She stole money from them and returned to Santa Elena. They tracked her there, to the laundromat where she was with her mother, and shot them both. The article lists the first, second, and fourth daughters as well as Rosa and Carlos as survivors. It mentions too that Rosa's husband had been killed ten years earlier for his union activities. "*Nadie sabe si Federico Alvarez, marido de Maria y padre de Carmen, Teresa y Raquel, está en vida. Hace cinco años partió hacia los Estados-Unidos y después nadie entendió nada de él.* (No one knows if Federico Alvarez, Maria's husband and father of Carmen, Teresa and Raquel, is alive. Five years ago he left for the United States and no one has heard from him since.)"

Así es la vida en Guatemala. Maria and Carmen would have been two of several killed that day. According to Google, 5960 homicides occurred last year in Guatemala's population of fourteen million. Grama would have said: "Bad news, darling, but we're alive and must soldier on until our time comes."

⇥ Carlos probably thinks I owe his family for lodging me—and maybe saving my life—my last thirteen months in Guatemala. Now I understand how easily I could have been killed in my reckless plan to sneak out of Guatemala into Mexico. In March he asked me outright for money to bring his mother here for his graduation. I didn't know about the car payments then. I didn't answer. He stared at me and feigned thinking out loud: Maybe he could credit the ticket and pay for it in monthly instalments, but there would be other expenses; he guessed she'd have to wait until one of her granddaughters graduated. I turned my head away and listened. The oldest niece, Teresa, twenty, was attending university part time in Guatemala City. The second, Raquel, had got married six months earlier, at seventeen, to a man her father's age. Then too Carlos had tested me to see if I would pay his plane fare so he could attend the wedding. I would have paid it if Jay and Grama (in a dream) hadn't objected. Sergio attended that wedding. Sent by Federico, Carlos felt.

⇥ Two weeks after Carlos moved out, Gina told me that he'd found a job teaching Spanish at Berlitz. May was a difficult month for me. His moving out, the realization that I'd made a fool of myself in marrying him and bringing him here, Bill's looming and eventual death—they took their toll. I felt myself bordering on depression as I stumbled through each day. I remembered the one I'd had at eighteen, and was determined it wouldn't happen again. If I could have concentrated I would have spent more time reading and writing. Instead I doubled my workout time at the gym, spent a couple of hours with Bill each day, and went to the movies at least twice per week. It helped that the AMC Forum is next door. Jay surmised what was happening and made me eat with him twice per week. And there were the occasional get-togethers with Gina and Emilia. I got through most days without wanting to kill myself. But there was the odd day when I was tempted to jump over my sixth-floor balcony. I gather that a Barbadian hairdresser had jumped to his death from this same building ten years earlier. I was afraid to ask from which apartment.

6

I PANICKED THE day Jay boarded the plane for England, where he would then fly to Ghana, his first stop in Africa. June 25. I phoned Gina as soon as I got back from the airport. She invited me over and cooked supper for me. Just before we ate Emilia arrived with a bottle of wine. We talked about a lot of things, mostly about our high school days and our relationships with our parents and siblings. Gina and Emilia said they envied me for having a gay brother. "Bi," I corrected. Gina rolled her eyes.

Emilia, her head resting on Gina's lap, said she no longer spoke to her mother: a Jehovah Witness who got hysterical and turned off the radio or television whenever there were discussions about homosexuality. More than once she'd told Emilia and her brother Felipe that if any of them were "like that" they should take their things and leave before she found out, and to forget that she was their mother. "Felipe is five years older than me. He dropped out of CEGEP. He and Mama were always quarrelling. She threatened to put him out unless he went back to school or found a job, he saying jobs weren't available. At home I was like kind o' silent. I had this feeling that if I like relaxed and behaved normal, I would out myself. I kept a journal that I used to hide at the bottom of the drawer with my panties. One day Felipe came in and caught me rushing to put it away. I was fifteen at the time. He got kind o' suspicious and demanded to read what I was writing. He pinned me against a wall and squeezed my hand until it went numb and the journal fell. I went into my room, grabbed a shirt and tore it into tiny strips while I wondered how to kill myself. It had the names of all the girls I wanted to make out with. A Black girl in church too that Felipe was trying to screw.

"After he finished reading, he knocked and came into my bedroom. My back was turned to the door. He sat on the bed and said to my back: 'So, Emmy, you're one too. There was this girl at Dawson I was dying to do. A killer for looks. When I moved in on her she said she was a dyke. Emmy, why'd you like want to be one of them?'

"I turned around and stretched my hand for the journal. He gave it to me. I got up, went to the stove, tore out the pages, one by one, and burned them. Felipe stared at me doing it. 'I guess that means you've decided to like go straight?' he said.

"'No, it means, fuck off before I set you ablaze too.' Then I went to my room and sobbed.

"Every day after that he'd hit on me for the money I got from babysitting a neighbour's kid, and he'd give me that like kind o' cute smile that said in everything but words, *cough up, girl, or I'll spill.* I coughed up. He never spilled, but I became a piggy bank that he constantly raided. I'd listen to Mama ranting about perverts, and dread the day I wouldn't have money to buy Felipe's silence. By the time I entered McGill I couldn't take it anymore. I decided to move out and to tell Mama why. A Friday afternoon. I'd had to leave class earlier and go vomit in the bathroom. That's how bad the tension was. I invited Mama to come sit beside me on the living room sofa, and I held her hand and I told her. She wrenched away her hand, laughed, closed her eyes, and said that of all the lies I could come up with, why did I have to choose that one. Why didn't I just say I'd found a man, *sin duda negro,* and decided to live in sin like Felipe? Did I not think breaking her heart was enough, did I want to give her a stroke too?"

Emilia paused then, a long one. "Mama couldn't believe me. She felt no child of hers could be gay. God couldn't play that joke on her, not after all the suffering she'd endured, all the privation her religion imposed. You see, Papa married her after he came back from fighting the Contras. He was an emotional mess. He left her when she became a Jehovah's Witness and stopped having sex with him, unless he became a Jehovah's Witness too. I was two when they broke up. Back in Nicaragua, Papa kept in touch with us, came and took us to the park, sometimes to a restaurant, and gave Mama whatever money he had. And we spent time with *Abuelacita*, his adorable mother.

"'It's the truth, Mama,' I insisted.

"'No, it can't be.'

"'I am telling you it is,' I shouted at her.

"Her face began to twitch. I got frightened and fled. Went to stay at the Y. From a pay phone I called Felipe. He had moved in with his latest girlfriend. I asked him to go to the apartment and see if Mama was all right. He did and he told her that what I'd said was true. Two days later I phoned her. She hung up when she heard my voice. She has never taken a phone call from me since. That's six years ago. I've stopped trying. I think her doctrine tells her she should cut all ties with me. There's a verse somewhere in the Bible that tells her to turn her back on her children, family, and everyone who doesn't follow her version of God. She probably wishes she lived in one of those countries where they kill gays."

"Is your dad still living?" I asked her.

She gestured kind of, gulped, then reached over to the coffee table for a paper napkin and dabbed her eyes ... "He was paralyzed in a work accident eleven years ago. He lives with my grandmother. She looks after him. It wasn't easy, but now Ortega's in power and she gets help."

I observed Emilia, her head on Gina's lap, a safe space where pain could be recounted.

"So what's the story with *your* parents, Meatman?" Gina asked, staring at me intensely.

I shrugged.

She gave me a wry smile. It created tiny wrinkles at edges of her eyes. "Meatman." She chuckled. "I remember how you got that nickname."

Emilia laughed. "Mrs. Bensemena now teaches at St. Luc's. I had to make a work visit there and I ran into her. She remembers you."

Gina chuckled. "How could she forget? Imagine you, you, of all people, telling her you wanted to screw her." She shook her head slowly. "Just imagine! Wonder *how* you would have done it."

"I told her you're studying to be a writer. She wants you to drop in to see her sometime and to bring a sample of your writing."

"Think you'll have the guts to tell her you're gay?" Gina asked. I didn't answer.

"She'd have understood your feelings for guys and the bluster behind that letter you wrote her." Her face grew serious. "She helped me. She was responsible for all the sex education we got. Remember? And she always said that if we had issues we wanted to discuss with her privately she would be happy to meet with us. Well, I went to see her when I was sixteen, and I told her. We met at least four times. She showed me how to get my dad to talk about the subject: ask him what he thought about gay marriage like; stuff like if he had a gay son who married a guy would he attend the wedding—stuff like that. When I tried it with Pappy—he was standing at the kitchen with his back turned, about two metres from where I was standing. He said without turning around: 'I don't have any problems with any of this, Gina; you should be talking to your mother.' Then the strangest thing happened. He turned brusquely and stared at me with a puzzled look. Next he walked over to me, pulled me close to him, hugged me, and said: 'Gina, I think all this innuendo is to tell me you're gay. Right?'

"I nodded.

"'Gay or straight, Gina, you'll always be my adorable daughter.' It's a good thing my bladder was empty. I hugged my dad and cried. He spoke to my mom about it that night. Next day she didn't speak to me at all, and to this day she has never allowed me to talk about it with her. But when she invites me home for supper she insists that I bring Emilia, and she tells Emilia: 'Please take good care of my Gina, but don't let her boss you around.' And she hugs Emilia twice as long as she hugs me. The other evening, I was tempted to say: 'Mama, like you've gone bi? You're trying to steal Emilia or what?'"

Their coming-out stories took me back to a Sunday morning when I was around fifteen and I told Ma to stay out of Jay's business. To the homophobic taunts too that I used to lay on Jay. But I didn't feel like sharing any of this with them. "I have nothing interesting to tell," I said. "I came out to Jay after my mother died. I'd suspected him.

Ma suspected him too. She'd felt he was having an affair with Jonathan, a white college mate. I don't know if he came out to her. It would have distressed her. She'd have knocked him from the pedestal she had him on, but she wouldn't have rejected him. No, I don't think she would have. She had her foolish beliefs all right—did she have them!—but she was my grandmother's daughter. My grandmother didn't have patience for foolishness. I should ask Jay if he ever came out to her. My father doesn't matter—never mattered. He's in St. Vincent. I hardly know him. My mother left him when I was two. He's some sort o' fundamentalist Christian too. Last time I went to St. Vincent I didn't accompany Jay when he visited him. I haven't the patience for the sort of religious gobbledygook he tried to lay on me when I was eighteen. Quite frankly, I don't care what he might or might not think or even if he thinks. Jay's the only living relative I'm close to, and I don't have to tell that he's one of the nicest persons on this earth; you know that already."

"He won't remain that way if Gúicho gets his net around him," Gina says.

"Life's full of paradoxes, but if Gúicho scores with Jay I would believe anything afterwards. I might even try walking on water ... Change the subject: were you two there the day Mrs. Bensemana gave Alfred that whammy for harassing Milford and John? ... Don't remember? 'What do you see in them that you hate in yourself? Go deal with your problem and leave them alone?' You don't remember?"

Emilia nods. "I don't think you were there, Gina, because I remember telling you about it."

We finished the bottle of wine. Gina gestured opening another. We shook our heads.

At home in bed that night, I fantasized about having my first novel published and inviting Mrs. Bensemana and all my former teachers, even the ones I hated, Bégin especially, to the launch. I thought too about Mrs. Mehta for the first time in a long while. Now she doesn't seem to hold the importance for me that she once did. She'd helped me keep my self-esteem from totally collapsing. Her enthusiastic response to a writing assignment she'd given me my second school year here had brought us close: "What I Like and Dislike about Living Here." For likes I'd written something about the vast wealth of print and AV material in libraries. I'd put my dislikes in a short poem that might have read something like this: *Winter's snow is pristine white and floods the rooms with light; outside, it bites. It does not bother me as much as that other snow that lives in winter and endures in fall and spring and summer too.* I hurt her feelings when I refused to be on the *Reach for the Top* team. It was only Alvin who could pull that off and not be called a fag. Today we're sensitized to the bullying that takes place in schools. Then I had the feeling that teachers felt you were a nuisance if you came asking them to protect you from it. Some felt that you courted it and therefore deserved it. One fact hasn't changed though: bullies and those whom bullying entertains still find it uncool when victims don't put up and shut up.

That night, while waiting for sleep to come, I remembered that once in Guatemala, shortly after I'd met Carlos, I'd dreamt that Mrs. Bensemana introduced me to her husband, and told me not to steal him. Later she was about to clobber me with a cricket bat, and I kept pleading with her not to damage my brain. Alvin looked on with arms folded. My screams awakened Carlos. I didn't go back to sleep. I spent the time reflecting on my high school days, specifically an encounter with Alvin. He'd invited me to go play pinball with him at the Côte-des-Neiges Plaza, but it was really a pretext to ask me whether it was true that I was selling drugs. He said he was disgusted with the way I was wasting my time at school. I suspected that Mrs. Mehta or Mr. Gaugin, my history teacher, had asked him to talk to me. I stared into Alvin's bulldog face and bulging eyes and told him to fuck off. He told Gina about it, because she sometimes looked at me and quoted her father: "'Those without brains long for it while many with brains squander it.' What say you to that, Meatman?" I wanted to tell her to fuck off, but even then she intimidated me. That night in Guatemala, aware of the stupid mistakes I'd made, knowing how I'd entrapped myself, I wished I could have reversed it all, and I vowed that if I ever made it back to Canada, I would embark on a programme of catchup.

⇥ By the middle of July I felt better and began writing again. I began to tackle the novel I'd told Jay about when he and I went to St. Vincent in 2007 to put Aunt Mercy, Grama's friend and household helper —gossipers said she was Grama's lover—into care. A novel about the townspeople accusing Grama of being lesbian and burning down her store only to discover afterwards that it had been instigated by one of her competitors. I'd made lots of notes about it. I began to put the plot details together and I hoped to have a working draft by September, when I would have to put it aside. I still have twelve unfinished credits to complete my BA. I never felt driven to finish it. After my first year, I took twelve credits per semester, rather than the usual fifteen. That way I got my loans and bursaries but also had extra time to spend on my courses.

In late July Gúicho's telephone number began to show up regularly on my caller ID. I chose not to answer the phone; there were no messages. Next it was a number from a public telephone, always the same number. Twice Carlos came by and buzzed. The closed-circuit TV showed him in the lobby. The third time he came to my door and rapped. I saw him through the peephole and didn't respond. I heard him try his key in the lock. I'd had the lock changed. I stood to the side of the door and heard him snort and stamp before he left.

The next week, Wednesday, around five, last week of July, I was returning home from watering Jay's plants and met him waiting for me in the building lobby.

"You no answer when I phone. Why?"

I shrugged.

He followed me to the elevator. I didn't go in.

"I give you fear! No. Is not possible. ¡*Increíble!*"

"With good reason."

"Joking. You make joke."

"If you follow me, I'll call the police."

"Is no necessary. I kiss. I no hit." He kissed his fingers loud, like a pop star flattering the audience. "I need talk with you. *En cualquiera lugar que elijas.* (Wherever you choose.)"

"I have nothing to say to you."

He stood in front of the elevator, blocking my entrance. The elevator door closed.

"*No me hagas eso.* No do me this." He wiped his eyes on his sleeves.

"What am I doing to you?"

"*Me rechazas.* (You're rejecting me!)"

A woman and a toddler came to wait for the elevator. All four of us got in. They exited on the fourth floor. We continued to the sixth.

"*Habla conmigo. Es todo que pido. Donde no importa.* (Talk to me. It's all I'm asking. It doesn't matter where.)" The elevator stopped. We got off. "Promise me. *Te pido. Por favor.*"

I agreed to meet with him at Atwater Park—Cabot Square—two days later, Friday, around noon. That night I thought several times of dialling Gúicho's phone to cancel. I was afraid I might succumb to his pleas. I felt empty and lonely and afraid—afraid that this might well be how the rest of my life would be. I'd seen my mother's loveless, arid life. I didn't want it. And I had seen Bill's. He had his superficial friendships at work, with people like Professor Bram. If he hadn't met Jay and me, he'd have probably died alone. Apart from Gina and Emilia, and a couple of their friends, I knew of no gay couples. John and Milford from my high school days broke up while they were both in CEGEP. Of course, in places where it's now legal for gays to marry—the latest is the state of New York—the media feature couples of twenty and thirty years who're happy that they can now marry. For contrast they show, in places hostile to gay relationships, couples of long duration lamenting the fact that they can't marry. I know of no married male couples personally. Initially I was sure my marriage to Carlos would last. Tenacity, I know now, is one of my character traits. Not always an asset: served me ill in my dealings with the Guatemalan cops. I don't know when to back off and cut my losses.

Friday Carlos arrived walking up Atwater from Gúicho's place. He wore jeans and a light green tank top, through which his growing stomach bulged. I'd paid a gym membership for him soon after he arrived, but he rarely went, or would leave with his gym bag but spend the time at Gúicho's place. Not starving at least. He sat on the bench beside me, and for a moment seemed taken with the itinerants in the park. To our left, four of them seated on a blanket were carrying on a drunken quarrel.

Then he turned his attention to me and asked if I was glad to see him.

"Are you well?" I said.

He nodded.

I too nodded but said nothing.

"Still love me?"

I looked away.

"I still love you."

I squirmed and inhaled deeply.

When I did look at him he was frowning. Six weeks ago this fellow engaged a lawyer to check into my assets, has been dissing me in the nastiest of ways, went week after week to fuck in the saunas—and now he was sitting beside me telling me that he loves me. It was a warm day, but I felt cold and saw the goose bumps on my arms.

After a long silence, I asked: "Why do you want to see me?"

He smiled and it puckered the corners of his lips and eyes. His eyes took on a dark glow—a look I know well, one calculated to disarm. He must have read something in my face too, for he said: "*La calma, por favor, la calma.*"

"*Y no la cama.* What's this meeting about?"

"I want make back up with you."

"So you want us to get back together?" I chuckled.

He nodded. "*Soy Guatemalteco. Tomo el matrimonio serio.* (I'm Guatemalan. I take marriage seriously.)"

Really! I chuckled. "How's work?"

He pressed his lips, paused. "*Perdí mi empleo. Faltaron estudiantes.* (Lost my job, not enough students.)"

"Well, we might get back together, if you had a job and could pay half of all the bills. Jay feels that he's paid for your food and rent long enough."

"We live together *mientras* I search work. When I find I pay you. *Te pagaré lo que te debo. El todo.*"

"No, you won't pay me. You'll move out. And there's all the money you'll need for your visits to the sauna."

His face got ugly. He took measured breaths; snorted a couple of times.

I turned my head away and smiled. I stretched and gave a fake yawn, then stared at him with a deliberate squint. "Our relationship is over, Carlos. I didn't leave you. You left me. You yourself told me that you started going to the saunas five months after you came here. A solid basis for an enduring, serious marriage, won't you say?"

He said nothing, and I got up to leave.

He raised his hand. *"Espera un momentito, por favor.* No leave."

I remained standing.

He spoke, his eyes turned away. "I search work. *Estoy buscando trabajo.* Teacher in United States. But if I find, I no get pay till September. I search work in Montreal. I find nothing. My English not good, and they not like my French. They take students. Is cheaper. I'm broke. *No tengo ni la buena consciencia."*

That's for sure. "There's welfare."

"Ese camino, no voy a tomarlo. (Not going down that road.)"

Then I suppose you have another.

His face darkened. He pursed his lips and clenched his teeth. His jowls bulged and he suddenly looked ten years older. I remembered Jay's admonitions to be kind to others, so I wished him lots of luck with his job search, walked off, and left him seated on the park bench. *Where do some people get their nerve!*

I crossed Ste-Catherine and Atwater and headed to the food court in the Alexis Nihon Plaza where I ate, then bought a copy of *Scientific American,* and read it. When I got home, there was a message from him. The caller ID showed he'd called three times from Gúicho's phone. *"Querido Pablo, eres mi querido y serás mi querido para siempre.* I know I treated you *malo* and I have *vergüenza.* I want stay in touch. I want be in your arms. I not know why I leave you. *Por favor* call me when you get my *mensaje."*

Enough sugar in this to give me diabetes. I became wistful, my thoughts returning to that morning in Guatemala City, five years ago, when I got the news of Ma's death. If I'd been more composed, I'd have phoned Jay, but I was under the spell that Ma's phone was monitored. I asked Rosa to charge my ticket to her Visa, and she said her credit balance wasn't enough to cover the cost of my ticket. "Believe me, Mama Rosa, you'll get back your money. My grandmother left me a little money. Besides, I plan to send for Carlos when I get back to Montreal." I hadn't thought this through. Yet I knew as I said it that I meant it. She seemed surprised, fell into reflection. She and Carlos moved a short distance away and conferred. When they came back, she'd changed her mind. Later she gave me an envelope with US$90. "Es un préstamo, (a loan)," Carlos said, as his mother handed me the envelope. "¿Comprendes? *No es un regalo.* (Understand? It's not a gift.)" Of course, I understood. In spite of her being an elementary school principal and Carlos' teaching salary, they had trouble making ends meet, partly because she sent money to Maria.

⇢ I came back from Guatemala and couldn't wait for the day when Carlos and I would be together. My eyes filled. Of course, I knew that most marriages run into problems. Jay has a better understanding of this than I. He'd seen Ma and Daddy's marriage come apart, and witnessed Daddy's descent into alcoholism. I think it's why he won't surrender his emotions to anyone. I haven't seen any marriages close-up. Breakups are supposed to happen to other people. If I didn't respect Bill like a father, I'd have told him to fuck off when he pushed me to put my inherited money out of Carlos' reach.

That July day, after listening to Carlos' message, I walked to the patio door of the living room, opened it, stood on the balcony and looked out at the traffic on Atwater and the many young people down there. Coming from Dawson College no doubt. Registration or orientation. Classes would begin in a month. I suddenly wished I had gone to CEGEP. Jay said it was like community college in St. Vincent but with many more options. Now that I've almost finished at Concordia, I know I would have enjoyed it. The teachers would have been better than the dullards I had in high school. I remembered for the umpteenth time coming by chance upon Jay watching a documentary about the nineteen sixties, how it led to my meeting Bill, and cemented my re-solve to keep from the destructive path I'd left when I gave up drug-pushing eighteen months earlier. Frightening to think that our fate often depends on such tiny incidents. The thought made me shiver. Each time I hear of police killings, I think of my run-ins with them. And that angry Arab jeweller from whom I'd tried to steal a ring in the Côte-des-Neiges Plaza, what if he'd had a gun and shot me? I envisage my inert body oozing blood in the corridor. Lucky if dead. Not so lucky—paralysed for the rest of my life—if the bullet had struck my spine. And what if the bullet had missed me and killed an innocent bystander? Never mind my being in the cross hairs of Nine Lives until he eliminated his competition and I ended up pushing for him by default. I attended two funerals of guys he'd taken out. I looked down at my trembling hands. There was a flash of lightning, then the rum-ble of thunder. In the distance around Chateauguay I saw the thick black clouds: a thunderhead. It might bypass downtown. I returned inside and closed the balcony door.

Just in time to hear the phone ringing. Luís Bondad, Guícho's official name, in the screen. "*Contesta*. You there. *Yo lo sé*. Mamá want talk with you."

I picked up the phone. "What does your mother want to talk to me about?"

"*No sé*."

"Okay. Tell her to call."

"No tell her I fucking around, okay."

"Why shouldn't I? How many men you've slept with since we've been together, Carlos?"

"*No sé. Ningùn.*"

"I think you mean thirty, and I might just tell Rosa."

"You no can. *No puedes. Son secretas entre gays.* No for straights."

I hung up.

In less than three minutes, the phone rang. "*Hola, mi querido yerno*," Rosa shouted, then went on to say that I was her darling son-in-law, and she didn't know what to do with that hard-headed ornery son of hers. If she were in Montreal she'd pull his ears and set him *erguido*: straight. (I restrained my chuckle.) That she'd ordered him to come and apologize to me for his stupid behaviour. The butter came in shovelfuls. Carlos had told her how nice and devoted I was, how I'd paid his school fees, taken care of him while he went to school, that I had the heart of not just one but several angels, so she knew I was forgiving, and now she was begging forgiveness on Carlos' behalf. He was always impulsive, but had a heart that was pure gold. (*That loves gold*, I wanted to interrupt.) That he always came to see the error of his ways. He would change. She'd vouch for it. The litany went on. No space for me to insert a word. "Pablo, you will change your mind and take him back. I said a novena to the Virgin. I felt peace in my soul when I came out of the church. It's a sign that things will be all right again between you and Carlos."

"Okay," I shouted into the receiver. "We'll see. *Vamos à ver.*" She'd said the wrong thing. From that moment it was my will against hers.

She continued talking. I put the handset down and listened to the indecipherable sounds. I put the receiver back to my ears and told her my doorbell was ringing, that I had to go, I hung up. *Rainwater does not wash out the leopard's spots*, I wanted to say. But even if I could have translated it, I wouldn't have got the chance to say it.

That night I dreamt I was in Guatemala, and Carlos and I were alone on top of the Gran Jaguar Pyramid in Tikal. (His sister lived nearby, in Santa Elena.) That Carlos fell off and I became afraid that the police would think I had pushed him. Later someone pursued me and I fell and couldn't get up.

Next morning he called me from a public phone. I didn't answer. He said that he would keep calling until I answered. When he called the second time, the message was that I had to help him, that he was in "*plena mierda*," that Gúicho had put his things on the sidewalk, that he was on his way to see me, that he was in the plaza, and knew that I was home.

I brushed my teeth quickly and headed downstairs, hoping to be out of the building when he arrived, but I met him entering the lobby. I decided to remain in the lobby.

He approached me. "*¿Recibiste mi mensaje?*"

"Yes."

"*¿Y qué piensas?*"

"*Nada.*"

"*¿Cómo nada?*"

Lint clung to his green sweater, his trousers were rumpled, his face glowed with grease, bags were under his frightened eyes. His armpits and breath smelled.

He stared at me and nodded. "*Dilo.* Say it."

"Say what?"

"I stink. I sleep in park. *Gracias a Dios que no hubiera llovido.* (Thank God, it didn't rain.) Ok, I fuck up. I treat you like shit, but you no can *sacarme. No soy basura. No es justo.* You must take *responsabilidad* for me."

"You're a Canadian citizen, Carlos. You're on your own. I can't help you with money. I have only enough to pay my bills and Jay is away travelling."

"Bullshit. *No soy tonto.* You have credit card. And you no let Jay go and no leave money."

I didn't have my wallet on me. I motioned to him to sit, and told him to wait there while I returned upstairs. Upstairs, I took a hundred dollars—almost all the money in my wallet—and returned and gave it to him.

He counted it. His face fell and his eyes narrowed. He snorted. "*!Cien dólares!* What I do with hundred dollars? *A Gúicho le debo $650.*"

"Carlos, I didn't put you out. All those years while you were waiting for your citizenship and going off to the saunas, I didn't put you out." *I could have done so, and more even: end the union and have you deported.* "I didn't. Now you're a Canadian citizen."

"You responsible me ten years." He gestured ten. "*Diez años.*" He shook his clenched fists.

For a while I said nothing and waited for his emotions to cool. "If that's the case, it means I can still have you deported."

He winced.

A woman entered the lobby and kept staring at us while she

waited for the elevator. She looked Mayan. I motioned to Carlos that we go outside.

We went to Cabot Square and sat two benches away from where we'd sat the day before. I toyed with telling him about the disrespectful things he'd been saying about me, but I didn't want to implicate Gina. He'd know it was she or Emilia who'd told me. But I couldn't resist totally. "Carlos, you don't respect me."

"How? No true."

"Because all the signs are there. Your nights at the saunas. Later your bragging about it."

"What you want me do? I young. I want fuck. You want write. You want talk with Bill. I go sauna and fuck. Your fault. No my fault." He shrugged his shoulders.

"*¡Púchica! ¡hombre!*" I said when I recovered.

He laughed. I said nothing. He resumed. "*Seas justo.* Be fair. You no can *sacarme como fruta podrida.*"

Rotten fruit all right. "One thing's now certain, Carlos. We won't be getting back together."

"Why not? *¿Y por qué no?*" He frowned. "You talk with Gina and Emilia?" He blinked uncontrollably.

"No. Do they know something that I should know?"

"Gúicho. Know how he … " He waved his fingers in front of his lips. "Why you smile?"

"We were in high school together."

Silence.

"You have *problema.* You want perfect man. But you too much late for *Jesu Cristo* and you go have share with eleven men … You no can leave me like this. You no can. *No puedes.*"

I said nothing.

"*!Contesta! ¡Habla!*" He raised his voice.

I remained silent.

He continued, loud: "You no can dump me like this. *No es justo. Es inmoral.*"

I stood up and started walking back toward the apartment building. He got up and began to follow me. I turned, looked him straight in the eye, and said: "Carlos, don't follow me. Don't. If you do, I'll ask the police to put a restraining order on you."

He froze. I crossed the street, then looked back to see him still standing there still as a statue staring at me.

I got upstairs exhausted. Lying on the couch, I remembered the dream, and wondered who had really fallen from the pyramid. I could see that my unconscious was already playing around with the notion of responsibility. Last night I did not know that he was now homeless.

I was awakened by the ringing telephone. There was no name. The digits on the caller screen suggested a cellphone. The caller spoke English with a heavy Spanish accent. "I secretary *del abogado* Alfredo Hernández. I leave message to Pablo Jackson. I tell you, Pablo, you no can stop support. You give support ten years. This the law."

I picked up the handset. "*Debe ser Gineta, la limpiadora y Carlos es su aprendiz.* (You must be Gineta, the cleaning woman, and Carlos is your apprentice.)" I hung up.

I went to the Canadian Immigration and Citizenship website and downloaded and printed the document that spells out that sponsoring spouses are responsible for their partners for three years. I highlighted the passage with a marker.

I SPENT THE rest of the day and evening anxious and unable to concentrate on anything. Drank juice and ate peanut butter sandwiches when I got hungry. I would lie on the couch for a bit, then get up and walk around, then return to the couch, before getting up again and walking around.

Around 11 that evening Gina phoned and ordered me to come to her place. "Now! If you don't want me to come over there and strangle you."

I got to her place after midnight. She was sitting on her couch with a half-goblet of wine on the floor beside her. She pointed me to an armchair directly in front of her. A book lay face down in it. She stretched her hand for it. I sat.

"What's so urgent? What's eating you?" I said.

"Carlos came to see you today and you spilled your guts about what I told you."

I shook my head.

"Then how come he called Emilia and cursed her out? Said we were gossiping about him. That you told him that you know he no longer respects you. Did you?"

"About respect, yes. But the reason I gave him was that he used to leave me at home on evenings and go to the sauna to have sex."

"You didn't tell him anything else?"

I shook my head.

"Sure?"

"Absolutely certain."

She tossed her head this way and that before calming down.

She picked up the wine goblet and took a sip. She pointed to the bottle on the kitchen counter and told me to help myself. I got up, poured half a glass, and returned to sit in the armchair.

I tasted the wine, checked my watch, and began to fidget, knowing that the metro would soon stop running. She patted the couch and said: "This is a sofa-bed and I have clean sheets and towels. I can even promise you coffee, but you'll have to make it yourself. I don't get up before ten." She looked at my wine glass. "Fill that; you will need it."

"I'm alright for now."

"So his mother phoned you last night."

"You know that already?"

"Whatever Guícho knows I know soon after, and you promised her you'll make up with him."

"Nope. She said something about novenas to the Virgin and when she came out the church she was at peace and certain everything would be all right. She exaggerates things. She used to tell the neighbours that her son-in-law was in L.A. waiting to take out U.S. citizenship. The said son-in-law had left to go to the U.S. and no one has heard from him since."

She pouted, seemed unconvinced.

"Gineta phoned me impersonating the secretary of Me Afredo Hernández." I did an imitation of her accent and recounted the message as best I could. We both laughed.

"Cheaper than lending Carlos $10,000."

"What?"

"You heard me. To pay Alfredo to track down your assets and get some of it for Carlos and himself."

"Did she?"

Gina frowned.

"Did she lend him?"

Gina put her hands on her thighs, threw back her head, and had a rollicking laugh. She wiped her eyes on the sleeve of her dressing gown. "Come on? The cleaning lady! She's the *cleaning* lady. She's looking for dirt. You're safe. If there's one thing Alfredo won't do is work pro bono … When did Carlos arrive here?"

"August 17, 2007."

"Gúicho says he's got his citizenship."

I nodded.

"Already! That was fast."

"The time he waited for his permanent resident visa counted. He made sure he had it before telling me about his nights at the sauna."

"*Quelle salope!* Should be grounds to revoke his citizenship and deport him."

"I won't do that."

"Use it to bargain with him. The Conservatives want to deport people like him who enter into bogus marriages for immigration purposes."

I remembered what Bill had said in this regard about his boyfriends. "What's the trouble between him and Gúicho?"

"I told you Gúicho lost his job. He's waiting to get on unemployment. He won't get it. His boss fired him for negligence. Carlos owes him for rent and food. They turned down Carlos' application for EI too. Not enough weeks or something. Montrealers need 595 hours to qualify."

I remembered that her research area was labour law.

"Then he can't. He worked twelve hours per week at UQAM. I don't know how much at Berlitz."

"Six. Negligible."

"He'll have to go on welfare."

"Says he doesn't want to."

She frowned. "He'd better not; not if he's serious about bringing his mother, his sister, and his nieces here. You know where he's staying? Don't look at me like that. Gúicho put him out last night. Slept in the park. Apparently he went to the sauna intending to sleep there and discovered that Gúicho had taken all the money he had in his wallet. Didn't even leave him enough to buy coffee."

"Well he has enough for the sauna for a few nights. I gave him $100 this morning."

"You bleeding heart! No wonder he thinks you have millions socked away. Boy, was he planning on getting some! Did you know he tried to borrow money from Gineta to apply for the family to come here? Emilia told him to stop being a fool. He'd only waste his money applying. He'd have to show he could support them for three years, the nieces until they're twenty-five. At Ville Marie Social Services she meets people all the time who've had to sell their houses to repay the government for what their sponsored relatives received in welfare when they moved out on them. You're lucky Carlos didn't pull that one on you."

"He wishes it were still ten years."

"You gay guys and your marriages!"

"Civil union."

"Same foolishness. Emilia and I are together now for how long? Let's see. I'm twenty-seven. We started dating when I was sixteen. Eleven years. No marriage for us. She lives in her apartment. I live in mine. I don't have to listen to anybody complaining about dirty dishes in the sink. She likes cats. I'm allergic to them. She can keep two hundred if she likes. I can't go to her place, so she comes here. And when she gets all worked up over her mother, I'm not there for her to dump on me. Marriage! Not for this dyke. Divorce lawyers are licking their chops. A new pool of clients. You know how you men are — straight and gay. Have to sample everything that comes your way. Why didn't I specialize in divorce law?"

"Stop your generalizing. Look at Jay. He's celibate. I've never cheated on Carlos."

"Then you and your brother are abnormal. Abnormal men and *very* abnormal gays." Her frivolous tone told me she wasn't serious.

I was back home by eleven the next morning. Jay left a message on my answering machine to say he was in Senegal. He left the name of the hotel and the number. I spent the rest of the morning and a good part of the afternoon recording in my journal everything that had taken place the day before.

IT'S 4:20 P.M., 11:20 P.M. in Kinshasa. I dial the cellphone number Jay gave me. I don't care if it wakes him. It rings ten times and then gives a busy signal. Wonder if he made a mistake in giving me the numbers. Did I copy the digits incorrectly? There was a lot of static on the line while we spoke; impossible to hear him at times. That foolish boy didn't even say which hospital he was in. I know he isn't dead. They'd have contacted me. Tomorrow I'll go to his flat and see if Jonathan's number is in his home phone. His plants need watering anyway. I'm sure he's given Jonathan the number. Might even be communicating with him. Where does Jonathan live? It's August, so he isn't teaching. Jay said he was putting together his dossier to apply for tenure. I'll check out his email at UQAM.

I'm restless. I should be like Gina's stereotyped gays and head to the Village and do whatever's needed to get laid. Haven't had sex since April, weeks before Carlos walked out on me. The odd occasion I walk from Atwater to Papineau, loll about in the section of Sainte Catherine that's closed to vehicle traffic, and glance at all the men eating, conversing, cruising on the outdoor terraces. It's sure raining men down there. *Men, men, everywhere.* Nary a one to hump with. Lots of fish in this sea.

Worth catching?

Won't know till you cast your net.

Get a net.

I don't know how to fish. I stare at someone, and when he notices, I turn my head away, and never look again. Prufrock. In my modern poetry course there was this guy — looked like a Viking: thick long blond hair that came down to his shoulders, piercing blue eyes, and almost two metres tall — who felt that Eliot was gay, that Prufrock fits the profile of a dysfunctional gay man. He didn't explain what a dysfunctional gay man was.

Maybe I should get Carlos to coach me. He certainly knows how to throw nets and where. I should try the saunas. Tried unsuccessfully to get into one before I was eighteen. Never interested me since. Bill went sometimes. "To get [his] rocks off." Bill: alive yesterday, dead today. When he died I wondered what life would be like without him. But you come to see that the sun rises just as it did the day before; that ingrates remain ingrates; that bad people remain bad and do their damnedest to make everyone else bad; that a few good people remain good and the remainder, discovering that goodness isn't profitable, become corporate directors and politicians. But there's still the need to get laid. Am I good or bad? I guess that depends on who's evaluating me. I could ask Jay. Would ask him now if he were here. He'd answer honestly, unless he was riling me; and if he was, he'd later tell me what he truly thought. I keep putting him on this pedestal and he keeps begging me to take him down. I hope he hasn't gone and made himself an invalid in Africa. Jay, don't do that to me. You are all the family I have, or care to have.

It occurs to me that I might find Jonathan's number on 411. I remember Jay saying he lives on St. Joseph. He sold his parents' duplex when he put his father into a CHSLD after he developed dementia. I find the number and dial it. He answers: "Yes, Paul."

"Have you heard from Jay?"

"Yes. Let's see. About ten days ago. Why're you asking?"

"Haven't heard from him in four days."

"That's not long."

I hesitate. Should I tell him Jay has malaria and is in hospital? I decide not to and feel pleasure from withholding the information.

"Funny you should be calling me. Is something wrong?"

I pause. A little too long.

"Something's wrong, Paul. Out with it."

"No. Nothing. I'm a neurotic when it comes to such things."

"*You!* You've changed."

That stings.

"Are you taking care of his plants? You know those are his children?"

"Yes, I am, and they're alive." He'd offered to look after Jay's plants. Jay told him I would and later said to me: "If plastic plants could die, Jonathan would kill them." In 2007, during the two weeks we went to St. Vincent to put Aunt Mercy into care and to sell Grama's house, Jay left him in charge of Ma's plants. (Jay insists on calling them Ma's plants.) When we returned the saucers were up to the brim with water. It took more than three weeks for the hibiscuses to dry out, and we couldn't save the amaryllis. He said he watered them every day, that Jay hadn't given him precise instructions. His mother kept a ceiling-high rubber plant in the dining room and a giant fig filled a corner of her living room. Jay had assumed he knew how to care for plants.

"Paul, you're still there?"

"Yes."

"Well, call back if you change your mind about telling me why you called. I'll be home all afternoon and evening."

Not to disappoint him totally, I tell him about the flood in Jay's apartment.

"He'll be pissed when he sees the damage to the oak floor he has just installed."

"I don't think so. He's not materialistic. You should know that. He had the carpeting removed to cut down on dust and to make it easier on me when I visit."

"I'm convinced that this isn't what you called to tell me."

I feel like saying, no, it's more than that, but because of your fucking smugness I won't tell you. Hope he doesn't think I want to have sex with him. One day I'll lose it and just let him have it. Never wronged the guy. Been his ally all along. The number of times I begged Jay to yield to his advances. Has it in for me because of the strain I put Jay through those thirteen months I was incommunicado while in Guatemala. As if it's any of his business. Makes an issue of it, as if it was he I'd stressed. And to think Jay wasn't even sleeping with him. Would understand if Jay's worrying had cheated him of sex and affection. I kept away from Jay's place while he was there recovering from burnout from all the shit his university put him through, his mother's sudden death, his aunt's descent into madness, and his father's dementia. Only thing left is for a truck to hit this sonofabitch. But I'm not wishing it. Back off, Paul. He's been through a lot, and you have no concrete proof that he has ever wronged you.

But I had good reason to stay away. On May 7 last year, Jay had a surprise birthday party for him, and invited Carlos, Gina, Emilia, and me. Alberto, an ex-student of Jonathan; Wendell, a gay friend of Jonathan since college days, now a high school history teacher; Tyrone, one of Jay's CEGEP colleagues; and Tyrone's partner Laurent, were there too.

Alberto, from Honduras, had moved from Moncton to McGill to pursue a master's degree in geology. He hardly spoke during the entire affair. Carlos tried to engage him in conversation, but he answered Carlos' questions in the fewest of words. Emilia had even less success.

Wendell was an altogether different case.

For a change I was wearing a plaid blazer of brown, blue, and beige squares. Wendell passed his fingers over it, and said: "Now I know what Don Cherry does with his suits."

Everyone laughed. Wendell wore a black t-shirt and discoloured blue jeans.

He continued. "Wanna hear a joke? There was this Frenchman travelling in the backwoods of Senegal, and he came upon this African wearing a loincloth. He said to the African: 'Would you like to eat me?'

"The African looked at him, smiled, and shook his head. 'Massa don't want eat. I think Massa want blowjob.'

"The Frenchman got an instant erection, dropped his pants, and pointed to his thing. The African kneeled and began to sink his teeth into it.

"'Ouch. Don't bite it. Suck it.'

"'How much Massa he pay for proper blowjob?'"

No one laughed.

"Okaaay," Wendell said, looking in turn at each of us. "You guys," meaning Jay and me, "speak with an accent. Where are you from?"

That question always gets my hackles up. I looked at Jay. He was moving around the room with a tray of canapés. "Jay, here's a question for you: Where are we from?"

"I mean like which part of Africa are you from?"

"Oh, I can answer that, but first why do you want to know?" All eyes on me.

"It's just that my family has a long involvement with Africa."

"Don't most white people?" Gina said.

"Not sure what you mean."

"I'll give you one example: the development you Westerners brag about was financed by the slave trade."

"I didn't learn that."

"How's your family involved with Africa?" Gina asked.

"My parents have a carved ivory tusk that my great grandfather brought back from the Boer War. One of his brothers even stayed behind and acquired a farm in Rhodesia."

"You mean Zimbabwe?" Gina interrupted.

But Wendell ignored her. "My uncle's descendants are still there. Papa follows African history closely."

"What does your father do?" Emilia said.

"He's an investment broker. He thinks that all those civil wars in Africa come from them getting independence before they were ready." He stopped talking. No one said anything for a while. He resumed. "Did you see that documentary in which the rebels in Sierra Leone were chopping off people's hands and feet? Gross."

"Guess what," Gina said, "they learned it from the Belgians."

"Oh, come on."

"Who's the historian here, you or me? It's one of the techniques Belgians in the Congo used to force the Congolese to go out and collect rubber sap. You know what that rubber was for? The burgeoning automobile industry. Bet your father doesn't know that?"

"I don't believe that."

Emilia chuckled.

"So," Wendell turned to me, "which part of Africa are you from?"

"The Diaspora. St. Vincent."

"I thought that was a Caribbean Island."

"It is and it's also Africa. Didn't Columbus call the Americas India?"

"Oh, come on, you're from the West Indies."

Everyone laughed.

Wendell frowned. "We're talking about The Islands. Right?

"You mean those near Kingston?" I said.

"No, I mean like Jamaica. Is it—I mean your island; what is it called again?"

"St. Vincent."

"Is it independent like Dominica?"

"Yes," I said.

"I took a side trip to Dominica when I visited Guadeloupe last year."

Total silence.

"What a difference in the standard of living between Dominica and Guadeloupe! Man, Dominica is kindo like something still in the Stone Age."

I bristled. "What's the connection between Dominica being in the Stone Age, to use your term, and your father's pro-apartheid stance?"

"You're *aggressive*." Condescending grin. "I saw some of the most gorgeous men ever in Dominica." He kissed his fingers. "They smelled like the earth. Pungent." He breathed deeply. "I like men who don't wear deodorant. Wow! Lean, brown bodies. My head spun." He whistled. "Ooh la-la."

"Were you wearing a loincloth?" Gina said.

We laughed.

Emilia and I exchanged glances. We knew the rest of the narrative. Even the use some Blacks make of it. I recalled this Black guy at Concordia telling a group of White males that Blacks will conquer the White race between their legs. They'd bristled and crossed their legs.

"Can't help it," Wendell said. "First guy that did me was Black.

Shoe polish black. I'm not kidding. Awesome. I was seventeen. He was twentyish. Forgot his name. Had this strong perspiration odour. Now it turns me on. I sneaked him into my parents' basement and we did it. You should see what he had on him." He put his hand on his chest and inhaled slowly, followed by a loud exhalation.

Emilia giggled.

"Since then I've been hooked. Man, if it ain't black, it won't track. Like my line? I score with it every time. I go to New York three times a year: March break, Pride week, and New Year's, and head straight to the gay bars where Black men congregate. Haven't found one yet like my first pickup, but I'm still looking."

He stopped talking and looked at each of us in turn. Assessing us or deliberately trying to shock us.

"Blacks don't have a monopoly on size," Tyrone said.

"How would *you* know?" He glanced at Tyrone's left leg. Tyrone walks with a limp. "I hear there's this organisation here, Arc-en-ciel, for Black gays. You guys belong to it?" He looked at Jay then at me.

We didn't respond.

"You know if they allow Whites to join?" He was now staring at me. Jay had returned to the kitchen.

I shrugged.

"Must be mostly Africans. *Ils sont machos en hostie!* Won't mind checking them out. Awesome, man."

"You won the lottery on the first shot," Gina said. "Fancy that. People play all their lives and never win. You win on the first shot and you want to win again? You're greedy."

He frowned.

"Robert Mapplethorpe is dead, but Phillip Rushton's alive. He'd be able to help you," Gina said.

"Is Rushton Black?"

We laughed.

"Does he have a big cock?"

"That's for you to find out. He certainly thinks he has a big brain, and will be sure you have one too," Gina said. She got up, nodded to Emilia, headed into the kitchen, and said something to Jay.

"What! You're joking!" Jay said.

She came from the kitchen, went into Jay's study and returned with her and Emilia's jackets. Jay came to the living room and stood there, looking distraught. Gina hugged him and whispered something in his ear.

"Hey!" Wendell shouted. "That's not polite."

"Fuck off!" Gina told him.

Emilia and Gina left.

The living room was quiet. "Did I say something wrong?" Wendell broke the silence.

No one answered. "I think I put my hoof in my mouth," he said frowning. He went to the bathroom. When he came back, he too put on his jacket and left.

The party became something of a wake afterward. The eight of us who remained tried to revive it, but it was futile.

⇾ When I chided Jay about it, he shrugged. "What you wanted me to do? He was there because of Jonathan. At university, nodding to him when we ran into each other on campus was all the interaction I'd had with him."

"You could have said something. You have the knowledge to put him in his place. I've read some of the books you studied: books by Basil Davidson, Eric Williams, Walter Rodney, Chancellor Williams. Yet you left it up to Gina to take him on."

"And you? Why didn't you?"

"It wasn't my apartment."

How could Jonathan not know Wendell's views? It's a question I've asked myself a few times. He sat there silently. Said nothing! What a fucking weakling! Looks it too. Back in Moncton, one of his students saw it and used it to try to turn a failure into a pass. Said Jonathan had cruised him, and he'd refused him, and Jonathan had failed him for spite. Fortunately, the revision committee upheld the grade and the scumbag withdrew the charges, claiming he might have misread Jonathan's cues. Jay was damn right not to give in to him. Couldn't/ wouldn't rebuke Wendell. Nothing but a spineless wimp. Likes his men *foncé*. Maybe that's part of what he and Wendell have in common. Maybe he too reduces us to dark meat. I should put Carlos on to him. Carlos would pig out on his salary and all that money he got for his parents' duplex. Purge him of everything. Would be more than enough to pay off Rosa's car and bring her and his nieces here, now that Guatemala has become a death trap for them. *Oh Paul, stop spilling acid. Go take your frustrations out on Carlos, or go to the Village, to the sauna yourself, and get humped. It's been a long time ...*

I look at my watch. I'll call Carlos and Rosa in an hour to see how things have gone. Some things we're obliged to do. Don't know how to talk about death. I'll probably end up saying the wrong thing. I remember how unfair I thought life was when I saw Grama in her casket. Death was for others, not my grandmother, and certainly not before I'd made good in her eyes. Broke down when I got back to Canada—bore my own pain and the pain she would have borne had she lived long enough to discover that I'd betrayed her, that I'd wasted my years in high school. And Ma, she too had to go and die before I could show her that crime wouldn't be my occupation. Death does indeed have its sting.

Bill made his easy for us. Said he'd had a rich though unfulfilling life. Apart from saying that he'd never had the life partner he yearned for, he never hinted at why his life had been unfulfilling. He was glad Jay and I were there to lessen his loneliness during his illness. Told us so many times. Glad too that he wouldn't be around to lie year after year in pee and shit in some nursing home staffed with exploited immigrant labour: people with every right to hate their jobs, he said. Worse still to do so with his intellect intact. "Just as well I go now. I've never felt at home in this world." That last sentence still haunts me. If he'd been in better shape I'd have asked him to elaborate. Fate was kind to him. He became weaker as the cancer took over: would have to wait a while and hold on to something whenever he stood; would on occasion begin to drip urine before he got to the toilet; but he had enough strength to get to the bathroom on his own or with someone holding him up. And he fed himself. On exceptional days he made himself tea. And wham! In a single stroke he was gone.

At the memorial for him I couldn't speak, didn't get to say how he'd been a father to me—the only one I had—and helped me find a purpose for my life. In fact I didn't know how much need I had for a father until I met him. The first sentence came and then the choking sobs. Professor Bram, who was officiating, put his arm around me, and Jay came and supported me back to my seat. Carlos called to say he couldn't come, that he had a job interview. I didn't expect him to.

◜ **9**

$\int$ENOR CARLOS. First his father's violent death, now his sister's and niece's. Will return here chastened. To bleakness. Times are tough. No jobs in the U.S. or here. School boards in the U.S. are laying off teachers as the country heads back into recession. Told Gina he didn't leave Guatemala to wash dishes in a restaurant for minimum wage. Can't say he's wrong. When he left here he was renting a room from a Salvadoran in Côte-des-Neiges. He's thirty-one. Celebrated his birthday on August 4. Told Emilia he's going back to school in the fall. Didn't tell her what he intends to study. Would he be able to now?

There's a soft spot in my heart for Rosa. She was good to me while I lived in her house. Her opinions seem so much at odds with her behaviour.

The evening Carlos left to attend the funeral for his sister and niece I gave him a copy of the Canadian Immigration document showing that I've acquitted my responsibility to him. Hope that will get him and his retinue off my back. That Gineta, she should put aside her pail, scrub pads, and gloves, and start a marriage extortion business.

-◜ Marriage. Grama opposed Ma's. Agonized over the upbringing we'd get in Daddy's home. Saw firsthand the brutality Daddy inflicted on Jay and was determined he wouldn't on me. Her journals are full of such entries. When she and our neighbour Mr. Morris talked about problem children in Havre, he'd say: "Ma Kirton, the fathers eat the sour grapes and the children's teeth are set on edge." I'm coming around to accepting Jay's view that Ma kept away from Grama and didn't tell her about my behaviour because she felt Grama would have accused her of tearing down what she'd built.

I used to wonder how Daddy's drunkenness would affect me. Whether I too would become a drunkard. No problem there now. I'm prohibited from drinking alcohol because of the anti-asthma drugs I take, although I cheat and have the odd half-glass of wine. Back in St. Vincent, when Grama and Jay talked about Daddy's drinking, they thought I didn't understand what drunkenness was. Havre had its town drunk: Percy. He sometimes staggered along Beach Road, singing as he went along and trying to kiss every woman he came upon and asking them to marry him. Once he came in the back gate, stumbled up the porch steps, and said: "Boy, where Ma Kirton is? I come to marry her." Aunt Mercy came to the back and began to push him down the steps. He tried to kiss her and they both stumbled and rolled down the steps. She was the first to get up. She helped him to his feet and pushed him out the back gate. I was laughing. She shook her head and said: "Don' laugh, Paul. Don' laugh. He been a respectable gentleman until his wife break his heart."

The fathers eat the sour grapes, and the children's teeth are set on edge. Jay still has nightmares from Daddy's cruelty. I hope not as frequently as when we were back in Havre and I used to hear him in his sleep begging Daddy to stop drinking. Granddad wasn't like that. Wasn't a womanizer either. Grama didn't love him. This marriage business. Business indeed.

Not sure what makes us know we love someone. It's easy to convince ourselves we do if we know there's some material benefit down the road. I think I know now why on my way up from Costa Rica, the Salvadoran guys I met in Scape were so interested in me. I thought it was because of my Africanness: my exotica, but now that I think of it, it was only after the word spread that I was from Canada that they began to crowd me. They spoke of relatives they had in Canada or the U.S. One said his brother got killed trying to sneak across the Mexican border into the U.S. Four of them gave me their addresses. They were all disappointed that I was leaving the next day for Guatemala. Two of them spoke impeccable English and translated for the others. "Delay your trip," one said. "Tomorrow's Sunday. We'll hire a car and go down to la Libertad. The sea is *estupendo*." Three of them tried to take me home that night. I had a bus to catch at eight that morning, and I knew that San Salvador had the reputation of being the most dangerous city in all of Central America, no place to get picked up in by strangers. It took force I didn't know I had to hold down my libido that night. I still hadn't slept with anyone. They were *handsome*, one in particular. When his brown eyes beamed on me, my knees shook, and I was forced to turn my head away. Think I understand what Odysseus endured as he listened to the Sirens. I never suspected then that their interest in me had anything to do with wanting to immigrate to *El Norte*. Carlos was no different. I wonder if the time would come when he'd be comfortable enough—or honest enough—to tell me the truth. Maybe he himself will never know the truth. Some truths never leave the unconscious, and when they do they're usually disguised.

Before Scape, three weeks earlier, in Manuel Antonio, Costa Rica's Pacific Coast, I'd met Joe at Liquid. He looked like someone from Southern India: dark skinned, petite body, average height; about twenty-two. He wore tight white shorts and a red skin-tight shirt. He was with Tino, a stocky older chap who looked in every way White—pale skin, auburn hair, blue eyes. I'd asked if they were a couple. Tino said Joe was his work mate and roommate. They'd come on to me as soon as I walked into the club. Joe pulled me onto the dance floor and began to grind his body into mine. At the first opportunity I told him thanks and moved to a bar stool. He followed me and asked me to buy him a beer. I did. He drank and grew restive. I saw Tino talking to a White septuagenarian. Soon after he came to Joe, who handed him a key, and he and the septuagenarian left. Joe requested another beer and peered into my wallet while I paid for it. He asked me what my plans were. I said I had none. A few minutes later he left for the bathroom. The bartender, who'd been taking furtive glances at us, rubbed his thumb and middle finger and told me, "*Dinero. Mucho pisto.* Money. *Es puta.* Whore. *¿Comprendes?*"

When Joe returned, we spoke but his eyes roved the bar. There were about a dozen clients in the bar, couples for the most part it seemed. It was still early evening, not quite 9. He said he'd been on his own since twelve. I asked about his parents. He said he had excellent relations with them. I'd already seen documentaries about street children in Rio, Bangkok, and elsewhere. I didn't think then that Joe's parents might have relied on his earnings.

A dwarfed, middle-aged, somewhat overweight man walked into Liquid. Joe's eyes lit up. He grabbed his beer and walked toward the man. Soon they were dancing and sticking their tongues into each other's mouths. The bartender looked at me and winked.

I left five minutes later to catch the bus heading to Jaco. In bed that night I tried to imagine myself in Joe's place. On his own at twelve and excellent relations with his parents didn't sound right to me. I came to Canada five months before I turned twelve, and Ma insisted that Jay come home before three so that I wouldn't be alone. Yet when I think about it, Jay was in large part responsible for me from the time he was twelve—five weeks before he turned twelve he began looking after himself and me the five days we spent each week in Kingstown. Sure, there was Cousin Alice in whose house we stayed, but apart from giving us food, she ignored us. Maybe I should have asked Joe what he meant by being on his own. In the Central American towns I passed through, I'd already seen the slums—from afar of course: acres of shacks: *covachas*, assembled with tin, tarpaulin, tarpaper, plastic, plywood, and whatnot. In Tegucigalpa, I was warned never to venture near them. Around the river they were still dealing with the after effects of hurricane Mitch from seven years earlier. On my way down to Costa Rica five days later I saw the shacks in Managua: igloo-like domes covered in black plastic, in la *Zona de Monumentos*. The temperature that afternoon was thirty-eight Celsius. How could they live in them? Yet they do. Our capacity to survive. And the slums, *La Limonada,* in Guatemala City are even more extensive, but, mercifully, contend with less heat. I guess that out of them come people like Joe and the *Pandilleros* who killed Maria and Carmen, as well as massive numbers of converts to Pentecostalism. The former, finding life absurd and knowing the police and military to be the arms of the wealthy, wrest away power however they can, indifferent to killing and being killed. The latter find religion easier and safer than seeking social justice from the thugs put in power by the wealthy to keep the poor in their place. And are not above dousing children with gasoline and setting them on fire for stealing a radish, like those effigies of the devil that Guatemalans burn every eighth of December.

I would later meet six- and seven-year old shoeshine kids and trinket sellers in the Central Park in Antigua, Guatemala. Children sent to work while the parents stayed at home. They begged me for money, and after I'd bought food for one, they all wanted food. They said they went to school at night. Not so, my teachers at the language school said. "And they are beaten when they return home without money." Children kept out of school and sent to work! How was this possible in 2005? I told one, Juan-Pablo, a very intelligent fellow who changed his age every time I asked him, that I would like to meet his parents. Thereafter he avoided me. Child labour is illegal in Guatemala, and he probably felt my curiosity meant trouble for his parents. Of course, this was before my arrest. I wanted to persuade his parents to send him to school. I knew I could convince Jay to replace the income that Juan-Pablo brought to the household; it wasn't much: for every client there were on average six shoeshiners, ranging in age from six to seventy. Most of their time was spent walking around the park or sitting on the benches or playing tic tac toe. I wondered what the future of a bright boy like Juan-Pablo would be like: would he join the *maras*, killing and getting killed, in the cities, towns and villages all over Guatemala?

Later I tried to sort out my feelings about poverty in several journal entries. Extreme poverty is not pretty. You react to it like you react to feces, and since you can't remove it, you run from it. Since my return I learned from a CBC documentary that many West Africans sell their children into slavery, to the owners of cocoa plantations. I don't remember the documentary mentioning the cheap price we in the Occident pay for chocolate. I've just finished reading a short story by Uwem Akpan about an uncle who sells his niece and nephew into slavery. When I read Grama's account of why she married Granddad — "for his house, his bank account, and his land. What's a poor girl to do?" — I was upset. Would I have idolized her as much if I'd known this while Jay and I were living with her? Now of course, I understand. Seems Ma and Jay must have talked about it. He brought up the bit in Grama's journal where she wonders at what point in the marriage she would have felt forced to horn Granddad. One time I told Ma it took someone with Grama's intellect to parent me, and she replied: "And someone with her morals would condone the things you do." I got angry and told her: "You don't know shit about morality; there's foam where your brain should be." Can't believe I said such things to my mother. Now when I visualize her, I see a sleep-deprived woman mumbling to herself, most likely about the struggle to be independent and to feed her two sons while holding on to her dignity. The pain I caused her. Maybe it's why she and Madam J continue to haunt me when I'm asleep. I wish she were here to see that I haven't turned out to be the wastrel she feared I would become. She begged Jay to keep at me, so that I won't throw away my life, and she admitted that she wasn't the mother I needed. Her big regret was that I wasn't there for her to tell me so in person. Mine is that I can't apologize for all the pain I caused her unnecessarily. If I believed in nemesis, I'd think Carlos' treatment is payback for the agony I caused her.

Mothers. Don't tell them negative things about their children. I must remember this when I speak to Rosa later. Apart from restating my condolences, I hope I won't have a chance to say anything more. I'm counting on her to chatter on until the phone card runs out.

How different is Carlos' behaviour from Grama's? Two things are clear: he came here with plans to bring his family after he got established; he broke up our relationship in part to get money to bring them here. He hadn't read the civil union contract. I bear some responsibility for his thinking. When Rosa resisted charging my flight to her credit card, and I told her I planned to marry Carlos after I got to Canada, she probably heard: if you charge my flight to your credit card, I'll reward you by marrying Carlos and taking him to Canada. Why did that thought first come to me at that moment? I had already told them I was travelling on money I'd inherited from my grand-mother. They certainly saw how broke I was; they couldn't have thought that there was any money left. *But they're Central Americans, Paul: people who risk all to come to El Norte. And you were visiting from El Norte. You may have run out of money in Guatemala but you would be returning to El Norte where there's money and op-portunity—or so they thought.* Funny I never saw Canada in that way. If I wasn't gay I'd return to the Caribbean. Wanted to return before I knew I was gay.

10

TODAY IS THE first day of classes for some CEGEP students. Jay would be teaching if he were not on leave. Son of a gun, as soon as he got tenure, he took unpaid leave to visit Africa. Left with plans to visit an orphanage in the Volta region of Ghana and another in Kinshasa that he sends money to. Don't know why he wanted to visit the DRC and put his life in danger. I remember how much he used to talk about visiting or even living in Africa; he even used it as an excuse to reject Jonathan's advances. Now I see he really meant it. I told him to send me pictures of what he's seen, but so far he hasn't. And it's four days now since he phoned to say he was in a Kinshasa hospital getting over malaria. And the damn number he gave me isn't working.

In less than two weeks I'll be back in school too. Looking forward to getting these last twelve credits over and done with and focusing on my writing. What would Grama think of this? She had a high regard for books. But West Indians want their children to become medical doctors, lawyers, or engineers. Guess she'd be okay with Jay being a historian. I can overhear her conversation with Haverites, had she lived:

"Ma Kirton, how your folks up in Canada doing?"

"Anna doing alright. You know she's a nurse. And Jay, her older boy, the light-skinned one, he is a historian. And Paul, well, he's still in school. They didn't tell me what he's studying."

"Paul, the genius. Ma Kirton, he still playing pan? I hear they does have steelband competition up there."

"Anna didn't say. I will ask her next time we talk."

And my meeting her if she had lived to travel here as she had planned to.

"So, Paul, darling, come sit here beside me and tell me of your wonderful accomplishments since you left St. Vincent."

And I, hesitant, walking slowly to the couch, my head hung low. "Grama, I haven't done much. Spent my time thinking about life." And I see her face tensing and her chest rising as she tries to control her disappointment and search for something innocuous to say. "Surely, Paul, you'll do something with all this thinking?"

"Yes, Grama. I plan to write."

"Well, who knows? You might be our third Nobel laureate for literature." *Both nuns and mothers worship images ...*

I edit out the possibility of Ma telling her about my earlier delinquency. Jay's no threat here. Even back in St. Vincent, he never told on me. Except for one time when I got suspended from school and tried to hide it, he never squealed on me, not even when he first caught me smoking pot in my bedroom.

I have imaginary conversations with Grama all the time, and they always end at this point because I can't imagine what she'd say next. I want to think that my grandmother, a self-educated woman, would know that you don't need to go to university to be educated. When I finish the remaining credits in December, I guess this part of the conversation will change to something like: "Grama, I did a BA in English with a minor in creative writing. Hope one day you'll read my books." You'd have loved my soon-to-be-published short story inspired by Mother Bernice.

Wish you were alive for me to ask you more about Granddad. Your journal entries on him make him out to be a miser and a buffoon. You both started out life as the poorest of the poor. Didn't have to be that way for Granddad though. His father had plenty of land. Lost it through philandering and drunkenness. Your mother had nothing. No mention in your journals of your ever meeting or talking to your father. Nothing about whether he was dead or alive. You mentioned him twice: when we visited Sauteurs in Grenada you told us he was Kalinago; and when Josephine gave you a message that she said she'd received from your dead mother, you said that your pale complexion came from him. Your mother got pregnant with you at sixteen. You certainly saw Granddad as someone who brownnosed White people. From the way you record it, he didn't see it as brownnosing, only as a means to advancement: becoming head of the janitorial staff. But if there was someone who could connect the dots, it was you. And you certainly made the connection between your financial independence and that brownnosing. And you knew you married him for his money and he married you for your youth. He was fifty-six, you nineteen. You never told Jay and me anything negative about him. For that we had to read your journals. You certainly exulted in the financial independence he bequeathed you. I remember when Eloise accused you of getting your wealth from dealing with the devil, and you told her it was your husband's thrift and your hard work. And you offered to put his spirit in her. And Eloise's eyes began to get big and frightened. At the time there was all the uproar about Jestina, who was said to be housing multiple demons. Jay and I still have this difference of opinion about whether you would have horned Granddad when he got older. I'm certain you wouldn't have. Jay isn't so sure.

You told Ma a lot more. Guess it's a case of women discussing their needs and how to manage their husbands. Now every time I think of you, I see you holding that kitchen knife, threatening to chop off Granddad's dick, if he hit you. It was one of the first entries that Jay showed me. Guess Granddad knew better after that. Ma couldn't stand up to Daddy that way. Then again, he broke stones for a living. And, thank goodness, does not have a stone heart. Later, after she left him, she ordered him to stop drinking and he obeyed. Jay's close to him. I feel nothing for him. When he came to visit us at Grama's, mostly at the store, I said hello to him and nothing more. Jay hugged him. He never asked me to and I never did. Funny, Jay said he never hugged him before Ma left him. Jay was always worried that he would go back to the bottle.

Jay likes his new wife. I didn't get a chance to meet her when we went to St. Vincent to arrange care for Aunt Mercy. I wasn't up to it the day Jay and I were supposed to go, and he went alone. Probably thought it was his duty. Too much learning required for me to establish an emotional connection with him. I'm positively certain it's not worth it. But I would have come home from Guatemala if I had known Ma was sick and dying. Risk the arrest and do so. I know Jay would dispute this. I still think he doesn't believe that I was afraid to phone home or write, but I believed those cops were looking for me to collect the $500 I "owed" them. But he's right. I shouldn't have put him and Ma through all that agony just for $500, and in the end the whole thing was a hoax. All that mattered to the immigration officers was that I had not renewed my visitor's visa. It was enough though for them to beat me up and take the $90 Rosa had lent me. They must have written something dreadful in my file to prevent my return to Guatemala; people overstay their time there routinely and are merely fined for it.

⇒ I glance at my watch. It's half past eleven. I'll call Rosa and Carlos in half an hour. Bought phone cards this afternoon. These days with interest rates at almost zero, my GICs earn nothing. Mutual funds have recovered from the Wall Street meltdown, but they say another recession is on the way. Jay convinced me to invest in ethical mutual funds. I have cut back on my spending. One reason I sent Rosa less money than I'd wanted. I'll move to a smaller, less expensive apartment as soon as this lease runs out.

What will I say to Señor Carlos over the phone tonight? All things considered I'm lucky not to have had any issues of physical violence with him. A miracle, given the violent society that shaped him. I better brace myself to resist all he's going to tell me to ingratiate himself back into my life. I'm sure he'll start by asking to stay at my place, hoping one thing would lead to another. I won't grasp that tree limb to find out if it will break. Grama wouldn't have taken him back, and when Ma finally got the courage to walk from Daddy, it was for good. If Grama were alive, would I have been able to ask her advice on this? Ma's advice would have been out of the question. Her religion already advised her to disown and even stone me—were it possible.

Would Grama have appreciated a novel in which the villagers

burn down her store? That woman Elka, who used to come to the store with her dress tied half-way up her wrinkled thighs—what will I do with her? Her excessive religiosity? Probably some secret deed she was atoning for. I should make her childless. Conceived for her brother (they used to sleep in the same bed, all of them in their parents' one-room mud shack, hear their parents having sex, and decided to try it themselves, and liked it; actually happened in a couple of families; we knew a boy born from it) and secretly aborted the pregnancy at fourteen. Damaged her reproductive organs. Unable to conceive. Have her set the fire to Grama's property. Put her on mourning ground —only the Spiritual Baptist religion would work for this—and let her deeds block her. Have her come blindfolded led by Mother Bernice, one morning at four to beg Grama's forgiveness. Have her travel to the river bank where she buried the foetus. Have Mother Bernice whip her on the spot to get her to confess.

Who would narrate the story? Grama maybe. How would she know what the community's up to? Her friend Sefus. He knows everything that goes on in Havre. Lots of room there for banter. "See, Ma Kirton, if you and me was man wife like I asked you to, I would o' protect you from these hooligans what call themselves Soldiers of Christ. Religion turn all o' them do(l)tish. That is the gospel truth, Ma Kirton. Remember them that did go up the hill up there and sing and pray and say they waiting for Christ to come? People that stupid will do anything. See? Now you know that no matter how strong a woman is, she still need a man to keep society from trampling on her. I know you got insurance, Ma Kirton, but it would o' been better if you had your store. They wouldn't o' tamper with you if I was your husband. They wouldn't o' dare to accuse you o' being lesbian. They would o' know you getting my sweet one-hundred percent pure man love, not this zamay whattamacallit foolishness." Yep, I'll make Sefus the narrator.

I'll have to play around with the chronology so I'll be able to tell Grama about my travail before I accepted my sexuality, and about my stormy relationship with Carlos, only to have her say: "Look, no need to fuss about your sexuality. Just accept it. Take me, for example:

at thirteen I realized I was sexually attracted to men and women, but never did anything about it until I met Mercy. She was liberal-minded enough to let me have her in secret while I was with my husband and after him Benjamin. After Benjamin I came to the conclusion that she was enough for me."

"So, Grama, Haverites suspected correctly?"

"Yes, they did but it was none of their business. Besides they couldn't prove a damn thing."

I laugh and remember Jay telling me one time that he thinks our imagination is our only salvation.

Reminds me too of the cuss-outs in Havre. Never heard Grama in any. Must have felt it was beneath her to engage in them. Not Aunt Mercy. She'd told Sefus to go look for love in Laird's stables where his father raised him. The shoppers laughed. Grama's face turned strawberry. Wonder what Sefus would have done if Aunt Mercy hadn't been behind the counter. He vowed he'd do to her what he'd learnt in the stables if he ever caught her alone at night.

Aunt Mercy and her neighbour Gwendolyn, who lived just above her, often went at it over Gwendolyn's waste water and rubbish that came downhill to Aunt Mercy's place.

"What you want me to do with it [the rubbish]?"

"Keep it in your house. You and it belong together."

About the waste water — "Where you want me to put it?"

"Drink it!"

This was at Aunt Mercy's new house. Before I knew her, she'd lived halfway up the hill. Jay told me that to get to her old house during the rainy season you had to wade through a lot of mud. The new house was built on the land where Granddad lived as a child; it bordered the Havre main road, a little way out from the centre of town, near Laird's Plantation. Jay said that when the house was christened they'd killed a rooster and sprinkled the blood in the four corners. They'd poured rum in the corners too. The house was built of imported pine, and Aunt Mercy sprayed it constantly with insecticide to control the termites that were threatening to consume it. Grama said she'd warned her not to build with wood, but she said it was what she could afford. At first it had four rooms: two bedrooms, a sitting room and a dining room and stood on cement pillars; her kitchen was a small building apart, and an even smaller building was an outhouse. She had electricity but no running water. She took her baths and did her own and her insane niece's laundry at our house. Four years before I came to Canada she got running water, and added an indoor kitchen and bathroom to the house.

Her niece, Joanne, who lived with her, was rail-thin like Aunt Mercy, and had whitish skin and wild grey eyes. She was an out-of-wedlock half-sister to the younger Lairds who owned the plantation over the hill, and a cousin to Pembroke and Alberta, the Anglican organist and deputy head teacher who caused a scandal in Havre when she became a Spiritual Baptist. Joanne was always laughing and talking to herself. Every couple of years she got violent and had to be admitted to the mental asylum for a few weeks. She'd studied nursing in England before she became mentally ill and returned to St. Vincent. It was her money that built Aunt Mercy's house. Joanne was supposed to come to Grama's house for her lunch every day. Some days she didn't come. On evenings when Aunt Mercy went home to sleep, she took food for her. Occasionally Aunt Mercy said: "I beg God night and day not to make me die before her." Joanne, not God, granted her wish the year after Jay and I came to Canada. One night she swam out into the sea and never returned. Fishermen discovered her body two miles offshore.

In the store, Haverites sometimes discussed Joanne. Some were convinced that somebody had done her in: worked obeah on her. Gwendolyn opined otherwise: in the cuss-outs she and Aunt Mercy had, with Joanne sometimes participating, she'd tell Joanne: "Shut up! You crazy bitch. Is all the belly you throw way in England that have you so." Joanne went around cradling a bruised blue-eyed doll that she called her baby, and would ask anyone near to her if they didn't see how much it resembled its father.

Gwendolyn's house—on the lot uphill from Aunt Mercy: cement, three bedrooms, living and dining room, and indoor kitchen and toilet —took up all her land. Her son, who looked White—Gwendolyn had deep brown skin, hazel eyes, and semi-straight hair—and who worked on a cruise ship, had built it for her. Before Aunt Mercy built her house on Grama's land, Gwendolyn had used the land as a rubbish heap and channelled her waste water there. She continued to do so after Aunt Mercy went to live there, and whenever Aunt Mercy asked her to stop, she'd throw her dress over her head and suck her teeth, and say: "Leave me alone, you lesbian bitch! Is *zamay* you want to *zamay* with me or what?" The bickering came to a head when Grama sent her a lawyer's letter. Gwendolyn brought the letter to the store, stood outside the door waving it, and shouted to Grama: "Get off my back and buy back your soul that you done sell to the devil. And send the lesbian bitch, your girlfriend, out here. Let her come face me. See if I don't put that dry roseau over me knee and pop it."

When Aunt Mercy had had enough, she went out to meet her: "Yes, whore, I come." By this time a crowd had gathered. "First thing, Gwendolyn, go find out who your son father is. Or go find a ship crew to service. That is what you and your sister used to do."

"You is sour, Mercy, sour 'cause man never want you. All you can do is *zamay*." She lifted her dress over her head, showing green panties. "All you is fit for is to kiss this. Here." She patted her loose backside, bent half-way, and offered it to Aunt Mercy. "Come. Why you not coming? Come kiss it."

"Is clap that bloat you so: VD got you *obzockie*; can't even bend. Bend a little more and see if I don't put my foot up your arse," Aunt Mercy said and began moving quickly toward her, fists balled. Gwendolyn did her best to run, her fat body waddling, her knock-kneed legs kicking sideways faster and faster as Aunt Mercy closed in on her. Then she tripped and fell as Aunt Mercy caught up with her. Standing over her, Aunt Mercy said: "Look 'pon you. In your favourite position. You slut! I should spit on you, but I won't waste me spittle."

"Kick her!" someone in the crowd yelled. "Kick the whore."

At that point Grama came out of the store, took Aunt Mercy's arm, and led her inside.

"Not fair. Not fair. We ain't even get to see Mercy pull out some o' that straight hair."

Gwendolyn struggled to her feet, dusted off her dress, and said: "Is a good thing I trip, else you all wouldo' been sweeping up bones 'cause there ain't no flesh there to speak of."

The onlookers sucked their teeth. Some laughed.

Grama took her to court. The judge ordered Gwendolyn to pay the court costs and to come to a mutually satisfactory way to resolve the problem. Grama let her install an underground drain on the land; the coming of garbage collection to Havre solved the rubbish problem. A year or so later she was again shopping at Grama's store. And she saved Joanne and Aunt Mercy's house from burning down one time when Joanne tried to set it on fire "to chase out the devil."

11

I PICK UP the phone card, dial the numbers, and effect the connection. My chest feels stiff and my head is throbbing. Carlos answers, and gives me a loud kiss. He goes on about how he can't think of anything but me. *Just buried your sister and niece and only thinking about me!* "I miss you. Is painful. I want be in my husband arms." There's a hum of voices in the background. The phone card is for eleven minutes. I tell him to put on his mother. She comes and says: "*Gracias, mi yerno*" at least five times, that the funeral went well, the *padre* gave them a great send-off, friends kept her from collapsing, neighbours brought so much food she'll have to give away some, she never knew she was so loved, etc. Then she switches to what a wonderful son Carlos is — "*¡Que bueno hijo!*" *Pero su independencia y su orgullo (arrogance)* get him into trouble, that she's convinced that I am Carlos' *alma gemela* (soul mate).

"You have one more minute," the operator breaks in.

"My time's running out," I say.

"*Prométame que ustedes van a reconciliarse* (Promise me you two will get back together.)"

"We'll see."

The conversation ends. I got through that all right. Thanks to the phone card. Good thing I didn't buy a twenty-five-minute one.

I turn the television on to watch the rest of "The National." Various people are talking about what Jack Layton meant to them. They say he was a sincere politician. (To me that's an oxymoron.) That he gave them faith once more in the political process. I wonder what would have been said about Obama if he'd died a month before taking office. Would have been nice to see Jack take power though and see whether he could implement his policies. I'm sure the wealthy would have waylaid him as they did Bob Rae back in the nineties, as they're doing to Obama right now. In democracies politicians are servants of the wealthy. Successful politicians manage to conceal this fact. You can only have a just society if you rein in those whose wealth comes from preying on the weak. And free rein and nothing less is what the wealthy have, and, to keep it, they destroy unions, foment wars, and overthrow governments. And warplanes, warships, missiles, bombs, armies, and police forces, paid for by the taxes levied on the middle class, are at their service. I read about this American rancher in Costa Rica who defied the Costa Rican government and used his private runway to supply arms to the Contra rebels in Nicaragua—and Costa Ricans couldn't do a damn thing about it.

I guess what's both admirable—and possibly dishonest—about the NDP is that they know all this and yet proffer a platform of social democracy. Bill felt that the provincial NDP were Liberals in orange clothing—North American capitalists would extend the leash no further—and that it accounted for the small presence of the Liberal Party on the Prairies. During the 2011 campaign he'd say, laid back in his recliner: "Remember Jack telling Liberals to lend him their votes in 2008? This time he doesn't need that trick. Canadians already see that Dippers are the new Liberals; some like Janice McKinnon are to the right of Pearson and Trudeau even. Chretien and Broadbent know this. It's why they're pushing for a merger. When you blend orange and red and add quite a bit of blue, what do you get? *Prairie-brown, I guess.* And the politics: an NDP like Brian Mulroney's Conservatives led by Janice McKinnon." It was all Greek to me, since I wasn't around during the time of Mulroney, and hadn't studied Canadian politics. One of the things that saddened Bill was how Saskatchewan, home of universal health care, enthusiastically embraced conservatism as soon as it became a have-not province. "Never fails," he said, sadly shaking his head. "When the poor get wealthy, they seek protection against those they left behind."

I recall the first time Jay took me to the seminar at your house. I think you never got over the trauma of Allende's overthrow. You told us that in 1972 you went to Chile to teach for free, giddy that a communist had been elected by popular suffrage: "I had enough money from Daddy's insurance to feed and house me for twenty years, if I lived frugally. Naïve. Was I naïve! When the fascists, capitalists, and the CIA unleashed their furor, I was glad to be able to return here with my life. Lots of Chileans weren't so lucky. I came back and did a doctorate in literature. My undergrad degree was in history, but I turned to literature: only place where you get hints of how what's lodged deep inside human nature controls us. I decided that I would teach only those courses that bring heightened awareness of the human condition. Too many of my colleagues hide behind the mask of aesthetics. Art for art's sake, they say. And I reply: 'Then let art create art, and let art study art and buy and sell art.' They accused me of being aggressive, difficult, obscurantist, weird. Talk about abusing language. Some even sent me hate mail. In the end I distanced myself from them. To have close relationships with more than a few people you must go along, or pretend to go along, with their anti-Semitism, their racism, homophobia—all their self-serving isms. I puke too easily for that."

Such an idealist. To the very end. You fell ill and had to come back from Toronto the day before the G-20 Summit began, the illness that culminated in your cancer diagnosis. You followed the G-20 protests from your hospital bed, and must have agonized that you couldn't be there. In the 1980s, you were present at all the vigils and demonstrations to draw attention to the victims of apartheid. You showed me a newspaper clipping of you wearing a Reagan mask hugging someone in a Botha mask below a headline that reads "Frosty Welcome for South African Ambassador Glen Babb."

Looking at the scandalous behaviour of Jacob Zuma, I asked you if you thought it was worth it. You said: "Of course. It's gross indecency to put limits on people's humanity based on their race. Now it's up to the majority of South Africans—be they of African, Asian, or European origin—to choose their government. Are they gullible and fall for the rhetoric of unscrupulous politicians? Of course they are—like humans in Canada, the U.S., Europe, Asia. Did the African National Congress learn something from the oppression they suffered? Yes. They enshrined same-sex rights in the constitution, the first country in the world to do so. Perhaps still the only one. Paul, we are such that even if we all depend on the same river, some will try to keep others from accessing it; others will soil their neighbours' section, boast about it, and use military might to continue doing so. It's the sad story of human history. But we can and we must educate people to think and behave differently. We don't have to be fatalistic about it."

Professor Bram would disagree with you on this.

I'd listen to you and have trouble imagining a time when Blacks couldn't vote, get a decent education, or health care. I shudder to think it was all true and was in place in South Africa during my infancy. Now the thought that oppressing others is a trait of my species makes me shiver. The difference between us, Bill, is that you believe all humans have the capacity to rein in such urges, and I believe that some people thrive on them and go looking for the opportunities to gratify them. It's clear from Churchill's biography that he loved war, and had no qualms about killing people. Looking at how U.S. soldiers behaved at Abu Ghraib, I'm convinced that for some of us humiliating those over whom we have power is akin to orgasmic pleasure. No, Bill, I can't go along with you on this one.

I miss you. Bill, I miss you. Our talks, sometimes until 3 a.m. Carlos was right: you were more important to me than I knew, more important than Carlos for sure. He catered to my libido; you to my intellect, my soul; you freed in me the moral decency that lay smothered under the anger and hatred in me. You helped me clear the debris and took to a higher level what Grama started.

But you preferred Jay over me. You and he went places, to cultural events, and you never invited me to come along. I never chided you about it, but it hurts, even now.

Apart from never having the lifelong mate you desired, you never told me why you felt your life was unfulfilled. *A lifelong mate.* You hated the need that took you to the saunas, that made you settle for the Enriques, Chais, and Ricks of this world. Bill, maybe we expect too much from life or fight the wrong battles with ourselves. Your boyfriends wanted what all animals need: food, shelter, warmth. You had all that in excess. To get it they allowed you access to their bodies. And you, of course, you had to give in. Men must placate "the devil between their legs." Not so long ago, wealthy men had harems. In Ibo culture men able to afford many wives leased them out to men too poor to have wives. I remember Sefus in the store trying to court Grama, aware of the wealth she had and he lacked and the sex he was sure she desired. Wonder how many times she teetered on the edge of ceding. Of course, she knew Sefus was mostly empty talk, that he had a daughter who worked as a maid in Kingstown and, although he never denied paternity, he'd never given her mother a penny to support her.

Grama had given in before, when she married Benjamin. Of course, all this would be idle speculation on my part if her friendship with Aunt Mercy was sexual. And Ma and that fellow in her church, Isaac, who wanted to marry her. Pathology, fear of men as a result of Daddy's brutality, figured in her rejection: she was right for the wrong reason. At what point does repression become pathology?

Sex. Sex. Sex. In spring all nature ruts or delivers the fruits of earlier rutting. The erotic perfume of lilac and apple blossoms permeates the air; their blooms (vulvas) delight our eyes. By June the dandelion seeds are wafting everywhere, and the maple and elm seeds coat the sidewalks and our balconies. Sex-crazed male birds flitter in the trees and call out and plead: I have nest, I have nest; or is it: sperm, sperm, sperm? In St. Vincent, as soon as twilight descends, the lamps of the fireflies signal: orgasm this way, orgasm this way; and nocturnal nature fractures the air with variant calls of: sex, sex, sex. The cacophony of testosterone shrieks and hums endures all night. On our seaside porch the cats took it to orgiastic heights. On the worst nights Grama was forced to chase them off. Every male that flies, swims, or walks battles to do it. Imperious desire. Yeats said he wanted none of it in his next life. But couldn't resist it in this life. Even tried the monkey gland operation. Born too early for Viagra.

"Wakeup" Johnny (Wakeup because the neighbours used to hear

him waking up his woman at night) was said to have come in one day and met his wife on her knees beseeching God to rid her of sexual desire. And he knelt right down right beside her and bellowed: "Lord what you take from her give to me." He must have got it. When I knew him he and his wife had long separated and he was fathering children with a woman the same age as his youngest in-wedlock daughter.

That devil between the legs—Priapus, a god, the Romans rightly deemed it, if we think of its power over us. I was at Sky one night when a man leapt over the bar and gave the bartender a bloody nose for having slept with his boyfriend. I've never felt like beating up Carlos or any of the men he slept with. Perhaps it's why he accused me of not loving him. Maybe I am indeed abnormal.

One evening last year, I was at Gina's place. Emilia was there too. Gina said: "We live in a small world. Sometimes we don't even know how small. There's this girl, Salwa, in the LLD programme with me. We get along superbly, and she's always telling me about her family, how they have some old man lined up to marry her, but she's not going to let them choose for her the way they'd chosen for her weak-willed brother. He had a White girlfriend that he'd refused to introduce to them, and one night he and the girlfriend went to a club, and while he was off somewhere with some friends, she left with another man. Her brother was so distraught that he took a whole bottle of aspirins and ended up in the hospital. After that his parents made him marry a woman he didn't love, the daughter of her father's business partner.

"About nine months after telling me this, Salwa invited me to her place, to a small birthday party she was having. Guess who showed up with a woman and a six-month old baby? Said."

"What?"

Gina nodded. "Boy, was he embarrassed! I didn't say: 'How ya doing, Mike.' Instead I said: 'Said! What a small world! Salwa is always mentioning her wonderful brother, and I would have never thought it was you. Aren't you introducing me to your wife?'

"He introduced her: Urshad. The baby, a boy, is called Ahmed. Paul, I had trouble keeping a straight face all evening. That White girlfriend."

We all laughed.

We already knew part of the story. In fact I knew the first part better than anyone else.

The third and last time I went to Sky I met him there. He'd already told us not to call him Said, to call him Mike. He was waiting for his partner to arrive. The section of the bar we were in wasn't crowded. A group of South Asians stood in a far corner eyeing us. I asked *Mike* if he knew them. He said no. While we chatted, Feliciano, the boy-friend, came. Gúicho came in a few minutes later. Feliciano stared at the South Asians while Gúicho carried on with his usual foolishness: feeling up Said's biceps, licking his tongue, asking Feliciano what he'd done to get this *papasito*. Gúicho, *Mike*, and I went off to dance. Feliciano stayed behind. When we returned to the bar, Feliciano wasn't there. Gúicho left shortly after to try his luck in another bar. I remained with *Mike* until the music stopped and the lights came on. Three of the South Asians were still there. They came to where *Mike* and I were standing, and one, gaunt like an Egyptian mummy, began to sing:

> "Me lover lost/ Find him.
> Is where he gone? Find him."

He stopped singing, stared at *Mike*, his eyes glowing, teeth bared, and asked with a distinct Trinidad accent: "How you doing, *Mike*?"

Mike bristled.

"Like you lost something?" another one said.

"Is your man you lost?" the third one said. "When you catch up with him, cut his arse."

"Good and proper."

All three laughed.

"Let's leave," I told *Mike*.

That was three years before Gina divulged this information. He'd never given any of us his phone number so, until Gina told me this, I didn't know the follow-up. Guess, however inadequate, marriage, for those who can handle it, is more solid than the vagaries of gay relationships. In Montreal, a large city, should he want to, he could split himself in two: Said when he's with Urshad; Mike when/if he goes to the sauna. According to Bill half the clients of saunas are men in heterosexual marriages.

Here you can be celibate, and it would be nobody's business. Not so in St. Vincent. Haverites looked with distrust and shouted unfavourable comments at men who weren't hitched to women. They were less harsh to Grama than they were to Aunt Mercy because there was no evidence that Aunt Mercy had ever had a man. In a tone of disbelief they'd say: "Mercy, you mean you going to meet your maker same like how you come? St. Peter should slam that gate in your face." Some offered to cure her of hanky-panky—code for the lesbian relationship they claimed she and Grama had. Even when I was present in the store, some men said that lesbians were that way because they hadn't been properly fucked, and they claimed to have what would cure them. Grama would look at me and then at them and ask them, please not to brandish their credentials.

They were very harsh with Job. Whenever he came to shop and met customers, he turned back. He was around fifty, short and small, with a protruding elongated bottom, and a voice as piercing as a pipiree's. Around sunset we'd often see him in short pants strolling with his knock-kneed gait along Beach Road. He lived in his deceased mother's four-room house on Havre's Main Road. He bore the taunts in silence, and for good reason. The one time I heard him try to flirt with a woman, she told him to cut it out, that if she were lesbian she would go for the real thing, not a counterfeit.

He didn't have a job but made frequent trips overseas. His trips abroad intrigued Haverites. When they asked him how he lived, he said he'd found gold in his mother's backyard. And some people believed him. A week before I left for Canada, a red-eyed, dread-locked, shirtless man, his ribs and collar bones protruding, perspiration odour searing, met Job in the store and told him: "We keeping a watchful eye on you. Hope you know that? Can't le' you go round the place spreading AIDS." He grinned, all his front teeth missing. "Brady and Jack get away. You not going be so lucky."

Job pretended not hear him.

"Gimme ten dollars. I hungry."

Job ignored him.

"I say gimme ten dollars. All that money you does go oversea and bull for, you can afford to give me ten dollars."

"Them pay you more than me," Job replied.

He boxed Job straight into the counter, and blood began gushing from his nose.

Grama ordered the man off her premises and took Job to the back and used ice in a towel to staunch the blood flow.

It probably explains why Neil Charles, who Jay said had a crush on his friend Millington, went Trinidad to study to become a priest. Not an option in Islam, or who knows what Said might have done.

Not the option Job chose either. I'm assuming he could have chosen. He was Father Henderson's acolyte. The two or three times I had occasion to be present in the Anglican church, it was he, in his religious regalia, who carried the cross in the ceremonial procession to the altar. At Grama's funeral he was still the acolyte—grey now, hunching forward, afflicted with ankylosis, his bottom still some distance behind him. Not sure if he continued as an acolyte after that because Father Henderson—he was always fond of Jay and me; our drive with him from town on Friday afternoons was usually a long unending chat, mostly with me; Grama thought he was a fraud—told Jay that he was retiring at the end of that year.

I still find it astonishing that Job could be so viciously persecuted. No one knew for certain that he was gay. So what if he looked androgynous. It was more that Vincentians, like Africans, strongly disapprove of celibacy. If you were male and seen visiting the Catholic presbytery alone, you could be sure someone was going to ask you about it. Father Henderson was unmarried but had two daughters. Haverites didn't criticize him for having his children, only for ignoring them. Henderson's mother, who lived in the Grenadines, sent them support money. Information that came from Sefus. Not that Sefus was well placed to criticize Henderson: he too was a non-parenting father.

12

THE PHONE'S RINGING, the short ring, followed by the long ring .The screen says anonymous. I wait until my voice mail message ends. "Answer the phone, Paul. It's me."

"Jay!"

"How you doing, dog?"

We both laugh for several seconds.

"You're in great shape. I know you are," I say.

"Yep. They discharged me today. Have to keep taking malaria pills for a few months, but I should be all right. It's messed up my travel schedule though. Small matter. I'm alive and almost well, for now at any rate. The occasional headache. But the joint pains are gone and my eyes are clearing."

I tell him that the funeral of Carlos' sister and niece took place today and relate bits and pieces of the conversation I just had.

He listens without comment.

"What made you remember that dog expression?"

"It's impossible to travel through Africa and not think about St. Vincent. You see all the same gestures here. You remember how women would put their hands on their hips and look upon one another with scorn and say: 'But look 'pon yo' nuh?'"

"Yeah. Cousin Alice's tenants."

"You see the same gestures here. You see them, hands on their hips, cussing one another just as they do in Havre. The same hand gestures when they talk, the same gaits when they walk. It's all here and reminds me Havre."

"Jay, don't ever stay this long without contacting me. I have to know where you are."

"Paul, this is Africa. The telephones don't always work. There's email of course if you can find access to an ISP. In any event during the worse part of the fever and chills, I didn't want to see a phone or a computer. They tell me there are excellent medical facilities in Lusaka. When I get there I'll go for a check-up to make sure there are no more parasites lurking in my blood. To think millions of Africans live with this all their lives; with over-sized livers; always sickly. One reason so many succumb to HIV.

"Boy, hospitals here are quite an experience. I had nothing to eat the first day. Here your relatives have to bring your food. And there's no guarantee you won't have to lie on the cement floor when they run out of beds. If you want to lie on clean sheets, you must bring them, and your relatives take them home to wash. You'll use toilet paper only if you bring it and if you can find it in the shops. Most people are too poor to afford it. The toilet you sit on won't have a seat. Broke a long time ago and there was no money to replace it. There's an open cardboard box beside it, overflowing with used newspaper and buzzing with flies. Some hit you in the face. The water they give you to drink will be polluted. If you can't pay beforehand for the drugs the doctor prescribes, you won't get them, and you're expected to have someone on hand who'll go to the pharmacy to get them. Most people here, before they go to the doctor or the hospital for treatment, must canvass relatives and friends for the money to pay for the treatment. Many die before enough money is collected. Many die too because the treatment stops when the money runs out. If you are poor, here's not a place to get sick. Worse yet, get sick alone. Here no one can survive long without family. You should see the stricken look on people's faces when they find out I'm travelling alone."

I'm shocked. "That bad!"

"The second day I paid a nurse to buy and bring me sheets, toilet paper, purified water, etc. She suggested I hire someone: her male relative, of course, a university student apparently, to bring me food and to change my sheets. The doctor overheard the price she quoted me, and interrupted her. Paul, you should see her face twisting with anger. He told me to pay her a third of what she was asking. Even so I'm sure it was a lot more than the going rate. I still ended up giving the relative a few dollars more. But before you blame her, consider this: apart from the pittance she gets after the doctors have taken their share of patient fees, she hasn't received her government salary for several months. Neither she nor the doctor has been paid. And that unpaid salary is around $10 per month. But there are things I have to be thankful for. At least they had the drugs to treat my malaria. They don't have drugs for much else. In Montreal my doctor gave me Aralen. It's no match for African malaria; not one tablet per week at any rate."

"Have you been careful with the food?"

"I haven't had any stomach trouble. But it's true that every time you eat here, you take a chance with your health. You smell the rot in the meat even though it's steaming hot. It was most likely bought at a market where it had been in the hot open air all day."

"When you get back here, you'll need to be tested for intestinal parasites."

"I have every intention to. Here on top of chronic malaria, a lot of children and adults have anaemia and gastro-intestinal problems because of worm infestation, caused by poor disposal of feces. Ghana is light years ahead of the DRC in its government and facilities, but when I visited the slave castle at Elmina, they told me there was a beautiful beach there. I took a beach towel. The sea was a beautiful blue, and the waves calm. Lots of people on the beach. Some in the water. But what do I see? This little girl defecating right there on the beach with indifferent people all around her. Then I noticed piles of excreta all over the sand. I decided to walk along a beach trail to a popular restaurant a short distance away. Big mistake. It was like walking through a latrine. I despair for Africa."

"Now you're sounding like Richburg."

"No, he was maligning the continent to advance his career. Justifying slavery and using language glibly and saying he wants to see *Jeffersonian democracy* in Africa. No Black person who's aware of

US history and the plight of Blacks during Jefferson's tenure would say that. He's parroting the master narrative. In fact that's what much of his book does. But I think it's experiences like mine that give his argument shreds of credibility."

"Victoria empties its raw sewage in the Straits of Juan de Fuca, and until fairly recently Montreal dumped its own in the St Lawrence. Scores of Quebec towns still do. Guess I won't be able to travel around Africa, even if I could overlook the homophobia."

"Being open about your sexuality could land you in jail here ... or in the morgue. But if you keep it under wraps, short trips to specific places is what I'd suggest. Some people don't mind the bother of living here. There are many Europeans here. For the climate, the heat. Some to profit from the suffering. But some of them provide what little health care and schooling there is, especially in the remote areas ... One subject you can't get away from here is progeny. Everyone wants to know how many children you have, and everyone expects you to compliment them for having many children, very profusely if they are male. It's unwise to talk about birth control here, and you never let anyone know you're gay, atheist, or agnostic."

I breathe out loud and change the subject. "Do you know Jack Layton died?"

"No! He did!"

"You should hear everybody saying he was a saint. I'm exaggerating. But you know what I mean."

"So he died. I was hoping he'd beat the cancer. Kind o' sad. Wonder if without him, his party would be able to displace Harper. He impressed me a lot. I only voted Green because of the way the media and the other parties treated Elizabeth May."

"Lots of chatter too about a Liberal-NDP merger."

"Dippers are too principled for the Liberals. Liberals take the shape of whatever they're poured into. They're almost as bad as Harper. So Jack succumbed. A great politician. I liked him. To be on the verge of winning the prize and then have it snatched away. But life's like that sometimes. How old was he?"

"Sixty-one."

"Too young to die. Ma died even younger."

"Fallen in love with anybody yet?"

"Not funny, Paul."

"I did in Guatemala."

"And look at the outcome." He chuckles. "Take care. We'll talk soon."

"Don't go so fast. I have unpleasant news. The fellow who lives above you left a tap open and it flooded your place. You'll have to redo parts of the floor and replace the piece of dry wall that partially separates the kitchen from the living room. I checked in your filing cabinet for your insurance policy. I called the company, but you have to get in touch with them to authorize me to get the work done. I still haven't met the culprit in person, only on his cellphone. Juliet, the president of your CA, showed him the damage."

For a few seconds, he's silent. "Email me the company's fax and telephone number and I'll work on it."

"Don't forget that you promised to send me some photos."

We hang up and I remain seated beside the phone. Snippets of what he said replay in my mind. I'd read in the Guatemalan press that in most countries in Central America there's a severe worm infestation problem. It's one reason visitors are told to avoid raw fruits and vegetables. But what about restaurant employees who use the bathroom and don't wash their hands? There's the problem too that soiled toilet paper is put with household garbage which is dumped on the sides of roads. I must remember to ask my doctor to order a stool test.

Richburg. His stance towards Africa is perhaps predictable; he knows there's an audience waiting for guilt relief, that would reward him for offering it. Africa's plight began with the Portuguese depredations of its coastal cities, followed by slavery and predatory capitalism. Richburg wouldn't emphasize that, nor would he say that for every billion dollars mining companies take out of the DRC the Congolese treasury collects $37,000 and, more importantly, why. He's all of a piece with Zora Neale Hurston, who, eighty years ago, wrote that slavery was the price her ancestors paid for civilization and that it was worth it. She too knew where the butter came from. She even supported the prevailing White American view that African Americans were childlike primitives.

The burden of all this propaganda. Do we confront it? Can we throw it off? Do we ignore it at our peril? And when we devote so much energy to it, what parts of our lives do we put on hold? Should my own writing tackle it? I don't know. This shit is heavy, too fucking heavy.

"*How you doing, dog?*" I recall Mother Bernice and laugh. At Grama's house you always heard Mother B before seeing her — beige skin, round-face, head swaddled in her purple Spiritual Baptist headwrap — waddling her way down the street, taking puffs from her pipe between each greeting. The greetings becoming louder, more distinct as she gets nearer. "Gertie, you there? ... How you do, Lawrence? ... Lawd, you don't see me here with the hard time? ... Mr. Morris, how you maugre so? You is disappearing. Why you don't married me? I will cook you up a good broth. You need skin 'pon your bare bones." Today, Grama is out front trimming the roses and can't hide from her. Ours is the last house down the street, so we get all the leftovers. "Ma, Kirton, how come you look so prosperous? Like you have a secret pipeline bringing down manna straight from heaven." Mr. Morris is still on his porch. "Ma Kirton, why you don't take Teacher Morris in hand, and put flesh 'pon his rawny body? A-a, Mercy is you that behind the clothesline and you not even saying, morning, Dog?"

"Morning, Dog," Aunt Mercy says.

Grama, Mr. Morris, Jay, and I laugh.

"Is dog me is for true. Dog that don't get *no* bone. 'Cause is just so Sonny treating me. Worse than dog. Up in Canada spending all he got 'pon White woman and forget he got a poor mother in St. Vincent. Jenny daughter tell me she see him with a White woman and two half-white pickney at some sort o' picnic that thousands of Vincentian does go to every year. She say is so he big and fat. The good life, and he don't remember me, his poor mother." She isn't thin. "Don't even write to say, Dog, you drink tea this morning? Dog, you buy a pound o' fish? Dog, how you does pay for your medication? I used to say when he born and his father left me, I used to say: 'Thank God, is not no gal pickney I have for go out and bring belly for me to mind.' But I know different now. Jenny own breed and left the pickney here for Jenny to raise. But every month Jenny can go to the post office and know a letter with money waiting for her. Ma Kirton, boy pickney. Ai-ai, me pipe gone out."

She empties the ashes from the pipe onto Grama's lawn, taps the pipe on a steel rail, pushes a hand into her pockets, takes out a roll of tobacco, breaks off a piece, and restuffs the pipe. From the other pocket she takes a box of matches, relights the pipe, takes a few pulls, and resumes exactly like a DVD she'd put on pause. "Boy pickney, Ma Kirton, all them think 'bout is where next to push that thing hanging between them legs. Me does pray for him every night. Me does beg God for guide him and bless him and prosper him and for remind him that me work like a slave for send him to school, that when me had only one penny bread me used to give it to him and go hungry. Ma Kirton, you ever see ungratefulness so?"

By now Grama has turned her back to her and the clicks of the shears have become quicker and louder. Occasionally she tears her eyes wide. But the monologue continues until Mother Bernice gets tired and resumes her trek to the beach to collect seaweed.

Mother Bernice's drama makes me reflect on what Jay said about the need for family in Africa. When Haverites spoke of the Sonnies, they would look uneasily at their still growing children, and say that God never sleeps, that the moon shines until the sun rises. Ungrateful children were sure to get their comeuppance. Even fathers who disowned the children while they were growing up expected them to take care of them when they were old. The shoppers talked about a Mr. Billy who had come back from Trinidad in a wheelchair and ended up on his daughter's doorstep. He'd left when his daughter was nine months old and never once written or sent a penny to support her. Bygones were supposed to be bygones. A father was a father. After all he'd provided the sperm. And many children complied, fearful of some sort of cosmic nemesis, haunted by the biblical admonition to "honour your father and your mother that your days may be long in the land which the lord your God has given you"—whether or not there had been parenting. Billy's daughter did, and Haverites said that God would bless her for it. Whenever Ma tried to lay that honour thing on me, I asked her what she and Daddy had done to deserve it, and she'd back off.

As Spiritual Baptist pointer and prophesier Mother Bernice was widely respected. She "piloted" the people on mourning ground and brought them back—for the 'Rejoicing.' Haverites and folks from the nearby villages assembled on the cricket ground to watch her in her white robes leading her latest successful mourner, dressed also in white and holding a lighted candle; behind her a man ringing a hand bell—summoning the African gods, Mr. Morris said—and hundreds of followers, all dressed in white, all with lighted candles bringing up the rear. On the cricket grounds they formed a circle, sang and prayed—and what prayers!—

"Lord I pray for Brother Percy."

Amen

"Give him strength for him to tarry."

Amen

"And I pray for our leader."

Amen

"Is a task with plenty worry."

Amen

"God, you is a rock for the weary—"

Amen

For us all to lean on.

Amen

"And you promise not to give us—"

Amen

"Anymore than we can carry ..."

And they got into the spirit and sang: "Rock, rock, hallelujah, rock/ Come and join hallelujah rock/Tell believer not for lay down there/ Come on, Rock , hallelujah, rock." Until they lost themselves in a frenzy—

Hekay boum, hekay boum.

Hekay boum boum
Hekay! Hekay!
Hekay boumma boumma
Boum-boum
Bumma, bumma boum, boum—

And eventually talked in tongues, until someone broke the trance and brought them back. And the last part where the mourner told what "joys celestial" she had encountered in her travels. For me this was always the best part. They spoke of all the deceased persons they'd met, how healthy they looked, what they were wearing, what packages they carried, and related the messages the deceased had sent to their relatives. A woman's dead father had ordered her to return to the man she'd left. Shoppers in our store discussed it for several weeks. "Ma Kirton, you hear Millicent father order she to go back to Bunjo?"

Grama would nod.

"Ma Kirton, you think she go go back?"

Grama would shrug.

"If she know what good for she, she will go, even on bended knee. You don't play with the dead. No, ma'am. You follow their orders. The dead don't skylark none tall."

Grama would nod.

It was Africa all right: ancestral worship, not as overt as in Benin or Nigeria. Before 1951 they would have been jailed for this. I read that in Eric Williams' *History of Trinidad and Tobago*, one of Jay's texts. And I heard Mr. Morris telling Grama that those *hekay boums* were for the drums they had been forbidden to beat. Father Henderson and Reverend Hennessy (the AMC Methodist minister) probably wished they could still be jailed. With every Rejoicing the Anglicans and Methodists lost members to "that diabolic sect"—Father Henderson's term. Mr. Morris would call out to Grama to tell her who'd been caught by the spirit. When Alberta did, he said: "Cynthia, listen to this. Henderson's ex-woman caught the spirit last night."

"Alberta did! Henderson must be wearing sackcloth and rolling in ashes this morning."

She had been his woman for many years.

Their conversation turned to Henderson's children. "Those young women were hoping to lift their stations. The scamp bred them and denied it." If it were today, they might have proved it with DNA tests. Not that they needed to. Both women resembled him. Henderson's mother, who lived in Canouan, had paid for their secondary education. One daughter taught primary school, the other was the district nurse in Layou. "You wait and see," the shoppers sometimes said, "is them same daughters he going call on when old age and sickness hit him."

On nights when Grama, Pembroke, and Mr. Morris met to chew the fat, they sometimes speculated about why Henderson never married Alberta. Grama felt it was because she wasn't White, or White enough, though Alberta was paler than Henderson and had "straighter hair. He waiting to meet some rich White spinster." (It reminded me of Gwendolyn who, when men in the store flirted with her, boasted that she had never gone down on her back for anyone darker than herself. "And never for free. Shout it from the mountaintop, gal," Sefus would respond and wink at Grama.) Pembroke felt Henderson was a natural womanizer and you couldn't blame him for keeping his options open. Pembroke was one too, but, in Mr. Morris' words, knew the value of keeping a cow in the barn; never said when Pembroke was present.

Alberta was deputy head teacher at Father Crowley's Anglican School: Havre's primary school. Jay, Millington and Neil Charles attended it. I didn't. In the old days when the church paid the salaries, Henderson would have been able to fire her. In any event, since 1979, the constitution provided for freedom of worship. "These not the old days," Mr. Morris said. "He can't do a damn thing to her. When Henderson or my man Hennessy" (Mr. Morris was AMC Methodist) "catch the spirit, that will be the day." He wagged his finger at Grama, who was on her porch looking across at him. "Cynthia, don't you dare say it can't happen."

"Bertie, you and I will go watch them and do a little hekay-boum ourselves."

Jay and I laughed.

"Won't happen to those two, Bertie. Won't. That spirit comes from Africa. Hennessy and Henderson have their roots in England; the branches down here but the roots in England."

"And what about a little cross-pollination, Ma Kirton?"

"A little, Bertie. Only a little." She raised her little finger.

Not everyone came back from mourning ground rejoicing. Some got "blocked." They became instant pariahs, for everyone soon found out—or imagined—what deeds had blocked them. Brenda had ended up in Mental Home, the insane asylum. Haverites said that Gladys, her husband's mistress, had stepped on grave dirt that Brenda had sprinkled on her steps, and thereafter Gladys became bloated and died. Grama was sure Gladys died from kidney disease because of the concoctions she drank to counteract Brenda's Obeah. But Grama was no match for Haverites, who were certain it was Obeah. And the proof that they were right was that Brenda could not get clearance on mourning ground and came back crazy. A decade later they still talked about it. "Ma Kirton, she work Obeah 'pon Gladys just because Gladys used for borrow her husband. Why she self didn't go out and borrow a man? What is sex, Ma Kirton? Is like water. You don't miss it till you thirsty. You drink it and you done with it, until you thirsty again. You don't have to go work Obeah 'pon a woman because your man enjoy she pum-pum. What you do is, get him for enjoy your own pum-pum. Ain't I is right, Ma Kirton?" Carlos would have told her yes.

Lena's "no-rejoicing" happened in my time. Where she escaped to no one knows. The only thing Haverites seemed agreed upon was that she'd overdosed Henry with whatever potion she had been given by Johnny-the-Obeah-Man, who lived over the hill in Esperance. I have read Wade Davis' *The Serpent and the Rainbow* and Zora Neale Hurston's *Tell My Horse* about voodoo potions, but I'm no further on in understanding Lena and Henry's saga. Henry went around the village muttering, "Lena no do me nothing. Lena no do me nothing. Is some mauby me drink." He seemed unaware of space and time. A couple years after administering the potion, Lena "caught the spirit" —or the spirit caught Lena—and she went on "mourning ground." No one in St. Vincent saw her after that. All Mother Bernice would say was: "She didn't get clearance, and me don't know where she gone. She put down she burden and run. And now all o' we have to take turns carrying it." And take care of Henry Haverites did. Grama sometimes gave him cheese and crackers, on occasion sardines and crackers.

Everyone knew parts of the story up to Lena's escape. Henry and Lena had been together since their teenage years. When they were around thirty, Lena discovered that Henry had made arrangements to sneak off to England to marry a woman he'd met while she was vacationing in St. Vincent. Henry never made it to England. Talk about a forgiving soul. On par with Christ: "Lena no do me nothing. Lena no do me nothing. Is some mauby me drink."

There wasn't a man anywhere in St. Vincent who hadn't been warned about the power of Johnny-the-Obeah-Man's potions and Lena's mauby, the name everyone gave to the mysterious potion that undid Henry. A shopper in Grama's store related that she'd administered deer horn and quicksilver to her son to counteract its effects. She named the young woman who'd given it to him. Sefus told her that quicksilver—mercury—was poisonous; it was why they no longer put it in tooth fillings. "How come you know so much?" she retorted. "Where you learn your Obeah?" Sefus guffawed and winked at Grama.

Lena's mauby. At Excelsior youngsters who'd never heard of Havre would tell others: "Boy, you behaving like you been drinking Lena's mauby." Brother, a mixed-race Barbadian, who was taller and stouter than the rest of us—his father was the manager of First Caribbean Bank—often picked on Trevor, a credulous, skeletal English boy whose huge head seemed too big for his turtle-like neck. Trevor's father was the manager at Cable and Wireless. In the schoolyard one recess, Brother told him: "Gorblimey, if I don' make you drink a bottle o' Lena's mauby." Trevor's face turned pink and his blue eyes grew big and glassy. "I shan't drink it," he said, closing and opening his eyes rapidly and shaking his head. "I bloody well shan't."

"*I bloody well shan't,*" Brother mimicked. "Who says you have to? I'll just pour it over your straw head."

"And wha' will happen?"

"Horns will grow on your head and you'll start eating grass."

"And my father will kill you."

"Oh no," Brother said. "When he sees you he'll start eating grass too. Your whole family will eat grass."

We laughed loud, and Miss Murray, our grade-four teacher, who was at the other end of the schoolyard, heard us and came over. Trevor told her the story.

She gave us a withering stare and sent everyone except Trevor inside. Brother tried other tactics afterwards but Miss Murray had successfully immunised Trevor. Wonder what has become of my Excelsior classmates. Fully half of them were the children of people whose companies had sent them to work in St. Vincent temporarily. At the end of every school year we said our goodbyes to those whose parents were moving to positions elsewhere. Brother left at the end of that school year. Trevor returned to England with his parents the year I entered high school.

When Jay returns I must ask him about eccentric Haverites. He'd know those who were around before I could remember. I was two and he was eight when we went to live in Havre. Stories useful for my fiction. I need insight into why and how people become eccentrics. I'll ask him too about Neil Charles whom some people called Nella because of his girly ways. Once he invited Jay to a birthday party but Jay did not go. I'll ask him about that too. Jay avoided the store and missed out on a lot of what I know. When he came to live in Havre, he witnessed a policeman in the store making fun of Daddy. Daddy had thought a knockout blow he gave Ma had killed her and had gone to the police station and told them to lock him up. Jay runs away from unpleasant situations. Has the temperament of a recluse. That policeman's antics wouldn't have fazed me. But then again I have no emotional attachment to Daddy.

➤ I brush my teeth and put on my pyjamas. Carlos disliked my wearing them. Somehow it doesn't feel right sleeping naked. In bed I take Ishiguro's *Never Let Me Go* from off the night table. I have fifteen pages to go. I took it from Jay's bookshelf five days ago. Guess Jay bought it expecting something like *Remains of the Day*. He, Grama, and I had seen the film together. The ticket seller had felt that I was too young to see it, but relented after Grama insisted that I should.

Professor Bram would say the style's abominable. Too many adjectives. "Let the verbs do the work, Joe. The language's not concrete enough." About the theme? I'm a long time thinking about this. Sometimes Bram echoes Nietzsche, the flee-the-market-place Nietzsche because there the people stink: the Zarathustra Nietzsche; sometimes Emerson's privileging of intuition over tuition. Bram's contemptuous of people who spend their lives dispensing charity. Says they're atoning for guilt. There are definitely whiffs of Ayn Rand in some of what he says—stuff like people should be left to live their insect lives in peace, that education promises gold but delivers mostly lead. At times he goes too far: "There are already seven billion on a planet that shouldn't have more than two or three billion. Would massive die-offs be bad?" He looked around the class. "No one's answering?" We shifted uneasily in our seats and said nothing. Should have asked him, why did he add to the problem by having a son? In class, there was this fellow from Saskatchewan, Brad. Mid-forties. A veteran of Desert Storm. The piece of fiction he presented for our critique dealt with a soldier in Saudi Arabia awaiting orders to attack Iraq. It was well written, and we all said so. Bram asked one question: "What drove a Swift Current young man to participate in that murderous orgy called war?"

Brad flushed and his head drooped forward. He was tall, lanky, with a pock-marked triangular face, deep-set, piercing green eyes, and closely cropped blond hair.

Bram stared at him, awaiting an answer. None came.

"Answer that question before you leave for other wars. And please read the *Mahabharata* before you do."

Brad's face turned amethyst.

The class broke shortly after. Brad didn't join us in the cafeteria that day. He never returned to class. We disliked Bram. Too full of his own self-importance. "Pumping iron," someone said, "won't put back the blue that's gone from his tail feathers."

I finish my reading, and I'm upset with the ending. I expected Kathy and Tommy to commit suicide. Guess not doing so underscores the power of state propaganda. I would have killed myself. I remind myself that it's all metaphor. What's the price of progress? Which humans are dispensable, which are not, should any be? For whose benefit do governments sacrifice the lives of the young men (and now women) whom they send off to fight wars? Now we know that many who return physically whole are psychically broken. In Brad's piece, his first-person narrator has nightmares of Iraqi soldiers in bearlike costumes stalking him. The end is something like this: "Now as I do my damned-est to revive the parts of myself that went numb, I remember that before we started fighting in earnest, I told my tent mate: 'Why all this waiting? Man, I'm just itching to get out there and mow some Hajis down, and be back in Swift Current in time for a slice of juicy home-cured Easter ham.'"

War. The focus should be on removing the injustice that causes wars, not on rules for fighting it. War is a crime against humanity. Those who foment it should be prosecuted vigorously. But we hold the lives of others—the non-us, the outsiders—cheaply. Haverites felt that Jack and Brady should have been doused with gasoline and set on fire because they were gay, and would have done so if gasoline had been at hand. The kind of routine burning that happens in Guatemala. A few years ago the minister of gender and ecclesiastical affairs in the government of St. Vincent and Grenadines wished he could incinerate all gays. Leaders broadcast their hate speeches—the case in Rwanda—and the masses begin the slaughter. I suppose it was issues like these that Bill said led him to give up history and study literature. I think they complement each other. Much of what I know comes from reading Jay's history texts.

I'm sleepless. Fragments of Vincentian memories from the earlier recall move across my mental screen like graphic scenes from movies. St. Vincent is my Eden. Jay never had an Eden. I think Daddy started flogging him from the time he was born, and when Grama rescued him, he continued to be beaten in school. Grama ensured that none of that would happen to me, that I would have an unsullied childhood. Professor Bram believes that serious literature mourns the loss of Eden, that literature—all art—is an elaborate mask we construct to mediate the post-lapsarian self; that evil is necessary, that it's one of the many pistons driving humanity. At times I think of my own evil, the pain I inflicted on Ma. Was it necessary? There's lots that's post-lapsarian in my short story that's soon to be published. It's about Mother Bernice and those who went to her seeking relief from hidden guilt. She fed Sonny as a mother would. He did not feed her, as Caribbean children should. My memories of her, put into fiction, will feed me for a couple of weeks.

13

IT'S FRIDAY, THE beginning of the Labour Day weekend. Carlos returned from Guatemala two days ago, and we've arranged to meet at the food court of the Alexis Nihon Plaza.

Where's he staying? The day before he left Guatemala he called to ask if he could stay with me when he returned. I said no and asked him what happened to the room he was renting. A mistake. I wasn't supposed to know this.

"I give back key. Left my things with *una amiga*. I want repair our *matrimonio*."

"We'll talk about that when you return."

"But you made promise with Mamá."

"No, I didn't. Your *mamá* heard what she wanted to hear."

It's 10 a.m. He is waiting for me. We get coffee and sit at a corner table. Very few diners.

I scrutinize his face. Skin the colour of Guatemalan earth: a cream-ish-beige limestone that you see in valley after valley as you travel east from Guatemala City. His hair, black and now curly, gleams. He must have spent his last quetzal at the *peluquería*. I recall the first time I noticed that his hair's actually blue-black, like the feathers of a male grackle. We were at the Temple of Minerva, a little way uphill from their house, and the sun was shining directly onto his hair. I breathe deeply.

He sees me staring at his hair, smiles, and says: "You like? For you I make it."

I sip my coffee. He hasn't tasted his.

"Where are you staying?"

"Is no important." He frowns.

I shrug.

"Miss me? Why you no want make up with me?"

I don't react. For a while neither of us speaks.

"Pablo, I speak you in English. ¿De acuerdo?"

I shrug. "Why not French?" He studied in it for three years, speaks it when he isn't talking to me, but insists on speaking to me in English because he's convinced that if he speaks passable English he'll get a job to teach in the U.S.

"You understand better if I no speak you in Spanish. Listen, I come Canada. I come from Guatemala hungry. I meet plenty food. I have big appetite. I eat. I no starve. Is normal. True?"

More than you can digest.

"Why you no laugh?"

Where's the joke?

He watches my face closely. "Here it is plenty *libertad*. In Guatemala it is plenty prison. Here it is plenty freedom. *¡Libertad!* I like. *La disfruto.*"

A deep line extends from the corners of his upper lip and contours the lower one. He's definitely ageing. Looks much older than thirty-one.

"You *responsable* for breakup too. You accept your *responsabilidad* for breakup too. Is too your fault. I love sex. Is good for my *salud*. You no like. You no like make sex. Is why you always *estresado*. You no can relax. *Nunca.*" He grins.

"Carlos, we were having as much sex as we had in Guatemala."

He shakes his head slowly, his eyes narrow, and his left cheek moves upward a couple of centimetres — his smile of embarrassment. "Was no *suficiente*. *Me masturbé* in bathroom four, five times *cada* week."

I'm surprised but try not to show it.

He's silent, his lips pulled back, questioning. "I no understand you. I no understand you. Why you like that?" He takes a loud breath and looks around the food court. "From start I want make contract with you for open *matrimonio*. We gay. We no be like straights."

"And what would the contract have entailed?"

He shakes head. "What? I no understand."

"*¿El contenido del contrato?*"

He grins, embarrassed. "Now is no important. I no want it now. I change. I no same person."

"So you wanted us to have the kind of sex you saw in the videos you used to rent and bring home when you first you arrived. Is that what you're telling me?"

He grins, turns his head away briefly, then glances shyly at me. "*Sí. Sexo apasionado en groupo.* (Yes, passionate group sex) I young when I first come. Now I no so young."

Another long silence. He breaks it. "You know I was no asking *lo imposible.* Is no strange. Your professor Bram he got family with woman and family with man."

He might set you up as his third. Might appreciate an amanuensis to put down whatever comes up.

His Adam's apple moves twice as he swallows his saliva and stares at the tabletop. "I love you, Pablo. *Te quiero mucho.* I no know why you no believe me. I always want stay *fiel* but you make boring sex."

We're silent. More than a minute passes. He fidgets. He says, "*Je vais dire cela en français. Je ne sais pas comment le dire en anglais. Je pense que les médicaments que tu prends pour contrôler ton asthme nuisent à ton désir sexuel.* You understand? *Así* is no my fault. You no want make sex when I want make. I want make every day. You must change *medicina* or stop take. Then we make sex every day. All kind." He's staring at me intensely. "All kind, no just vanilla."

I breathe deeply. *Let that one pass.* I smooth my hands on my thighs and look around at the tables slowly filling up with the early lunch crowd. *Now he wants me dead. Stop taking my drugs and choke to death.* I'm tempted to ask if this is advice Gineta gave him.

"*Hay otra cosa.* You always looking for third foot on rooster. You always looking for hairs in soup. Today I take cadaver to *cementerio.* I want you do same. *Lo mismo. Echémonos la tierra.*" He stares at me intensely. "No?" He's closing and opening his fingers.

I don't answer right away.

What would Bill have done in this situation? That would depend on which Bill: young Bill or older Bill. What would Grama have done? Jay wouldn't even be in this situation. My head begins to shake even before I speak. "Carlos, I want to have somebody in my life. In fact I so much want somebody in my life that when I should have left you, the fear of being alone stopped me. Then *you* left. I'm glad you did. I've lived through the pain. Now it's not so bad." I stop talking and think: I'll grant that we are sexually incompatible, and I shouldn't blame you for that. Would I reconcile with you if I hadn't known you diss me behind my back? Moot point. I know now. My hands are sweating and shaking. I put them under the table and between my knees so he won't see. "Spoke to Rosa since your return?"

He frowns and nods.

"How's she?"

"*Estresada*. Sad. *En luto. Preocupada por la nieta.* (Stressed. Mourning. Worried about her granddaughter.)"

"Must be terrible what she's going through. Will Guatemala ever become a peaceful country? They say the murder rate is dropping."

He frowns. It's not what he wants to talk about.

"How are you managing for money?"

"I no have. No have *ni un centavo.*"

"Are you staying at your friends for free?"

He shakes his head.

"How are you paying?"

"No pay yet."

"I can't help you. I gave you all the emergency money Jay left me. If I run into difficulty before he comes back, I'll have to borrow some from Jonathan."

"*Sí. Puedes.* No leave me en *el arranque.*"

I don't respond.

"I want make up. In Guatemala was only thing I think in and *después mi regreso. No sé* how convince to you. Have me confidence. Think I tell to you this because I want money? No. I am *sincero.*"

For a few seconds we say nothing, then he resumes: "I see it how easy life leave. *Veo con tan facilidad se pierde la vida* ... I take note

... *me doy cuenta*. The important it is our *matrimonio*. With small *ajustamientos* we live together till die."

Without my asthma medicine mine will be quick.

"What you say?"

I stare at him and remember the first time we made love: the first time I made love. I was the awkward one. He was the one with experience: experience he'd gained on campus. I want to say yes but know I must be resolute. "No, Carlos. There's too much damage to repair, and I can't stop taking anti-asthma drugs. Won't risk my life. Maybe I could try different things in bed. But with someone else, and only after I've won his confidence." I think back to the time he infected me with crab lice and tried to convince me that I had been unfaithful to him or had picked it up at the gym. Up until then I'd wanted to believe that his staying out until three and four in the morning was because he was at Gúicho's place. Why should I think he isn't lying now? Following the crab lice infection he became the model partner for about three months. Of course, he was waiting for his citizenship. I shake my head and think, you'll repeat the pattern, Carlos, and find new excuses: 'Rainwater cannot wash out the leopard's spots.' *No, we won't be getting back together.* Fearful he might persuade me, I get up and stretch out my hand to shake his. He doesn't take it.

"No close the door. *Hazme confianza. Te amo.*" His grief-stricken face turns into a horrid mask.

I walk away quickly, to a cubicle in the toilet to cry, then head home.

When I get home, I change my voice mail greeting to: "For the moment I'm not available. Please leave a message. I'll contact you." Of course, that's not true. I'll answer when the phone numbers of people I want to talk to show up on the screen. The greeting is to avoid being waylaid by Rosa, Carlos, Gineta, Afredo, and others of their ilk. He didn't use his sister and niece's death to weaken my resolve. Surprises me he didn't bring it up. *Stay your ground, Paul. Don't weaken. Remember Grama's strength. Even Ma's.* She was thirty-one when she left Daddy. Grama couldn't have been much older when she left Benjamin. She had Ma at twenty. Ma was eleven when Grama left Benjamin. Grama was thirty-one too. They all came from a line of women who didn't take shit from men. Grama's mother was quite feisty too, even after she became paralysed. Funny. Carlos is thirty-one, two months older than Jay.

→ It's a beautiful Friday but humid and hot. Great start to the Labour Day weekend. A week ago we were all nervous about Irene. They're still recovering from her devastation in the U.S. Atlantic States. Vermont too has been hard hit. Flooding and washed-out roads in Eastern Quebec and Atlantic Canada. In Libya, they haven't ousted Gaddafi yet. Some members of the National Transition Council are offering amnesty; others like David Cameron are clamouring to bring all those involved in war crimes to justice. Yesterday there was only one Gaddafi stronghold left. Today it's two. *Truth is the first casualty of war.* You hear the reporters stumbling, sifting their information, censoring themselves. You suspect they're all wondering, journalists and politicians, whether the thugs they're tossing out today will be replaced by thugs they'll have to toss out tomorrow.

The only objective element in all this is the suffering of Libyans. No matter how NATO dresses this up, this is about Libyan oil and revenge for Lockerbie. As to Libyan democracy, if it comes, it had better be led by someone the U.S. approves of. Hope Libyans aren't fooled by rhetoric. George Bush and Tony Blair destroyed Iraq, in their words, to free Iraqis from Saddam Hussein. Many of the soldiers who fought there said they never distinguished between warriors and civilians. In Brad's words and the words of many Coalition soldiers, Iraqis were Hajis, not humans. The U.S. and NATO blithely ignore Saudi Arabia which is using its wealth to foment trouble around the world. Too much at stake: Saudi oil, Saudi money that keeps American and European banks solvent. Just as well they leave Saudi Arabia alone. What begins as a quest for human rights always finishes in a race for profits or becomes the catalyst for civil war.

The world is broken. My life is broken. Don't even know how to fix that. I'd go for a walk but it's too hot, and at this time the downtown streets would be too crowded. I pour myself a large glass of lemonade, take my copy of *Leaves of Grass,* and go out to the balcony to read.

Traffic is heavy on Atwater. When I move from here it will have to be to a quieter street. My mind returns to Carlos' pleading. Wonder if any of this is strategy he planned with his mother. He may think he's sincere but I don't have to believe him. When Millicent, who lived with her husband five houses up our street, ran off with her lover, Aunt Mercy told Grama: "That coonoomoonoo! It serve him right. When she run 'way with Bassy five years ago, he been foolish enough to take her back. Dress pig up in the finest silk and put it in a palace and see what it do outside when it meet mud."

Carlos' contract. Wonder what excuse he'd give if he couldn't point to Professor Bram. Bill Clinton? John Edwards? Eliot Spitzer? The Kennedy brothers? Berlusconi? I head back indoors for my journal. These thoughts might come in handy for future fiction. Professor Bram, with his bulging deltoids, biceps, triceps, pectorals, and femorals; unwrinkled face—uncanny for someone sixty-eight—thick auburn curls descending from his scalp onto his shoulders (Bill said it's a wig); his skin-tight jeans and spandex t-shirts. Makes you think of Dorian Gray and Mephistopheles.

We were twelve students in his class. He'd selected us based on our writing portfolios. He asked us to print our names in bold letters and put them on our desks. "So you all want to write in this post-literate age." His turquoise eyes ablaze (might have been contacts for all we knew). No frowns anywhere in his face. "Brenda, who will buy your books?" He stared at the young woman sitting on my left.

Silent, bug-eyed, she looked at him.

"How wealthy are your parents?"

Brenda frowned.

"I guess they're not. You may be in the wrong class—class in all its meanings. This class, my class, is for writers of literary fiction. If you're going to pursue this line, you'll (a) be a parasite and live off your parents, your spouses, or lovers—the sex had better be good—and if you don't already know how to, start learning how to fawn; now as in times past, honest writers need patrons; or (b) spend your time slaving away at some hateful job like I'm doing here and have little time to write; or (c) live in abject poverty."

He stopped looking at Brenda. Now silently, he looked at each of us, one after the other, seated at two conference tables joined together. "I've been at this long enough to know each of you secretly think you'll be the next Atwood or Ondaatje or Hill." He stared at me. "It won't happen." For a few seconds, he stopped talking. "If you want to live off your writing, write for TV or Hollywood. Not easy. You'll have to understand how the illiterate mind works, what gives it pleasure, and stick to one-syllable words and a vocabulary of three hundred."

He paused, took a quick glance around the class. "Some of you are damn good looking. It helps. You stand a better chance of making it into the office, onto the couch, and even having your scripts read." He paused. "You haven't walked out? Good. This is my first lesson. If you are going to write literary fiction, you must chuck politeness and political correctness. Your task is to invent blade-sharp language that dismantles the skeletons of convention and slice into the sinews of hypocrisy to expose what they hide, uphold, and bind."

He closed his eyes and recited: "I wandered down the chartered streets/ Down where the chartered Thames doth flow ..." — Blake's "London" — in its entirety. "You will have to write with that sort of candour. Not that it will matter. It didn't matter for Blake while he was alive, and he lived at a time when literary art had meaningful matter. Few people will read it, and if it's truly literary fewer still will understand it. We live in a post-literate age. Want to become a famous writer? — I didn't say a good writer — rob a couple of banks first and ensure that you're caught. Or threaten to blow up parliament. Helps tremendously if you can break out of prison and stay on the lam for months at a time. Readers lap that stuff up. Can be arranged with the guards" — for cash, he gestured, rubbing his fingers. "And when you leave prison, create a character with your name, who describes all you did and might have done. That or walk on your knees from Bonavista to Victoria. The herd needs heroes. Writers are wimps."

By now some of us were laughing. A couple days later I told Bill about him. It was then that I learned about Bram's two families. They live in separate residences: one partner, a Black woman in her late twenties, his ex-student and mother of his only child: a six-year-old son. "Some of us won't believe it's his unless we see the DNA results," Bill said. The other is a Korean man, Kim, in his early thirties. (Explains why he tortures his body to try to look young.) "One time he brought them both to a party at Concordia. Neither partner knew that the other would be there. I was told that no sparks flew. I no longer go to staff parties. Put some excitement in those dull affairs. It was the topic of faculty gossip for a long time. Just what Bram wanted. Bram's angry the Hippie movement ended."

I'd shared all this with Carlos, expecting him to be shocked. He was supposed to be a fervent Catholic. At the time he was going to mass every Sunday—to the 11 a.m. one at Marie reine du monde. He said: "*Un hombre libre. Sin complexidades. Y tú, Pablo ¿no quieres ser como él?* (A free man. Without hang-ups. And you, Paul, don't you want to be like him?)"

I'd find out that being without hang-ups meant living on the edge. How could he think I'm conventional? I was a month short of twenty when he met me in Guatemala, and I had run the risk of bringing him here. And he knew of my delinquent past, though not the full story of how I ended up in police custody in Guatemala. Conventional? Jay and Jonathan, yes. I? Definitely not. This discussion was before he'd slept out or infected me with crab lice.

For all his unconventionality, Professor Bram didn't want us calling him by his first name, though he didn't care enough to call us by ours. Guess nothing would be unusual about his two families if one wasn't gay. Having a wife and mistress(es) is commonplace. According to Thorstein Veblen, until fairly recently men displayed their status and power by the number of slaves they owned and the size of their harems: an earlier form of conspicuous consumption. (Jay once read me a passage from the *Mahabharata* about a king who lost his kingdom, his sons, his wife—they were all property—himself too, playing dice, and was reduced to a life of beggary in the forest.)

The slaves are still with us, except that they're now called bonded labour and servants, and we take stock only when the press reports that some Middle Easterner travelling in the West gives a good hiding to his/her "servants." There's the occasional documentary too about slavery in East, West and North Africa. And polygamy, remnants of the harem, is the next big battle Western governments will have to tackle. Last week I heard a man complaining on the radio that the Canadian government prevented him from bringing his wives here. Guess he wasn't prepared to do like the others: declare one and, depending on their ages, sponsor the others as sisters or daughters. More difficult now because of DNA testing.

Polygamy without the financial constraints would be just right for most West Indian men. Those who haven't travelled to White countries invariably ask those returning from them how much White meat did they eat. "None! Man, you ignore all them White women over there begging Black men to fuck them? Man, you don't see how them flock down here every winter to get fucked?" I guess Rushton came upon some of his ammunition honestly, except that he mistook fantasy for reality. You wonder how these notions begin and why they're believed. In St. Vincent nothing's more hateful to the middle class and pleasing to the lower than to see White Peace Corps women entering and leaving the shacks of barefooted Ras this or Ras that. On mornings, we sometimes saw one who taught at Esperance Secondary walking downhill from Ras Selah's shack. She always carried a pillow. The neighbours would look at one another and wonder why. And sometimes they asked Ras Selah if he didn't have pillows. For an answer he gave a belly laugh and a toss of his waist-length locks.

And there was Lloyd who lived in a mud hut up under the rocks, and helped himself to people's chickens, the occasional goat, and whatever vegetables he needed to complete his meal. He created quite a bit of chatter in Havre when he showed up with two women he brought from Kingstown. People called one Short Gal and the other Tall Gal—collectively they were called The-Town-Gal-Them. Most days if you were on Main Road around 2 p.m., you'd see them trudging in the direction of the river over the hill: Lloyd in the middle, the women flanking him, bath towels slung over their shoulders. They lived like that for a couple of years until one night while he was chopping off the tail of a cow belonging to the Lairds someone filled him with bullets that shattered his prostate and severed his spine.

⇥ Professor Bram's published output totals fifteen short stories. They're reminiscent of Ionesco's *Rhinoceros*. Several of them had been shortlisted for prizes; two had won. "Most of what we write is chaff," he'd tell us when critiquing our work. "Chaff without grain. A great invention the computer. A good bin for verbal crap. You can hold on to it all. On occasion it comes in useful as fertilizer." More than once he quoted Thoreau's statement about why he read the *Iliad* in Greek; Eliot's, that some of the best poetry is poetry he didn't understand; and Joyce's, on reading *Finnegan's Wake*. He thought *FW* the most creative novel ever written, "better even than *Gravity's Rainbow*," which he'd made us read. "If you are going to invest all this effort for no pay, make sure you create something that you, if no one else, can be proud of." His rank is still assistant professor.

"'Hot shit, huh, and still assistant prof," a couple of my college mates said.

"Forty-plus years of teaching. Fifteen short stories."

"One short story every three years."

Someone must have been finking on us. At one point he asked us if we'd read Wordsworth's *Prelude*. No one had. "Crap for the most part. A nugget or two in fourteen mounds of slag ... But you find that then too writers were dissed, like you folks diss me now." He paused, with more than usual drama, picked up a thick volume from his desk and read: "Impostors, drivellers, dotards, as the ape/ Philosophy will call you." He frowned—a long silent frown—and stared at the floor. "Yes, there are those who brag that it's beneath them to read fiction." He sighed and turned his face away from us. "In the end, Wordsworth too sold his soul, he did; became poet laureate, hacked out the lines needed for ceremonial occasions. Guess like me, he too had to eat and feed his family." He faced us again, this time calmly. "He too—I mean Wordsworth—began with the illusions we all start with." He turned over a few pages of the volume and read: "Prophets of Nature, we to them will speak/ A lasting inspiration, sanctified/ By reason, blest by faith: what we have loved,/ Others will love, and we will teach them;/ Instruct them how the mind of man becomes/ A thousand times more beautiful than the earth/ On which he dwells." He guffawed. "Of course, Wordsworth was not alone: Shelley, a worse poet than Wordsworth, believed that poets are the unacknowledged legislators of mankind. If you have any such illusions, I beg you, please dispel them. Disillusionment is not beautiful."

I felt that beneath all that contempt, he had a grudging respect for Wordsworth. Bram never lost a chance to impress upon us that writing won't pay the bills or win us acclaim. About a month after we began his course, Brad told him that if we followed his advice, he would be out of job. Perhaps this had something to do with the dissing he gave Brad's piece. Guess Bram's like most people who don't enjoy eating the shit they serve others.

What will he think when he sees my short story in print? *Chaff?* I felt it wouldn't meet his standards. Too light-hearted. Too folksy. I've seen copies of *Bacchus*, the journal that's bringing it out, on the floor of his office. If I were comfortable with him, I'd invite him for coffee and tell him I'm paying for his coffee with the proceeds of my fiction. But his personality is too caustic for me. Bill was ambivalent about him but admired his daring: his being able to have the kind of family arrangement that suited him oblivious of what others thought. But Bill restricted their interaction to the campus. During Bill's period with his boyfriends, Bram had invited them to socialize with him — then he identified as gay rather than bi — but Bill found excuses not to. "Bram's the sort that makes a virtue out of necessity. If you want a peaceful life you keep away from them; otherwise, you'll suffer their never ending sanctimony."

They couldn't be friends. Were too different. Though I'd better not say so. Many relationships defy logic. None more so than Grama and Aunt Mercy's. Bram wouldn't have appreciated Bill's anger over injustice. I couldn't imagine hearing him say to Bram — as he'd said to me: "The day Harper cancelled the Colonna Accord, I felt ashamed to be White, and Harper later rubbed salt in the wound when he patched it up with an apology for the residential schools horror. And while he was on the West Coast apologizing, Pierre Polièvre, a member of his caucus, was on the East Coast expressing contempt for the First Nations' way of life. It was a well-orchestrated charade. Imagine that: you destroy a people's way of life and then blame them for the trauma you've inflicted." I could see Bram shrugging and saying, as he said critiquing a piece that Brenda wrote: "Ethics work when it's meshed with biology. Capitalism is triumphant because it accepts and rewards the fact that humans are selfish. Even its victims agree. It's why poor Whites in the U.S. are mostly Republicans."

⇜ The air feels heavy. Its humidity is good for my lungs but not the allergens, the gunk, it picks up and brings in its passage here. There's been a tight feeling in my chest these last few days. At times my head feels like it's ballooning outwards. Psychosomatic, I'm sure. My unresolved feelings over Carlos probably. I'll see my doctor in an hour. There's a new asthma medication he wants me to try. I return indoors, close the patio door and all the windows, and put the air conditioner on low.

14

I AWAKEN AND for a while it seems as if I'm lost in fog. Slowly the fog becomes a white wall. There's something in my nostril. I lift my hand to remove it. Someone stays my hand. It's Carlos. How did he get in here? Then I remember. I was on my way to catch a cab to the hospital. The feel and sound of air going into my nostrils register. I know now. I passed out and somehow got here. I feel a burning in my left hand, lower my eyes to look, and see the IV connected to it. I try to speak, but my throat is rigid. I try to speak again. I force. The pain is excruciating, and I'm forced to stop.

A nurse enters. "Mr. Jackson, I see you're awake. I'm injecting prednisone into your IV. It will reduce the swelling in your throat. You suffered an anaphylactic shock, but you are on your way to recovering. How's your throat?"

With all my strength I force to speak but no sound comes. I point to my throat and shake my head.

"I understand. The doctor will be in to see you presently." She takes my blood pressure, records it, and leaves.

It's the new medication that Dr. Brant gave me.

Carlos comes to the right side of the bed and holds my hand. My first impulse is to pull it away. How did he know? How did he get here? I stare at him.

"No lose you this time," he says. "If you no careful, lose you next time. *Surpris de me voir ici, n'est-ce pas?*"

I can't reply.

"*Après ton départ, je suis resté dans le Plaza. Je me sentais découragé. J'avais pas la force de me lever parce que je n'avais pas réussi à te convaincre que je reconnais mes bêtises et que je voulais tourner la page.*" He takes a loud breath. "*Je me suis mis à réfléchir: comment arriver à te faire comprendre que je t'aime? J'ai essayé de comprendre pourquoi j'avais pris notre relation à la légère.*" He shakes his head slowly. "*Honnêtement, tout ce que je voulais ce matin c'était de me jeter dans tes bras et pleurer et te demander pardon.*" His voice is choking. "*Je sais que j'étais bête. Que je me suis laissé porter par Gúicho. Oui, c'est en grande partie ça. Je jouais le clown, niasais á ton dépense. J'ai honte, Pablo. J'ai honte. Ce matin je n'ai pas su comment le dire et comment te demander pardon.*"

He's taking advantage of my situation. This morning you blamed me for your infidelity; now you're telling me the breakup is your fault! Of course, it's your fault. You cheated. You walked out, hoping to get money. This morning you hinted about wanting a deal where you could sleep with other men, and now you say all you wanted to do was fall into my arms and cry. Are you one person in the morning and another in the evening? At least you've come around to confessing that you routinely made fun of me behind my back. I don't want to hear any more of this. If I could speak, I would tell them to send you away from here. I strain to say stop. The pain's excruciating, and I spend several seconds recovering.

He's silent for about half a minute. "*Tu ne veux pas savoir comment je suis ici?*"

I don't respond.

"I left Plaza little *antes* ... 6 p.m. I see *abarroto* in front your *edificio* and I went see what happen. I see you on ground. Barry, *concierge*, he say ambulance coming. I put my hand on your chest. You no have breath. I take EpiPen from your pocket and give you shot, and I pump chest and you get back breath. Then come ambulance and I come with you to hospital."

So now you feel you've saved my life, and I'm indebted to you forever. It's the new medication: *Matasma.* I took the first pill in Dr. Brant's office. He kept me for half an hour and told me to go. I was to take a second pill at 17:30, after that it was twice a day, upon waking and around 10 p.m., at 12-hour intervals. If I had any serious side effects, I was to go to emergency. Within five minutes of taking the second pill I began to feel dizzy.

A South Asian woman comes. She introduces herself: Dr. Indira Ganesh, and asks how I am.

I point to my throat.

She nods. "You'll see the difference by tomorrow morning." She looks over at Carlos, sitting on the window side of my bed. "A good thing your partner came onto the scene in time. He gave you a shot of epinephrine and restarted your heart. You'll be okay. Everyone got there on time."

I want her to shut up, to stop boosting Carlos' ego. I signal to her that I would like to write. She pulls her prescription pad and a pen from a pocket of her smock and hands them to me. I write: *Saw my doctor this afternoon. Took a new drug: Matasma. Reacted to it.*

She reads it, writes on the pad and hands the pad and pen back to me. She asks for the doctor's name and the location of his practice. I write them down and hand them back to her.

She nods. "We'll contact him. Don't hesitate to press your bell if you need anything." She leaves.

Carlos is quiet. He gets up and says he's going to get a cup of coffee in the visitors' lounge.

While he's gone, I think back to what he's just told me. I hate being in this state. Now I owe him something. Situations have a way of trapping me. You could say he rescued me in Guatemala too. When I arrived in Hue I had $225. In a $10-a-day hotel plus buying food, the crudest sort, it would have lasted at most two weeks. And now. Just when I'm ending our union, I collapse on the street, and it's he who rescues me. Looks like fate has turned us into Siamese twins.

He comes back with his coffee. I'd like a cup too but I can't swallow. My skin is tingling all over and I'm uncomfortable. Jenny the nurse returns. An older woman, nearing retirement, semi-corpulent, hair all grey, skin extremely pale; British accent. She goes to the oxygen gauge, says she's lowering it. She asks Carlos if he's staying overnight. He says yes. I try to catch her eye, to signal that I don't want him to, but she doesn't notice. She tells him she'll find him a pull-out bed. She leaves.

He looks at me, notes the fury in my face, giggles, and says: "*La calma, por favor. Ahora, no tienes la brida.* (Calm down. Right now, you don't hold the reins.)"

I fear anxiety would keep me awake all night. I press the bell. Jenny comes. I gesture that I would like to write. She returns to the office and comes back with pen and paper. I write: *possibility of insomnia. Sedative?* She says she'll consult with the doctor and let me know.

She leaves and returns with sleep medication, which she injects into the IV. She tells Carlos someone will bring his bed shortly, and leaves.

To avoid looking at Carlos, I close my eyes while I wait for the sleep medication to take effect.-

15

I **AWAKEN AND** see it's morning. My chest feels normal. During the night the oxygen was disconnected. Carlos is snoring away on a bed pulled out from an armchair. I hear a nurse talking in French to the patient sharing the room with me. I cannot see them because there's a screen separating us. My bladder feels ready to burst. I press my buzzer and tell the nurse in a hoarse voice that I need help to go to the bathroom. Jenny comes. I'm surprised to see she's still on duty. Then I remember Ma sometimes worked three twelve-hour shifts in a row, in this same hospital, then would spend a full day recovering at home. I think she worked in OR, in the recovery room; at least she did in the early days when we were civil to each other. Jenny disconnects the IV, saying I no longer need it. She lets me stand and makes sure that I'm not dizzy. I walk to the bathroom alone. Carlos has come awake through this and is sitting up. He's in a green hospital gown.

¿"*Mejor?*" he calls to me as I approach the door of the toilet.

I nod. Our unresolved issues return, and I don't feel so good now. While in the bathroom, I remember that it's the Labour Day weekend and that I'm supposed to have supper with Gina and Emilia today. Would I be able to go? Except for a slight hazy feeling, probably because I haven't too long awakened, I feel fine. How much of this will I tell them? This is my third anaphylactic shock: in St. Vincent when I was six after eating *lambi;* and when two police officers arrested me putting graffiti on the door of the Plamondon Metro, pepper-sprayed me, took me to the station, and roughed me up—I was fifteen at the time. So far I've been lucky. Where they happen and who's there spell the difference between life and death.

When I get out of the bathroom, a slender, Eurafrican young man in surgical green is placing towels on my night table. I can't see his name tag. He tells me that the shower is outside the door, across the corridor. He stares at Carlos and tells him he'll get him a towel too.

In the shower I reflect on how much we take our well-being for granted, how easily an allergen can shut our bodies down and kill us, and my problems with Carlos seem distant. I'm grateful my voice and lungs are almost normal again. Functions we take for granted. I leave the bathroom feeling hungry. Some of it the result of prednisone, but all I want to do is to eat—anything, even a human steak, I joke to myself, and remember the tall tales Ma told Jay and me. That too, come to think of it, was in the first few months of our arrival here. She nixed all that after she went back to fundamentalism, would have found storytelling sinful. She once said that reading novels was sinful because they were lies. One of the few quarrels I ever heard between her and Jay. She'd got her tall tales from Paddy, a nurse who worked permanent nights on the psychiatric unit here in the Jewish. Rachel, a young, white nurse, was his most eager listener. "'Want to know why we Jamaicans so good dancing limbo? It's because out in the Jamaican countryside, people build their houses in the tallest tree branches and get in and out of them by climbing up and down liana vines. They learned it from Tarzan.'" He was a good limbo dancer, and when they had their staff parties at the Jewish, they'd ask him to do the dance.

"'You know why Jamaicans have so many children?'

"Rachel waited, bug-eyed and blushing.

"'Guess,' he insisted.

"She shook her head.

"'For revenue and medicine.' He kept her waiting. 'The mother rewards those that grow fast and fat.' He stopped again, pretended the story had ended.

"'What's the reward?' Rachel asked.

"'She sends the fattest one, usually a girl, to gather firewood and orders her to put on a cauldron o' water. When it's boiling loud and the steam almost hitting heaven, she throws the child in. When all that turns to jelly, she parcels it out by the ounce in banana leaves and takes it to Kingston and sells it, and makes enough to feed the family for five years. People line up for miles to buy it because if you eat it twice per year, you will never get cancer, and if you're a man you'll never become impotent. Better than all those bogus products on the market here. That's why so many eighty- and ninety-year-old Jamaican men have sixteen-year-old girlfriends, and Jamaican men can't satisfy with just one woman, and why so many of you Canadian women visit Jamaica. Rachel, when you go to Jamaica, make sure you try it. Miracle Jelly, that's the name. I shouldn't be telling you this 'cause it's a national secret.'" He'd look at Ma and wink.

When Ma upbraided him for spreading false stories about the Caribbean he'd say: "Anna, Rachel going repeat that story, and her friends will visit Jamaica to find Miracle Jelly. I can see them all over the place asking for it. And the young men-them asking: 'Missis, you sure is not something else you asking for?' All I doing, Anna, is boosting Jamaican tourism. It got people who still looking for Eldorado. Well I offering them Pleasurado."

After that, Ma intervened when he told his stories. "Why you keep telling lies about the Caribbean?" And he'd reply: "You all don't bother with Anna. She from dull St. Vincent. She don't know drat 'bout Jamaica."

One of the rare occasions that I agreed with my mother. I felt it was wrong to create such stories about the Caribbean. Now that I know stories portray humanity's psychic history, I'm even more convinced that Paddy's stories were wrong. *Are you sure about that, Paul?* If I were comfortable with Professor Bram, I'd ask him what he thinks about such stories. Paddy's audience must have been putting him on. In *Pleasures of Exile* George Lamming mentions English factory girls who asked their male West Indian workmates to show them their tails.

I dress and return to my room, and Carlos goes to the shower.

Some of Paddy's tall tales were good: one in particular, about four men: an Indian, a Chinese, a European, and an African. They lived in a village of a thousand people, "somewhere behind God's back in Jamaica." Everybody in this village bathed naked in the river, the women in one section, the men in another. But these four men were never seen bathing, and worse yet none of them were ever known to have affairs with women. Whispers went around, people observed them closely to see if men went into their houses. They came up with nothing. Then at two one morning, the African went to the river to bathe, and just as he was about to enter the water, he heard footsteps coming down the path. He grabbed his clothes and hid behind a big stone. It was the European who'd come. He took off his clothes and the African understood right away that they had the same problem. "Brother," he called out, and the European picked up his clothes and began to run. "No run, man," the African shouted. "Me and you got the same problem." The European returned and they commiserated. Part way through their conversation, around 3 a.m., they heard footsteps and hid. It was the Indian. He took off his clothes. He had the same problem. European and African cleared their throats. Indian made a run for it, but European was quite a sprinter. "No run, man. We is one." And he showed him what they had in common. By now they suspected that Chinese had a similar problem. They waited but Chinese didn't come. They agreed that they would stake out the river beginning midnight the next night. Sure enough, just after midnight Chinese showed up. When they cleared their throats, Chinese fainted on the spot. They went to revive him and saw right away that he did not have their problem. But he did have a problem. He had a penis and a vagina. Paddy would stop talking then. "So what was the problem with the other three?" his listeners would ask, and Paddy would look at Ma and wink and say there's where the story ends.

Night after they'd ask him to retell the story on condition that he disclose the problem of the other characters. He'd tell it and they'd feign interest until he got close to the end, and he'd shake his head. "Tonight I can't tell you. Maybe tomorrow night." Eventually he told them: "The end is like death; you yourself can't know how or when you die. All you leave me alone. I don't know everything."

Ma stopped telling us these stories after she became a born-again Christian. I'm pretty certain she and I would have gotten along better in the later years if she hadn't returned to fundamentalism. It's always one extreme or the other: Carlos grabs too much and soars without knowing how or where he'll land; she tried to turn into a ghost. I should be the last person to criticize extreme behaviour. Last person.

I'd like to meet Paddy, get him to tell me some more of these stories. Wonder if he still works here. Probably retired. I don't know his last name.

→ As if on cue Carlos comes into the room, dressed in his street clothes: jeans and a beige T-shirt. I remember that the forecast had said that it would be hot today. He sits on a chair across from me. I catch myself opening and closing my fingers. I feel caged and he controls the latch. I'd feel better if he left but I remember that it was he who knew I had an EpiPen on me, that his intervention probably saved my life or at the very least prevented me from becoming brain-damaged.

Edith, a nurse practitioner I'm meeting for the first time, comes. Ma and her colleagues called NPs know-nothing doctors. Edith wears her hair in a brush-cut, is in her forties; is from Sierra Leone and was trained in England. She intersperses this information and questions about St. Vincent into the conversation we have about the medications I'm taking. My early medical charts are here at the Jewish, during the time Ma worked here, and haven't been updated for at least five years. The later ones are at St. Mary's. Edith leaves and returns with Theophylline, my regular medication.

They bring breakfast: dry cereal, apple juice, a shelled boiled egg, toast and coffee. Out of habit and politeness I offer to share it with Carlos. He shakes his head and says there's a Second Cup on the ground floor. I wonder if he has money to pay for a proper breakfast. For the first time I wonder who has my wallet. I don't ask because I don't want to make a link between his breakfast and my wallet. He leaves.

I swallow everything on the tray—would have eaten the utensils too, if ...—push away the table, and close my eyes. What a difference twelve hours make!

"Mr. Jackson."

I open my eyes. A diminutive, bespectacled barrel-chested man is standing near the head of my bed. He introduces himself as Dr. Joseph Olinski and asks how I am.

"Won't say I'd run the marathon, but the 300-metre might be tempting."

He smiles. "Good attitude. But take it easy for the next few days. I'm ordering a brain scan for you," he says while writing in my chart. "We contacted Dr. Brant and he said you've been complaining of headaches. If everything's fine, we'll send you home later today. Everything should be. Just routine. I take it your spouse is still here?" He stops writing and raises his eyes to make eye contact.

"No. Yes. Yes."

He frowns.

"He's not my spouse. Well, he is. We're separated. Not officially."

He lowers his eyes, seemingly embarrassed.

"It's all right," I say. "Carlos admitted me and identified himself as my spouse."

"In that case we need to know that there'll be someone with you for at least twenty-four hours after you've been discharged."

Carlos re-enters in time to hear him. "No problem," he says.

I watch Olinski's stricken face and give him a reassuring nod. His frown disappears and his facial expression returns to neutral before he turns around to face Carlos. "I'll leave you two to resolve this. I'll check back to see you around eleven. By then we would have had a look at your brain—just a precaution, we don't expect to find anything amiss—and we'll discharge you."

He leaves. I'm furious over the conditions for my discharge, but know I haven't an argument, so I shut up. Carlos pushes the pull-out bed back into its armchair form and sits on it. He knows me well enough to stay silent.

16

RAOUL, A MIDDLE-AGED Hispanic man, in green clothes, comes to get me. He has a gurney. I tell him I can walk. He hesitates, then presses my bell and speaks to the nurse. She lets him hold on a while, then tells him the doctor says it's fine. *Why's everyone treating me like an invalid?* I follow Raoul. We take the elevator to radiology. They put me lying on a shelf projecting from something that seems to come from the *Star Wars* set, and I wait to be launched into orbit. The technician, a woman, asks if I'm comfortable in enclosed spaces. I nod. I want to say I once inhabited a womb, but you never know what will get people uptight. She mentions a few other banalities. I nod to everything. I just want to get into space and be over with it. She goes to sit on a raised platform about three metres away and fiddles with buttons. She asks me if I'm ready. I tell her yes but want to ask, where are the 3D glasses? The shelf moves inward and my head enters into what I can only describe as an unheated oven. Feels like I have entered fairy-tale country. The technician's voice breaks in and tells me to hold my head perfectly still. Then the shelf glides out, but she tells me not to get up. Not even a whirl, never mind an orbit.

About fifteen minutes later a couple of men: one African, one South Asian, in white smocks, come to the dais where the technician is. Their eyes rove over what I'm sure is a screen, and they're looking at images of my brain. The technician descends and tells me that a few of the images are blurred, and so they have to repeat the procedure but differently this time, with iodine. I wait for another twenty minutes, and another doctor comes. She asks about allergies. I list all that

I know of. She says she'll have to inject me with something else but doesn't say what.

"Why, must you inject me?"

"Just another way of doing it so the pictures would be clearer," she says, looking away from me. She injects whatever it is directly into a vein of my left hand.

"I'm already flying," I say.

She laughs. "Don't go too fast or too far. We want you within reach."

The technician and the two doctors remain on the dais. The shelf moves inward and the procedure is repeated. When I come out, the two doctors have left and Raoul is waiting to take me back to my room. I meet Carlos sitting on his armchair-bed.

➤ It's 1 p.m. Carlos has been talking about the large number of Guatemalans being deported from the U.S., but I've only half listened, wondering what has taken Dr. Olinski so long. I've decided I'll defy them and go to Gina's supper party this evening. I'm eager to leave. Olinski shows up around 2. His face is tense. He asks me to follow him. I feel my skin tightening. I look at Carlos. He's bug-eyed. I get up, with fake enthusiasm.

Olinski swallows audibly.

I follow him down a corridor. He opens a door into an office with a conference table, computers, and bound manuals. There's a telephone on the computer desk. Olinski picks it up and says that he and Mr. Jackson are waiting. Ten more minutes and the doctors who'd been looking at my brain images walk in. Men in their thirties. They introduce themselves: Kwesi Mbolo and Ramesh Boodhoo. Olinski and I sit on one side of the conference table; they sit across from us. My hands are moist.

Mbolo asks if I'd ever sustained any sort of trauma to my head.

I shake my head.

"Have you been suffering from headaches lately?"

"Not so much headaches but the feeling that my head is ballooning."

"Dizziness? Darkness of vision? Blurring?"

I shake my head. "Just a tight feeling around the temples on occasion."

"Any loss of feeling in your extremities?"

"I suffer from cold hands and feet."

Boodhoo goes to the computer desk, picks up a remote, and resumes his seat. The lights in the room dim, and a large screen appears on the wall to my right, taking up half of it. I watch the cursor moving to the left side of the screen. It clicks and the screen divides into two. It clicks again on an icon in the left screen and a picture appears. Boodhoo says it's the occipital lobe of a healthy brain. He zooms in on the outer edge and drags the cursor along what I know are called the meninges, stuff I learned in high school biology with Mrs. Bensemana. He explains all this and I say nothing. He clicks on the right half of the screen and tells me that's how my occipital area looks. He zooms in on an outer area and moves the cursor to a dark, dime-sized spot. Again he points out the meninges and the cerebrospinal fluid. The dime-sized spot holds my attention. I see clearly the outline in the dura mater. It extends to the arachnoid mater. He puts the cursor on it. "See this? It's most likely a benign tumour."

"Benign meningioma," Mbolo says. "It doesn't put any pressure on the brain tissue yet. If it grows we'll have to remove it."

"A crash landing," I say, remembering my comment about getting high.

They exchange puzzled looks.

"Go on," I say.

"Usually, it's when they're big enough to distort CSF balance and affect brain function that patients become aware and seek treatment," Olinski says. "You are lucky; we caught it early."

"Following us, Mr. Jackson?" Mbolo says.

"Yes," I say, wanting to turn the whole thing into a joke. But I hear the tremor in my voice and the tips of my fingers feel frozen. The doctors keep on talking but I've stopped listening. They say misfortune comes in threes. Mine comes in fours: breakup of my relationship, Bill's death, anaphylaxis, and now a brain tumour. "How long did you say I have to live?" I stare at Olinski, then Mbolo, then Boodhoo.

"Probably to a hundred. It's bad news only because one day it could mean the inconvenience of surgery and rehab, but with this type of tumour there's a 91% cure rate with simple surgery. Yours is in a location where it's easy to operate without ever touching brain tissue. At this stage it doesn't require surgery."

It will be my luck to be in the nine percent. They aren't telling me the whole truth. The tumour is just above the visual centre. They don't say it but I know this from biology and from poring over Ma's nursing manuals.

They say nothing for a while and I too am silent.

"Will I have to give up my studies? It's likely that soon my sight would be affected."

I watch Boodhoo exchange glances with his colleagues.

"Your sight shouldn't be affected. If you have the remotest issue with your vision, blurring, dizziness, whatever, you are to contact us. If we get around to surgery it would be simple. Nowadays this type of surgery is precise. We can keep the swelling of the meninges to an absolute minimum. We have multiple ways to prevent discomfort." This from Mbolo.

"About my studies?"

"Just keep on doing them as before, as if you've never heard any of this. It could be another ten, twenty, thirty years before you require any intervention. What are you studying?"

"Nothing extraordinary: a BA in English. Creative writing. I have a semester left."

"What do you hope to write?"

"Already write. Fiction. Just got paid for my first story."

"Congratulations!" Olinski and Mbolo chorus.

They look at one another. Mbolo presses his lips. Olinski closes his eyes. Boodhoo's face is expressionless. He says: "Whatever action we take will depend on whether the tumour is growing. Usually they remain unchanged for decades, and there'll be no need for a craniotomy if the tumour's not affecting you."

Mbolo adds: "Usually in a case like yours we take a look every three or so months. If it's stable every six months. But, to reassure you further, we'd like to see you in a month.

"How do you feel?" Olinski asks.

"Dazed. A crash landing." I want to laugh but can't.

They say nothing.

"I'm alright. I'll be alright. I know I'll be all right." *I must be alright.*

"Need to talk to a psychologist before leaving?" This from Mbolo.

I shake my head. I saw one when I was twelve. It was a waste of time.

"Sure, you'll be alright?" Olinski asks. "Is Carlos going to be with you?"

I look at him and nod. I wish he didn't know my business.

"If you feel distraught when you get home, call the nursing station and ask them to contact me," he says.

Yeah. Right. PR babble. If I really needed to contact you, the nurses won't be able to find you. Certainly not on a holiday weekend.

I walk back to my room, and throw myself onto my bed, and begin to cry. At some point, I feel Carlos' hand tapping my shoulder and hear him asking, *¿Qué pasa?* I turn my face away from him. He places his hand on mine. He's silent for about a minute, then he asks again.

"Nothing," I say. "Just overwhelmed by all that's happened."

"*No soy tonto.* Tell me. *¿Qué pasa?*"

I remain silent. After a while, I tell him I'll have to throw myself on his mercy since they won't release me unless there's someone accompanying me home.

"*Me da pena.* That's painful. Is what you think?"

I don't reply.

Edith comes and tells me I'm discharged. She gives me a prescription for choral hydrate. I'm to take a dose when I get home and go to bed. Carlos leaves with her and comes back with my personal belongings: a Ziploc bag with my wallet, a pen, and a small notebook, and takes my EpiPen and puffer from the drawer of the night table.

WE TAKE THE elevator down in silence and head out the main door. Before the bad news I'd have walked down to the Côte-Ste-Catherine Metro and taken public transit home. Now I don't want to be in a crowd. We take one of the cabs waiting outside the hospital. When we get to Sherbrooke and Atwater, Carlos asks if I'm letting him in.

"Didn't you tell Dr. Olinski you'll stay with me for the next twenty-four hours?"

He replies yes, but says he knows I told the doctors what they wanted to hear so that I could go home.

We get out the cab. Carlos hesitates at the door. I shrug. "Look, you don't have to come up if you don't want to. I can call an agency." He enters the building. We take the elevator to my apartment. As soon as I close the door, he embraces me in a bear hug and tries to kiss me. I turn my head away. He releases me. I sit down on the sofa — Ma's sofa, I suddenly remember.

He sits beside me. I scowl at him, but he ignores me. He holds on to my wrist and orders me to tell him what the meeting with the doctors was all about.

"About the care I should take to avoid a repeat of what happened yesterday."

He shakes his head slowly, knows I'm lying, must be seeing fear in my face.

I shrug.

He asks what I would like for supper.

I say nothing, but I give him $140 — all the money I have on me

— and tell him to go buy whatever groceries he needs. I hand him the prescription, my Medicare card and tell him which pharmacy to go to.

He pushes the money into his pocket, stares at me for a while, and tells me to swallow my pride, just as he has swallowed his. "*No eres Superman, Pablo. Tú y yo somos seres humanos frágiles.* (You're not Superman. You and I are just fragile human beings.)"

I say nothing. He leaves.

When he returns, he says: "See what I brought you? *Tu fruta favorita. Guanaba.* Soursop. Ripe." He holds it up, with his thumb depressing the skin, for me to see. "See. You smiling. First time today."

Won't be for long.

He prepares a soursop drink for both of us, puts the pitcher and two glasses on the coffee table, and sits beside me on the sofa. I enjoy the soursop. I rarely have it. Unless I buy them already ripe—the rare good ones—they rot before they ripen. Nowadays there are claims that it can cure cancer.

"You go tell me what the *medicos* said?"

"No."

"How I go help you then?"

"You don't have to help me." *Maybe not even they can help me.*

His face is stricken. I remember he saved my life yesterday. I reach for his hand and squeeze it. "Sorry. I don't mean to hurt your feelings. Thanks for helping me out."

He gets up to cook.

I go over to the phone to check for messages. There's one from Jay. He's in Lusaka. He left the hotel's telephone number. Says he has internet there and will email me. His cellphone doesn't work there. Gina left a reminder about supper.

It's almost 4 p.m. I am loathe to call her. What will I say? That I have summer flu? Knowing her she'll offer to come over and look after me, and to find out if I'm lying. If I tell her I've just been released from hospital, she'll definitely come over. Last thing I want. I'm not going to tell anyone about the meningioma. If those doctors are right, it's a secret I could keep for decades. If wrong and I must soon have surgery, Jay's on leave of absence. He'd be back here in an instant. What am I going to tell Gina? *Tell her you're in a bad mood and you don't want to spoil her party.* She's Madam Candid herself, so she should understand. If she doesn't understand tell her to fuck off. Can't tell her that. No, not Gina. She could tell me that, and it would be all right.

I dial her number. She answers.

The usual greetings. "Gina, I'm begging off from supper tonight. I'm not up to it."

"What!"

"You heard me."

"Boy, if you don't get yourself together and come over here, you won't hear the last of it from me." I hear the chuckle in her voice.

"I think I'm coming down with something like a summer flu. For the moment it's a kind o' dry fever and headache.

"Okay, take care o' yourself. If it worsens and you need anything lemme know. That scamp Carlos should be the one you could call on. In tough times, friends … they're all we can count on."

We hang up and I breathe more easily.

The choral hydrate is taking effect. I need to check my emails.

Jay's is there:

> Got to Lusaka three days ago. Did it by bus and train from the DRC in stages. Exhausting but a good way to experience Africa. Spent the first day getting my bearings. Yesterday visited the Munda Wanga Environmental Park. The picture of the lion is one of many I took there. Camcorded quite a bit of it. You'll see it all when I get back. Spent all day today at the Lusaka National Museum. Very educational. Taking it quiet this Sunday. Will be on the campus of the University of Zambia on Monday and Tuesday. On Thursday I head south to Livingstone, to Victoria Falls (thought the name had been changed, so much for African independence.) Set off for Botswana on Friday.

⇥ My eyes are closing. The smell of chicken from Carlos' cooking wafts into the bedroom as I lie down.

⇥ I awaken gasping for breath, from struggling to free my arms from a group of women who had them pinned behind my back. The dream: I'm in a conference room somewhere—a university classroom maybe. I'm at a lectern giving a presentation, when I suddenly feel my hands pinned behind my back and a chorus of female voices saying: "Apologize! Apologize," Gina's voice dominating the others.

"Apologize for what?" I say and struggle to free my arm and turn my head around.

"You know what for." Ma's voice.

The apartment is dark. There's no sound of traffic on Atwater. I look over at my clock radio. It's 3:41. I get up and head to the kitchen. The door to Carlos' room is open. He's snoring away. I drink a tumbler of orange juice and go back to bed, but I can't fall asleep. I get up, pick up my journal and record what has happened to me over the last thirty-six hours. I leave the dream for last. I wonder about its significance. I'm not misogynistic. Okay, there was that stuff I sent to Mrs. Bensemana, in which I turned her into a sexual object. Once Jay had said that my treatment of Ma was because I hated women. But he couldn't have meant that. He knows how much I adore Grama and Aunt Mercy. I think back to the Black girls in secondary two who outperformed the boys. They didn't outperform me then. I didn't resent them. If I could have spent time with them without being called gay I'd have done so.

Paul, your mother died without having the frank discussion she wanted with you. You wanted to apologize for the torment you put her through. Isn't that something to apologize for? Awake you think you've made peace with the dead. Asleep you discover you haven't. I hope, profoundly hope, this is all there is to this dream.

I turn the pages backward to read my recording of a similar nightmare:

June 17, 2011.

I'm naked and lying paralysed on my back on a table in a large empty hall while Madam J, Ma, and three of her church sisters debate what they should do to me. I hear Grama and Mr. Morris talking and coming toward me, then scampering feet and shouts of "Get out! Get out, you infidels!" as the church sisters rush them. The torturers return. From her purse, Madam J takes a whip and flicks it. It slices the air with hissing sounds. Her eyes glowing, she approaches me slowly, the whip held high above her head, and says: "Turn him over and tie him down." They open their purses and take out coils of rope. I try to scream but no sounds come. I come awake with my heart thumping away, my throat parched, and my tongue heavy.

This is serious. I can't deny it. I don't know what to do. I sit there stunned as the impact of all that has happened sinks in. I reread what I've written about my meeting with Carlos in the plaza. My mind flashes across what he told me about seeing me on the ground, images of him on the ward, now here sleeping in the next room. We are fate's fiddles, and are luckiest when she abstains from playing us, and lucky when she doesn't play in F or G. I think of Carmen trying to slough off delinquency and paying the price with her own and her mother's life.

I don't know how to deal with the reality that I have meningioma. It had better not be malignant.

And if it is, what the hell will you do about it?

Don't go down that road, Paul. Don't.

How am I going to manage this information? I can't tell Jay about it now. He's having too much of a good time travelling. I won't wreck his vacation. I forgot to tell Carlos not to share the info with his friends. Shit. By now, Gina probably knows I lied to her. I'm sure he phoned Gineta to tell her he won't be in. (I suspect it's at her place that he's staying; he refused to tell me where.) If only to vaunt his victory and wallow in the fact that he saved my life. Information Gineta would have already transmitted to Gúicho, Gúicho to Emilia, and Emilia to

Gina. I tap my chest and take a deep breath, relieved that I haven't told him anything more. The thought of people whispering behind my back, *You know he has a brain tumour,* would be unbearable. And with each teller the story would gain garnish, including how much time I have left to live. From what the doctors said, a lot of people would be long dead before I have surgery. Look on the bright side. Be the Paul who outwitted the Guatemala cops.

You did! Much good it did you. Your mother died without your making peace with her. Now the cause of many of your nightmares. And you're barred from re-entering Guatemala for five years. And the seemingly one good thing you got out of it, your relationship with Carlos, turned out to be bogus.

What will I tell Carlos when he gets up? There are his pleas—at the Plaza and again at the hospital—that we get back together. The only clear fact in my head yesterday was that he would be here for twenty-four hours. Now I don't want to be alone. I'm anxious. How am I going to swallow my pride and ask him to stay? How am I going to face Gina and Emilia, Gina more so, if he moves back in? She already thinks I'm masochistic. I can just hear her: "Enjoying it? Does he whip you?" That smirk spread across her face.

I won't overtly beg him to stay. *And if he moves out voluntarily? And if he moves out voluntarily?*

He won't.

You mean you hope he won't.

Life's fetters. I take a deep breath, tears are close. Once they're on, only life can remove them, and sometimes she's blind to what's there and binds you some more.

You're going to sit down with him when he wakes up and tell him you're in a vulnerable phase of your life, shaken by the shock you've just come through, and would like him to stay with you for a few days. But it would be food and lodging in exchange for his company. There won't be sexual relations between you, and he's forbidden to bring his friends to the apartment. If by some fluke he hasn't yet spread the information about "the heroic rescue," ask him not to talk about it, make it a condition for his staying with you.

And if he says you don't have the right to impose conditions on him? You don't have the right, you know. You don't. Now you need him more than he needs you.

I sigh. Whew!

Cut it out, Paul. It comes like an epiphany. *What you're going through is part of what it is to be human. What you're calling dignity is arrogance. You should be able to say to Gina: I need Carlos, and not be apologetic about it.* One time Jay upbraided me about this. He acknowledged the rotten deal that asthma is, but reminded me of the gift of intellect. Easy for him to say. He doesn't have to endure any of the shit I do. I torture my body to avoid looking like a walrus, and would torture it even more if I could get it to look like his. He's completely indifferent to his body and doesn't care whether or not people are sexually attracted to him. The things you lack you long for, the things you have you are indifferent to. He never speaks about his longings. Before he left for Africa, you'd have thought the only thing missing from his life was this visit to Africa. He must have his concerns and fears though. Everybody has them. It's just that he doesn't talk about them.

Wonder what he'll say about the tumour. Probably nothing. He'll hug me and say he'll try to be there for me as I try to deal with it, and he'll encourage me to tell him my feelings. But he won't say much more. He's made his peace with existential suffering. Guess after spending eight years with Daddy beating the shit out of him and Ma, he's reconciled to pain. I am the one who wants God to exist so I could sue him. Jay doesn't care whether or not God exists, but how humans cultivate whatever goodness they have. I like to think he took nothing from Grama, but he took that. Recently he has been urging me to read the *Mahabharata*, but that will have to wait until I finish my courses. If he were here now, my head would be on his shoulders and I would be crying, because I would feel safe doing so. His arms would be around me. I can't interrupt his vacation. He's been responsible for me most of my life. Incredible. Ma must have felt guilty about this. Probably explains why she was partial to him. Hope my dependence isn't beginning all over again. Better not be. I don't want it. I won't accept it. *Humility, Paul, humility.*

18

I KNOW NOTHING about meningioma. I should check it out on the internet. I check article after article, and see that the doctors were right in what they said. It wasn't a case of minimizing the problem. Besides I see that from where it is it would be easy to operate when the time comes. The only risk could be temporary impaired vision from oedema, and even that would be far-fetched. The only doubt is that nine in every hundred are malignant. 160,000 diagnoses each year in the US. Divide that by ten for Canada. Nine percent of 16,000: 1,440 — every year 1,440 Canadians get the shock that their meningioma is malignant! My hands begin to sweat.

I hear water running in the bathroom. Carlos is up. He mustn't see what I'm researching. Of course I could tell him it's for the novel I'm working on. But my voice and facial expression would betray me. I turn the computer off and promise myself I would read no more about it.

≈ He comes into the bedroom and stands over me, behind my back. I turn to see he is wearing my burgundy bathrobe.

"¿Cómo estás?"

"Fine," I say.

He moves to the front of me and tells me that last night he had the strangest dream: that he and I were travelling on foot in the gorge through which the Interamericana runs along the banks of the Selegua river — between Huehuetenango and La Mesilla — and at one point when we got to a bridge, he heard a loud splash, and couldn't find me. He wanted to go and look for help but found he couldn't move.

I stare at him intensely. I'm tempted to say: No, you dreamed you pushed me off the bridge. "Well, here I am in real life. I haven't disappeared. Thanks for spending the night here. Thanks too for saving my life." *Would I want my life saved if it turns out that the meningioma is malignant?*

"What you thinking?"

"Nothing."

"*¿Qué estás escondiendo?* What you hiding? What bad news you get? Why you no tell?"

"They certainly didn't tell me anything that would make me want to commit suicide, if that's what you're thinking. Your dream hints at that."

He's shaking his head. "I certain is bad thing. I stay with you for while. Okay? This is situation I no like. You hide from me something."

I don't answer. I'm glad it's he who offers to stay, that I don't have to go to him on my knees.

He moves to my back, stands behind me, and lets his arms fall down to my chest. Instinctively I hold his hands, and before I know it tears begin to flow. I feel his own fall onto my neck. We remain like this for several seconds.

He leaves and goes to the living room. I hear the first notes of Massenet's *Méditation* from one of my favourite collections of violin adagios. When he and I began living together, he'd go off to mass on Sunday morning, and I would play classical music. Listening to classical music on a Sunday morning was something we did at Grama's house. I wonder how different things would have been if I'd continued to play the steelpan. I read in *Montreal Community Contact* about the work Salah and the Albino brothers do and recently attended one of their Steelband festivals at Parc Émilie-Gamelin.

The smell of coffee drifts in from the kitchen, and I hear the tiny sounds Carlos makes chopping fruits for my breakfast. He brings me a cup of coffee, black and strong, the way I like it. When we were together he always insisted that I buy dark-roast coffee from his area in Guatemala. I'm sure that's what he bought yesterday. I can taste the strong acidic difference. He says that I should come to the table in about five minutes and returns to the kitchen.

He has his bowl of cornflakes and milk, orange juice, scrambled eggs, and toast for himself; for me, a fruit salad of blueberries, strawberries, kiwi, and pineapple along with black cherry yogurt—my favourite, must have bought it yesterday—toast and peanut butter. I tried to get him to change his diet after he got here but without success. While we were still together I took over the cooking to avoid the copious amounts of butter he added to everything. Apart from butter he wanted nothing in his rice. I needed lots of vegetables. And he pigs out on fried potatoes. It's his life. Hope he doesn't regret it. Probably won't matter. It's I who have asthma and now a brain tumour. Grama ensured that we had a healthy diet. No match for the flaws in my body. Without them Jay got the benefits, has good dietary habits. He doesn't go to a gym, but, unless the day is excessively cold or windy, he's up at five for his daily hour-long walk. I think back to our days when we lived on Linton, while Ma was alive, and I tried in every way to show I was superior to him. I see the pathos of it now. I see too how right he was: now the nickname Ma Kirton's Genius feels like a curse. Fate's hand is there too, hidden in the community that imposed that name on me.

Carlos puts his hand on mine and jolts me out of my reverie. "Eat," he says scowling.

I look at the food and realize I haven't touched it. I eat the fruit. He gets up, brings the coffee pot and tops up our cups. I have no appetite for the yogurt, toast, and peanut butter; I push them away and shake my head.

He finishes his breakfast. He's a fast eater, but I think today it's because he has probably had trouble eating his fill since he came back from Guatemala.

"Thanks," I say, looking across at him and smiling.

He returns the smile, then chuckles and shakes his head. "First time you give me real smile in plenty months."

He's probably right.

I get up and begin walking toward the bathroom, but remember that when we lived together I washed the dishes when he cooked and vice versa. I stop, turn around, and say to him: "I need to lie down. Sorry about the dishes. Hope you don't mind."

He nods his okay.

After brushing my teeth I return to bed. Classes begin on Tuesday. I'll have to shake off this torpor. There's also the novel I'm working on. Life has to go on. I pick up my journal and decide to write whatever comes into my mind.

> *I'm glad Carlos is here with me. How will I explain his presence to Gina without revealing my health problems? Jay is away. I don't need to tell him. If all goes as the doctors say, Carlos would be gone by the time Jay gets back. The only person who could snitch on me would be Jonathan and he has no way of knowing unless he calls here and Carlos answers the phone.*
>
> *What does his being here mean? What does it mean? Where will it lead? Not to us getting back together, I hope. I'll admit that I've been lonely. Bill's death and Jay's travelling have left me bereft. There's only Gina, and she's so censorious. There's not a great deal I can tell her. I need to broaden my social circle. Try maybe to meet gays online. I don't want to go to the gay clubs or the saunas. I urge Jay to go, but the truth is, I know now I don't want to be anyone's sex toy for a night.*

I hear Carlos' footfalls coming toward my bedroom. I close the journal quickly and put it away before he manages to catch me writing. He knows I keep a journal, but because of what's happened in the last couple of days and his sure knowledge that I'm withholding information from him, he's likely to resume pestering me with questions. He enters and sits on the armchair across from my bed. We say nothing for a long while.

"*¿Por almuerzo* lunch, *w*hat you want ?"

"Hombre, please. Don't turn yourself into my servant."

"*¿Y si quiero?* (And if I want to?)"

"I appreciate your being here with me at this moment. I once had depression, you know. It lasted a few months. Following my grandmother's death. A long story. I forced myself to go to work every day. Taking customers' orders and filling them, like an automaton, distracted me. I didn't know Bill then. If there'd been someone like him to talk to I'd have never got to that stage."

He stares at me intensely. "*¿Cómo, por qué?*"

"I was full of hate: hatred for my mother, hatred for life, hatred of myself. And guilt—guilt that I had betrayed my grandmother. One time I got dressed to go hurl myself in front of an oncoming car on the Decarie Expressway. In the end I felt it was unfair to the people who might have been killed or severely injured. And then Bill, Jay's professor at the time, was offering a course on writers I admired. I begged Jay to ask him to let me sit in on the class. That's how I met Bill. He saved my life. I'm pretty certain I'd have like slipped back into depression, because I still had serious issues to deal with. That course and the interest Bill took in me set me right. You met me because I went travelling to test my ability to survive on my own. He'd urged me to."

"You sorry for meeting me?"

I don't like the question, and I'm a long time answering. My mind turns to times in Guatemala when we were lying in bed or sitting on the patio and he'd lean over and whisper, "... *mi otra costilla*"; (... my other rib) sometimes "... *mi media naranja;* (... the other half of the orange) or just simply, "*mi querido.*" Initially I did my best not to laugh at the strangeness of the expressions.

"You silent. You answer yes. You no want hurt my feelings."

I shake my head as I try to find language for what I'm feeling. *It's not sorrow I feel. It's ambivalence. Remember, you are the first and only person I've had a relationship with. I learned a lot about myself while we were together. I saw the gaps between what I thought and what I did. Imagine me advising Jay to go out and meet strangers and have sex with them, only to realize that I myself haven't the willpower to do so.* I glance at him. He's attentive, waiting for my answer. "I think you believe I blame you for what happened. Initially I did. Your deception. Gúicho's influence. Gineta. I gave up on you then. But I've heard what you've been saying lately, and I understand that you too had some growing up to do. Some adjusting too. I've lived here since 1997, even went to high school here. You came at twenty-seven."

He nods. "And make myself ass."

Gúicho certainly rode you and Gineta had her saddle ready.

We're silent for a long time. He turns his head away and says: *"Je veux te poser une question. Ne te fâches pas."* He glances at me quickly and turns his head away again. *"Jamás* I believe story you tell about your mama will." He glances at me again. "Gúicho and Gineta convince me you lie. Alfredo he think it too. You know what make me *sospechado? Mes frais de scolarité.* You pay it: $11,000. If Jay give you allowance, you no can pay." He stops talking.

"Go on," I say.

"Is all. *Ya terminado.*"

I remember the day he was to meet me at Concordia's EV Building and never came and went off gallivanting, of his expensive habits in Comitán and Mexico City, but I know that talking about them would lead to recrimination, and Jay taught me the value of steering clear of that. But I can't fully avoid responding. "And the $1,000 that you wanted to investigate the wills?"

He chuckles. *"Fue una prueba para ver tu comportamiento, tu reacción. Supe que tú mentías, que jugaste sucio conmigo.*(I was testing you to see how you'd react. I knew you were lying, that you played dirty with me.)"

I'm tempted to ask him about the $10,000 loan he tried to get from Gineta. Asking him would get me in trouble with Gina. He's on another fishing expedition. "Carlos, your speculations are interesting, but my grandmother's and my mother's wills are still Jackson family business. They concern Jay and me, not you."

"I want know if I have truth. *Hoy, quiero ir al grano.* Go to bottom of affair. *Nada más.*"

"Right or wrong, top or bottom, my parents' wills are none of your business."

"Estás trompudo conmigo. You pissed off because you know I have truth."

"If you're going to spend your time accusing me of this or that, we'll have to make other arrangements."

"*Soló quiero mostrar* ... show that it has deception my side and your side. Today we take all to *cementerio. ¿Echémonos tierra?*" He gestures tossing soil and brushing his fingers.

I don't respond. He's staring at me expectantly.

"Something else molest me: *Piensas que vivo a la gorra.* You think me a *mantenido, un parasito.*"

I shake my head. I see how saying that I should have demanded that he pay his share of the expenses when he first came might have led him to think this.

"Is what too think your friends. Gúicho he tell me so. *¿Comprendes?* I no looking hairs in soup. I telling truth."

I do my best not to laugh. "Maybe that's Gúicho's opinion of you." *It* is *his opinion of you.*

"*Fíjate.* I want you understand good. When I encounter work, I pay you all. *El todo.* I take out *seguro* too. If die before finish pay, you get money."

I shrug.

"*Ahora, cierro el pico.* I shut up. *¿Echémonos la tierra?* Final burial? *Okay?* What you say?"

I'm silent.

He fixes me with a stare. "*¿Qué dices?*"

"I'll think about it."

He comes over to me, puts his hand on mine. It's cold. Usually it's I who have cold hands. He smiles. "*Entonces, consulta con la almohada.* (Sleep on it)." He leaves.

I take my journal out from the night table and record all that's just transpired.

19

JAY AND I are sitting on the ward where I'm recovering after the bout of radiation I received three hours ago. I look over at him. "Jay, would I be able to lead a normal life after this?"

Silence.

He's taking too long to answer. Caught between honesty and diplomacy. *Might as well say no.* "When did I ever lead a normal life?" I angle my head so I can look into his eyes and hold his attention. "You never led one either." *You're a voluntary eunuch.*

"Paul, that's a question for the doctors."

I almost say: *What, eunuchs?* "Now you're being a hypocrite. What did they tell you?"

"Nothing they haven't told you."

I hold his gaze. I know when he's lying, much like he knows when I am. He withholds information and is never able to look me in the eye. "Are you telling me the truth?"

"As much of the truth as I know."

"That's not an answer."

"Paul, what do you want me to tell you?"

"You haven't figured that out?"

He gulps his saliva.

"I want you to say: 'Paul, you will be well. You will write many novels. You and I will travel to places together. We will buy a house together and maybe adopt children orphaned by the civil wars in Africa. Paul, you will take care of me in my old age.'"

He's smiling and nodding. "Great attitude. With that spirit we'll probably do a couple of those things."

I shake my head. "Remove the *probably*." I'll never get him to say with conviction: 'Paul, you will be well and will lead a normal life.' It's a quality I both hate and admire in him. I decide to tease him. "Jay, you know you're a father?" *Eunuch and father, Paul, they don't go together.*

"Who's the mother of my child/children?"

"You're *so* conventional. You don't have to inseminate a woman to be a father."

"All right. Where are my adopted children?"

"Open your eyes. See what's in front of you."

"Paul, *you're not* my son."

"Gee, you're quick on the uptake. I'm not! Kid yourself. You've been a father since you were twelve. *My* father. I tried to tell you so at the airport when I was leaving for Latin America. You thought I was bullshitting you, right?"

He blushes. "That's a horrible thought, Paul. I loved Ma, but not that way, and I only five." We both laugh. He shakes his head. "At the airport you said brother. I'm sure that's what you said. I'm more comfortable with that." He falls silent.

Children. When Carlos and I legalized our union, I wondered if we would adopt any. That notion got quashed pretty quickly. Poor fellow. Came here and went wild with freedom. After his imprisoned sexuality in Guatemala. Now he understands what happened to him here; analyzes his own behaviour without any help from me or any psychologist. In the end, I felt he was sincere about wanting to mend the break. I could find no fault with him during the time he stayed with me. In fact, the Tuesday after Labour Day when classes started, if he hadn't been there to push me out of the apartment, I wouldn't have gone. And once I became engrossed in my school work, the love of learning took over. At home I even found time to work on my novel. It was nice again to come home and meet somebody there, or, if he wasn't there, know that he would be there. I knew for certain then how much of a hole his leaving had left. He stayed in at nights. I said I hoped it wasn't on my account. He shrugged and smiled without comment.

⇥ Two weeks after he came to stay with me, he came into the apartment one late afternoon beaming. *"J'ai un poste, Pablo. Finalement!"* He'd been hired by Quebec Immigration as a Spanish translator. *"Maintenant, je peux partager toutes les dépenses et rembourser mes dettes. Il n'y a plus de raisons pour que nous ne revenions pas ensemble. Tú me manques."*

I was happy for him. Happy he'd be able to send money to his mother and niece, and perhaps bring them here.

He still didn't know about my meningioma. Because of it my life had begun to take on an inexplicable urgency. It could be malignant. I felt I did not need to be as discreet as I'd been. I decided not to let bygones be bygones and to be candid with him about his behaviour. I told him he'd made fun of me behind my back, had entertained his friends with what went on in our bedroom. I was sitting at the dining table. He was sitting on the sofa, about three metres away.

He stared at the floor and said nothing for a while. He got up slowly, came over to me, placed his hands on my shoulders, and remained silent for more than a minute. "I am sorry. I beg you pardon," he eventually said.

I didn't answer. The wound was deep. Forgiving others who've hurt me — an issue Jay and I have talked about many times — isn't something I do easily. It wasn't just a question of forgiving him. Forgiveness in his case meant resuming the relationship. My body went cold at the thought of having sex with him again. The one thing I wasn't going to talk to him about was whether or not I'd lied to him about my mother's and grandmother's wills. After our discussion the Labour Day Sunday, he dropped the subject.

He wanted us to reconcile, and was clumsy at saying so. It's one thing to say that gay men obsess over gym rats and are mostly interested in the young and handsome. Quite another to tell me we should stay together because we weren't *papasitos, mangos;* that he looked like a papa rhino and I like its calf; that the only place we might be able to find sex once in a while was at the sauna and we'd get lucky about one night in four, when ugly old men couldn't find anyone else. Ouch!

⇥ Going to the sauna. That's something I should screw my courage and do if I still have any sexuality left after the thwacking this radiation is giving me. *You, Paul, go to a sauna! That will be the day. Your hands and feet will be dripping sweat and you'll begin to tremble when the first man looks into your cubicle.*

"Ever went to a sauna, Jay?"

He shakes his head. "I should have?"

"Yes."

"Why?"

"To educate yourself and tell me what it's like."

"Aren't you the one educating me about sex?"

"When you came down with malaria, I said: Jay seems to be having the same experiences I had in Central America, wonder if he's going to come back here with his own version of Carlos." My real objective is to find out if he's had any sexual experiences in Africa. He has told me about a whole lot of things, but not a peep about that.

"I didn't fare as well as you. No man ever came onto a bus and asked to fondle my beard and give me his phone number. Or invite me to live with him and his mother. If I'd thought about it beforehand I'd have grown a beard."

I laugh.

"But if I were as extraverted as you I might have got into a little trouble." His eyes brighten. "In Kumasi I stayed two days in a run-down hotel, where I never saw more than one employee. There might have been others but I saw only him. I was one of two guests. The other guest—he stayed one night—was a history professor from Burkina Faso.

"The hotel employee's name was Kwame. Thirty years old. I'd already noted how beautiful men in Accra were. But Kwame was more beautiful than any I'd seen. Within hours of meeting me he poured out his soul. He wanted to leave Ghana; life there was oppressive; every time he went back to his village his father pestered him about getting married; the last time his father took him to see a shaman who prescribed potions, because his father thought he was impotent. At this point he stopped talking and gave me a long stare. When he resumed he said: 'I told my father—my mother and my younger brother, father of three boys, were there too; they'd brought him along to shame me into getting married—I told them I didn't want a wife and children. I want to go away and study. I'm different. If you're ashamed of me I'll stop coming home.' He stopped talking for almost a minute and stared at the floor. We were in the hotel restaurant. I was sitting at a table about two metres away. He was standing with his back leaning against the counter with the cash register. Still staring at the floor, he said: 'I'm different. Different. If they know how different they would want to kill me.' He lifted his eyes to see my reaction. 'I want to leave Ghana. I want freedom. I want to go to London, or New York, or Toronto.'"

Jay takes a deep breath. He's embarrassed. He swallows and resumes. "Later that day when I went outside to get a cab into downtown Kumasi, I met him waiting for one too—without his navy blue uniform and white apron, wearing beautifully laundered black slacks and a lilac shirt that complemented the blackness of his silk-smooth skin. He was truly stunning—palm tree straight, sleek, in every way symmetrical; intense glassy black eyes. Only flaw: no butt to speak of. When I checked out two days later, he gave me his address and begged me to write to him. When I got back here I wrote to him and wished him well in the pursuit of his dreams." He stops talking and stares ahead of him, his forehead wrinkled. "Who knows? Some traveller looking for African beauty might meet him, hear his story and take him to Europe or North America, where for a while he'll be a trophy, and, I hope, eventually establish a life of dignity."

"You'd have gained something from having sex with him: experience. He might have wanted you to, just for the experience."

"I doubt it. It would have been wrong to take advantage of his vulnerability. Besides he was looking for a saviour."

"I heard that all right, and know a lot about that. But you're still alone, Jay, and will die alone if you let all these opportunities pass you by."

"That wasn't an opportunity, Paul. That was a trap. In the meantime life goes on."

"It's by falling into traps and getting out of them that we grow. I grew ten years in the nineteen months I went travelling because of the traps I fell into and extricated myself from."

I feel suddenly nauseous. I pick up the kidney basin beside me and spit into it. Not spitting so much today. My second round of radiation. The spitting was a lot worse last week. Radiation knocked out my white blood cells too. Had to rush back here for a blood transfusion two days later.

I take several deep breaths and wait for the nausea to pass.

"No women chased you down? I hear they eagerly hunt down Western men. Once they grab your sleeve, you have hell getting away."

"And many fall for husbands online and end up in brothels all over Europe and in Turkey. There's a plethora of films dealing with the subject. Yet women continue to take the bait, confident that what has happened to others won't happen to them."

"No women, eh? You mean you're no longer bi?" I giggle.

He shrugs.

"Time to get off the fence, Jay-boy. Time to become Jay-man. You've just turned thirty-one. You should have resolved all this by now."

"It's why you have to get better quickly—to show me how. Once upon a time I tried to be your guide. Now it's your turn to guide me in areas where you're the expert."

"Cop out! Okay, would you like to go to a sauna with me when I'm over all this? Though, according to Carlos, I shouldn't go there with you. You'll score and I'll be ignored. Just kidding. It's something I wanted to do when I was under eighteen. Now, even though I'm tempted, I won't go."

He's silent.

"Say something. Share your thoughts."

"My thoughts: I have none."

We fall silent again.

"I wonder if the fellow whose brother got killed—the Mohawk, who worked with Ma; his brother's body was found covered with cigarette burns in the parking lot behind Place Bonaventure; you told me about it—I wonder if he and his two gay brothers did things like this together."

"There are quite a few cases each year of men murdered by homophobes they've picked up, men they didn't know before. It explains why some men choose to go to the saunas. It's a safe place to have sex with strangers."

"I hadn't thought of that."

He falls silent. He doesn't like to talk about sex. I'm lucky to get this much out of him. A replica of Ma. "Jay, you're still afraid of displeasing Ma. Right?"

He rolls his eyes and looks up at the ceiling.

"When I took you to Sky a few years ago, I told you that brothers who sin together bond better. Remember?"

"There's nothing sinful about sex when the partners respect each other."

"And one another?"

He frowns at me.

"More than two, Jay. Carlos, for example, loves orgies."

"Paul, 'Everyone cuts his cloth to suit his fit.'"

"You haven't seen a tailor yet or bought anything off the rack for that matter."

He chuckles.

"Ah, Jay, you just don't want to grow up." I sing a few stanzas of "I Don't Want to Grow Up."

He chuckles as I sing through the list "I-don't-wannas."

What would I do if my treatment team tells me my tumour's terminal? Initially they were sure it was benign. Quite possible that they released cancer cells into the cerebrospinal fluid during surgery. They don't seem concerned about that. They've ruled out chemotherapy for the time being. I'd have preferred it to this radiation. "Not so easy," they said, "for drugs to cross the blood-brain barrier. For the time being, we'll spare you the havoc they wreak on the body." More havoc than this radiation is causing? They insist that my reaction is uncharacteristic. I told them that I'm worried about my sight, that I'd rather live six months with vision than two years without. In the end they persuaded me to go along with radiation therapy. "The measurements are precise. They won't damage your brain tissue."

I answered: "Nor should I be here, *the tumour is benign*. Remember who said that?"

None of the three looked at me or bothered to correct my deliberate distortion.

"I'm going to the visitors' lounge to use the computer there," Jay says, breaking into my recall. "I'll be back so we can have lunch together."

"That's why you should have an iPhone. You being a Luddite isn't going to save Africa."

He gives a yes-no headshake and leaves. When he's here I'm less anxious about my health. When I begin stumbling in prognosis' dark alley, he holds my hand and guides me back into the light.

My cell phone is ringing. I look at the screen—Carlos. He calls me twice a day, near lunch time and again after supper. I don't tell him that I'm at the hospital. In fact I haven't told him yet that I'm undergoing radiation therapy. He asks the same question: "How're you feeling today?" Issues the usual orders: "Don't spend the day moping; work on your novel," followed by a loud lip smack, and says good bye. He reserves chitchat for the after-supper call.

If Ma were here would she be spouting her platitudes? "It's all in the hands o' the Lord, Paul. Take it to the lord in prayer." I would like to get my hands on that Lord. Jay would have warned her not to. "And if I is right and you is wrong? It gwine be too late when the fire start to burn up your backside. There will be wailing and gnashing of teeth; you better repent," Madam J, Ma's work colleague and church sister, once told me. I stared at her dentures and resisted saying: *When you start gnashing your false teeth will fall out.*

Guess that's how they waylay frightened people on their deathbeds. *Paul, you think about your mother too much.*

Señor Carlos the morning on my way to surgery. Holding my hand, his eyes closed, praying silently, then saying: "You no believe. I believe. God listen to me, no you. You come back. You change mind. We go back together." And I tempted to say: Yes, if Benedict 16 officiates at the marriage ceremony.

He'd found out about the surgery on October 8, three days before it happened. He'd come to my place around seven in the evening with a cheque for $200. "I begin pay you back my *frais de scolarité*. I know you no believe me when I tell you I pay you back. I start now."

I shook my head and told him to pay Gúicho what he owes him, and send some money to his mother. "I might need this money down the road. Right now I don't." Mentally I had already agreed that the $11,000 I'd paid for his school fees would be my de facto separation settlement.

After he found work I remained firm that we wouldn't get back together, and I persuaded him to move out—although it pained me to do so—so he could rebuild his life. His libido is huge. I opted to save both of us from the anger, frustration, or guilt he'd eventually feel when he could no longer be faithful. It's unhealthy and ultimately futile to be at war with our physiology. "I want you to be free," I told him. "In a relationship with me, you won't be." If I had known the brain tumour was malignant, would I have let him go? On October 1, he moved into a furnished studio apartment in the building adjacent to the one Bill lived in.

When I went back for a scan on October 3, the tumour had grown by two millimetres. My treatment team was alarmed and wanted to operate immediately. I told them they had to wait until my brother got home. He was in Lesotho. Those four days while I waited for Jay to arrive were difficult. I spent them mostly in bed. On evenings I went to the cinema, but hardly followed the films.

Jay arrived on October 7. I underwent surgery on October 11.

The evening of October 8 when Carlos came with the money, I told him that I was having a quiet Thanksgiving because I would be having surgery on Tuesday. "Please don't tell your friends. I'll tell Gina myself when I'm out of the hospital. I don't want to be overwhelmed by visitors."

"Surgery! Why?"

"I have a small tumour in the outer membranes of my brain. Don't worry. *No es el cáncer.*" I watched his eyes bulging with fear and his trembling hands. "I'll be all right, Carlos."

"You sure?"

I nodded.

"You afraid?"

"*!En absoluto!*" I shook my head.

"You know this since September 2. *¿Verdad?*"

"Yes. But not about the surgery."

He clenched his teeth, swallowed. Then asked what time the surgery was.

At 6:35 the Tuesday morning, when Jay and I arrived, we met him waiting in the hospital lobby.

I'd judged him wrongly, dismissed him as egotistical and callow. But I can't square this and his shenanigans with Gineta. I guess he's too easily influenced. That or his father's assassination made him cynical or for that matter ruthless. No, he isn't ruthless. Weak, not ruthless. It's why he quickly abandoned the scheme Gineta put him up to. In Guatemala we'd got along well. Like school friends. Marital relationships are plunges into the dark. Some things you can only know in hindsight. You can never predict whether your individual evolutions would bring you closer or push you apart.

On the day of my surgery, apart from Jay, who spent all day at the hospital, Carlos, Gina, and Emilia were the first visitors I had after I returned to the ward. Carlos had ignored my advice not to tell them; he even told them that I didn't want them to know. When I tried to upbraid him, he said: "*Es injusto sufrir solo cuando uno tiene amigos. En este caso no tengo culpa ninguna. Quieres controlar todo.* (It's wrong to suffer alone when you have friends. I don't feel any guilt whatsoever for telling them. You want to control everything.)"

Certainly can't control my body. Nor can the doctors. Everything that wasn't supposed to happen did: excessive bleeding, oedema, and what should have been benign was malignant. One of the 1,440 annual cases. The exceptionality no one wants.

⇥ Jay returns from the Visitors' Lounge.

"That was quick."

"Only had a couple of emails to reply to."

"I should have given you an iPhone for your birthday."

He ignores me and looks at his watch. "I'll go get my lunch so we can eat together."

I look out the window. It's a blustery November day. The trees around St. Joseph's Oratory have already lost their leaves, are stripped down to stalk and bark. Last week when I came for my first round of radiation they were still golden. In a week the wind and rain changed all that. From green to gold to grey. Today their bare twigs are tossing in the wind. Wonder what winter will bring to Montreal and me. Environment Canada forecasts a colder than normal winter. It's a *la niña* year. The July I arrived here, fourteen years ago, and found Montreal just as warm as St. Vincent, I couldn't have anticipated the ice storm that struck at the beginning of January. In all my years in St. Vincent I'd never experienced anything comparable. On TV we certainly saw the damage hurricanes did to the other islands. We collected money in school to send to the victims. Can't remember a year when there wasn't a collection tin on the counter in Grama's store, but St. Vincent was never struck by a real hurricane while I lived there. A category one struck last year. But it in no way resembled Ivan, the 2004 category four that flattened Grenada.

Right now they're rebuilding the bridges and sections of highways that Tropical Storm A12 washed away in Central America, and scrambling to find food and shelter for the more than 100,000 whose homes have been flooded or destroyed. Billions in damage. Thirty killed in Guatemala. Over a hundred in all of Central America. Stan struck while I was in Guatemala and buried a lot of people alive. Ma died wondering whether it had killed me. Emilia is collecting money for Nicaraguans. I gave Carlos some for the Guatemalan Association here. Haven't heard if Gúicho is doing anything for Salvadorans. In normal times close to half of all Guatemalans are malnourished, the government says. The UN puts it at seventy percent. To have even the little you have destroyed. Fate's harmonics. To which Central Americans seem resigned. All the same Central Americans are fatalistic. Not far beneath their feet there's bubbling lava. Pacaya, Masaya, and Santiaguito are perpetually erupting volcanoes less than twenty kilometres from major cities. In Guatemala hardly a week passes without the earth shaking, reminding you who has ultimate power and who does not. Central Americans take it all in stride and continue to worship a divine being who they believe responds to their supplications. ("Don't let anyone here know you're an atheist," my Spanish teacher warned me. "It could get you into serious trouble.") The ancient Mayans, who lived by conquest, venerated Nature's destruction. They held volcanoes sacred, saw them as the sun inside the earth, and paid them tribute: the same sort of tribute they expected from their conquered subjects. During the civil war the Guatemalan military found their craters useful for the corpses they dropped from their planes. "To save Guatemala from communism," say the newspaper ads opposing all attempts to bring them to justice.

⇥ The dome of St Joseph's Oratory, Brother André's oeuvre, is draped in clouds. Many terminally ill people are in there right now praying in front of the crypt containing Brother Andre's heart and hoping for a miracle. An illiterate doorman at a college whose curriculum must have mystified him. A miracle worker too, a miracle worker who became a Catholic saint last year. The drizzle obscures the steps leading up to it, or I would see people climbing them on their hands and knees. Easier than a 780-kilometre pilgrimage on foot to Santiago de Compostela. I heard a devout Catholic, voice disguised, saying on radio that he undertook it at age fifty-two to find out if he should leave his wife of twenty-seven years and become a practicing homosexual. At the prodding of the journalist, he said that he eventually decided to hold on to his marriage while leading a secret gay life outside the city he lived in. He could not, he said, bring himself to declare his homosexuality to his children. I suspect it's people like him who climb the stairs on their hands and knees. Easier, I suppose, than vocalizing the cause. Plumbing the psychic depths of the human beast will require much more than the unravelling of the human genome. A lot more. If this tumour doesn't maim or kill me and I finish my novel, I might penetrate a millimetre or two into that darkness.

My mind turns to my journal entry two days ago—something to this effect: Nature outside of me, following nature's rules: storms, earthquakes, volcanic eruptions, to be expected. Not at all puzzling once we understand the intricacies of high and low pressure, tectonic movement, the earth's molten interior, subduction zones, etc.—all under the governance of natural forces. Nature inside me is a different matter. Cells abandon their usual function and begin to destroy my body. The what and how of it science knows. The why they speculate about. Smoking causes lung cancer, they say. And those who've never smoked and get it? *Second-hand smoke*. And the smokers who live to be octogenarians, nonagenarians and even centenarians? *Good genes, good attitude, good diet, lots of exercise.* These priests of physiology. Priests of religion concocted life after death to satisfy our lust for immortality, justify life's agonies, and palliate death's pain. They were once the diviners and healers. Now priests of physiology create their own myths to fill the voids where anxiety might fester: explanations no more scientific than the reasons we give for loving war.

Makes me think of Josephine. She came into the store breathless one afternoon and demanded to see Grama. Lucy, the shop assistant, was in the back doing some paperwork. Grama wasn't there. She'd gone up the hill to take soup for a dying woman who had no relatives. "Sonny, tell your granny I get a' important message for she from the other side. Tell she I coming back here at four o'clock and she is to wait right here for me."

Grama waited. Josephine came: pale-skinned, petite, a mole the size of a pea on the tip of her nose, head swaddled in white, which meant she had some sort of office in the Spiritual Baptist religion. She asked Grama to describe her mother. Grama hesitated. Josephine insisted. "This ain't no joke, Ma Kirton. No joke at all. It is serious." While Grama spoke I perused Josephine's face, observed the tiny movements of her lips, her dilating pupils, tiny frowns, wrinkling of the lips, gentle nods.

"Well, Ma Kirton, that is the same woman who come to me in my sleep. She tell me: 'Go and tell Cynthia I say that somebody is jealous of her success and is trying to harm her.'"

I was sitting on the high stool Grama had put there for me so I could watch and listen to the shoppers. A few shoppers reproached her for having me there. Felt that the issues discussed were too raunchy for my ears. I think I was around nine when Josephine brought her message. Grama was standing beside me, her arm around me, as if protecting me, while Josephine spoke.

"Tell Cynthia she must wear only black underwear, keep a black candle burning all the time, check her steps for grave dirt before she step outside, and be careful who she take gifts from. That is the message your mother give me. I didn't know which Cynthia the message for. I didn't even know your name is Cynthia, so I didn't know who to tell. Then your mother come back a next night and tell me that if I didn't deliver her message something bad will happen to me. Ma Kirton, I had to ask around to find out all the Cynthia-them so I could deliver the message. Is so I find out you is a Cynthia, and I see you is light-skinned, and the woman that give me the message is light-skinned too, and now that you describe your mother, I know the message is for you."

Grama was silent for at least fifteen seconds. Finally she said: "Thanks for the message, Josephine. I will follow your advice and obey the instructions."

When Josephine left, Grama said to me: "Not a word about this to anybody. You hear me?"

I nodded. "What if Josephine tells other people?"

Grama shrugged.

"Are you going to follow your mother's advice?"

"My *mother's advice*! Paul, my mother died a long time ago. And her skin was darker than yours. I got my complexion from my father. If you go looking for evil you will find enough to destroy you several times over. If you call yourself a diviner you could always convince some people that you see things they can't." I asked her what a diviner was; she explained it to me and then said: "Josephine would have better luck with Mercy. Maybe I should invest in black candles and black underwear, and hire her to do the divining." She laughed then looked at me asquint. "It's why I want you and Jay to be well educated so people won't make fools of you."

"Why didn't you tell her that the woman she described wasn't your mother?"

"Because I didn't want her to go looking for someone else to make a fool of."

Now I wonder. Josephine no doubt sent many people looking for the source of imaginary Obeah. But she didn't ask Grama for payment. If there was any benefit to her work, it came from the status it gave her. She was a labourer on Laird's estate. When Jestina, who was neighbour to Jay's friend Millington, became possessed by multiple demons and began to attract a lot of attention, it was Mother Bernice and the Spiritual Baptists—not Father Henderson, her parents' priest—they called upon to exorcise and drive away the demons.

Grama didn't let me go to see it. She disapproved of what was being done to cure Jestina. She didn't believe in demons. The chasing of the spirits took place on a Sunday. If Grama had been away I'd have asked Aunt Mercy to take me and to hide it from Grama. I'd got to go with her on a week day two weeks earlier. About twenty of us stood in the road and listened to Jestina's voice change from an old man's to an old woman's to a clucking baby's as she spouted all the obscenities that she knew: Vincentian, Jamaican, and even Black American. It was the first time I heard the expression mother fucker. She seemed to be enjoying herself. The Sunday of the attempted exorcism, I stood on our front porch and watched the minibuses full of Spiritual Baptists from all over the Leeward Coast heading up Pasture Road where Jestina lived. I watched Aunt Mercy leave. Grama was on the back porch reading. Jay didn't go either. Next morning Aunt Mercy described the exorcism to Mr. Morris. Several pointers had come. Mother Bernice worked on dislodging the female demons and Pointer John on the male ones. "Them call the spirits them by all kind o' funny names what I can't even pronounce and ordered them to come outta her. And while they was doing that, the rest of us was singing and beating the sides of the house and the ground with coconut and sago branches. The last thing Mother Bernice and Pointer John do is sprinkle the ground with Dettol and turpentine."

"I heard the singing all the way over where I was in Esperance," Mr. Morris told her. "Did you all see the demons running away?"

"Teacher Morris, you want to get me in trouble, is that you want?"

For the first four days, Jestina appeared to have regained normalcy, and shoppers in the store praised Mother Bernice and Pointer John, but on the morning of the fifth day, they found Jestina's lifeless body entangled in one of the fishermen's seines.

After that the shoppers said that the demons had left too suddenly and unbalanced her. One woman, a Spiritual Baptist herself, was sure that Jestina's spirit would reveal to some future *mourner* why she'd killed herself. I never heard Aunt Mercy or any of the shoppers in the store say that it ever did.

⇥ Mother Bernice. In my short story, I show her two-room wooden house on Main Street, perched on storey-high cement pillars, an external cement stairway without a railing. Far in the back and half-hidden by fruit trees was her mourning shrine, a small hut, where she piloted mourners. Her house was the only one of its kind remaining on Main Street. It stood out not only because it was small, two rooms, but because of the vast yard space and the two lots of land to the back where she grew sorrel, ginger, and saffron. Just before Christmas you'd see her sitting on a stool underneath her house—where she also had her kitchen, a small space fenced in with galvanized sheeting—cleaning ginger rhizomes and bagging dried sorrel, which people came to buy to prepare ginger beer and sorrel for Christmas. And she would be singing or humming:

> *Sowing the precious seed*
> *Sowing the precious seed*
> *Reaping time is coming by and by*
> *Some day in glory you will find me*
> *Singing and shouting eternally.*

⇥ When Jay and I returned home in 2007 to put Aunt Mercy into care, we found Mother Bernice looking after her: preparing her food, washing her clothes, and making sure that she had a bath. By then the pillars of her house had been walled in and two additional rooms added to the back. It was still small compared to most of the other houses on Main Street. She told us that Sonny's children had visited her and given her the money to enlarge her house. "Them upbraid Sonny. Them make him shame. Now he does send me a pittance every now and again."

Jay comes back with his food: a smoked salmon wrap, fruit salad, and coffee. I tell him that I was just thinking of Jestina, Mother Bernice, and Josephine, and ask him if he'd managed to track down his school friend Millington.

He shakes his head.

"These days with internet and Facebook, it's easy to find priests and pastors." Last he knew, Millington was an Authentic Methodist Church minister in Barbados.

"I'll try to find him for you," I say.

The food wagon stops outside the door. A scrawny East-Asian man, in white, his hair covered with a hairnet, puts a food tray on my bed table.

Jay moves his chair closer to the window so I can adjust the bed table over my armchair. Before I remove the plate cover, I smell the fish on it and I'm overcome by nausea. I point to the kidney basin on the bed. Jay reaches over and gets it for me just in time. When the heaves settle, I go to the bathroom. Since my first bout of radiation a week ago, I've lost five pounds. I return to sit in the armchair and watch Jay eat his lunch.

Is this how one dies? My own death is the last thing I want to think about. I turned twenty-five two days ago.

"Are you alright?" Jay asks, alarmed.

I nod. "Tell me about Africa," I say, "about the beautiful fellow you were attracted to in Ghana."

"There's no more to tell. I know about his physical beauty, my interpretation of it, but I don't know if he was truly beautiful in the ways you and Bill talked about—the ways that really matter. You know, should know, that our beauty and ugliness have to be judged from our behaviour. The body—I think Bill told you this—is a bio-degradable, beautifully carved or clumsily carved urn. What it contains, that's what matters." He pauses, as if doubting himself. "Besides, Paul, even if I were interested in Kwame, I'd already heard him say his father took him to shamans and made him take all sorts of potions. He and I belong to radically different worlds. You knew of Carlos' Catholicism: his *andas* and whatnot. It didn't deter you. But it would have deterred me."

"Is that why you've rebuffed Jonathan?"

"No. It's as I've told you: I'm not sexually attracted to him. I know Jonathan almost as much as I know you. We are better off as friends. It's as a friend that I need him."

"I worry about you. Here you are thirty-one and, apart from the disaster with Tamara, you've never had a relationship."

"It doesn't bother me, Paul."

"It should. I am getting ready to leave this world, and you are going to be alone."

He frowns. "What are you talking about, Paul?"

I smile. "I'm talking about wanting to see you in a nurturing relationship. Go out. Meet guys. Fool around. Let go."

"You just want to see me afflicted with PCBs." He grins.

"PCBs! What does sex have to do with PCBs?"

"Post-coital blues. "

We both laugh.

"No laughing matter. Jonathan says they always afflict him the morning after a pickup. Says it's an empty feeling that comes on im-mediately after the orgasm and worsens as the guy goes out the door; and he knows that next day or next week, if they run into each other they might not even acknowledge that they know each other."

"So he picks up guys. He's not an abstainer like you!"

He continues as if he didn't hear my comment. "Once they've bedded you, you're like the deer that's been caught and eaten. They're on to other prey."

I've never had to think seriously about any of this. Carlos came into my life when I was on the verge of finding out and forestalled all that perilous exploration. If I get better, I'll find out for sure. Abstinence isn't for this cat. "I'm glad Jonathan got around to sleeping with guys. Jay, since you have to deal with his—what do you call them?"

"Post-coital blues."

"Wouldn't it be easier for you to be his lover: less work and some pleasure?"

"I seem to think we've had this conversation about casual sex before: the Sunday after your return from Guatemala."

"Don't remember. But if we did, you didn't take my advice. I took the advice you gave me regarding Carlos. Remember? You told me to be patient with him, to understand the frustrations he would face as an immigrant in a strange environment without his family?"

He nods, presses his lips tightly, and swallows.

"Well, you see what came of that. But I don't care anymore. I'll be dead soon anyway. At least I hope so. I don't want to live with a damaged brain. This shouldn't be happening to me. It's the only gift I've got from life. Now she's taking it away."

He comes to sit on the armrest and puts his arms around me and rocks me gently. "Cheer up, man." I feel the convulsions, next the warmth of the tears rolling down my cheeks.

I hate being like this. When the convulsions stop, I say: "Thanks. I'll try to control my emotions better."

"It's all right, Paul. It's a raw deal all right. Don't worry about my feelings." He reaches over to the bedside table for a couple of tissues and hands them to me.

"What time's it?"

"12:46."

"Wonder if they intend to keep me here all morning and all afternoon too. I'll give them thirty minutes more. I won't call while half of them are on their lunch break. I want to be home in my bed. Can you stay with me the rest of the afternoon, maybe evening? I'm anxious. Worried. I need the distraction."

He nods.

"When we get home I want you to rent a few comedies. Things that will make me laugh, keep down the nausea, and help me eat." I feel the tears filling my eyes again as the weight of what's happening in my body refuses to leave.

⇥ My mind turns to my first meeting with Bill in his office at Concordia. He seemed so confident, so sure of himself. Little by little I discovered his insecurities. So candid about needing Chai and others. We know what we would like to do, but will is only one element in this inscrutable colossus we call self. Then again, we pare ourselves, even damage our psyches, to hide those traits that displease others. What Freud calls civilization's discontent. I try to envisage Bill as a younger man. On the gay desirability index he was one rung above bottom. Visibly androgynous. Walked with a wiggle. In St. Vincent he'd have been harassed the way Job and Neil were. When I met him he had a skinny slouching frame, a protuberant belly, bandy legs, and a gawky look. His nose formed a humungous ridge in his narrow face; his sad hazel eyes, deep in their sockets, were ringed with wrinkles. His piping voice made people turn to see who was speaking. A target for sexual exploiters and bullying homophobes. He came of age when homophobia was legal. He never spoke to me much about this. Not easy to talk about. You relive it. And you'd be baring yourself to the listener, who'd think you were begging for sympathy. Never a good feeling. I'd felt so ashamed of myself after I dumped my sorrow on him. He comforted and reassured me. Not sure if he'd had anyone to do that for him. I'd wanted to ask him about that while he was dying, but felt it would evoke painful memories.

Jay gets up to put the wrapping from his meal in the garbage bin. "Have my food," I tell him. "I can't eat it. Should have asked for Gravol before." I think of having the small cup of apple juice, but the thought turns my stomach queasy. I press my buzzer, and tell the nurse who answers to bring me Gravol.

Jay picks up the book he brought with him this morning. Daddy forbade Ma to read anything but the bible to him. Grama corrected that. How did she manage to rise above her culture? Must have been because of the books she'd read. I wonder if Jay understands how exceptional she was. What would our lives have been like if we'd lived with Daddy? If we hadn't had her? We were lucky. Jay less than I. What if Ma hadn't walked out of her abusive marriage? Daddy would have dragged us off almost every evening to the villages around Georgetown to "win souls for Christ." By the time we got to adolescence our backs would have been scarred from the welts left by his and teachers' straps. There are five on Jay's back.

I remember what Grama said when she and Jay discussed "Among School Children": that in her school they memorized facts, like William the Conqueror conquered England in 1066; that they sang *Rule, Britannia, Britannia, Rule the Waves* and did not know they were praising Britons for enslaving Africans; that they were tested annually by the inspector of schools. In the early years he was a white man from England. After the inspector left the headmaster flogged those students who'd failed: the girls in their hands, the boys over their backs, and bloodstains would later show on the backs of the boys' shirts. The flogging continued down to my time. Before I went to school in town I remember Jay coming to the shop one day with blood on his shirt. He refused to tell Grama why. He had fever and was put to bed. Aunt Mercy stayed with him. Grama held my hand and we went up the hill to where Millington lived. She asked Millington what had happened to Jay in school. He said that Jay had had ague and the teacher had flogged him for getting his math problems wrong. The teacher, Mr. Branch, lived where Havre bordered Laird's estate. Grama and I took a shortcut along a muddy track to his house, one with two-rooms. A woman was in the yard tossing corn to chickens. Grama called out to Mr. Branch from the road. He came to the door. She told him: "If you put your hand on Jay again, it will be the grave for you and the gallows for me. You hear me? You beat a child unable do his work because he's sick! What sort of brute are you? I wouldn't hire you to look after cattle, never mind children."

And so she sent me to Excelsior, where children weren't beaten, and the brighter they were the harder they were made to work. She intervened once at Excelsior. I was in junior three at the time, and while removing a book from the bookshelf in my classroom the book-shelf tumbled down. Nobody was hurt.

The teacher screamed at me: "You're clumsy! Don't you know that curiosity killed the cat?"

My classmates laughed.

Stung, I said: "You don't have the right to scream at me. It's not my fault your bookcase is rickety. You're lucky I didn't get hurt. My grandmother would have sued you."

When I told Grama what had happened she said: "I am going to ask your teacher if she scolds Thomas Edison for his curiosity when she turns on her lights and toasts her bread." The following Tuesday the principal called me into her office to find out what had happened. After listening to me, she stared at her desk for a few seconds then said: "Your teacher was probably having a hard day. She meant nothing by it." Two days later the bookshelf was replaced by a sturdy book-case.

I watch Jay turn a page. "Jay, have you ever wondered what our lives would have been if we hadn't come here."

He marks his place with the bookmark, and is silent for a few seconds. "On occasion, yes. But we came here, so I don't waste time pursuing such thoughts."

"You remember when we went home for Grama's funeral, four of your classmates from elementary school came looking for you to drag you off to the rum shop?"

He arches his eyebrows, squints sceptically, and purses his lips. "You're sure that's not part of the fiction you're writing?"

"No. When they wouldn't leave you took out your wallet and gave them some money and told them to go have a good time."

"I'll take your word for it."

"I wanted to see you go with them." I chuckle.

He puts the book on the trolley. "Why're you chuckling?"

I laugh.

His frown deepens.

"I was just trying to imagine what it would be like seeing you drunk, and Ma witnessing it all."

He snorts.

I wish I could get into that head of his to know what he's thinking. For a while we say nothing. He gets up, stretches and sits again. It seems as if he's gained a few pounds.

"Come closer," I say.

He does and I put my hand on his flanks and tap his sides. "You're getting love handles, Jay."

"But I don't weigh a gram more. It's flab."

"You should go to the gym. Why don't you? Afraid you'll look so good, guys and girls would chase you down?"

He shakes his head. "You're over-obsessed with looks and sex. Life's a lot more than that."

"Wrong. Life *is* about sex. Your kind of sex when you meet *your woman.*" I chuckle. "As long as there's an orgasm in the offing, male praying mantises don't mind being eaten. Life is the end-product of sex—some might even see it as the dregs of sex."

"Well, dregs of sex or not, I won't be creating any."

"You *won't* be having children! That's new."

"Come on. I already told you that bit about wanting children and a wife was to put Jonathan off. But we have to help to feed some of the starving children around the globe. You see what's happening right now in Somalia?"

"And how do you get those who survive the famine to stop their irresponsible breeding? Catholicism and Islam urge them to breed."

He doesn't reply.

"Catholicism and Islam don't feed them."

"If we accept the golden rule we can't let others suffer when we have the means to help them. Remember, children are not responsible for their parents' stupidity."

"You're right. In Guatemala, I found it surreal watching fifty-year-olds and six-and-seven-year olds competing for shoes to shine in the parks. Some days not even making enough for a meal. When these youngsters become teenagers and see their future in these fifty- and sixty-year-old men ... Just imagine if we'd been born into those circumstances. What would you have done in their place, Jay?"

"I don't know. In Africa, it was more children selling in the markets instead of going to school."

"It's why many Central Americans become *pandilleros,* and live by extortion ... If instead of sending you to school, your mother has been taking you since you were six or seven years old to pick coffee so that she could earn enough for tortillas and beans, and every day you walked by the *finquero's* mansion, cars, and dogs better cared for than you—how would you feel? Many of those workers are Mayan, and they know that the land the *finquero* calls his own was taken by force from their ancestors. Can you blame them for wanting to take it back?"

Jay stares at me, the fork in his brow quite visible. "There are guerrilla fighters in Latin America and Africa who say they are doing that. But the peasants whose crops they destroy and whose children they rape or kidnap and turn into killers might want to differ. I'm not discounting their legitimate grievances, but I don't countenance the remedy."

—➤ The distraction has helped. Forms of misery different from my own. I look at my watch. It's 2:03 p.m. I press my buzzer and ask to talk to Harriet, who is caring for me.

She comes and I ask her around what time I'll leave. After a long pause, she says she doesn't know, that Dr. Cantor will have to give the all-clear before I can go home. I ask what time he'll come by.

She says: "Sometime before five."

"But I want to leave now."

She frowns and gestures that it's out of her hands. She leaves.

Jay picks up the book from the trolley. He buys so many books he'll soon run out space in in his apartment to put them. Suits me fine. I get to read them without having to buy them. He's reading an author I don't know: A.S. Byatt, "Read me a passage," I say. He reads, and in the passage I recognize the lines from Tennyson that Byatt's character is quoting.

"The style's so antiquated," I say.

"That's the point. The story takes place in Victorian England. So the characters use Victorian diction and syntax. From what I've seen so far it's about the tension between religious faith and science, with a heavy helping of romance thrown in. It's an ideas novel for the most part. It's your field."

"Is there violence in it?"

"So far I've only seen it in one character."

"Wonder what Bram would think of it. He'd be sceptical if there isn't violence. He cites Freud all the time. Says good fiction is an oblique inquiry into the human condition, and because sex and violence are the engines of life, writing that elides them—elide, his word —is dishonest. One day he brought in a copy of the film *Naked* for us to watch to illustrate what he meant by honesty. I think he enjoys watching people squirm.

"'Angels and Insects.' Interesting title. Forget about angels, and I'm not being sarcastic. My comment's based on biology. Did you see that Nova programme 'What Darwin never Knew'?"

"No."

"Well, if it is to be believed, all land creatures evolved from a single species that came out from the water. And all the genes of that creature have been passed on, to be turned off or on in specific species depending on the demands of the environment and eons of survival selection. You know what I think? Since we are at the top of the evolutionary chain, we embody the genetic codes of every creature that is below us, either in the decodable genes—the genome—or in the remaining mass of DNA. Those Wall Street bankers who've plunged us into this economic crisis and put hundreds of thousands of people out of their homes and tens of millions out of work are no different from bees and ants that expel their unwanted members to die when their services are no longer needed."

"I think Byatt would agree with you. The novel mentions those ants." He takes a deep breath and fidgets. He's signalling that I should change the subject.

"Depressing topic, right?"

He doesn't respond.

"I know, I know. I should be thinking of comic stuff, but I can't. I'll leave you to read quietly. I'll lie down for a while and try to doze."

I lie down. My mind plays with the idea that if these therapies don't work, horror and death are waiting. I am twenty-five and cancer strikes—just when I am trying to make up for wasted time. I shiver. Tears follow. My back is turned to Jay. I'm glad he isn't seeing any of this. It's unjust for him too, a cruel way to spend the half-year sabbatical he took in order to travel. Now the rest of his time will be spent learning to care for a brother undergoing radiation therapy. I bring my lower arm up to my eyes and sop the tears with the sleeve of my hospital gown then turn around to face Jay.

He looks across at me, frowns, and says: "You're crying."

I shake my head.

He gets up and pulls his chair closer to the bed and puts his hand on my wrist.

"Tell me the honest truth, Jay. Don't you at times wish I hadn't been born?"

He scowls. "What sort of question is that?"

"In your place, I would."

"Well, that's why I'm Jay and you're Paul."

"I don't have the right, Jay. I don't have the right."

"Quiet, Paul."

"Taking up your time like this. I've been doing this since I was five. You should be pissed."

"Don't tell me how I should be. "

"You're too good. You should be angry with me. I want you to be angry with me. I would feel better if you were."

"Right now you seem angry enough with yourself."

"You're right. Stoicism is not my strongest trait ... I should take up Olinski on the offer to see a counsellor before these feelings shatter my sanity. You're nodding. You agree." *Maybe you should see one too. All that calm—you should find out what's beneath it.* I remember how I was never able to make him angry. "You amaze me, you know that? You amaze me."

He shrugs.

"Jay, I don't want to die. I don't want to become a vegetable. If I was going to die, it should have been when I wanted to—while I was in high school. I travelled and I lost my death wish. And then I met Carlos. A disaster. Jay, I want to write at least one novel before things worsen. I don't want my life to be useless."

"You're not sure things will worsen."

"What would I have done, if you weren't here?"

"Carlos would have done his best."

I nod. Yes that part of him surprises me. "He may yet have to, to spell you. Remember how it was with Bill: the CLSC during the day, I in the early evening, you at night?"

His face is taut.

"The wrong topic. Right?"

"Go on, talk. Doesn't mean I agree with you."

"As soon as I get home, I'm going to phone Gélinas."

"Why?"

"To make my will. Brain tumours can be unpredictable."

"And who will you be phoning about your will to live?" He snickers.

"Don't mind what I say. I have plenty of that. Triple, quadruple what I had as teenager. Nowadays, gathering material for my novel, I spend long hours mulling over my life in St. Vincent. In spite of my asthma, I had a superb life. Even at Cousin Alice's house. I had so much fun at school. In Junior five, when I finished my work ahead of time, I helped the junior two teacher correct her students' work; sometimes I tutored the junior one students who were having trouble learning to read. Later you and I at the library; on the weekends and school holidays back home at Grama's chewing sugar cane on the back porch, the juice running down our elbows, heaps of chewed fibre beside each of us. One time—I couldn't have been more than seven—I stripped down to my shorts and turned the garden hose on myself, and Aunt Mercy gave me a tongue-lashing, saying it would cause my asthma to flare up. Remember that, Jay?"

He shakes his head, seems himself to be in deep thought.

"But the best part of it—truly the best part—know what it was? The days in the shop, listening to Grama's customers commenting on what was going on around them and in the rest of the world. Some of it plain foolishness. And I could always question Grama about what I didn't understand. She never missed an opportunity to feed my curiosity and make me feel wanted."

"You're sure you're not seeing the past as better than it was?"

"No. You only understand how privileged you were when you see how in many places children are a burden, burdens to be loaded onto others, or tools to make money, or satisfy the desires of the ruthless and perverted."

He does not comment. For a long time we say nothing.

"Grama gave me confidence ... I came here and it vanished, and I became like a pebble that everyone kicked around."

"Really? In Ma's house you were a tsunami threatening every moment to drown us."

"Ma couldn't protect me, you couldn't protect me, the principal couldn't protect me. Sleep-walking, pissing my bed. If Grama knew this would have happened would she have sent me here? Remember that poem I sent to Mrs. Bensemana? Because of the attention I knew it would get me. Remember that? Imagine me, a fourteen-year-old, inviting my teacher to have sex with me."

Jay is silent, the fork in his brow pronounced.

"I remember you back in St. Vincent, quiet and sombre. When I came back from travelling, you said: 'Paul, when Ma fled Daddy's house and didn't carry me with her, it left a hole inside me, and it only half-filled when I came to join her in Canada.' I wrote that statement down in my journal. I understood then why back in St. Vincent you always looked so unhappy. And your personality hasn't changed. It's as if you don't expect to find happiness anywhere, as if you expect betrayal, and can't risk trusting anyone." He's staring at me intensely. "Surprised I know you so well. Right?"

The fork in his brow deepens and the furrows move further up his forehead. He snorts. "Go on. I'm listening."

"It's all I have to say. Well not all. When my relationship with Carlos was going well, those were happy days. I want you to experience something like that; even better: a relationship that lasts. If anyone deserves it, it's you. I used to think you should be with a man, but now I see beyond gender and think only of companionship; just be honest with her—or him—from the start."

"Put that in your will when you make it: 'To Jay I bequeath the right to share his life with a woman or a man and to be always honest and happy.'"

We both laugh.

"I am managing all right, Paul. The psyche has its own rules that no one, not even psychologists, understands. I think I'm doing quite well, all things considered. And don't worry about your care. I'm sure you'd be better by the time I return to work. In the worst of all scenarios, we'd simply use the money we've inherited to pay for your care. After paying my bills, I always have a little left over from my salary. And since travelling through Africa, that little has become a lot more, because all sorts of things that I thought were essential, I saw that they weren't and now I bypass them."

"Like what?"

"Owning lots of expensive clothing which I hardly ever wear, lubricating my skin with expensive creams ... going to expensive restaurants."

"Restaurant owners and workers won't appreciate that. Neither will our governments: less sales tax. You're not helping the local economy. Your spending keeps people working."

He shrugs. "I wouldn't have even bought the condo I have. I'd have bought something further away from downtown for a few thousand dollars less, and it wouldn't have a Jacuzzi."

"No need to feel guilty over being comfortable. They're the little hugs we give ourselves. Look how hard Ma worked and how little she gave herself. So if we get her pension and insurance money and have a comfortable life, it's nothing to feel guilty about. Granddad brownnosed enough for the money that set Grama up in business. They paid their dues, Jay, they did."

"And we must pay ours."

"You should talk. Look where I am and the state I'm in."

"How do your health problems square with world hunger and preventable diseases? You're missing my point. It doesn't matter who earned what or did what. We don't have the right to gorge while others starve. I'm not speaking specifically of myself, but of all of us— society as a whole."

"So you want to live like those folks who devote themselves to —what do they call it?—voluntary simplicity, and give your extra income to the NGOs who pay themselves hefty salaries and give crumbs to the people they say they're helping?"

"That's an unfair generalization."

"Don't you hear the stories about food aid being sold in markets in Somalia, about guerrilla groups intercepting the food, about the huge sums celebrities receive for the fundraising campaigns they undertake, about the affluent lifestyle recipients of cancer research money lead: jet-setting around the world, staying in five-star hotels? There was this woman who lived in Laird's Shanty who used to stand outside Grama's store and sell the soy milk the clinic gave her to supplement the nutrition of her children."

"Let's change the subject. You won't convince me. You're not seeing the whole picture."

Dr. Cantor arrives. He's in his early thirties. He wears thick lenses that make his eyes seem cavernous. The top of his head is completely bald; elsewhere his hair is raven black, including his very thick beard and moustache. He's a trifle taller than I and has massive shoulders and bulging biceps—definitely spends a lot of time at the gym. He smiles at me, nods at Jay, picks up the clipboard with my chart, and writes on it. He puts the chart back onto the trolley and asks how I feel.

So-so, I gesture. "Couldn't eat lunch. Felt nauseous."

"I see you got Gravol earlier."

"Too late to make a difference."

"I could let you go home now, but you must try to eat when you get home. And drink lots of fluids. Or you could stay here for another two-three hours and let us run an intravenous."

I shake my head. "I prefer to go home."

"Okay. Harriet will do a final check and then you'll go."

He writes a prescription for more Gravol, and then leaves.

Harriet comes at 4:17, takes my blood pressure and gives me the okay to leave, reminds me about being hydrated, to make sure I have Gravol on hand and to rush to the emergency here if any unusual side effects develop. She talks, staring alternately at Jay and me, implying that he should make me carry out her orders.

We leave. It's almost 5 p.m.; rush hour has started. I think of the smells in the metro. Now meat, fish, or egg smells make me want to retch, and perfumes and colognes in the minutest amounts cause me to wheeze and my chest to tighten. Two mornings ago the smell of bacon came through the ventilator in my apartment, and I vomited until my stomach was all that was left to come up. Before this it was always touch and go in small spaces crammed with people. Three months ago I chanced it to the Comedy Nest at the Forum; halfway through the performance I began to wheeze and had to leave. "We have to take a cab home," I tell Jay when we get to the lobby. This is getting to be expensive.

When we get inside the apartment, I say: "I'm taking a dose of choral hydrate and heading straight to bed."

"First try sleeping without it."

"You don't understand. I want to sleep for as long as I can—until after sunrise tomorrow morning."

He says nothing.

"Perhaps not even wake up."

He frowns and scratches his upper lip with his right forefinger and pretends not to hear me.

"Fine. You can pretend. You're not the one whose life is hanging in the balance. This murderous shit in my body is what I wake up to every fucking day! Each week I go and they fill me with deadly shit to fight other deadly shit." I drop heavily onto the sofa. Jay sits beside me and puts his hand on mine.

After sitting there silently for about ten minutes, I remove his hand. "Thanks. It must be hard for you too." I remember his cry for freedom in 2007 when I proposed that we continue living together.

"Why the frown?" he asks.

"Nothing."

I go into my bedroom, pick up my journal, sit in the armchair, and begin writing in it:

> There are days when all this writing, especially of my novel, seems futile. Today is one of them. While we boarded with Cousin Alice, Jay joked once that if at birth I could have chosen between Ma's nipple and a book, I'd have chosen the book. Now I wonder how much sustenance there is in books. Helpless now anyway. Beyond satiating our curiosity is there anything more? In Gravity's Rainbow, there's a section where Pynchon's narrator is exploring the loss of innocence that literacy brings to a community that's now under Soviet influence. Right now books and their ethereal knowledge feel like a burden. If the end of knowledge is to solve problems, the time I've spent amassing it has been wasted, and reading has turned out to be just another addiction. If we faced the truth, we'd admit that we are hardly more than what our senses are assessing—the eye mostly, with the other senses subserving or complementing it. Immediate reality is that point, real or imaginary, that the eye fixes on, oblivious to all else. It's true that what our senses apprehend is mediated by what we already know. But even that knowledge is restricted in its usefulness, depending on whether it was acquired abstractly or practically—a point those who argue for hands-on education have been making strenuously since John Dewey.
>
> At some level we fear that we are nothing, and do the utmost to convince ourselves otherwise—via offspring, via the records we leave behind, via belief in an afterlife. When the offspring go, we'll still be swallowed up in the oblivion of time. Unless we are a Shakespeare, a Shelley, a Michelangelo, an Auden, or a Leonardo da Vinci and leave stellar works behind us—but they're no substitute for the living self. If the gods had offered them a choice between art and eternal youth, I have no doubt which they

would have chosen. Longfellow urges us to emulate great men and put footprints on the sands of time. He must have known some would do so by being Hitlers, Stalins, Pol Pots. And what's the value of footprints after we're dead! At its nadir living is finding activities that distract us from the weight of time. And if we think that some activities, intellectual pursuits, for example, are better, it's only because we've been manipulated into thinking so.

And as to the belief that we will live again after death, it's a wilful turning of our faces away from the decay that inheres in nature and sustains nature. "Humankind cannot bear much reality." I'm with Tennyson's Lotus Eaters: Why should we alone toil ... And make perpetual moan, / Still from one sorrow to another thrown ... ?

I close the journal and get up to take my pills, and I'm tempted to take them all and might have done so if I were alone. Jay would intervene before they take effect. I see now why doctors want someone to be with us at such times.

10

JANUARY 1, 2012. First hour into the new year. Jay is in the adjoining bedroom. His light is still on. He's probably reading. Together we welcomed in the New Year—without champagne, without fanfare. I begged him to go off somewhere and have fun, told him I'd be all right. I especially wanted him to accept Lionel's invitation.

Lionel is this fellow that Olinski sent to talk to me, to help lift my spirits. He'd beaten Ewing's sarcoma after several bouts of radiation and chemo and triple recidivism. Cancer struck him at age twenty-three just as he was about to finish a master's degree. Jay and I met him for the first time on December 9. He came back to the ward on December 16 and invited us to his place to ring in the New Year.

"Thanks," Jay said. "We'll think about it and let you know."

"Your ... partners are welcome too." He sucked in his breath and pushed up his shoulders.

Jay shook his head almost imperceptibly, signalling that that we shouldn't respond.

Lionel's eyes brightened. And right away I knew. He was attracted to one of us.

When we got home I told Jay we would hear from Lionel.

"How do you know that?"

"If you were looking at him, you'd have seen it in his eyes. I won't mind casting my line in those waters. That is if you don't mind."

"Whoa! Whoa!" He shook his head slowly. "Cool it. Your immune system isn't up to hanky-panky. Did you say: 'If *I* don't mind'"?

I nodded. "His eyes might have lit up for you, in which case I should keep to the sidelines."

He stared at me alarmed, his arms raised, his head shaking.

"At this pace, you'll break your neck."

"I want you to call Lionel and to go to the party. I can't go. You know—the smell thing; my body might crash. You go. I'll be all right."

He shook his head with an emphatic no.

"Call Lionel then, and tell him why we can't come, but invite him —and his partner, of course—to come visit us."

"In that case, it's you who should invite him to visit—it's your apartment. I don't want to be here when he comes."

"It could be to your apartment."

He's shakes his head. "Oh no. I'm not the fisherman here."

"Okay, just call him." I couldn't tell him then that my hope was that Lionel's eyes had glowed for me and not him. Just the sort of person I want to be with now. Went right back to school, finished his degree, and now teaches philosophy at a CEGEP. Born in England from Grenadian parents. Moved to Montreal when he was seven. About five centimetres taller than I, big-boned—ox-like haunches and thighs like hockey and football players—with a layer of fat spread on solid muscle; deeply bowed legs, walnut skin; flattish nose, intense dark-brown eyes, thick lips, and a deep voice.

Four days after this conversation, I called Lionel, because Jay wouldn't, and almost choked when a woman answered the telephone. She put him on the phone, and I told him that because I'm hypersensitive to smells and have an aversion to meat and fish products I couldn't come, and Jay didn't feel that he should leave me alone on New Year's Eve. "How about paying us a visit: the Saturday after New Year's perhaps? Bring along your partner." There was silence for about ten seconds. I broke it. "You could come for supper but it would be vegetarian: tofu, beans, salad, that sort of thing."

"I don't mind vegetarian food. It's just that I'd promised this girl that we'd go see *The Iron Lady* that Saturday. I'll check with her and see if we can change the date, and I'll call you back."

On Boxing Day he called and said he'd come. I told him his partner was welcome too.

"I'll come alone."

I so wanted to ask him who the woman was that answered the phone.

Jay, who overheard my part of the conversation, asked why I was so excited.

"He'll come, Jay. Woohoo! He said yes."

"Your eyes are glowing. Don't drop the phone."

"Keep *your calm* and see if you don't lose out on everything."

"Everything! You're smitten!"

"Okay, I'll level with you: my first choice would be that he wants me, but my second choice would be that he wants you."

"Put yourself on pause. You don't even know if the guy's gay."

"You're right. But I'll find out. I'm sure that at the very least he's bi. That won't stop me. I don't know how long I have to live. I don't have time for your scruples."

"You're breathless. If you keep this up, you'll get a stroke."

"You can talk. You don't have a death sentence hanging over you. Lionel will understand."

Jay fell silent.

That was ten days after my last round of chemo, and my aversion to odours had diminished to the point where I could eat cheese without retching. I could persuade Jay to prepare a casserole that he's good at: with cheese, eggplant, and spinach. Things improved further, to the point where today I had my first chicken meal in three months. Chicken marinated in ginger, lemon juice, and white wine; it went down and stayed down.

⇴ Gina and Emilia invited us to come by tonight as well. Even if I risked the perfumes and food smells, Gúicho and Carlos would be there. Those two are thick again. Since Carlos began paying him the rent money he owed him, bygones have become bygones. Gina, Gúicho, and Carlos have their cuss-outs and afterwards it's as if nothing ever happened. Offend me, and there's hell to pay. Our weaknesses, Jay tells me on occasion, are our deadliest enemies.

⇥ I'm propped up by pillows in bed, my journal open, supported by my thighs. A battle is going on in my brain about what to write. It's the beginning of a new year. My next check-up is in five weeks. At least there are no bouts of radiation therapy scheduled for 2012. Let's hope it stays that way until I die, several decades from now and with Lionel or an equivalent at my side. I laugh.

Since my arrival in Canada, my New Year journal entry has always been a summing-up of the year that's just ended. I don't recall ever writing anything about my hopes for the beginning year. Can't even remember what I would have written while in St. Vincent; maybe just how I spent the day, what Jay, Grama, and Aunt Mercy did and said. Something about Joanne too, the few times Grama and Aunt Mercy managed to persuade her to have New Year's dinner with us.

There would have been no comments about Daddy. Comments about him are only in the entries on days when he came to visit. I'd stare at this strange, molasses-coloured man, same complexion as mine, who was supposed to be my father: slumping gait, staring at the ground, lips quivering when he spoke to Grama. One time he handed Grama some money for us—I was around six—and she said to give it to Jay. He glanced at her and frowned. Thereafter he always gave Jay the money he brought us. His visit never lasted more than ten or so minutes. During the school year he'd come on a Saturday and go to the house, knowing that Jay would be there. It probably gave them a chance to talk more comfortably to each other. Jay and he would then come to the store. Jay would be half a step ahead of him holding his hand, as if he were the adult and Daddy the child. Grama would invite him to the backroom. He'd say the perfunctory: "How are you, Mrs. Kirton? ... How you doing, Paul? ... Behaving yourself? ... Not giving your grandmother no trouble?" He'd fidget while Grama was getting him a drink and cookies. He'd down them quickly, resume fidgeting for a couple of minutes, then signal Jay with a stare that he was ready to leave. Jay would accompany him to Main Street and wait there with him until the bus for Kingstown came. When he left, I treated the visit like yesterday's weather report. One time Grama asked me if I would like to go with him and Jay to the bus stop. I shook my head. She didn't insist and he seemed indifferent.

When we went to St. Vincent in 2007, Jay gave him and his wife money to replace a worn-out fridge and to install a telephone. Since then, they phone each other regularly. When I wake up later today, I'll ask Jay for the number and call to wish him a happy New Year. He'll be surprised. He probably feels Grama raised us to look down on him, probably congratulates himself that she didn't succeed with Jay. I think her disdain for him—maybe disdain is too strong—had the opposite effect on Jay, made him protective of Daddy. What will I say to him? If he starts talking about religion ... The longest conversation I had with him was on the day of Grama's funeral, when he tried to convert me to his religion. I antsy to go off and smoke a joint and he holding me back with his preaching. I giggled as I thought of handing him a spliff and saying: "Smoke this and clear your head of foolishness."

I hope Jay hasn't told him of my illness. He's under strict orders not to discuss my health with anyone. He's in touch with some of Ma's friends. A week ago he visited Lea Abromavitch whose life I made miserable with the noise I created above her head. Every once in a while he tells me that Beatrice says hello and that I must give her a call. Of course, I don't know who knows me at the Jewish General. "You're Anna's boy, right?" Adeline, the nurse who prepped me for surgery, asked me, and then went on to say that she and Ma belonged to the same church. For a few days I worried that Madam J and her crew would show up, bibles in hand. I can just hear Adeline telling all and sundry: *Remember Anna? Her boy Paul—the second one, the one that gave her all that trouble, that we used to pray for—he had surgery for a brain tumour.* That confidentiality stuff is a shell game.

⇥ This novel I'm writing about Grama is forcing me to re-examine a whole lot of issues. Guess I'll have to speculate about her and Ma's feelings toward Daddy. I'll have to begin with what's in her journal. Her relationship with Ma would have to be more than what's in the journals though. I think Ma felt no particular attachment to her. Except for the two trips back home that Jay says Grama paid for: one to see us, which I vaguely remember—Jay has had to fill me in with the details—and one when she came to accompany us to Canada, she never returned home while Grama was alive. She couldn't have had any deep attachment to Grama. When I confronted her over the fact that Grama had offered to pay our fares to come and visit her, she brought up the argument about being independent, and Jay sided with her. Since her death, I've asked Jay about this. But I don't trust his answer: the same one he gave when Ma was alive—about not wanting to spend other people's money. Why shouldn't I if they offer it to me? He's too emotionally invested in Ma to be objective. He wouldn't even know he wasn't being truthful. Ma filled his head with negative stories about Grama: that Grama was very impatient with her when she started going to school; that when she had trouble understanding something, Grama would say: "What's difficult about it?" and make her feel like a fool; that Grama would go through her school books and correct the mistakes that the teachers had overlooked; that around thirteen, she asked Grama why she didn't have a second child, and Grama told her: "So it would be easy to walk out on your father if I had to"; and Ma replied: "You should have had another child, one that could please you, because no matter how much I try I can never meet your expectations."

She got that last part right. I told Jay that this was Ma's version, that Grama's journals show Ma as weak-willed and gullible, and that even he couldn't find fault with that assessment.

"In case you've forgotten, Grama died, and if she rose from the dead nobody saw it. The way you go on about her a fool would think she was divine"—said it with a sneer too. Still feels the need to defend Ma. "Maybe you should ask another question: whether in dealing with us Grama wasn't compensating for the mistakes she'd made raising Ma."

"Mistakes like what?"

"In one of her journal entries she said if she didn't have Ma she would have gone to Britain to study. In the early years Ma seemed to have had difficulty learning. Grama might have felt angry that she'd had to sacrifice her own dreams to raise a mediocre child."

He had me there. At least he admitted that she was mediocre.

"Paul, you seem to have forgotten that Grama didn't do anything to discourage Ma from abandoning her house and go to work in Laird's fields. Ma said it broke her heart that Grama didn't. Grama had to know better. It's quite possible Ma never forgave her. Difficulty forgiving others is something you know about. I'm sure Grama wouldn't have done something like that by the time we went to live with her. And weeks after Ma walked out, Grama felt bad about it and sent Aunt Mercy to bring her home."

"So Ma talked to you about this?"

"Yes. And she wanted Grama to admit that she hadn't done the right thing, but Grama never did."

Whether his speculations are true I don't know, but he bought Ma's story about the second child, and he thinks I became that second child. Now I wonder whether Ma felt I'd displaced her or if she'd told him that I had. If she thought I had, it would have been difficult for her not to resent me, at least at the subconscious level. Nowadays, from all the stories we hear about parents who murder their children, and what we know about human evolution and our genetic connections to those species we consider below us, we can say that humans are capable of any behaviour found in other species. I shouldn't harbour such thoughts about my mother.

Back in St. Vincent when Jay and I played at quarrelling, I said bad things about Daddy, and he would tell me I shouldn't, and I would say I didn't give a hoot because I didn't want his daddy to be *my* daddy. He'd come back with: "I don't say bad things about Grama." Recently he said to me that Grama had trouble being impartial, that on Friday afternoons when we returned from town, her eyes always lit up when she saw me but she never even noticed him, and that when we were home her world turned around me; some hocus-pocus too about her being so taken up with me the morning we were leaving for Canada that she almost forgot he was there.

"And what about all the time she spent in July and August going over your literature books with you? All that other reading you both did together? And I heard her praising you for passing your subjects with good grades. The money she gave you when you were coming to Canada? She didn't give me any. You're not being fair."

"She gave Ma an equal amount for you." Then he twisted his lips and tossed his head just like Ma used to, the closest he could come to agreeing with me. I never thought the attention I got pushed him into the shadow. I should tell him it's because I learned early how not to be ignored. He's hinted on occasion that all that attention has been bad for me. Was it? I don't know. In any event we came here, and he, who was conditioned to endure harsh treatment, met none. I, who'd been pampered, met it all—in one gulp. And fate has been mocking me since my first asthma attack at age six. How else can I explain this difficult life? Thought I'd turned the page when I returned from travelling and began university. Now, one semester before I graduate, the blow falls, and I have had to withdraw from my classes. But I'm not giving up. I won't give up. I'm resuming classes in three days. And the glow in Lionel's eyes had better be for me. I'm going to grab all opportunities that come my way.

Slow down, Paul. Slow down. You have no certitude Lionel's gay. It's the beginning of 2012, a new year. Don't start it with wild speculations. Change the topic. Write your journal. I begin writing, an account of the major blows I received in 2011.

Halfway through the writing Jay comes to the door of my bedroom. "Sorry. Saw your light on. Didn't know you were writing your journal."

I close the journal and place it beside me on the bed. He's still standing in the doorway. "Come in." I point to the armchair at the foot of my bed.

He wrinkles his forehead and tosses his head to the left. Hesitating.

"It's all right. I'm not sleepy." I pile the pillows up to a more upright position.

He sits and we are silent. To break it, I tell him about my decision to phone Daddy.

"He'll be surprised and pleased. They've probably just gone to bed, after coming home from Watch Night Service."

"I won't know what to say to him."

"Ask him how the rainstorm that washed out the bridges and destroyed several homes affected him. Ask him if the bridges have been rebuilt, what crops he's growing, what sort of prices he's getting for them, what politics is like in St. Vincent these days. And don't forget to ask how his wife is."

"What's her name again?"

"Beulah."

"Not an easy name to remember."

"For Evangelicals, it is." He sings: "Oh, Beulah land, Sweet Beulah land!/ Upon the highest mound I stand./ I look away across the seas/ Where mansions are prepared for me,/ And view the shining glory shore:/ My heaven, my home forever more."

"After all these years—you were eight when you left his home —you remember that!"

He shrugs. "Maybe I heard Ma singing it years later."

"What else can you tell me about Mrs. Beulah?"

"She cooks a wicked goat stew."

"Beulah. Goat stew."

"She made ginger tea for me, to prevent me from catching cold."

"Ginger tea against catching cold." I pull out the drawer of my night table and take out a writing pad and make a note of all this.

"This will be his happiest New Year in a long time."

"Really?"

"Paul, he no longer asks me about you. It's too painful. I'm sure he blames himself."

"Then maybe I shouldn't phone him. It might bring back bad memories."

Jay shakes his head vigorously. "The exact opposite. If I know my father, he's praying to God for this."

"How do you know that?"

"I know my father."

"And if he starts talking to me about religion?"

"He won't. He knows Grama raised us to question it. If he were talking to Ma, he would. With us, no. He knows you were laughing at him when he tried to talk to you about it. He told me so. He'd be so glad you're making the contact; he won't do anything to jeopardize it. And if he begins to talk religion, just say it's a topic you're not interested in. Daddy has come a long way. Suffering has taught him a thing or two about his limits and maybe what God won't do for him."

After that we fall into silence. I feel my eyes closing over. The phone call will have to be made tomorrow.

Jay says goodnight and leaves.

$$\cancel{} 11$$

LIONEL LEFT TWENTY minutes ago. Jay is washing the dishes. Don't know why he didn't just put them in the dishwasher. Old habits, I guess. He's humming "What shall I do, dear Lionel, dear Lionel" and turning his head around to glance at me, sitting at the dining table.

The joke's on me all right. Lionel came around 6:30 pm. For the first time I saw that his gut overhangs his belt, that he walks with a roll, and what with his bow legs, it gives him a kind of Roly-Poly look. Made me desire him even more. While we ate and drank the bubbly that I'd insisted Jay get, Lionel, Mr. Talkative who visited me at the hospital, became Mr. Taciturn. If he'd already seen the painting that I got from Bill—the one of three naked full-sized males: Asian, African, European, with intertwining bodies—I would have attributed his reaction to that, but it's on the wall facing the bathroom so it won't be in people's faces. If I'd had some place where I could put Bill's penis sculpture—Bill offered it to Jay, but he didn't want it—I might have displayed it where Lionel could see it, just to get his reaction. Maybe he disliked the food. I couldn't read Jay's thoughts from his facial expressions. Even when Jay put the platter of chicken, steeped in lemon and ginger for my benefit, and I explained that I'm now able to tolerate chicken, he merely nodded. By the time we got around to dessert, a Black-Forest cake that Jay bought, I was beginning to wonder whether he thought we were doing this to entrap him.

After dessert he opened up a little. Took all that time for the bubbly to reach his brain. We went to sit in the living room, Jay and he on the sofa, I on the armchair, so I could observe his body language.

I decided to force the issue. "I'm kind o' surprised," I said, "that you didn't bring your partner. Is she your wife, your girlfriend?"

Lionel looked at me with a squint. "Does the term matter?"

I shrugged.

"Perhaps we have an open relationship."

"Meaning?"

Jay gave me a *don't-probe* glare.

"She sleeps with whom she wants and I with whom I want."

"O-o-kay," I heard myself saying.

"You don't seem comfortable with that."

Fixing me with his sternest stare, his look telling me not to prolong this, Jay said: "We hold the view that all humans are unique and must tailor their lives to suit their needs."

"You sound like a professor." He chuckled. "So you think it's a question of need, huh?"

"Guess so," I said.

Lionel guffawed. "The woman's my sister, my only sibling. Her name's Muriel."

He must have heard the rush of air coming out of me, but nothing in his body language implied it.

"You two must have an excellent relationship?" I said.

"The best there could be. We've always got along well. I am four years older. Mother, Dad, and I always thought her behaviour was perfect, and then when she was on the cusp of nineteen she did something that sent us into shock." He stopped talking and we waited.

"What did she do?" I asked.

Jay tore his eyes at me, and I shrugged to let him know I didn't care.

"It's all right. It's not a secret. In the end everything worked out all right." He paused and then added: "It could have been catastrophic though. Our lives could have become entangled with the law."

Jay looked over at me. I knew what he was thinking. I hoped he wouldn't start blabbering: we had a similar problem with Paul.

Lionel scratched his temple. "It was a Tuesday in February. I was sharing an apartment in the McGill ghetto with a friend from high school days. It was my turn to cook that day and I was preparing spaghetti, when the phone rang and Mother asked me if I was free and could come over right away. Something had happened but she didn't want to discuss it on the phone. I turned off the stove and left a note for Gene. I took a taxi to my parents' house in Pierrefonds.

"I met Mother with her back leaning against the kitchen counter and crying. I went to her, put my arms around her, and asked what was wrong. All sorts of scenarios were playing in my head, that Dad had died of a heart attack or had a stroke or an accident. Never once did I think it concerned Muriel.

"'Take a look in Muriel's room.'

"I went, holding my breath. Apart from the bare mattress, nothing registered. I went to her clothes closet and opened it. It was empty. I returned to the kitchen and put my arm around Mother. 'Did she leave a note?'

"Mother shook her head.

"'Was there some sort of quarrel with you?'

"She shook her head.

"'With Dad?'

"'None that I know of.'

"'Should we call the police?'

"'Not yet.'

"'Does Dad know?'

"She shook her head. 'He'll find out when he comes.'

"Mother was no stranger to children running away. She was, still is, a social worker with Batshaw Youth Services.

"Phones with caller IDs were then the new gadget, and my parents had one. Cell phones were already popular, but Muriel didn't have one. I got a sheet of paper, went to the phone, and began to record all the numbers in it. There was a 937 number that stood out from the suburban numbers, but there was no name attached to it. Of course, Muriel was at Vanier at the time, so it could have been one of her friends from school. I dialled the number and asked to speak to Muriel. 'Muriel!' a gruff voice with a Caribbean-Canadian accent said. 'Who's calling?'

"'An ex-boyfriend.'

"'How you get this number?'

"'From the police. I am her brother. Tell her to get in touch with us before the police come to get her.' There was a long silence.

"'All right. I will give her your message.'

"Muriel phoned ten minutes later, just as Dad was walking in the door. He listened in on what Mother was saying. Dad hung up his coat, came and stood beside Mother, and put his arm around her. Unusual for him. Goes with his occupation. He's an accountant. When Mother hung up the phone, she motioned to Dad to sit down. We all sat down and talked about what happened. Dad had this sort of agreement, linked to his insurance policy, where he could consult a lawyer for general advice. He called the number. The person at the other end told him that Muriel was no longer a minor and, beyond persuading her to return home, there was nothing he could do.

"Over Mother's objections Dad decided to phone the police. An officer, quite young, bilingual, French Canadian came to the house. Dad gave him the telephone number. He ran it through their system. He stared at Mother and Dad and he said: 'I'm going to give you some information that I shouldn't. If you repeat it I'll deny that I ever told you. It's as a father that I'm telling you this, not as a policeman.' He told us that the telephone number belonged to a drug dealer who was under their surveillance. He gave us the address where the boyfriend lived: Lincoln, two buildings in from here. 'Try to get hold of your daughter and persuade her to leave. Anything could happen to her.'

"Mother. What a woman! 'Jim,' she told my father, 'we must pretend we're not angry with her. At her age the sex hormones are calamitous. We'll tell her we're glad she has found a boyfriend, but that there was no need to break with us in the way that she did. And we must invite the boyfriend for supper.' Dad got furious. 'I don't want any drug dealer in my house: sitting at *my* table, eating *my* food. No sir. I don't know how many people he already killed.' Mother asked: 'So how do you plan to get Muriel out of his clutches?' He hung his head, hunched over, swallowed, and his eyes filled. 'Juliet, I don't know. I don't know.' His voice choked. Mother looked at me sitting on her right—she and Dad were sitting at the far ends of the dining table—'Jim, you can't catch flies with vinegar.' Dad straightened up, and looked at her with his palms up, facing her, 'Okay, you handle it.' He's always good that way. Both of them in fact. They adopt the better solution, regardless of who proposed it.

"The following Saturday we waited to meet her and the boyfriend, but Muriel came alone. She said something came up and Ronnie couldn't come.

"We frowned at her. 'Ronnie,' Dad said, 'since when his name became Ronnie?'

"We later found out he'd told her not to give our parents his real name. The false name was the cue Mother needed. She took Muriel into her bedroom. They remained in there for more than an hour and when they came out, they were both crying. She never returned to his apartment. He was killed two months later by a rival. She later confessed that if I had not mentioned the police in my phone call, Hilcox —his real name—would have kept her from communicating with us. 'You mean until you recovered your senses?' Mother said.

"'My senses. I don't know about that. I was like hypnotized. You broke it the Saturday I came home. Know why he didn't come? The area north and west of Décarie is no-man's land for him.'

"I said: 'Muriel, you mean, you knew he was a pusher and you still moved in with him?'

"She shrugged. 'You don't understand.'" He paused. "I think my sister has issues with her body."

Who doesn't?

He was silent for a while. He resumed: "Our already close relationship became closer. Three months later, just after she began university, I had my diagnosis. She, Mother, and Dad were there for me all the way. When I wanted to give up, I remembered how much they wanted me to live. For three years I underwent radiation and chemo. I don't want to remember how miserable those years were. The tumour would shrink almost to nothing, our hopes would rise, and then it would start growing again, sometimes to the point of paralysing me for brief moments. Then it shrank and stopped growing indefinitely. Touch wood."

There was a long silence.

"So how come Muriel's living with me? She did two degrees in political and social thought at McGill, and, after short stints working for politicians and their aides, she became discouraged. Mother and I told her she shouldn't force herself to do work she hated. When she asked us what then, Mother told her to find out what she really enjoyed doing and to let her know. She opted for social work and returned to university. She lives at my place. I'm just a three-minute walk from the Prefontaine Metro station, a short commute to McGill. Mother and Dad help her with her other expenses. She's doing her last courses in social work. She'll graduate this June."

He got up to go to the bathroom. The light in the corridor leading to it was on. He'd see the painting. I waited for the toilet to flush. Then he came out and stood at the door gazing at the painting.

He came back, looked at his watch, thanked us for inviting him, said the next time we'll come to his place, and left. Not a word about the painting. My body felt as if anaesthetized. As soon as he was out the door, Jay began to laugh, and if I had the energy to do it, I would have hit him.

→ Jay wipes his hands, hangs the dishtowel on the towel bar of the stove, and turns to face me. The smirk returns to his face. I raise my right hand, a plea for him to stop it.

He sits down at the other end of the table. My mind turns to Muriel's story. I wonder what Lionel would think if he found out I'd been a pusher.

I decide to be mischievous. "Jay, you're bi, why don't you make a go at Muriel and leave Lionel for me?"

He looks at me and raises his right hand slightly aft, palm facing me — his gesture for: that does not deserve an answer.

"You're a noble soul, Jay. Even if she turns out to be ugly that shouldn't deter you. Wonder what issues she has with her body. Guess I shouldn't be talking. I only have to smell food to gain weight."

"If Lionel wants you, he has a unique way of showing it."

"Don't take me seriously. I'm just trying to hold myself together."

He gets up, frowns, then sits back down.

My body feels as if encased in lead. I struggle to my feet, go to my room, and drop onto the bed. I haven't even the energy to clean my teeth. For a while I lie there examining the scenarios I'd woven from caprice and need. If he invites us to his place, I won't go. Jay could go if he wants to. It would be too painful. He might even fall for Muriel. What made me think Lionel was gay? Maybe he's uncomfortable with being so. Stared at the painting and didn't utter a single comment. *Because he didn't have hiccups over you doesn't mean he isn't gay.* Well, I wanted him to have hiccups over me, and he didn't. So even if he's gay, straight, bi, lesbian or transgendered, it still doesn't matter. Times like these I wish I could be like Gúicho—put him on the spot, at the very least ask him what his sexual orientation is.

I feel better now and become hyperconscious about my dirty teeth, especially given the poor state of my immune system. Dr. Cantor warned me against gum infection. I go to the bathroom and brush them. On the way back, I knock on Jay's door and enter. He's propped up in bed reading.

"Boy, wasn't that a downer. I feel better now." It's all I want to say. I return to my bedroom, get into bed, pull the covers over me, and hope I fall quickly into a deep sleep without nightmares.

≫⫶ 11

THE NOISE OF water running in the kitchen wakes me. It's still dark outside. I look over at the clock radio and see that it's 5:16. Jay must have had trouble sleeping. I'm usually awake long before him. In fact this is just about the right time for me. I get out of bed, put on a dressing gown, and walk to the kitchen. He's standing there waiting for the microwave to finish what he has in it, most likely tea.

"Sorry. The noise woke you."

I shake my head. "You know I'm usually awake around this time." I rarely sleep for more than five continuous hours.

"I'm going to feel miserable today," Jay says. "My body is sluggish when it doesn't get seven hours. I awoke from a nightmare. I'm at a party. It looks like your friend Gina's apartment. Gina and Emilia are there. Lionel, Carlos, Bill, Wendell, Jonathan, Gúicho, and you are there too. In the dream it seems as if there's a relationship between you and Lionel because you are threatening Wendell with an empty wine bottle. Then the rest becomes confused because Ma enters and asks what's going on in her house. I remember thinking to myself, but this is Gina's apartment. How Ma could be saying it's her house? Then, you leave Wendell and begin to head for Ma with the bottle raised above your head. I try to get to you and the effort awakens me."

"Interesting." I think about the dream then tell him: "It's your fear that I might get emotionally worked up over Lionel and suffer for it. Somewhere in there is your own discomfort with your sexuality. It's why Ma enters the dream and makes the claim. Her house probably means our bodies."

He purses his lips in protest but says nothing.

"Jay, did you ever discuss your sexual orientation with Ma?"

"Yes and no."

"What does that mean?"

"Just what I said. When your friendship began to develop with Bill, she became worried that there was something going on between the two of you. You can't blame her, Paul. Evangelicals are taught that gays are pedophiles who lure young people into homosexuality. They even have a name for it: 'the homosexual agenda' and a spurious text circulating, supposedly penned by gays, about their plan to turn all of humanity gay. They have to believe that nonsense otherwise their theology would unravel."

"Explain."

"You know the story of Zacharias? Christ told him he should be born again, meaning that everything sinful would be cleansed out of him. Daddy used to say it's like gold that's heated till it melts and all the impurities in it are burned away. I used to think it meant that when people got saved their insides glowed red-hot. Evangelicals believe that we're gay because we reject their 'offer of salvation.' It's why they go to such extremes to exhibit gays who claim they're born again and that it made them straight—the Exodus boondoggle."

I nod.

"It's easier for them to declare war on us than to revise their theology."

"Makes me think of Galileo. Forced by the Catholic Church to say the sun revolves around the earth and put under house arrest for the rest of his life ... So you're saying Ma believed that gobbledygook?"

He nods twice and takes a sip of his tea.

"What exactly did you tell her?"

"I told her I didn't think you were gay, but that if you were and had a relationship with Bill, you were old enough to make that decision."

"And she didn't have a heart attack?" I chuckle.

"Next she asked: 'And what about you?' I think it was your taunts, the sermons she was hearing in church, and Harper's statements about undoing same-sex marriage legislation—remember all those ads opposing same-sex marriage that his party put in *ethnic* newspapers?"

I nod. "So what you told her?"

"I said I didn't know. She did a lot of wincing during that talk. I told her that any religion that taught her that she should reject her children for whatever reason wasn't worth belonging to."

"How did she respond?"

"I don't remember. The subject never came up again."

"Maybe it was then that her heart began to fail. Just kidding."

We fall silent. He leans with his back to the kitchen counter. I make tea in the microwave and we go to the dining table and sit there with just the kitchen light on.

"How old would Grama be if she were still alive?" I ask.

"She was born in 1935. Seventy-six."

"July 22 this year she would have been seventy-seven."

"She wasn't quite twenty-one when Ma was born."

"Seventy-six. That's not old. Looks like we'll have short lives. Both Grama and her mother had strokes and died kind o' young. Ma was what, fifty?"

He nods. "Her mother's stroke was caused by an accident, so it doesn't count."

When I gave Mbolo, Boodhoo, and Olinski the family's medical history, I'd forgot that bit about my maternal great-grandmother."

"There's Daddy. He's alive. He's sixty-five, looks older, but as far as I know, he's in good health."

"When's his birthday?"

"March 16."

"You must remind me. We'll both call and wish him a happy birthday. I'm glad I called him on New Year's Day. Do you call him on his birthday?"

"Yes."

"How come you never told me?" His back is against the light and I can't see his face, but I'm sure the V is stamped in the middle of his forehead.

He breathes loud. "I don't know."

I want to hear what he thinks. But it's another one of those truths I won't get out of him, so I drop it. "We're all of a sudden obsessed with family. These last three months I've thought more about St. Vincent than I have in all the other fourteen years here put together."

"It's normal. You're trying to understand what has shaped you. Now that you're writing. As you create your characters, you probably can't help reflecting on what has shaped your own."

"That's good." I shake my head, impressed. My mind returns to his nightmare. "That nightmare, Jay, don't attach too much import-ance to it. It's just your unconscious trying to deal with situations and people we've encountered. I'm not going to pursue Lionel. For a while there I got carried away. If ever I invite him here again, he wouldn't be the only guest. Maybe he's like you, afraid to trust his instincts."

"Not that again, not today. I'm going back to bed to see if I can get a bit more sleep. Maybe I shouldn't be having this tea."

"Ah, but we had a great conversation."

He gets up. I remain seated at the table.

When he closes the bedroom door, I turn on the light over the dining table, then walk over to my bookcase for Caryl Phillips' *New World Order*, which I started reading two days ago. I fall upon his essay on Marvin Gaye. I read about Marvin's cross-dressing father, Marvin's own cross-dressing, his five gay paternal uncles. There's enough in the essay to imply that Marvin's father fought body and soul to avoid being the sixth gay brother, and in the end the price was horrific: he murdered his son. Even his God betrayed him. The infor-mation sets me hyperventilating, and I have to go get my puffer in my bedroom. I never thought it was possible to have that many gays in the same family. We will never know the full facts of why Marvin's father killed him. I'm sure too that his father didn't know.

For the first time I wonder if lurking in me somewhere is the feeling that it's wrong for Jay and me to be gay. One of us would have been okay. But two, that's too much. I remember the story about the three Mohawk brothers, one of whom worked with Ma, another who was found murdered in a parking lot. I felt theirs was a unique situa-tion. And yet I was pleased when I found out Jay wasn't altogether hetero. I don't know how strong his feelings for women are. With Tamara he came even before he could enter her. I'm sure he regrets telling me this. I'd spiked his wine with vodka before asking him. Since then, I haven't been able to get him to drink more than half a glass of wine. Wonder what would happen when he does eventually go with a man. His story about Kwame tells me he's definitely attracted to men, until then I had doubts. At one level I'm glad Ma and Grama aren't here for us to have to explain anything to them. I wonder if Jay told me the truth regarding what he told Ma. Could he endure displeasing her?

This one essay's enough. I haven't the energy to continue reading. I return to bed, and my mind drifts from subject to subject, image to image, and settles on Lionel's contemplation of "Three Men." I wish he'd commented. I think his silence means he disapproves. Maybe he's just being coy or behaving like some fucking prima donna. I catch hold of myself and tell myself to change the subject. It would help if I read something that takes my mind away from this. I return to my bookcase and take down volume three of *La Calle Donde Tú Vives*, fiction inspired by Guatemalan folklore.

⁂ 13

I PLOP DOWN on the couch. I have a quick decision to make. Ran into Prof. Bram this morning at the foot of the escalators on the ground floor of Concordia's Hall Building. At Bram's side a youngster the colour of cork, about seven, with a huge semi-Caucasian Afro. I asked the youngster his name. He said Fyodor, and I remembered Bram vaguely talking about the depth of intellect in Dostoyevsky's novels even as he decried Dostoyevsky volubility.

"My son," Bram said and gave me an evaluating stare.

"Oh." I pretended I didn't know about him, and held back from asking how old Fyodor was.

"So you're about to become a published writer."

I looked at him puzzled that he would know that.

"I have my sources."

Fyodor looked up at him, seemingly impatient to move on, but Bram didn't notice.

"There's something I've been meaning to talk to you about. It has been on my mind since last semester. By the way, how's your health?"

"Fine, I think. It's why I've resumed classes."

"Good because your studies are what I want to talk to you about. Bill asked me to."

He must have seen the surprise in my face because he slowly nodded while staring into my eyes. "Do you have classes this afternoon?"

I shook my head.

"Then come and see me between two and two-thirty. Hope no students would be blocking the doors. Stupidest decision ever. Stupid strategy, this strike. Hurting themselves. Most of them don't want to be in classes anyway. They should go to classes and refuse to pay tuition next semester and show up for classes. You go on strike when you can bring the company to its knees."

I went off to the cafeteria wondering what Bill had discussed with him. I never thought Bill and he would have spoken about me. Then again, knowing Bill, I was sure he wanted to know how I was doing in my courses. I don't expect professors, except maybe those in law — most people in fact — to respect the niceties of confidentiality. *My studies.* What did he want to tell me about them? My grades are good, so it can't be about that. My lowest grade was A- and it was in one of the two courses I took with him. In that course, most of his students got C.

Around 2:20, half a dozen students held placards at the Maisonneuve entrance to the Hall Pavilion. When I got to his office, the latest number of *Bacchus* was on his desk and open at the page announcing the upcoming authors. With his index finger on the information, he said: "That's my source. Congrats. It's hard for beginning writers to get published." He was suddenly so human I was taken aback.

He pulled open a drawer of his desk, took out a manila envelope. "This is an application for the graduate program here." He stopped talking and looked at me for about ten seconds. I was too surprised to say anything.

"I want you to fill it out this evening and take it to the faculty of graduate studies no later than tomorrow. Bill asked me to push you to continue your studies, to the point of getting a doctorate. There's a strong possibility you'll get a bursary — a few of your professors will lobby on your behalf; I've done the preliminary canvassing." He smiled, seemingly genuine. "Your professors like you. There'll be work too as a teaching assistant ... Bill said you have notions about only doing what you want, and all that jazz. But that's not how the world works, my boy. The lucky few drink watered wine. The majority drink water, and rarely of the best quality. You could be foolhardy and hope to earn a living from writing, but unless you're damn lucky, the luck of lottery winners, you won't make enough to pay bus fare, never mind food or rent. Bill told me too that you've inherited some money. That would be gone in ten to fifteen years. Sooner if you live comfortably."

I folded my arms and pressed them to my chest to cope with the surprise of having this sprung on me. I have had absolutely no plan to go to graduate school. My unique ambition has been to finish my courses and then work full time on my novel.

Bram remained silent, sometimes looking at me, sometimes at his desk: behaviour, now that I think of it, I wouldn't have ascribed to him. Until then my unique impression of him was that he was a bully—a vicious one since his weapons were language and grades—a clown, and an exhibitionist.

→ I unzip the section of my satchel where I put the application and put the envelope beside me on the sofa. Graduate school. I bite my nails. I love learning, no ifs and buts about that. I think and think and think about it, and chuckle to myself remembering "Miniver Cheevy." My mind goes back to high school, to my English, French, and history teachers, to the lecture Mrs. Bensemana gave me about not seeking valorization in sex. I wonder how they remember me today, or if they remember me. Mrs. Bensemana does. All right, I'll apply to grad school but with the condition that I choose what I'll study, and have time to finish my novel. If grad studies interfere with that, down the garbage chute grad studies will go.

The bursary would be nice. He touched on a sore spot. Wouldn't have thought Bill was discussing my business with him. Their friendship was closer than Bill let on. That or Bill flapped his mouth too much. The end-of-year investment statements have been coming in. They bring tepid news. In spite of loans and bursaries, from 2007 to now, I've burned through $76,000 of the principal and every cent of the earnings. And I can't blame it all on Carlos, and none of it was for Aunt Mercy's care. We couldn't bring the money we got for Grama's house and land here, so we've been using it to pay for her care. Jay and I will go to see her during spring break. We'd planned to go in December but my meningioma scuttled that. Jay uses his spring breaks to visit her. The last time he did she didn't remember him or who Grama was.

Bram's right. When I no longer have bursaries and have to repay the loans and live solely from this money, it will disappear like ice in summer. Like it or not I'll have to find supplementary income — or find a sugar daddy. I laugh. Even if I were so inclined, who'd want to pay for or play with my body?

I should talk to Jay about grad school. It's 4:17. He might not be home yet. My going might just be the jolt he needs to complete his doctorate and remove that thorn from my conscience. I go over to the armchair beside the telephone table. The message light on the phone is blinking. I see the number: Lionel's. Jay first. I dial. It rings and the voice mail comes on. While I'm telling him to call me, he picks up the receiver. I relate the events of the day — all except the bit about not being able to earn a living from writing — and ask him what I should do.

He's silent for a while, then asks: "What do *you* want to do?"

"I don't know."

"Come on, Paul. I seem to remember having a little brother who was always reading my textbooks sometimes even before I could get to them."

I chuckle. "Maybe that's because they weren't pushed on your little brother by some bully of a teacher."

"Paul, you know the answer. Why are you bothering to ask me?"

"What's the answer?"

"What would Grama have told you?"

"That's not fair. I never ask you, What would Ma think, even though I know that a lot of what you do even now is to please her."

"You're always saying that."

"If Jonathan were honest with you, he'd tell you the same thing. I'm sure he's bright enough to have figured that out."

"He told *you* so?"

"When the sneer he gives me for a smile becomes a genuine smile, I'll ask him."

"Grama and Ma are gone. Those two had their share of disagreements. Let's leave them alone. Sorry I mentioned Grama. Look, Paul, you're like Grama — oops, did I say Grama — she couldn't see a book without wanting to know what was in it, and neither can you. You'll be studying for as long as you have sight, and even if you didn't have sight, so get the diplomas that say so ... Paul, are you there?"

"All right. I'll fill out the application and take it in tomorrow." We hang up.

I press the listen button for Lionel's message. He asks me to call him either at home or on his cell. I call his cell first. It's turned off. I don't leave a message. I call his house. He answers and says he's having a party the Saturday before Valentine's day and Jay and I are invited. He pauses and adds: "You could bring along a couple, maybe even three or four of your gay friends. That would help to even out the number between gays and straights."

The receiver feels slippery as my hands begin to sweat.

"Are you there?"

"Yes. Yes."

"Anything wrong?"

"No. Nothing."

"Don't you and your boyfriend have gay friends?"

"You mean my ex-boyfriend?"

"What! You two have broken up!"

"What are you talking about, Lionel?"

"Isn't Jay your boyfriend?"

I laugh, and laugh and laugh, and each time I stop for breath and try to talk, I begin to laugh again. Finally, after a series of controlled breaths, I say: "Lionel, where on earth did you get that idea?"

For a while he's silent. "One of the nurses told me that your boyfriend brought you to the hospital in a coma and while doing routine tests on you they came upon your meningioma. Since you were the patient I assumed Jay was the boyfriend."

The word boyfriend sets me off again. I swallow and clear my throat. "Didn't we at any point in our conversation let you know that Jay and I are brothers? That's strange. We usually introduce each other as brothers. Only one person ever thought he was a lover I was passing off as a brother, and she meant it as a joke."

I hear his breathing. "Sorry for the misunderstanding. Now that I think about it, it's probably because they told me about the boyfriend but nothing about Jay."

"So you don't mind if we bring gay friends to the party. Does that mean you're gay too?"

"It doesn't mean anything. Call me back to tell me if you and Jay are coming and whether you're bringing any friends."

"Wait ..."

But the receiver clicks and I don't have the courage to dial his number again. I'm reminded of that woman in the film version of *For Colored Girls*—I don't know the actress's name, but she tells off the character played by Janet Jackson, who'd kept her waiting and then brushed her off with a curt no to her request for aid to her organization. Madam J, Gúicho, that woman, Grama—maybe—they all have an assertiveness that I lack. Back in high school, I used to think I had it but it was all bluster.

I have to talk to somebody. I dial Gina's number and hope she answers the phone. She does and I'm relieved, but says she can only give me ten minutes. I tell her what has just happened with Lionel.

She laughs. "He told you, 'It doesn't mean anything.' That's a strange answer. It means the guy's into playing games. Meatman, you have the hots for him. Fess up."

"A little."

"Take a purge. He'll fuck up your head. Life's too damn short. You know that better than me."

You can talk. You have Emilia. "Will you and Emilia come to the party?"

"I'm definitely curious to meet this guy who's about to hang you on his clothesline. I better come. I might have to unpin you. I'll mention it to Emilia. She didn't say she had anything planned."

"Oh, and by the way I'm applying to go to graduate school."

"Great. Now you're talking sense. You made a fool of yourself in high school. Alvin and I talk about it all the time. Now it's time to redeem yourself. I hate people—especially Black people—who waste their intellect. Now all you need is somebody to play with that lonely willy, but don't let desperation push you into doing anything stupid. Meatman, I have to go."

I dial Jay's number. The answering machine comes on, and I tell him to pick up the phone, that it's important. He does.

"Did you know that you and I were lovers?"

"How do you come up with such foolishness?" I hear the impatience in his voice.

"Lionel didn't think it was foolishness."

"Lionel. What's this with Lionel?"

"Jay, all this time he thought you and I were a couple." I relate the conversation I had with Lionel

"I'm speechless," he says. "Well, it's true that in appearance we don't look like brothers. I didn't think medical workers had the right to relay information like that."

"They don't, but they do, especially if they're homophobic."

"But if he thought we were lovers, why did he say we could bring our partners?"

"That's true. He did say that. He was playing games with us. Probably thought we were playing games too."

"I don't think I want to go to his party. You go. Take Carlos."

"I'll pretend I didn't hear that. I've already invited Gina and Emilia. I can't back out now. And if Lionel's interested in you?"

"That would be Lionel's problem."

"You exasperate me."

"Can't help it. I have to go. Have a lot of reading to do for a class tomorrow." He hangs up.

I sit for a few minutes, then get up and pace, and a weight of aloneness comes upon me. I was not born to be alone. Yes, Gina, I want someone to play with my willy, and other parts of me too. I envy Jay his self-sufficiency, though sometimes I think it's a mask. Even Grama, strong as she was, opted not to be alone. As I work on establishing her character, I've been puzzling over her relationship with Aunt Mercy. It would be too simple to say it was a covert lesbian relationship. I still don't understand how and why they got along so well. In everything they were opposites. Never saw Aunt Mercy reading anything.

Not even sure she could read. She held all the superstitious beliefs that Grama rejected, but that didn't seem to bother Grama. I used to think their relationship began on a servant-employer basis. But it started before Granddad's death. Granddad would have sooner sent Grama out to work as a domestic and demanded her wages so he could invest them. Aunt Mercy did the domestic tasks, not because Grama told her to, but like a regular member of the household. If there was something on TV that Aunt Mercy wanted to watch, and it was near supper time, Grama took over the preparations.

I can only speculate that she became the sister Grama never had. Jay thinks so too. And, like healthy sisters, they took each other's strengths and weaknesses in stride, and shielded each other from loneliness. Maybe that's why Lionel has Muriel living with him. And had Gene, the roommate, during his days at McGill. *Roommate, my eye. His boyfriend.* I'll get around to finding out about him. I'll pretend I forgot his name when I bring it up. Would be a way to get him to name others, if there are others.

"Uh, that fellow you shared an apartment with — forgot his name ..."

"You mean Gene?"

And I shaking my head, "Gene, Gene? Name doesn't ring a bell."

"Michael?"

Headshake.

"Bing."

Headshake.

Even now the goose-bumps are rising.

Jealousy will undo you, Paul.

If I mention this to Jay, he'd advise me to go see a psychiatrist.

14

I CAN'T BELIEVE it has happened. It's a little past 5 a.m. and sleep has abandoned me. The hot shower I took after Bernard left is partly to blame. Anyway it's Sunday. I have some choral hydrate left over. I could take one and unplug the telephones. Hope it won't dull my concentration. I have to prepare for my exam on Wednesday. Anyone who desperately wants to leave a message can leave it on my cell.

This has been quite a week. After you've been subjected to bad news for a long time it's as if you have to reset your body's receptors for good news. My check-up, this past Tuesday, shows that my immune system is back to normal, and there's not even a hint of adverse activity in my brain. "Everything is healed." Mbolo had to tap me on the shoulder to get a response. Olinski stared across at me silently. Boodhoo was absent. Finally it registered. I'm fine for now and could plan for the future. Even if there are relapses, as happened with Lionel, I know they won't necessarily be fatal or incurable.

At Lionel's place tonight. I ate like a pig. Sampled everything except the seafood. Freedom to eat.

Wouldn't mind getting a place like his. Has the middle floor of an older triplex, those built at a time when French Canadians had large families. It's sparsely furnished with a combined living and dining room that has windows on two sides and a fireplace in the inner wall. Painted in pale beige with varnished doors and baseboards. Kept thinking, Jay should have bought something like this instead of that cell in the beehives real estate developers now throw together; they begin to fall apart before you move in.

I got to Lionel's place around ten. There were six guests. Jay, Gina, and Emilia weren't among them. I wasn't sure Jay was coming. Earlier I'd cussed him out and hung up the phone on him when he said he didn't feel like going. Gina and Emilia arrived just before eleven. Gina said they went to see a film at the LGBT Afro-Caribbean Film Festival. I didn't know one was on. She seemed surprised when I said so. "Jay and Jonathan were there."

The bastard! Jonathan probably told him not to invite me.

"So what did you two see?"

"*Être Noir et homosexuel.* I think that was the title. Emilia, what was the title of the other one?"

"*Leave It on the Floor.*"

"Don't know about being black and homosexual. It was too short. Eight minutes. It gives the impression that all Blacks are homophobes and use religion to justify their homophobia. It's not fair. Take my father, for example; besides, I've seen a whole series of articles in *Montreal Community Contact* written by straight people condemning homophobia."

"And the other film?"

"Great," Emilia said. "Superb dancing and singing."

"Great themes too: solidarity among the down and out, honest expression of feelings. Burning off your frustrations in dance and performance. What else?"

"Forgiveness," Emilia said.

⇥ All evening I had the feeling Lionel was avoiding me. I'd try to talk to him and he'd shuffle off to do something. In the end I gave up.

Muriel was something of a surprise. Given Lionel's bulk, I didn't expect her to be thin, but I didn't think she'd be obese. *I think she has issues with her body,* Lionel's statement came back to me. She was dressed in silk, black pants and a loose black top. It made no difference. She moved as if her haunches and legs were a pedestal and the upper part of her body were loaded with springs. I wondered if she was already like this when she ran off at nineteen. She and I chitchatted and she introduced me to Bernard, a Rwandan she'd met at McGill. He's an information technology specialist. I got her to talk with Emilia because of their interest in social work and moved away when they began discussing job prospects in the area.

When Jay arrived, Bernard was telling me about his hobby: painting. It was almost midnight. Most of the food was gone, not that that would bother Jay. I excused myself from Bernard, met Jay at the door, and began upbraiding him for not telling me about the film festival.

"Get down from your high horse. I didn't know about it either. Jonathan phoned to tell me about it right after you hung up the phone on me. We got there just as the film was beginning."

"So why are you arriving so late? It's disrespectful, you know. You shouldn't have bothered to come."

"You just want something to quarrel about. Who's the fellow you were talking with?"

"We'll get around to that. Why didn't you bring Jonathan?"

"He didn't want to come. That fiasco with Wendell is still affecting him."

"And so it should."

"Who's the fellow you were talking with?"

"Muriel is waiting to take your coat." She was at a respectful distance from us and must have known we were quarrelling.

He gave her his coat.

"Go greet Lionel, grab some of what's left, and come back and I'll introduce you." I left him at the door and returned to talk with Bernard. Gina wandered by and whispered in my ear: "Looks like you've found yourself a man," slapped me on the back, and began moving on. I grabbed her arm and told her to meet Bernard. Bernard's barely taller than I and skinny. Gaunt. Don't think he could get skinnier and still be healthy. He wore a dark green shirt. Inside its sleeves his arms looked like twigs. The shirt pleated excessively where it was tucked into his skin-tight jeans — poor choice, I thought: they accentuated his bone-thin legs. He looked like he had been flattened and the sides shaved off. He reeked of cologne.

Jay came back, and I said: "Honestly you shouldn't have bothered to come at this late hour."

"I was afraid if I didn't my brother might make a fool of himself."

"That's the most pathetic joke I've ever heard."

Bernard looked from him to me and back again and started to move off. I held his sleeve. "He's my uptight brother. You can stay. Bernard, Jay." They shook hands.

Jay hung around for a minute or so and looked uncomfortable before drifting off again to the food table, where Lionel joined him. They moved into the kitchen, which was hidden from view, and I lost sight of him until I was ready to leave. He was in the kitchen chatting with Lionel when I told him that Bernard was going to drop me home. The open V registered above his nose and his eyes arched.

I turned my head away and said: "He lives in Burgundy, Jay." I looked at my watch and saw that it was 1:17. "I've already missed the last metro." I watched his Adam's apple as he swallowed. I knew the warning that would be in his eyes so I avoided them.

Bernard waited for me at the door while I went over to Gina and Emilia to say goodbye.

When I bent over to kiss Gina, she said: "Seems like you've found yourself some not so *tenderloin*."

"It's only a lift, Gina."

"Then make sure that what's lifted gets put in a *safe* place. And please, don't break any teeth on that jerky."

Now it occurs to me that Jay was talking with Lionel from the time he arrived.

Don't go there, Paul.

But I have to. He prefers Jay over me. The bastard!

Yeah, but you got Bernard.

Some consolation prize. Hope he's no bullshitter. At least we exchanged phone numbers and he wants me to go see an exhibition with him at the Museum of Fine Arts on Saturday. I cross my fingers. Wonder what this twig of a man sees in me. I'm sure he weighs not a gram more than 50kg, if that much. Whatever it is, it better be more than a one-night stand. I better stop being so hepped up about him. One orgasm does not a marriage make.

Now my mind turns to Jay and I have an image of his body

encircled by Lionel's huge arms while he sleeps peacefully. I'm the one sleep has abandoned. Jealousy surges through me. I wonder what kind of sex they had. I'm sure it wasn't vanilla. Lionel's no neophyte.

Your imagination's controlling you. Get up, take a choral hydrate, and unplug the telephones.

25

JAY'S VOICE IS calling out to me from a ridge on the opposite side of a valley. I try to see where he is, but there's no sign of him. The call comes again. I open my eyes. Slowly the fog of sleep clears, and I see him standing in the doorway of my bedroom. Something about his posture and his face tells me he's in distress.

"I tried phoning you several times, but got no answer."

Quickly the events of the night return: the party, Bernard, Lionel. "Had trouble falling asleep. Took sleep medication and unplugged the phones." I wait for him to speak.

He says nothing.

"Well, what's so urgent?" *Did Lionel break your heart? Last night you two seemed to be everything except married.*

He remains unresponsive for about fifteen seconds. "Paul, Aunt Mercy died around two this morning. Daddy phoned to tell me. I left several messages on your cell."

"Aunt Mercy died. Damn it! Why didn't you phone me at home right away?" *I'm glad you didn't.* "You said Daddy phoned to tell you. How did he know?"

"Paul, you get on my nerves sometimes. Daddy and Beulah, I put them in charge of her. Remember spring break 2009? I wanted you to go with me to see her. You took Carlos to Miami. I told you when I got back, and you didn't respond."

I don't remember the conversation ever taking place.

"While I was waiting for you to return my call I booked our passages online. You and I have to be at the airport at five tomorrow morning."

"I can't. I have an exam on Wednesday morning. Have you paid for the tickets yet?"

"No. I have to pay by the latest 6 p.m., an hour from now."

"When's the funeral?"

"Thursday."

"Make it Friday, so I can write my exam and have enough time to make it home. I might just be able to find a late evening flight on Wednesday. If not I'll come on Thursday. When did you book the return for?"

"Sunday. I have to teach early Monday morning."

I remember my date with Bernard on Saturday. Why did she have to die now?

"It would be nice if we arrived home together. I felt awkward when I arrived home with Ma's ashes and you weren't there."

The blow connects. For a while we say nothing. "Tell you what, Jay. Make the departure for Tuesday. Tomorrow, I'll arrange something with my prof. Keep the burial for Thursday and let's return on Friday."

He shakes his head. "I'll be too tired. You can arrange to come back on Friday if you want."

One half of my brain tells me the dead are already dead and shouldn't muck up the plans of the living. The other half reproaches me. My full bladder feels as if it's about to burst. I get out of bed and head to the bathroom. While in there I think more calmly. The date with Bernard will have to go. If he doesn't understand why, he's not worth going after. It seems so logical, why didn't I think of it before? When I get out of the bathroom I meet Jay sitting at the dining table. "Okay," I say, "let's make the departure Tuesday and the return Saturday."

"Thought you'd wanted to spend some time with Daddy?"

"We could do that on Friday."

He nods.

"How much do I owe you for the ticket?"

"Nothing. Grama took out a $20,000 insurance policy for her. It will more than cover all the costs."

"Who's making the funeral arrangements?"

"Daddy."

"Where are you burying her?"

"In the Kirton plot."

"In the Kirton plot!"

"What's your objection?"

"Just that ...

"*Just that* what?

"Forget it. People will talk."

"What will people say?"

"You know the lesbian stuff ... Ma Kirton, her husband, and her lesbian lover in the same space. I can just hear the comments, the jokes that Sefus and others will invent. Some calypsonian might even take it up. Remember the calypso last year about the guy who raped a sheep?"

He closes his eyes and waves his arm dismissively. "Let people say or sing what they want. Remember Aesop's fable about the boy, the man, and the donkey?"

I nod.

"She was baptized Methodist, so I told Daddy to contact the Methodist minister. Go make yourself some coffee, two cups: one for me too. After that we'll put the obit together."

While emptying the dregs of yesterday's coffee I ask him what time he got the phone call.

"Shortly after 3 a.m."

"Stop me if you think I'm prying. What time did you get in?"

"2:10 thereabouts."

"Alone?"

The V and tri-frown come, along with his squinting eyes. "You're funny."

"Well, you and Lionel were closer than two dogs coupling."

His cheeks balloon and his eyes are squeezed shut. He's offended. But I press on. "Can't blame me for thinking you spent the night in his arms."

"You're blurring the lines between reality and the fiction you're writing."

I know he won't ask me about Bernard. Too credulous to think beyond what I told him when Bernard and I were leaving.

After I've set the coffee brewing, I lean against the kitchen counter and look across at him. The thought comes to me that the people who shaped our lives are going. Have almost all gone in my case, since Daddy doesn't really count. I wonder how Jay feels about Aunt Mercy. I don't always know when his actions are out of love or out of duty. Once dementia struck her, I couldn't relate to her. Jay had to remind me to call her. Sometimes I did and sometimes I couldn't stand it, especially when she no longer knew what to do with the telephone. Her caretaker would hold the phone to her ear and she'd mumble incoherently at first. Eventually nothing that made sense came from her. I feel the tears coursing down my cheeks, not because she's dead: she's eighty-three or eighty-four; but because of the state of her life for the last four years — our helplessness in the face of fate.

I wonder if Jay feels this to the same degree that I do. Maybe he needs a life-threatening experience ... Getting malaria is the worst thing that ever happened to him. Some days I feel like worshipping him, other days like making him disappear from my life. Right now it's neither. I pour the two cups of coffee and take them to the table and go in search of my laptop so we can write the obit.

FEBRUARY 19. Back home in Montreal. Home: ambiguous word that. Depends on where I am. Nice to leave with above-zero temperatures and return to above-zero temperatures. It's 6:10 a.m. and still dark outside.

I'm tired. Must be the travel, the ordeal my body has just come through, and the momentous developments of this week. I should remain in bed, but Bernard wants me to meet him for brunch at the West Indian restaurant near Atwater and Notre Dame. I can't say no to that. I'd have preferred an invitation from Lionel, but as Aunt Mercy would have said, I'll cut my cloth to suit my fit. Or maybe it's a case of when you can't do better, you say no matter.

Aunt Mercy's funeral was a routine, subdued event. And there was nothing unusual about St. Vincent, except that people were still talking about the piece of a Russian spacecraft that was discovered on one of the Tobago Cays back in December. It's the dry season, and Kingstown was dusty and dirty. The few garbage bins I saw were overflowing. Elsewhere Styrofoam and plastic were omnipresent. Literacy week was being celebrated by the ministry of education, and I wondered how they defined literacy. I don't doubt that many of those promoting it would fail. It would take more than talking—libraries in primary schools, and understanding culture to be more than carnival, steelband, and calypso—to transform St. Vincent from an oral to a literate society. I heard that when the community college was built, the plan didn't include a library.

In Havre all the talk was about Mother Bernice's funeral. She was buried two days before Aunt Mercy. The Vincentian media covered it and thousands of Spiritual Baptists from St. Vincent and even as far away as Trinidad and Barbados converged on Havre. It had to be held on the cricket grounds. Mr. Morris—he now has a fulltime caretaker but all his neurons are firing—said that her granddaughters and four great-grandchildren came from Canada to attend it. She had died suddenly. A granddaughter visiting her from Canada thought she had been in the bathroom for too long, went to check, and found her dead.

I was happy to see Marcella, Cousin Alice's caretaker. She gets more beautiful as she matures. She's now a senior civil servant. The tenants are all gone from the downstairs of Cousin Alice's house. Some of the walls have been knocked out and the space completely remodelled so Cousin Alice can move around in her motorized wheelchair. Her head droops over her lap and old age has scribbled all over her face, but nothing else has changed. She asked if I was still the brazen youngster she knew. I chuckled when she reminded me that, when I first came to stay with her, I'd asked her if Mr. Bolo was her boyfriend.

Jay and I had a couple of surprises. Millington came to the funeral with his mother. He gave a moving tribute. I never know how to take funeral orations. During my delinquent days I attended a couple of funerals, and the glowing tributes I heard had nothing to do with the cold-blooded killers who'd had their comeuppance. He was probably at the house with Jay when I was at the store—that's why it took the memory of the trip to Mr. Branch's house for me to remember him. Jay said that for the first three years when he first came to live in Havre he and Millington spent lots of time together. Grama liked him, even helped him with school supplies, and I'm sure that when Aunt Mercy was dishing out goodies she wouldn't have treated him differently from us and maybe even gave him extra to take home. Jay said that he sometimes shared coconut fudge with me that came from Millington's mother, but I don't remember. For one reason or other Jay had never got around to tracking him down in Barbados where he was posted as an AMC minister.

Outside the church, before we walked to the cemetery, this Eurafrican fellow two heads taller than I, with watery blue eyes, thin blond hair, and crinkly skin came up to me. A Laird, I thought, and wondered why he'd be there. He asked with a Bajan accent if I remembered him.

I shook my head.

He grinned, showing large teeth, and said a glass of Lena's mauby might jolt my memory. He extended his hand. "Brother. Remember me from Excelsior?"

"I certainly remember Brother" *but you don't look remotely like him.* In those days he was chubby. Apart from being gangly, he seemed like someone in his forties. He couldn't be more than twenty-six, twenty-seven. Even in the open air his cologne was strong and seemed to be duelling with a rank meaty odour.

He said he was in St. Vincent doing some consulting work for the government, and that he was in touch with five Excelsians who're still living in St. Vincent. He recognized my name in the obit announcement and came to the funeral hoping I would be present. I invited him to drop by our hotel in Kingstown, and he promised he would.

Jay and I arranged for Millington and Brother to visit us on Friday evening after we returned from visiting Daddy and his wife. Millington was first to arrive. He met us waiting for him in the lobby, and suggested that Jay and he go to the bar for a drink while I waited for Brother to arrive.

"I thought Methodists aren't supposed to drink. At least not in public," Jay told him. The statement was out of character for Jay.

"Oh," Millington said, then paused. "I'm agnostic."

There was silence.

Jay broke it. "We are too. Paul prefers to say he's atheist."

"Goes without saying; Ma Kirton raised both of you."

"Does that mean you're no longer a minister?" I asked.

"Yes, it means that."

"What are you doing now?"

"Looking for a job."

"Your mother must be devastated," Jay said.

"Well, yes. She is and would be even more so if she knew the rest."

"For example?" I said.

Millington looked at Jay and motioned the bar. "Paul, you stay here and wait for Brother. Come join us when he comes."

I took it as a cue that Millington wanted to say things to Jay that he didn't want me to hear.

Brother didn't come for another twenty minutes. When I mentioned going to the bar, he shook his head and said he keeps away from alcohol, that he was diagnosed with type-one diabetes while he was still a toddler, that he used to have insulin shots when he was at Excelsior. Explains his aged look, rank smell, and overuse of cologne.

We remained in the lobby. I ordered a pot of tea. While sipping it we caught up on each other's lives.

When I mentioned the kerfuffle with Mrs. Bensemana, he laughed and said: "And they didn't expel you for good? In Barbados, you would have been expelled and barred from other schools."

I told him nothing about my delinquent activities but a lot about my travel to Cuba and Central America; my pot experience with the police in Guatemala; Carlos and prison I edited out, and made it appear that under a false identity I was able to find work in Guatemala and support myself. My return to Canada. University studies . My hopes of becoming a writer. Nothing about my illness.

He said his eyes were weak, that he'd already had surgery to correct retinal bleeding, and so he avoided overtaxing his eyes with reading, but he would definitely want to read my books.

He'd done a commerce degree at the University of the West Indies in Trinidad and now worked for a consulting firm. He turned on a tablet and showed me photos of his three children — twin girls aged three and a boy eleven months — and his wife Merlene, who, he said, was an administrative secretary at UWI Cave Hill and a great-niece of ex-Barbadian prime minister Errol Barrow. There was one photo taken of the entire family at the front of Oistins Nazarene Church.

We exchanged contact information and promised to stay in touch. I doubt we would. He belongs to an Evangelical church. A huge difference between Jay and me is that I don't have time for people to whom I have to justify or explain my sexual orientation. No need for their opprobrium or pity. I'm convinced that you can no more cleanse

West Indians of homophobia than you can purge trees of the chemicals they've been absorbing for decades. I won't holiday in the Anglophone Caribbean or anywhere in Africa, with the exception of South Africa. I went to Miami and New Orleans a few years ago but I won't return, not until Louisiana and Florida recognize our rights. I sometimes wonder if all these gay cruise-ship passengers who're greeted with insulting placards and pelted with stones in the Caribbean—when they're allowed to land, that is—aren't a trifle masochistic. Jay feels otherwise: that we should accept people at their level, teach by example, and interact with those who despise us in order for them to see that our humanity is no different from theirs. Quixotic, I say. My days for quixotic pursuits are over. Life's too short. Let the dead bury the dead, leave them to decompose.

Jay is the great beneficiary of this trip. I chuckle. If he overheard my thoughts, he'd say I'm calling him a vulture. After he first spoke to me about Millington back in 2007, I had the feeling that he felt guilty that he'd allowed their friendship to fizzle. So after Millington and Brother left and Jay and I returned to our room, I pushed him to tell me about their meeting. I itched to know what devastating information Millington was withholding from his mother. I lay in bed propped up by pillows. Jay sat in an armchair at the foot of the king-sized bed and seemed loathe to speak.

"He regrets that he didn't drop out of theological college when he began to doubt Methodist theology," Jay said in a voice tinged with sadness, his eyes focused on the wall behind the bed. "But it was complicated. He'd received a church scholarship. He wants to work in education, counselling or social work, but he'll have to return to school, and he doesn't have the funds. He had an interview for a position in the civil service today, and is waiting to hear if he's been hired."

"Is he married?"

The V and deep frown appeared and he stared at me. "Why do you ask?"

"It's a normal question."

He was a long time answering. "This has to stay between us. He's gay. It's why he wanted to have a private moment with me."

"So that's what would devastate his mother."

Jay nodded. "And an aunt in the US who helped pay for his secondary education. She continued giving him money for extras while he was in theological seminary. He entered the ministry thinking he could be celibate."

"And discovered he couldn't be?"

"Possibly."

"Whose husband he stole?"

"No one's, as far as I know."

"He's damn good-looking, that much I can say. Desirable."

"Eventually he became disgusted with himself and left the church. Caribbean Methodists don't tolerate homosexuality in their ministers. Apparently British Methodists do. In any event he found himself performing rituals he no longer believed in. So he told his superiors that he was in conflict with Methodist doctrine and left." Jay sighed, looked away. He bit his lip and swallowed.

We fell into a long silence. I broke it. "Jay, if Millington remains here, he'll destroy himself. He needs to be in a place like Canada where people don't have to feel guilty about their sexual orientation. Why don't you help him to get away?"

"How?"

"Jay, Millington was your first love. Come clean with me. I had a suspicion when you mentioned him in 2007. If I'd known he was gay I would have contacted him on your behalf."

"Love? I don't know that I'd call it love. There might have been some sort of attraction. He was a nice person: disciplined, never said anything cruel about anyone. Loyal. Maybe I'm idealizing him."

"He's damned good-looking. Do you love him, Jay? Do you still feel *some sort of attraction?*" I couldn't help chuckling. "What do you feel for him now?"

"Paul, I'm meeting him again after fourteen years."

"Answer my question."

"I wish his life hadn't turned out to be such a mess." He swallowed loud and wiped his eyes with his sleeve.

"Jay, you have to help him."

"How?"

"I don't know, but I want you to do something."

"I'm Jay, not Paul. He's Millington, not Carlos."

"Cobwebs! Sweep it away."

"No. It's not cobwebs. Millington and I parted company fourteen years ago. True he has developed a tall, well-proportioned body and a beautiful face, and his values don't seem to have changed. I have changed, physically and otherwise."

"Did you tell him you were in love with him?"

"Why would I? I'm not Gúicho, Carlos, or that fellow that wanted to fondle your beard on the Guatemala bus. In any event, I'm not sure I was."

"You were. You're blushing. Your eyes are glowing. Bet your hands are sweating."

"Slow down. This is the same sort of behaviour that could have got you in trouble with Lionel."

"Oh! So you and Lionel have been discussing me?"

"What are you trying to say?"

I chuckled. "I'll leave you to figure that out."

"I'll figure out nothing. If you have something to say, say it."

"You're in love with Lionel. That's what I want to say."

"So that's what the coupling-dogs remark was about. Paul, I don't want Lionel. If you think I have sexual issues, you should get to know him."

"Nothing you can't straighten. You're patient, long-suffering. Masochistic even."

"For someone who couldn't wrench himself away from Carlos' abuse, you're very perspicacious."

Our exchange was becoming a quarrel. I got out of bed and sat on the armrest of his seat and put an arm around him. "I want us to promise each other something. I've been thinking about this on the plane coming to St. Vincent. I want us to pledge to stay close together and never let boyfriends or husbands, friends, whatever get between us. I want too that if we say anything hurtful in anger to each other, we'll retract it."

He lifted his head to look into my eyes. "Even if it's true?"

"We'll just have to find a kind way to say unpleasant things."

"You'll have a hard time keeping your pledge."

"Then I'll have more retractions than you. Just say you promise." I put my free hand on his.

"Fine by me. I did a long time ago, since I was eight and read Ma's note telling me to help Grama take care of you."

"And you've done a fantastic job. Now I want it to be mutual. And now I must tell you that Millington is a stunningly beautiful man on the outside and from what you've told me, he's beautiful on the inside too. I know you love him, Jay, and now I'm urging you to let him know. A change comes over you every time you talk about him. Your voice alters. Given Grama's admiration for him, he's the guy she'd have wanted for you. Think about it. Do you want him, Jay?"

"Uh, uh uh!"

"Stop stuttering and give me a clear answer."

"Maybe if we'd stayed in touch and ..."

"That's good enough for me. What's his email? Does he have a cell?"

"You're moving too fast."

"Hand it over, Jay." My hand stretched out in front of him.

He sighed, got up, took out a piece of paper from his wallet, and gave me Millington's cell number. I got out my iPhone and texted:

> *Millington, Jay bn in love with u since hschool dsnt no how 2 tell u. Do u luv him? Meet us at the airport 7 am if u can.*

Next morning Jay was up before me, before the alarm. He looked tired. "What's wrong?" I asked.

"I couldn't sleep."

I checked my emails and text messages. There was no response from Millington. Our flight from E.T. Joshua was at 8 a.m. When we got there, whom do we see standing near the LIAT counter? Millington. His eyes lit up when he saw Jay. They hugged. He whispered something in Jay's ear. Jay hasn't told me what, but I have a pretty good idea. I saw the tears gleaming in Millington's eyes. I couldn't see Jay's eyes, but I'm sure they weren't dry. Mine were let's just say moist.

On the plane back I told Jay: "You're not going to muck this up. I'm not going to let you. Even if he comes here and you have to support him till he dies, and even if you two have to undergo sex therapy, he's the person for you."

Jay was quiet. Then he gave me the best answer he could: he put his hand on mine and squeezed it.

—≫ I'm ashamed to say that during that week in St. Vincent I never thought of Bernard. I felt guilty when I got home and found his message asking me to call him when I get in, regardless of the hour. I know now what Jay meant when he said he wasn't sexually attracted to Jonathan. But I'm not Jay. I'll work at it and see what happens. Now I must get ready to meet Bernard down the hill. I brought back nothing for him. I'll give him the T-shirt I intended for Gina. I won't be able to give Emilia the one I bought for her. A message on my phone from professor Bram says that I'm on the short list of candidates pre-selected for a bursary but the final decision will be made when I complete my courses and final grades are in.

—≫ It's nearing 5 p.m. I look again at the blinking new-message light. I saw it when Bernard and I came back to the apartment. Leaving the restaurant, we bounded up Atwater. It felt like spring in February, outside and inside me. I even unzipped my jacket. A few metres from home, it occurred to me that Bernard didn't know about my illness. Doubts came then. I want this to last, at least until he or I lose interest. Maybe I shouldn't tell him. But when he begins interacting with my circle it will come out. And it's fair that he should know. At the door of the building, he asked: "Why the sudden gloom?"

While we were at the restaurant we played footsie under the table. Desire glowed in his dark eyes, but at home the passionate sex I looked forward to turned tepid from the anxiety of not knowing how he'll respond to my illness. And afterwards, he too seemed lost in thought, his eyes far off somewhere. While he was showering, I thought of writing a note and giving it to him with instructions that he read it only after he got home, but changed my mind. If he went straight home, he should be there now. I should call and clear this up before he gets it into his head that I no longer want him.

I check my telephone messages. The first one is from Lionel. After welcoming me back and saying he hopes burying our aunt wasn't too painful, he asks me to call him.

This guy who didn't want to talk to me at his party! I remember Jay's remark about his being complicated. Coming from Jay, that's a lot of criticism.

The second message is from Jay. It's brief. "Paul, call me when you get back and before you speak to Lionel."

I dial Jay's number right away. "What's this about your message?"

"Did Lionel call you?"

"Why? Should he be calling me?"

"Around ten he called and asked me how things went in St. Vincent and we chitchatted. Then he asked what I was doing for the rest of the day. I said I had a week's work to catch up on. He said I should forget about the work for a while and come to his place for a bit of fun, that his dick was already hard waiting for me. I told him: 'I couldn't come even if I wanted to.'"

"'Would you want to? Was that a pun?'

"I didn't answer.

"'Tell me something: Do you guys ever get laid?'

"I said nothing. He laughed. 'Maybe, I'll have more luck with Paul. He seems more in touch with reality.'

"'Maybe you would.' I hung up the phone."

Now it's my turn to laugh. "Shit, man. Jay, you shouldn't have gone and met Millington. But there's no need to be faithful. Just practice safe sex. Strike while the iron's hot, Jay. There's nothing to gain from abstinence."

"You sound just like him. 'Recreational sex with single or multiple partners. No attachments, please.' It's what we were talking about at the party. He regaled me with stories about the places he'd travelled to and men he'd slept with, even in Africa; said his gaydar never failed him. I asked him if he wasn't afraid. He said no, that in Montreal he doesn't worry about bringing guys home because Muriel is there. Sometimes he goes to the sauna. He invited me to go with him."

"Bet you said, yes?"

"I just wanted to let you know. It's up to you if you want to get involved with him, but I thought you should know what you might be getting into."

"He called and left a message, but I heard yours too and called you first."

"What does his message say?"

"Just to call him. I will. Remember I'm grateful to him for letting me know malignant meningioma doesn't have to be a death sentence."

I hear his nervous breathing. "But don't feel that you have to sleep with him to thank him."

"And if it's to our mutual benefit? These days if I had the courage to, I'd go looking for some recreational sex myself. You can keep yourself pure for Millington. You've been doing that all along though you didn't know for whom."

He says nothing.

"Don't worry, Jay. I'm just playing with you. I won't take up any offer from Lionel before I get to know him. Thanks for sharing this, like the good brother you are. Take care. I'll call you back."

I sit in the armchair beside the phone. Something about this conversation—maybe Lionel's honesty about his needs—reminds me that I haven't been honest with Bernard. I dial his number. His message comes on. I hang up without responding. Just as I put the phone down, it rings, and Bernard asks why I didn't leave a message. I'm at a loss for words.

"What did you want to tell me?"

"I probably shouldn't do it over the telephone."

"Then come to my place. Gives you a chance to see where I live."

"Okay."

He gives me an address on Delisle. I put on my coat and head back down Atwater. He meets me at the door. He's wearing an emerald-green dressing gown over his street clothes. His eyes are alert, focused on me. The apartment smells of the paints he uses. Not sure how long I could remain in it. While he's putting away my coat I note the modesty of the place. On the right, as soon as you enter, there's a kitchenette with a short counter with a tiny fridge under it; a two-burner hotplate that takes up half the counter space. Above the counter are three cupboards. Ahead is a small living room, and beyond that are the doors that lead to what I think are the bathroom and his bedroom. In the living room are a brown vinyl couch, a green arm-chair, and a coffee table on which there are African carvings. The floor is covered with a grey industrial rug. The walls are painted bone white and covered with his canvasses. They're full of green hills. In about half of them, there are huts but no human beings.

I feel his back against mine and his arms pulling me close to him as he gently pushes me toward the couch. When I sit he says he has to turn up the thermostat. He comes back and sits beside me. I tell him to open the window a crack so I could breathe more easily.

"Now what's the crisis?"

I say nothing.

His face is taut with tension. "What, you think I can't handle it? I'm Rwandan. We didn't do anything that will make you pregnant."

I laugh, then take a deep breath. "Meningioma. Do you know what that is?" I stare at his wrinkled forehead and his Tutsi face appears even narrower than it is.

He shakes his head.

I explain what it is and what I've just been through.

He says he thinks Lionel went through something similar, that Muriel told him about it.

I nod and say that that's how I got to meet him.

He pulls me to him and kisses me. "That means I have to make sure you take extra care of yourself. I don't want to be widowed any time soon." A cloud comes over his face. He pulls in his lips, looks away, and takes a deep breath.

For a while we say nothing. I break the silence. "So you are serious then?"

"You thought I wasn't? And you—are *you* serious?"

"Serious enough to want to continue."

He holds his fingers up in front of my face. "I'm not too bony for you? Not afraid of my chicken bones? Gays like muscle-men." He laughs with his face turned away. "I once tried to hook up with a Trinidadian who told me my saltfish was too hard and bony for him."

"He was quoting a calypso." I sing it for him: "I don't want no bone/ Give me flesh alone/If your saltfish hard and bony/ You ain't talking to me ... No need to worry, Bernard. I have enough cushion for both of us and some to spare. Did you score with the Trinidadian?"

He shook his head. "No. I was too hard and bony."

We chuckle.

He pulls me close to him and our lips meet. I feel as if I'm floating. I remember Carlos, remember this was how we'd started. "I have to head home now; to study for an upcoming exam." My throat is itching too. I shouldn't be here.

"Think you can give me two days a week: one on the weekend and one during the week: Tuesday? We could profit to see films at half price."

I want to say, you're a reasonable guy, but instead I lean toward him and kiss him and nod.

I float up the hill. I throw my coat onto the couch and phone Jay and tell him about Bernard.

He listens without interrupting me. "When am I going to *really* meet him? I mean you introduced him but we never got to talk."

"I'll see if we can arrange to have supper together next Saturday, but you must leave right after."

"You've spoken to Lionel?"

"No."

"Are you going to?"

"Yes, and I'll tell him I'm not available. I'm seeing somebody but I won't tell him who."

"When Lionel finds out about Bernard, don't let him influence you with what he calls his ultra-liberal modus vivendi. He doesn't understand why guys enter into long-term or even short-term relationships. He said that his father has a workmate who never wears his wedding ring and leaves his wife at home when he goes out because: 'When you go to a restaurant you don't carry your lunch.' He gave me a long lecture on the relationship between Sartre and Simone de Beauvoir and Aldous Huxley and his wife Maria. Apparently Maria trolled for Aldous; in exchange Aldous let her pursue her lesbian relationships. Lionel describes the world's men as 'dishes at a banquet, *all* are worth sampling.'"

"How's it he didn't dine on you that night? You seemed already on his plate, condiments and all, just cutlery missing."

"Bye, Paul." He hangs up.

I'm not phoning Lionel tonight. I'm going to try to have a nap before I begin putting my thoughts together for my exam.

11

25 AUGUST 2012.

It's noon and ten of us have met for a picnic at Parc Lafontaine: Jay and Millington, Gina and Emilia, Carlos and Marc-André, Muriel and Lionel, Bernard and I. Gina said there'll be an eleventh person, someone from our high school days. S/he isn't here yet. I haven't been able to cajole the information out of her. My mind races over the possible suspects: John, Milford, Said (highly unlikely unless he's left his wife), Doc (I would love to see him, to see how he's evolved); pretty sure it won't be Alvin. Most likely Milford.

I am standing with my back leaning against a maple, about three metres from where Gina and Emilia are spreading green vinyl tablecloths on two picnic tables we've joined together. They secure them against the breeze that's threatening to billow them. The surrounding trees sway gently and their leaves trill. On my bare arms the breeze creates a cool, pleasant sensation. I'm still wary of being directly in the sun. No problem here. It's a comfortably cool day. The sky is cloudless and a rich azure — beauty above enhancing beauty below: the trees are at their greenest, just before they begin to yellow. From the pond a short distance away come the sounds of ducks. The notes of a redwing pierce the air and intermix with the whistles and trills of what must be chickadees and tree swallows: p-wit, p-wit; we-use, we-use ... Apart from the omnipresent seagulls and pigeons waiting for what's offered accidentally or deliberately, the sparrows, flitting from tree to tree, are the only ones visible. When we arrived two cardinals eyed us sceptically then flew away. My once-upon-a-time interest in birds seems such a long time ago.

Jay and Millington stand talking with their backs turned to Gina. Millington squints and digs his elbow playfully into Jay. Jay grins. Millington arrived in June. He and Jay got married shortly after. I haven't had much time to get to know him. Jay and he must be still in their honeymoon period. Millington volunteers at a food bank while he waits for a work permit. Began there two weeks after he arrived. Everything—his angular face, aquiline nose, limpid amber eyes, glossy black hair that furrows like a washboard, and sleek trim body a trifle taller than Jay's—combines to make him strikingly beautiful. Bernard thinks I exaggerate his physical beauty, but likes him for his "calm disposition." I think Jay and he make a very handsome couple. And now Jay has added a gym workout to his daily walk. He insists it's because he's in his thirties, that it has nothing to do with Millington. How little we know ourselves.

Bernard and Marc-André are talking a little to the left of the picnic tables, about a metre from Gina. Marc-André tells him something and he's grinning from ear to ear. This is the fourth time I'm meeting Marc-André. Carlos phoned me one evening at the beginning of May to ask me if he could come by; he needed my opinion about something. His eyes gleaming with mischief or triumph, he showed up with Marc-André and introduced him as his new boyfriend. I doubt he knew about Bernard because, at the time, apart from Jay, I'd told no one else about him, so Carlos probably wanted to make me feel jealous. Marc-André is pale to the point of being pink, has light blond hair and sky-blue eyes. His narrow waist, bulging deltoids, biceps, triceps, pectorals, and thighs like tree-trunks grab your attention. If you were into muscle he'd be quite a catch: a *mango,* a *papasito.* We chitchatted for a little more than an hour. I learned that he was a personal trainer. And I wondered if he'd come by his muscles honestly.

About half an hour after they left, Carlos phoned to ask me my opinion. I joked that maybe he should keep him under surveillance 24/7. He insisted that I tell him more, but I couldn't. I told him I'd intuited nothing negative, that I had no opinion.

He later told me that they'd met at the sauna, and he'd passed the entire night in Marc-André's cubicle, and they'd talked about what they wanted but couldn't find. They agreed to meet again, and now they were trying to build a relationship. When they visited me it had been six weeks since they'd agreed to date seriously. I wanted to ask him if it was an open relationship, whether they were into group sex, etc., but reminded myself that it was none of my business. Marc-André is thirty-eight.

I stare at Bernard turning away from Marc-André and speaking with Gina. When he found out I was about to end my lease, he told me not to, that he didn't like living alone, and would like to move in with me. The night before he made this offer, we were lying in my bed, and he'd fallen asleep on his back. I listened to his breathing and stared at the outline of his frail form, and I wanted to read Arnold's "Dover Beach" to him, and hold him, and fuse his body with mine, and say into his ears — to keep it a secret from the very air around us — *Bernard, let's create a relationship that will blend our individual selves; let's sustain each other.* But he might misunderstand my plea and interpret it as a desire to possess him. I reached over and kissed him on his half-open mouth, and his body, still asleep, arched towards me. His proposal to move in with me came the next morning while we were having coffee. After he left I agonized over it. That night I dreamt that Grama and I were walking hand in hand along Beach Road, and she said to me: "Paul, have you ever considered that the earth might be a living organism and that we live on it like fleas in the hairs of dogs and cats, and that when we die, it's because the earth has caught us?" The rest of the dream became confused but I remember her saying at one point: "Can you encircle the moon with your hands? Can you silence the ocean? Can you still hurricanes? In our battles with nature we are like adders who've lost their fangs."

I've surrendered to Bernard. I wasn't born to be alone. He gave up his apartment and moved in with me. Sold his car too; free parking is difficult where we live, and paid parking is prohibitive. The second bedroom has pretty well become his studio. He keeps the door closed, and when he's painting he opens the window a crack. I don't kid myself. With him I don't feel the erotic passion I felt for Carlos or the skin-tingling that came with the thought of what it would be like encircled by Lionel's arms, but I prefer this quieter feeling to the anxiety I endured the years Carlos and I were together.

Of course, some nights Bernard's screaming and sobbing awaken me; and I have to shake him awake and clasp him close until he's calm. He was eleven when the Rwanda genocide took place. From his hiding place, under a pile of hewn branches still with their leaves, at the bottom of a ditch, he'd heard the death screams of his brothers, his parents, his age mates, his grandparents, his neighbours. Later, when night came and the death screams died down and the death squads moved on, he crawled out and stumbled over bodies with vultures, visible in the moonlight, already perched on them. Stealthily he wound his way through the charred remains of houses: dodging, crouching, sometimes playing dead when bands of killers were near, until he escaped into the forest. For twenty-three days he walked in the night and hid in the day until he was rescued. Eventually he contacted his only surviving sibling, an older sister who was studying in Belgium, and came to Canada via Belgium. His three brothers, older than he, weren't so lucky. Neither were his parents and grandparents.

He seemed so self-assured that night when I first met him. Placid exteriors ... How's it possible to hold, to carry, to live with, such memories? Jay said that he and Ma had had a conversation about carrying painful memories. She'd done her clinical psychiatric training at Douglas Hospital, and some of her patients were Holocaust survivors. Surviving and staying sane. Many do or seem to: Morgentaler, Bettelheim, Weisenthal. They survive and seem not to hate humanity. How do they do it? Probably why Bernard's so bony. Must take lots of calories to keep his demons caged.

I would have preferred not to know his story. It has forced me to look into myself and at others and see the volcanic violence in us waiting for the right seisms to erupt ... or held in check like New Orleans dikes holding back the sea until Katrina comes. World War II. Bosnia. Rwanda. Burundi. Nigeria. Sudan. Libya. Syria. I remember Grama, her eyebrows raised, telling two Jehovah-Witness women who'd just related Job's story in their attempt to convince her that God was just. "You and I reason differently," she said. "I'm on the side of Job's wife."

Bernard looks across at me and starts walking toward me. "In deep thought," he says when he's half a metre in front of me. At home he says this often, then gives me a peck on the forehead and sometimes a squeeze of the hand before he wanders away from me. On occasion I pull him back and embrace him; easy to do: his body is so slender. Once or twice, he chided: "You can hold me like this forever and I'll love it, but don't blame me if your novel never gets written."

"In writing mode?" he asks. "We're at a picnic. Remember?"

"Just thinking. Thinking how happy I am."

He nods, smiles, and holds my hand and leads me toward the picnic tables.

At the picnic table Marc-André is holding a Frisbee and looking around him for players. He's wearing a tank-top. His screaming muscles remind me of Carlos' remark when I eventually introduced him to Bernard. "Es *un paquete de huesos*. He's a packet of bones. Couldn't you find someone with a bit more flesh—*alguien con más carne?*"

Lionel gets up from his folding chair, leaves Muriel sitting on hers, and begins removing the items from their picnic basket. He finishes and joins Marc-André. They move to an area with fewer trees and begin to toss the Frisbee. Bernard joins them. Jay opens the picnic cooler that he has inherited from Ma and takes out two gallon-size jugs: one of ginger beer and one of mauby. Millington made the ginger beer and Jay made the mauby. Bernard and I brought nothing. They told us not to. We joined them at Jay's place and paid the taxi fare to the park. None of us owns cars.

Bro Millington joins the players. About a month after we got back from St. Vincent, Jay told me that my experience with meningioma had helped him make up his mind about Millington. He'd asked himself, what if it had been him, and what if it had been fatal. So he decided to take the plunge and enter into a relationship with Millington.

I call him Bro Millington so he'll understand that I appreciate his presence in Jay's life. Nowadays I go to Jay's apartment more often because he's there. I try to understand how he feels about moving here. He should get his work permit sometime in the next six months but will have to wait two years before receiving permanent resident status. It was a lot easier when Carlos came. In less than four years he became a citizen. It's complicating Millington's plans to return to school: he won't be eligible for student loans and bursaries during this time.

I read somewhere that in T.S. Eliot's earlier years, a time when Eliot was in dire financial straits, Bertrand Russell gave him a couple thousand guineas that he'd inherited. Russell had seen its use in developing the talent of a young artist. (Eliot gave it back years later when Russell fell on hard times.) The way I see it, nothing should stand in the way of cultivating intellect. But Millington assumed financial responsibility for his mother after his father's death three years ago. She has always been a housewife, is now sixty-two, and has severe arthritis.

At times I see such responsibilities as lead—the lead of custom—that prevents us from soaring, and I admire those who can cast it off. (It's what I have Sonny thinking in my short story "Mother Bernice.") In saner moments I know that to do so is to renounce our most humane traits: generosity and compassion. Millington feels guilty too that he can't pay for his share of the living expenses. Things shouldn't matter, certainly not when Jay has the resources. Yet they do. No one wants to feel like a parasite. Bernard and I are lucky. We share all the household expenses. I'm grateful for the money my grandparents and my mother bequeathed me. Fate curses and fate blesses.

I hope Millington and Jay are happy. Sometimes I catch hints of anxiety in Jay but I'm loathe to ask him about it. Millington's definitely stressed. Often fidgeting a lot, seemingly lost in his thoughts, his hands almost always sweating. Must be the weight, the tension, of waiting for a work permit and his visa.

Two months ago, they formalized their union. Gina and I—Gina mostly—arranged the party that followed. Jay says that Millington is afraid to tell his mother. I should ask Jay if he has told Daddy. Wouldn't I love to see the expression on *his* face as images of Sodom and Gomorrah overtake his mind.

I look across at Lionel throwing and catching the Frisbee. He's the best of the three players. Sometimes he scoffs at us for going into what he calls "voluntary bondage." He and Gina are now quite close. Our main loci for socializing are his condo and her apartment.

They haven't been in touch with Gúicho for a month. He met a sexagenarian from somewhere in Alberta and moved there with him. "If he makes the news, let's hope it's on the back of a bull," Emilia said, and we all laughed.

Jonathan's the one missing today. Can't say that I like him but I hope he and Jay reconcile. When Jay told me he would propose to Millington, I told him that if Millington accepted, he should brace himself for Jonathan's response.

"Meaning?"

"If he reacts with only short-term anger, you'll be lucky."

Jay invited him and me for supper one Friday and broke the news to him then. Jonathan began sulking as soon as he saw me. I think he was looking forward to an evening alone with Jay and my presence pissed him off. Too bad.

For the most part we ate in silence. It was grilled salmon with Jay's special rice, cooked in a spinach and tomato sauce. After coffee Jay gave him the news. Jonathan blanched and held on to the table. Then he got up and went to the bathroom. We heard him vomiting. He came out looking wan, threw his jacket over his shoulder, and left without saying a word. That was mid-May. Since then he hasn't replied to any of Jay's phone messages, or to Jay's letter explaining the evolution of his relationship with Millington. In the letter—Jay had me read it to make sure the tone was the right—he told Jonathan that "on matters of the heart, we have little control," and that no matter what happens he hopes they'd continue to be friends. From what Jay knows, he hasn't sunk into another depression.

I contrast this with the shambles I was in when I returned from Guatemala in 2006. Not bad at all. Wish Ma could see me now. In two weeks, I begin the MA programme. I was lucky to finish my semester. Only a few of Concordia's departments embraced the student strike. In May Bram called me to his office, told me I'd got the bursary and handed me a print-out of an email Bill had sent him with instructions to give it to me when I finished my BA. Bill advises me that there's little likelihood that I'd earn a living from writing, that my love for knowledge and ideas makes me an ideal candidate for academia, and that I should get the requisite doctorate. "I suggest, too, that you arrange your life so that you could live off your own earnings, like Jay, (you will feel better for doing so) and like him, give the proceeds of your inherited money to the needy. You told me how distressed you were by child labour in Guatemala. Help some of those children to get an education. Compassion is meaningless and becomes mere voyeurism when we can ease suffering but don't."

I wonder if he discussed any of this with Jay. I'm contemplating his advice. It's unfair that he delivered it from beyond the grave, when I can't argue with him. We'll see. For now, with the MA bursary and Bernard sharing half of the expenses, I'm able to manage. At some point, I'll talk to Jay about Bill's letter.

A hand is waving across my face. It's Gina trying to draw me out of my reverie. The other hand holds a paper plate with three fish cakes.

"Boy, where are you?"

I grin and take the plate from her. I look to my left and see that Emilia is dishing out potato salad. The Frisbee players are approaching. Carlos is sitting with his back to the food and munching on carrot sticks. Near him is Muriel, definitely smaller. Her sides no longer overhang the chair she's on. Six months ago this canvas chair wouldn't have supported her weight. I'd noticed in my last two visits to Lionel's place that that she wasn't there, and got around to asking him why. He shrugged and said she was at their parents' place. Later I learned from Gina that in May she'd had bariatric surgery in a U.S. hospital, and was staying with her mother, who'd taken time off work to be with her during her convalescence. I want to congratulate her, but I'm not supposed to know about her surgery, and any comment I make could rebound one way or other to her obesity.

I hear the tones of Gina's cellphone. Next the directions she's giving someone. A minute later I see him, Alvin, lumbering like a mobile tree trunk, barely five feet, across the bridge over the pond. Even with his cap and dark glasses, I cannot miss that bulldog face, the skin retracted in a huge smile, like a receding wave. I want to run to him and hang from his neck. He comes, takes off his backpack and kisses Gina, Emilia, and me on both cheeks. Gina holds on to him as if she's afraid he'd turn and run away. My eyes follow him and Gina, who's holding him by the hand and introducing him to the people he does not know. I feel happy. I wish Milford and John were here. Perhaps next year. In a different world, Said would be here too.

Quite a different August from last year, this one is worthy of its name. Here, in this green oasis, we've put aside our private storms and come to reify our links. Better not to look too closely at what they are. Today, let the heart hold sway.

I turn this way and that to look at each of them. My family. From Canada, Rwanda, Guatemala, Nicaragua, the United Kingdom by way of Grenada, Jamaica, St. Vincent. Brought together by accident, war, desire, need. And I can truly say I'm happy … for the time being.

Acknowledgements

I offer my thanks to Ilona Martonfi for coordinating and hosting a writing group to which I belong and whose members—Ilona Martonfi, Susi Lovell, Roz Paris, Robert Winters, Michael Primiani, Michael Emanuel, and David Gates—read and critiqued sections of this manuscript; to Michael Mirolla for his excellent editing, especially for pointing out the excrescences; and to David Moratto for the cover design.

About the Author

H[ubert] Nigel Thomas was born in St. Vincent and the Grenadines and has been living in Canada since 1968. He was a mental health worker, elementary and high school teacher, and eventually professor of US literature at Université Laval. He is the author of several essays in literary criticism as well as four novels: *No Safeguards* (2015), *Return to Arcadia* (2007), *Behind the Face of Winter* (2001; translated into French as *De glace et d'ombre, 2016*), and *Spirits in the Dark* (1993); three collections of short fiction: *When the Bottom Falls out and Other Stories* (2014), *Lives: Whole and Otherwise* (2010; translated into French as *Des vies cassées, 2013*), and *How Loud Can the Village Cock Crow and Other Stories* (1995); a collection of poems: *Moving through Darkness* (2000); and two scholarly texts: *Why We Write: Conversations with African Canadian Poets and Novelists* (2006), and *From Folklore to Fiction: A Study of Folk Heroes and Rituals in the Black American Novel* (1988). In 1994 and 2015 he was shortlisted for the Quebec Writers' Federation Hugh MacLennan Fiction Prize for *Spirits in the Dark* and *No Safeguards* respectively; in 2015 *Des vies cassees* was shortlisted for Le Prix Carbet des lycéens. In 2000 he received the Montreal Association of Business Persons and Professionals' Jackie Robinson Award for Professional of the year; and in 2013 was awarded Université Laval's *Hommage aux créateurs*. He is the founder and English-language coordinator of Lectures Logos Readings, a monthly reading series.